age

Murdering Tosca

An Opera "Shocker"

Margo Miller

PublishAmerica
Baltimore

BROOKLINE PUBLIC LIBRARY

Coolidge

3 1712 01251 8232

© 2008 by Margo Miller.
All rights reserved. No part of this book may be reproduced, stored in a retrieval system or transmitted in any form or by any means without the prior written permission of the publishers, except by a reviewer who may quote brief passages in a review to be printed in a newspaper, magazine or journal.

First printing

All characters in this book are fictitious, and any resemblance to real persons, living or dead, is coincidental.

PublishAmerica has allowed this work to remain exactly as the author intended, verbatim, without editorial input.

ISBN: 1-60474-993-8
PUBLISHED BY PUBLISHAMERICA, LLLP
www.publishamerica.com
Baltimore

Printed in the United States of America

For Colin

Markings in the Score

That evening, the opera had begun, *Vivacissimo con violenza,* fast with violence, the orchestra in full cry, as Puccini wanted. So long ago, a lifetime ago. He was tired, elated. Free of them! He had only to cross the stage, go out the fire door.

From a great distance, he heard the orchestra build to the finale, *grande slancio,* the impetuous surge that promised him—from somewhere in the gloom high above him—Tosca should jump to her death.

All was well.

Then came a creak as something dissolved underfoot. It was working. Then nothing but the rush of air and a confusion of costumes. But whose?

Why had they done this to him?

John Austin Othmar Presents

TOSCA

Melodrama in Three Acts
Music by Giocomo Puccini
Libretto by Giuseppe Giacosa and Luigi Illica after Sardou

The Palladium Theater, Pallas

Thursday at 7:30   Saturday at 2   Thursday at 7:30   Saturday at 8
March 22   March 24   March 29   March 31

The Cast

Floria Tosca, soprano.....................Margarita Dettori
Mario Cavaradossi, tenor...............Liugi Luongo
Baron Scarpia, baritone.................Bruno Cappetto
Cesare Angelotti, basso.................Johnson Jones
Spoletta, tenor................................Rollo Shaw
The Sacristan, baritone.................Edgar Nelson
Sciarrone, basso..............................Alexander Avery
Jailer, basso...Giorgio Spelvino
Shepherd, soprano............................John Joseph McLaughlin, Jr.

People of Rome..............................People of Pallas

Conductor: Victor Pompelli

Chatham County Philharmonic, F. Macdonald Gilson, music director
Chatham County Chorale, Hunting Smith, conductor

The action takes place in June 1800

Act I: Morning, La Chiesa di Sant'Andrea della Valle
Act II: Evening, Scarpia's chamber in the Palazzo Farnese
Act III: Dawn, Ramparts of the Castel Sant'Angelo

Music Management: Gillespie & Associates, New York

1.

At last they were gone. Good riddance! He was out of their clutches. The theater was his again and would stay that way. In the gloom of the auditorium, the new carpeting grabbed at his sneakers. A good sign, he thought. They certainly didn't stint on the restoration. He hurried up the steps to the stage. Darker here. Only instinct told him where he should find it. There it was, in a wing, and he walked the ghost light out to center stage. He felt for the switch.

"*Lux fiat!*" he said and held his breath, as though he was doomed once again to disappointment. He had gone further than most in the opera world, but no further, and not because it was his own fault. There was a sudden warmth, a glare. "*Lux fiat!*" he said again, but with a theatrical push on the vowels that made him smile. Then, because as an opera director it was second nature to translate the merest scrap of a foreign language, he pronounced:

"*Lux fiat,* let there be light."

And light there was. In its cage of metal, the great bulb of the ghost glowed yellow and began to beat back the darkness.

"Limelight," he crowed.

He began circling the stage, hesitantly at first, like an animal marking territory, and then faster and faster, as though propelled by the cape of an opera grandee, Don Giovanni or the Duke in "Rigoletto." He could feel the tug on his shoulders, the slap against his calves as he slowed. The music would lead him on, the rising phrase of the vocal line commanding gesture till, with a flick of the lace at his wrist, he opened his hand to heaven, splayed wide his fingers, and hit the money. Oh, God, how he held the note! Oh, God! how it boiled out of him and widened. Just try doing that with your hands in your pockets. Oh, God! how they yelled and screamed. Corny, corny, crony, but pretty damn wonderful. The people who complained that applause drowns out the composer's last great chordal colors—he quoted from a review—had never been on stage. He winked at the ghost light.

Now there are people who think the ghost light is on stage to prevent people from toppling into the orchestra pit, and those jerks call it a trouble

light, and there are those people who know the ghost banishes evil spirits—
and this last is what he believed. The ghost light always meant a new start. It
was right and proper that he lit this ghost light. In six months he would present
his first production of "Tosca" in this very theater. And when it was all over
he would stand alone on this stage. As the director, he would take his solo
bow. More than the director, he was the impresario, his name on the marquee:
John Austin Othmar Presents…He liked his name. Sonorous and mysterious.
The "Othmar" he had cribbed from an obit.

He could see himself at the solo bow, slender and severe in black. With his
tux, he might wear a simple silk turtleneck as they were doing these days. His
bow would be quiet, profound, yes…an *hommage* to art. Then, beckoning to
the wings, he would summon the whole company. Yes…the turtleneck was
exactly right—he in black, standing center stage, everyone else in costume.
He would swoop up the hands on either side of him and lead the cast forward
to receive the plaudits of the house. It would be his triumph. Behind him,
already fading fast, was the humiliation of—but why even mention it?
Behind was the sabotage at—but that he would avenge! Again he circled, for
the first time giving voice. "E-e-e-e," he squealed. "Ou-ou-ou," he moaned,
and "ah-ah-ah." He began to laugh.

The cape melted away. He stood facing out into the dark, the ghost light
behind him casting his spectral self over the first several rows of orchestra
seats. He must sing. His voice must be the first his theater heard. He would not
sing the arias in his considerable repertory. Those too were in the past. The
proscription did not apply, however, to the simple vocal exercises that "a
humble *amateur de chant* might practice as part of his faith in the lyric art that
is opera." To quote from himself.

The cloak of humility has many pockets and stowed deep in one was the
sorry fact of something that had happened to him many years ago in a small
German theater, when a sudden flash of gold doomed his opera career. It was
a "Bohème" and he sang Schaunard the Composer. Shit, he had to start
somewhere. It wasn't so much he forgot what happened back then, or blocked
it. More that he moved on. "Found my true calling," as he liked to say. Any
idea that he had connived, however innocently, in his downfall had been
given a quicklime burial in the part of his mind that lay beyond thought.

Glancing now out to Row D, say, where they had sat, he gave them the
finger.

Center seats. She was blonde and wore a blue sheath in hammered satin
that was not kind to her figure. In the Artists Room after the performance, her

husband made much of adjusting her chinchilla stole, of pushing her forward to fawn over this singer and that. "The Krauts actually do click heels and kiss hands," he told Gilly later.

"Not this American," he had vowed. He bided his time as the couple worked their way down the cast. The Mimì curtsied. The men bowed, the Rodolfo staying in character with a head-snap. He was the last of the least. "But prepared." And when you thought of it, the means of his revenge, how simple it was, how natural, how wonderfully *theatrical* to use the theater against them.

"Another of our Americans," said the opera house intendant, but not, of course, mentioning him by name.

The handshake he now gave her was only what they all deserved—the preening husband, the vacant wife, and he as their victim.

The intendant, hissing with shame, hurried the couple out. "Americans," he could be heard saying as if that explained all. Needless to say, he never sang there again. "Industrialist," said the intendant when firing him, as if "industrialist" explained or excused.

He never again sang professionally on any stage. But to abandon the world of opera, which he loved, would be the act of a coward. Or as he preferred to say, "I'd be a fool to leave when I have put so much into it." So, to salvage his dead self as performer he took up opera directing and renamed himself John Austin Othmar.

Other men have come to this calling by different routes, some from stage design or directing, the great Tito Gobbi from acclaim as a singing actor, and Boris Goldovsky, by his own admission, from hating opera. It may be that Othmar loved opera too well. He sometimes thought that. "Defending the music against singers" was how he put it. Some people—singers—thought he was too pure, too puritanical as a stage director. So, he'd been found unworthy as a performer? Well, then! (he loved arguing with himself) Well, then, he would never ever again sing on stage—except, of course, except to hum a phrase or passage that he was trying to persuade some brainless tenor or soprano to see it his way, and thus "make the public see the music happen." (Quoting again.) They were all brainless, singers—and those that weren't were on ego trips.

Alone now and basking in ghost light, he did his old warm up. He sang scales, he sang intervals in various combinations, he sang nonsense syllables. His was the classic baritone voice, with neither the real lows of the bass-baritone nor a credible tenory top, and was well-produced if a bit colorless.

"The voice of celery" was the verdict of one of the more gnomic critics. "Gotta be a typo" Othmar still believed. But a "useful" voice, the kind music managements could find work for in oratorio if opera failed. "A tenor may get the girl but I get the gigs" was an early pronouncement.

After singing the scales and intervals, he did another exercise, the swooping, downward sighing on "ah," that a particularly gossipy singer told him was one of the tricks of the trade taught by the great pedagogue—but why dignify gossip with that name, when it had worked for Othmar.

The more he sang the more he felt himself come alive. There was the feeling of resonance in all the right places in his head, the coolness between his ears and the buzz behind his eyes when in the upper chest register, and the sound "coming out of his forehead" when in his mixed register.

"Gonna bust my buttons!" he sang to F-sharp and unnotched his belt. Should he, he wondered, start wearing suspenders? With the right shirt, they had the sort of theatrical flare that might go over well in this dump of a town. The "uniform," of course, for rehearsals was blue jeans, turtleneck, sneakers. He could feel his body fill. Not entirely with air—"Not the lung but the diaphragm is the engine of voice," he would say grandly when he lectured on singing to women's clubs. "Singing comes not from the heart but," and here he would pause, "from the gut," and be rewarded by the audience's faint gasp at a vulgar word. For good measure, he would tell about the voice teacher who divided his fellow pedagogues into two groups. There were the "in and uppers" who believed in blowing from the diaphragm. And there were those like himself who were the "down and outers" who pressed down on the diaphragm to expel sound. "And not just a 'down and outer'," Othmar would tell the ladies, "but this teacher called himself a 'de-fe-*ca*-tor'." And every time he told this story, there were gasps, and then giggles, from the ladies.

What Othmar did not tell the ladies was that singing was putting on another self, donning a costume, going beyond. He could feel that now, feel himself swell with a sense of accomplishment and importance. And, it must be said, with desire.

After all these years he still lusted after the image of himself as stage presence. He had been a costumer's dream, blessed with a long neck that swanned from open collars. He could dress "period," conveying the seedy elegance of the Composer in "Bohème"—his first and only stage role—that was implicit in black checked trousers, careless jabot and blue flyaway tailcoat. He was on the tall side, but it also has to be said he was narrowly built and stick-like. Had he been a lanky man, a more supple man, a more physically-confiding man, people would have warmed to him more. "I refuse to sell myself," he once said in another context. Nor did his face welcome scrutiny and people's eyes tended to skate over his features. He wasn't exactly pop-eyed but his "baby blues," his "peepers," as his dated slang had it, looked stuck onto his face. He wore his hair long and full, combing it back from his considerable brow to fall in wings. This style looks wonderful on men with prominent ears but his were small and clapped to his head. Too free a hand with pomade made his hair waxy and he would prove the sort of blond whose hair turns yellow before it grays.

Fully warmed up, he cast his voice round and round the empty theater, listening, as singers do, for dead spots. There were none. This only served to confirm his feeling of great good luck. This could be it! This would be it! The wilderness years were as good as behind him.

"Mine, mine, mine," he sang. "All mine."

The empty theater, as sentimental as any matinee audience, erupted, showering him with motes of dust that hung in the ghost light, an applause of gold. He bowed deeply to the house. "God bless," he said. "God bless you all."

God knows, that September day had begun without promise. He left Manhattan in a borrowed car in the driving rain of a tropical storm. Ahead lay a three-hour drive north to the fair city of Pallas, where he was to stage "Tosca" in March. At noon he would meet formally with the town fathers and receive the keys to their precious theater. It was called, what else? The Palladium—and he was sure it would be a bad joke. Still, he had worked in theaters that scarcely deserved the name, in seedy movie houses and college gyms with bleacher-seating that creaked and a token stage at one end. He did the lighting for the "Così fan tutte" staged on the elm-girt lagoon of a public park with the stilly water standing in for Mozart's Bay of Naples. The audience sat rapt in the beauty of it till the body mikes on the singers began broadcasting the radio frequency reserved for taxi dispatchers. "Top at City Hospital...Who wants a Pizza Hut delivery?" He'd been assistant stage manager for the "Carmen" done in the round in a brewery warehouse, a venue so cold that people kept their coats on. Moreover, it smelled from the real horses (for the bullfight) and their attendant manure, stinks that he excused on the grounds this was *verismo* opera. There was the opposite of *verismo*, the terribly tasteful "Alceste" put on in a college chapel with the set consisting of a single column of white chiffon—a production forever after known as "Modess...because."

13

Opera was everywhere these days, arts money flooding any town that could find a congressman willing to birddog grant proposals for his artsy constituents. Thus Pallas, thus "Tosca." Thus, John Austin Othmar, driving north on a prayer and a shoeshine (he was a soldier's son) to sell opera to people who weren't sure they wanted or needed it.

The classical music station he liked began to quit at Hawthorne Circle, the "Pastorale" surviving an attack of static only to fade away like Haydn's "Farewell." He was tired to death of news, which seemed to consist of one damn war after the other, wars that no one knew how to end or begin. The ever-spreading mess in Vietnam he had viewed smugly from the safety of a high draft number, and advancing years (he was thirty-nine). It was far easier to be for the War on Poverty, the ceremonial announcement of which he heard during a costly taxi ride as the black cabby, slowing to catch LBJ's every sorrowing word and running the meter, moaned "my man, that's my man."

On Othmar drove, unable to open the car window because of the storm and stewing over his slow progress. The truck route had been recommended as the fastest way north, but bursts of speed only came in the brief intermissions between one shabby town and its dreary twin. If he had cared to notice, they weren't identical. There were brick and granite towns, and there were wooden towns with clapboard houses and a shingled church. One or two even boasted a town green, but he had little use for scenery, except on stage. And anyway the towns tended to run together because two days of rain had plastered the Labor Day bunting to store fronts and light poles making a patriotic blur which dragged on for miles. Just when he spotted a straightaway with broken line, a school bus bounced toward him with its freight of screaming kids and the wash dowsed his windshield. Glancing down at the dashboard, he found he was low on gas.

People who lent you their car, he thought sourly, ought to fill it up and let you replace what you used. But that was wealthy people for you, the nicest people in the world, and why not? but mean over the little things. He thought of Gilly—it was Gilly's car—and how Gilly could afford to be generous, could afford to carry him when money was tight, Gilly never hurting, Gilly able to weather the ups and down of the music business because Gilly's father up in Boston could always bail him out. Gilly managed singers and conductors. The Pallas "Tosca" had been Gilly's idea.

"Just a matter of enlightened self-interest," Gilly had said in his easy way. Behind that deprecating statement was Gilly's need to find work for his growing roster of promising young singers. Left unsaid was ol' pal Johnny Othmar's greater need.

14

"Piece of cake," insisted Gilly when Othmar waffled. "The good people of Pallas wouldn't know 'Tosca' if it bit them. You'll be doing them a favor. Bring culture to the masses and when it's all over, take home a little something for yourself." Othmar stiffened. That was Gilly, never letting him forget certain items of furniture and objets d'art from a production of "Werther" that followed him back to New York. What business was that of Gilly's!

As the highway began to climb into the hills, the rain gave way to the drizzle that doesn't need the wipers on full time. Othmar, amusing himself by calculating just when he had to give in for visibility's sake, cleared the windshield too late to read the road sign for the shorter way to Pallas.

"Sorry to be late," he said, and affecting sympathy, "You're all such busy people."

"Welcome to our theater," said the lone woman in the group of men. She was belted into a trench coat on the lapel of which was pinned a big shiny yellow button (a "Smiley" button Othmar was sure) and she carried a clipboard. He knew the type. Madam chairman. And the men were her committee. One would be the treasurer, and he would be the man to cultivate. It had rained hard, too, in Pallas and they stood damply in the theater lobby, the men in car coats. Othmar raised an eyebrow. Car coats! Except behind the wheel, was there a sillier coat than a coat which ended at the knees? Car coats, Othmar thought with satisfaction, reduced the town fathers to gumdrops.

"Welcome to our precious jewel," thrilled the woman. "I am sure you will do us proud."

He bowed. "Madame is too kind." Women always liked that.

The men he could see would rather be elsewhere. They shifted on their feet. Othmar's own raincoat did not exactly inspire confidence. It was dark green, a waxed cloth, a fine English make that fell almost to the ankle, second hand (but who here would know?) and he wore it loosely belted at the hip. More than one of the car coats thought it looked like a lady's bathrobe, and wondered at the implications of that, not for opera but for Pallas.

"I know you have to get back to the office," said Othmar taking charge. He imagined them selling insurance and foreclosing on mortgages, and the one who smelled of clove must yank teeth. Still they stood, clustered, a cauliflower of balding heads, dead eyed and tightly buttoned.

"The keys!—He must have the keys," the woman called.

Like an actor handed a prop, they gladly sprang into action and were all over him. One plucked at him (and how he hated being touched): "You'd better sign this." Another poked papers into his chest. "You'll need to look these over." A third, the mustache who foreclosed, said "they" would "want to see the final figures."

"Yes," he promised, and stepped back out of reach. "But of course," he agreed and stepped forward so firmly they must needs retreat. He smiled at himself: you could convey menace in the simplest of movements. He gave his most charming smile to the woman. "I think you mentioned the keys."

"I want you to have this," she replied and swooped to pin a big yellow button on him. Looking down at it, he spelled out "T-O-S."

"Wrong side to!" she exclaimed, screwing the button around. "You're reading it backwards! It's SOT—for Save Our Theater."

"Ahhh," he managed.

"You'll find we are be-sotted here."

"My theater," he said, when finally he had shooed them out. "My theater, not theirs. Mine, mine, mine."

His theater, and yet he sat, hunched in an aisle seat like a man who has arrived too early for the matinee. He was exhausted, content for the moment to shut his eyes. There was the tinsel sound again in his ears. When, after many minutes, he was able to hear past it, he listened for the theater's own sounds. High in the fly loft, the wind played in the cables. He opened his eyes. The stage was a black void and the auditorium lay in darkness but for the EXIT signs over the doors. Their blocky red letters cheered him. They said, yes, this is a working theater. We have our own rules, own language, own spaces. We deal in illusion but illusion is only craft made manifest. Opera is, well, opera…As long as he knew what opera was, he didn't have to define it. Better not to. Trust to instinct. His cast—he wondered about his cast. What did they know? Working together for a month, six weeks, what would they come to know? Would there be the ensemble that lifts the routine to the sublime? The four small roles were on their way to being filled with good young singers, all with but little stage experience. Calls were out for the principals, Tosca and the Scarpia and the Cavaradossi. That these three would certainly know their way around was something Othmar would have to face. He scowled. Better a bunch of kids who knew nothing, whom he would mold into an ensemble. Old habits die hard, opera habits never, reinforced, as he knew, by tradition and underwritten in the music. And the vagaries of the opera house acoustic! The singers don't hear much of the orchestra, which is seated under and ahead of them. The conductor hears little of the voices, which stream out over his head. Opera is, opera is…absurd.

With that thought forcing a smile, Othmar stretched, got up stiffly and walked back up the aisle to a lighting panel he had seen in the lobby. He found the buttons for the wall sconces and the chandeliers. Whoever had done the theater restoration had gone all out. With the old paint removed, the plaster decorations were immaculate, the roses in the garlands buxom and the ribboned swags crisp.

"Not such a dump," he murmured. "Not such a dump at all!"

Leaving the sconces on, he made for the stage. The steps to the side of the orchestra pit were dusty, and he expected the stage would be, too. No one had swept.

"Kitchen brooms," he said (he was one to make lists). "And a janitor's broom." Theaters had their own special dust, he'd tell anyone who cared to listen. Theater dust was like nothing he had ever seen, and he knew dust and dirt: he'd cleaned a million houses to pay for voice lessons. There was the street dirt that people tracked in with them, and in the city it was sooty and black, but in Boston, where he'd also worked, it was reddish and shiny. Stage dust, as opposed to dirt, was the sum of everything in the theater, the steam heat, the flaking paint, sawdust and metal filings, crumbs from the Danish at rehearsals, Kleenex—God knows how many boxes a cast went through—to say nothing of the upholstered seats that exhaled plush every time a patron sat down. He rummaged in the wing by the stage manager's corner. Ah, there it was. Right where it should be. The ghost light.

"Now we're in business."

2.

Sarah Smythe stood in the dark theater lobby peering into the even darker auditorium. In her right hand was her reporter's notebook. She had many little fears, one of which was keeping people waiting, and so as usual she had arrived well ahead of the agreed-upon time. Good manners only prolonged the agony, for today's assignment was not without its challenges, and she was already slippery moist with anticipation. She liked to think she was a seasoned reporter, able to cope with most events that people in the small city of Pallas (population 41,777) threw her way. This story was bigger than anything she had covered. "It will put us on the map," her editor teased, and he had reserved space on Page One.

For on this theatrically-bright October morning Sarah would finally interview the man who would bring grand opera to town. It was to be a production of "Tosca." Not an opera she knew, she had to confess, even by title. At the moment, her main concern was whether she could call the opera producer an "impresario," and if so, was impresario spelled with two SS's? Best to put both in and let the copy desk decide.

She was suddenly aware of a darkness darker than the dark theater. And a smell. Men's cologne. There were two kinds of cologne, the kind her darling Denny had worn and the other kind that stuck on you when you shook hands and stayed in your hair, and this one was that.

Lights snapped on.

"Are you Mr. Orthwin?" Blinking, Sarah stepped forward. She had a tendency to crowd. The man did not move. There was a near collision.

"I am not Orthwein. Whomever he may be."

Sarah wondered about the grammar. Shouldn't it be "whomsoever?" She heard a handclap.

"I am, however, John Austin Othmar. As in—a roll of drums, please—Othmar the Magnificent! And you must be Sally Smith."

She found herself being herded into the theater auditorium. Othmar threw on more lights. Chandeliers blazed and sconces twinkled in the boxes. He clearly knew his way around.

She thought she must say something to show the Palladium was her theater, too. "The Palladium retains its original mushroom cellar."

"Which," he pealed, "'by sliding open its ceiling vents, released cooling air into the theater.' I quote from one of your exhaustive articles on the restoration. Really, very comprehensive. Go to the head of the class! Shall we go for coffee?"

"Coffee?" she said doubtfully. Was he trying to buy a favorable story?

Sarah Smythe was a born worrier. Worrying was as much a part of her natural condition as her fair hair and blue eyes. She had been spared the worrier's frown. Instead, her little pink mouth curled into a perfect O! of surprise. Men had liked to pounce on that mouth and kiss it, and she married the one she called "Darling Denny," otherwise Peter Denison Smythe III. The few years of marriage were her happiest ever. Denny ran her life and she basked in his demands. Just when she began seriously to worry she wasn't getting pregnant, he went out fishing and drowned. She hadn't much liked the Smythes. Denny's mother called her Miss Mouse or The Nun; and Sarah worried it might be true. So, after a decent interval as widow she returned the antique Smythe silver that had come to Denny on his marriage, packed up the things that were hers, and moved back to Pallas where she had been born and raised.

There, she went to work for the local newspaper, The Clarion Voice. She wrote features. She covered society. "Whatever that is these days," said her Aunt Evey. She wrote the weekly food page, which could be recipes or an "essay." She wrote about the arts. The Clarion Voice did not print reviews. In small cities, opinion causes more trouble than it is worth, Sarah's editor said. The way around that was to write nice features that explained what the arts were, stories that educated the public. Sarah liked her job. She used to worry she was tolerated only because her family owned a chunk of Clarion stock and her brother was the paper's lawyer. She knew she couldn't be fired, and for this she was beginning to be grateful. She was now thirty-nine. "Life Begins at Forty" had been a best-seller in her mother's bookcase. Sarah worried that might be true and worried that it wouldn't.

A natural worrier does not necessarily make the best reporter. Sarah tended to worry herself out of facts she knew she knew. But she could be depended on to get everyone's middle initial correct, and that counts for a lot in places like Pallas. She worried about spelling things right. She had been born "Sarah with an H," as she was always reminding people. It followed she would marry not a Smith but a Smythe. It also followed that most people, in fact anyone who did not live in the county, would hear the fair name of Pallas as "palace." She was accustomed all her life to spelling things out. As a feature writer, she crammed in more facts than were good for the reader's immediate comprehension. Some months ago, in announcing the first-ever performance of "Tosca" in Pallas, she devoted a fat paragraph to the Napoleonic wars that figure offstage in the libretto but neglected to place Puccini's opera in music history.

Her next dispatch was read by a trio of interested parties in far-off New York City. It contained a recipe for Chicken Marengo, named for Napoleon's victory that defines the loyalties of the characters on stage.

"Made with *canned* mushrooms?" Liz was disbelieving.

"Johnny, what are you getting us in for?" That was Gilly, for whom Johnny Othmar was something of a meal ticket. "Can't you sex it up and tell her it's known in the trade as a shabby little shocker?"

"You have only to hear her once on the phone to know there's not much upstairs," said Othmar. He moaned. "Why does this always happen to me?"

"Here we go again," said Liz to Gilly later.

"Oh, yes! Let's go for coffee!" said brave Sarah. "On me, on the Clarion Voice," she insisted. It was more professional that way, she thought. If the paper paid, then it would not appear that Othmar was buying publicity. She would take him to Kulda's Koffee, which was just across from the theater.

"Follow me!" she said gaily to Othmar. Traffic along South Main was steady and sluggish, and she darted through, bestowing on one car a big smile and on the next a little wave of thanks. "I don't usually jay-walk," she said, full of herself. But there was no one to hear. She looked back across the street. Where was he?

Darkness dissolved Othmar as he stepped back into the shadow cast by the theater marquee. From this haven, he watched Sarah gain the sidewalk and turn to catch him up. She had a trim figure, he noted, and good legs—what you could see of them. "Miniskirts have yet to hit beautiful downtown Pallas Athene," he said to his New York self. He found a dowdy Sarah reassuring: He'd had enough of Liz's fashion wars. But what most struck him now was Sarah's to-and-froing. She would walk a few steps and turn—and to what purpose? He waited for her to look his way—and could hear himself directing the scene: "Sweetheart, lift your hand to your brow against the sun, tha-a-at's right, and squint, yes, squint." But as he couldn't look into Sarah's mind, and know her code of manners, he could not fathom her delay. Sarah could not look for him so obviously. Oh no, that would put him on the spot for not crossing the street with her, and to point that out would be rude.

Amused, he settled further into his shadowy lair to see how this little drama would play out. "Why doesn't she cross back over and try to find me?" he wondered. "I would, if I had lost something." They (he meant women) say men won't stop to ask directions if they're lost. His mother was always at his father: Stop at the farm stand and ask; stop the policeman and ask. "This is different," he said with satisfaction. "Sarah Smythe has lost me."

Behind the pacing Sarah stretched what Othmar supposed was a representative sample of Pallas's small businesses. There were surely more where the commercial district continued on North Main, for he had yet to spot a movie house or a department store. Still, the scene in front of him could tell him something useful. As an Army brat, he had grown up moving base to base. Sometimes there were mountains on the horizon, and sometimes not, but always there was grass that looked shaved rather than mowed and flags every where. The year his mother planted spills of pink petunias when pots of cemetery-red geraniums were the flowers appropriate to his father's rank was memorable for his father's rage. As an opera impresario, he first made his name in college towns, none without their charm but whose life revolved around the campus. Pallas would be different. Already he could tell it had its own civic identity—it had once seen fit to build a splendid theater—and this made him hopeful. He thought of himself as an injection, that is, he was something they—that is, Pallas—had never experienced. It would be his game, his show, this "Tosca." His to say what "Tosca" was as opera and should be. Pallas was the clearing in the woods, the way out. Pallas today, tomorrow the world, and the Palladium was the stage that would accomplish this, make his name.

"They'll put a plaque up to me here."

As grand as the Palladium bulked, it was diminished by the company it was forced to keep. The only hotel worth the name rose, a grimy granite pile, at the corner where South Main met North Main. Once upon a time, the business block opposite the theater must have seemed the wave of the future. For one thing, it was built of stucco when older merchants still believed in the fastness of brick. And weather had proved them right, for the stucco was crumbling and stained. The October sun exposed fading signs identifying the insurance company doing business behind closed venetian blinds, the stationer's with its display of engraved wedding invitations as solemn as tombstones, and the drugstore holding health at bay with bottles of colored elixirs and shiny white boxes. The bakery was observing Halloween with a mountain of cupcakes iced like pumpkins. The dizzying revolution of a striped pole marked Joseph Patti's barbershop. Othmar grinned. By local standards his hair was too long, and, God knows, too blond. But his eye gladdened at the sight of the news stand awning with its promise of the New York papers. Next to a vacant shop was Kulda's Koffee where Sarah continued to wait.

Back and forth she walked, her shoulder bag swinging. He'd probably gone to the john, she rationalized. It was really funny, he thought, all that activity for so little result.

"Tells you something," he said to himself. "She can't find her way out of a paper bag." That was good news. A Sarah who was not too inquiring might be very useful. If she did not know what to ask, she was not a problem. "Eternal vigilance is the price," Othmar quoted to himself. Then, because he was feeling on top of things, he murmured: "Snow jobs as needed."

Stop lights had emptied the block of traffic. "It's nice to be vanted, dahling," he said to the Othmar who was his best audience. "Time to make our entrance." And slipping on brilliant black sunglasses that glared back at the world, he strode across, jacket dangling from his shoulders.

And yet Sarah didn't see him. Or rather she saw a man she didn't know but who seemed to know her.

"It's your sunglasses," she declared. "I couldn't see your face."

There was something else about Othmar, an image that would replay itself later, something about his walk which was as worrying as sunglasses in October. It came to Sarah the next morning. Othmar was "suave."

But now she hurried ahead to Kulda's to open the door. He entered as though she didn't exist. What was he supposed to do? Othmar was annoyed. Pull out a chair and seat her? Impossible in a joint that consisted of six booths along one wall and a counter with a dozen stools.

"Mr. Kulda got the idea at the '38 World's Fair," Sarah prompted. "The tile and the black and white décor. It's Moderne. The only one in the county."

A good thing, Othmar muttered. Soapy film from a dishrag was visible on the first table Sarah chose. "Not that one," he said.

Othmar saw an elderly waitress rise from the back booth. Her black nylon uniform sagged. Irish, by the look of her.

"Miss."

"Hello, Catherine."

"Yer egg and olive?"

"Too early for lunch. What would you like?" Should she call him by his first name? What if he wasn't John but Jack?

Othmar said coffee would be fine.

"The muffins are home-made." Sarah was Kulda's only regular patron who did not know the muffins came from the bakery next door. But Othmar could not be tempted.

"Cinnamon toast, please, Catherine. Such a treat!"

Othmar's gorge rose. Did he really want to spend a month or more in dumps like this? He toyed with the salt and pepper dispenser, two vials in a plastic case, and pressed the white knob. Obedient to the force of gravity a cone of salt rose speedily from the table.

Sarah giggled. "You're supposed just to tap."

"Milk or cream with yer coffee?" The waitress was on his case.

"Oh, have the cream!" said Sarah.

"Milk," said Othmar.

The coffees came, his with cream, and the cinnamon toast running butter.

Catherine returned one further time. "Milk," she said, setting a brimming glass before Othmar.

It wasn't long into the interview before Sarah found two more things to worry about. "Tosca" had no overture. She would have to banish that word from her coverage. A pity, as she had been playing with the idea of using opera language to make the production unfold for her readers. "Aria" she assumed still applied, and "duet." From the local music store she had already ordered an LP of "Tosca." There was also something called a "piano-vocal" which had the music and the words. She would get Aunt Evey to play it.

Othmar was beaming at her. Or was it a glare? She had better listen.

"Of course, my 'Tosca' is a steal from the old Sarah Caldwell production." He winked. "I call it my homage to the Divine Sarah."

"But she didn't sing, did she?" Sarah, who took an interest in other Sarahs, was at a loss.

"You don't know much," said Othmar. "Not Bernhardt—the Boston Sarah. But we've got all winter to educate you."

Sarah began to fidget. Her first deadline was at four, when her editor would want to see the lede and first couple of grafs. The story that would tell the readers of the Clarion Voice how lucky the city of Pallas and county of Chatham was to host a professional production of a world famous opera. "Host" was her editor's choice of verb.

"Tell me about your role in 'Tosca,'" said Sarah hoping to get him back on track.

"I am The Attavanti."

Sarah wrote that down. Not a name she remembered from reading the synopsis. Perhaps "attavanti" was Italian for prompter.

"You first see me at my devotions. In drag."

She took a deep breath. Her editor wasn't going to like that.

"I shall wear blue contact lenses."

"But you have blue eyes," she protested.

"Honey, my peepers won't read past the pit. I need blue eyes that will bounce off the back wall."

"Like Ethel Merman's voice," Sarah said to show she understood.

"Very good! Very good, Sarah!"

Opera is theater, he went on. Opera was illusion, and pretend. "Magic time," he said Sarah Caldwell called it. Sarah had the feeling she would be hearing a lot about the Divine Sarah.

"And if we impart a truth or two, we're home free and dry."

His voice, thought Sarah, was too glitttery for Kulda's. Nor was she sure how all this would shape up as quotes. Would it read funny? Or flip? Worse, she hadn't been able to get in her questions about the budget. Her editor was big on figures. She wondered how old Othmar was. How should she describe what he wore? "Natty?" Those pants were a windowpane plaid. And a bit tight. Perhaps "theatrical" was the best word and people could figure it out for themselves. He was very blond. She wrote down "sandy" for his hair.

"The Attavanti even has her own tune." He conducted as he hummed.

It didn't sound much like a tune to her.

"Well, who is The Attavanti?"

"I thought you'd never ask."

In this production of "Tosca," as Sarah would inform her readers, the stage curtain is up while opera patrons take their seats. As the house lights go down, the stage lights illumine a tableau beyond a panel of netting called the scrim. The setting is a chapel in a Roman church, Sant'Andrea della Valle. A woman enters, carrying a wicker basket. She kneels near the altar. This is the private chapel of the Attavanti family and Attavantis have always been buried in the crypt below. That small wooden door leads down to their tombs. For years, Attavantis have come to pray to the simple figure of the Madonna on the altar. Now there is to be a painting of the Magdalene to adorn the chapel. "Tarting it up a bit," Othmar had said to Sarah's shock. If there was one thing frowned on in Pallas it was jokes about religion. The artist painting the Magdalene is Mario Cavaradossi. The model—well, she isn't a model in the usual sense—is the Marchesa Attavanti. The Attavanti. Cavaradossi has discovered her lost in prayer and given her blond hair and blue eyes to his Magdalene. That the Magdalene will have her features flatters the Attavanti family, Sarah would write. Reading this two days later in New York, Othmar groaned. "Where did Sarah ever get that idea from? If she's anything, she's an Angelotti—Angelotti's sister." Liz laughed. "At least she got it right that the blue eyes will send Tosca up the wall."

"What's her first name?" Sarah's editor was going over her copy.
"The Attavanti doesn't have a first name." Sarah hoped there wasn't going to be trouble. This was not exactly a news story, not the Attavanti part. "They never gave her a first name. She's a plot device. She's not that important in the story. It's just the Attavanti chapel. The Attavanti never actually appears in the opera, though you hear her music. Her music sets up Cavaradossi's first big aria."
This bored the editor. "Then why is she on stage."
"Well, there's no overture, just some menacing music from the orchestra to set the mood. Our, that is, this production shows you the woman Tosca is jealous of."
There was no stopping Sarah.
"The Attavanti has blue eyes, *occhi azzurro.* " Sarah read from her notes so she wouldn't seem to be showing off. "Tosca's eyes are dark, *occhi nero.* Cavaradossi loves Tosca. Well, if that's so, says Tosca, why not give the Magdalene my dark eyes. As The Attavanti, Othmar threatens to wear blue contacts. And a very blond wig. He's a hoot. You really would like him—if you knew him."
This Sarah doubted.
She rushed on. "You see, with The Attavanti on stage, you actually see why the Sacristan hears whispering in the chapel, and says what he does. Which only enflames Tosca. You see The Attavanti drop her fan. With the crest that identifies her. 'With dire consequences,' as Othmar says. Well, Othmar sweeps off stage. The scrim rises—the netting I told you about. The

opera really begins. Othmar drops his costume in a corner and goes back to being the stage manager."

The editor turned away. "Just don't become part of the story."

That afternoon, Othmar sped back to New York in his borrowed car. As the miles increased between greasy Kulda's and dopey Sarah the happier he became. The thing to remember was the theater. It was a little gem, red brick with white stone, as elegant as a Broadway playhouse. It was his. It could lead to bigger things. He would…what was the new word?…he would "invest" himself. Opera by opera he would build "inventory." There would come a time when "John Austin Othmar Presents" guaranteed a classy production by the best (available) singers. He thought of a slogan: "Prepared in Pallas and proudly shared with all." At the last big traffic circle before the city he stopped at a pay phone and called Gilly.

"Dinner's on me."

They met at a Hunan place way up Broadway, thrifty Gilly traveling from work on the 104 bus and Liz, for whom parking spaces always opened up, honking from her VW convertible.

Othmar ate like a man sentenced to life without Chinese food. "The town's totally dead," he announced.

"What did you expect?" parried Liz.

"But not without possibilities," said Othmar, who felt that if there was dishing to be done he should do it. "The theater is truly, truly marvelous. It could be the start of something big. A real, regional opera company. Far enough away from New York and Boston not to be swamped by them. But attractive to young singers because it isn't the back of beyond and they might just get reviewed. You know how I feel about ensemble opera and with you steering the best of your kids, this really could take off."

"To the future!" Gilly gave a mock toast with his beer.

"How was the Divine Sarah?" Liz, who worked four days a week at a Madison Avenue gallery, saw enough of the art world not to suppose the same human frailties existed elsewhere.

"Actually, a pleasant surprise," said Othmar.

"Not ditzy?"

"Really less than we thought," he said, deciding to rehabilitate Sarah. "She doesn't know anything, especially about opera. She's humble. Asked me why I said "The" before every character. The Attavanti. The Tosca. The Scarpia."

"And why do you?" wondered Liz. The "The" conjured an Othmar pushing the characters around the stage at his bidding. "Puts them down, it seems to me."

"As I was saying, Sarah's really glad to have me explain things. Told me—I didn't have to ask—she would read me my quotes before they went in the paper so she'd get it right. I think she can be very helpful."

"Sounds like our boy is on his way," Gilly said to Liz as she drove them home.

"I can't wait to meet Evey Titus."

"She's our little secret for now."

3.

From her newspaper desk in far-off Pallas, Sarah Smythe had no reason to believe that a cast was not already in rehearsal for "Tosca." Rehearsing was John Othmar's business, as she saw it. Hers was more humble—to help build an audience—and she saw it as a civic duty to interest enough people in "Tosca" to fill the Palladium, which she took to calling the opera house.

"Nine hundred and thirty-eight paying customers?" Her editor was incredulous.

"Times four."

There were to be a total of four performances, three as announced and the fourth, planned and budgeted, as the "Tosca" "brought back by popular demand." At least once a week Sarah would write something interesting, or charming, or even newsy about "Tosca."

Pallas was virgin territory for opera. It was an old mill town. A few hundred might turn out for the pops concert by the local orchestra but the ball park was always full. When restoration of the Palladium was first broached, letter after letter to the Clarion Voice told the city fathers to get their priorities straight and spend the money fixing up the ball field. It flooded in spring, delaying the season, and for most of the summer batters had to face into the setting sun. Sarah's editor was one hundred percent for the ball park when he sat behind home plate. He was one hundred percent for the arts when delegations from various arts councils sat in his office and told him how much the arts would contribute to the local economy. He was amused they put it that way as if the bottom line was all he was expected to understand. "What's that you're wearing?" they said to him at Rotary when he sported one of Millicent French's bright yellow SOT buttons.

There was, as he could appreciate, a real news angle to "Tosca." It concerned the theater itself. Its restoration was part of the grand plan to put life back in down-town Pallas. Like so many old cities elsewhere, it was fast losing shoppers to the malls and commercial strips springing up in old cornfields. Even the movies had moved to the mall, to something called a "cinema." That the city had this jewel of a theater was owing to an earlier impulse to put Pallas on the map. For most of the nineteenth century, it had been little more than a thriving mill town where two railroads crossed. With prosperity came the urge for civic betterment. A library was built. When a fire destroyed the old Music Hall up over Driver's Emporium the call went out for a real theater and a young architect named Joseph McArthur Vance answered that call. To settle on a name for the theater, the Clarion Voice ran a competition. While "Palace," which punned becomingly on Pallas, got the most votes, "Palladium" was declared the winner. "The very name," stated an approving editorial, "conveys the dignity of civic enterprise."

The Palladium's first seasons wisely mixed edification with entertainment and Sarah's grandfather pondered Sarah Bernhardt as Hamlet and cheered James O'Neill as the Count of Monte Cristo. Little girls with a crush on the Boston Stock Company ingenue begged to carry her valise to the theater and were rewarded with one of her monogrammed hankies. Sarah's father preferred vaudeville and saw Fred Allen as "The World's Worst Juggler" long before he heard him on the radio. And when "the talkies" came to stay, the Palladium became a movie house called the Palace. Sarah used to go as a child—when the polio scare permitted. And when television doomed the Palace, the theater was bought and turned into a hardware store. The new owner simply boarded up the stage area, took out the seats and lined the auditorium with bins for rolls of linoleum and carpeting and shelving for cans of paint. It was called Upton's and the marquee advertised specials. Like the Sleeping Beauty, the Palladium slumbered till another form of civic betterment came to her rescue. When, in the distant state capitol, it was decreed that cities of a certain size should each have a community college, Sarah would editorialize in the Clarion Voice that "education for all was coming to the City of Athena, goddess of wisdom." Not enough money came with the community college for a real theater. "Sound bodies in sound minds" was one thing, the arts another, and, no matter how hard you pretended otherwise, the student center was only a "suburb of the gymnasium." Sarah wrote in another editorial. "The magic smell of greasepaint has no chance against swimming pool chlorine."

In one of those ironies of modern life, the shopping strip actually saved the Palladium. Needing parking, Upton's Hardware moved out to the little mall as a "home decorating center." Millicent French, hitherto occupied with making playgrounds safe for children, plunged forward, heading up the committee of local citizens who bought the Palladium. That is, they "went on" the note to the bank, in Sarah's editor's phrase. He should know: he was a bank corporator. He loosed Sarah on the story. It was she who managed to float an idea or two that hadn't actually occurred to the people keenest on restoring the Palladium. One day they read in the Clarion Voice that it would serve as the theater for the community college. Another day Sarah wrote the high schools could use the Palladium, too. And the civic orchestra. Also the Pallas Players, "that merry band of amateur thespians," as she called them in an editorial.

"Well, something has to be staged that people will come to see," Sarah's editor told them at Rotary.

It may have been Sarah's Aunt Evey who put her up to the idea of opera for the Palladium. While they appeared the firmest of friends in public, Evey Titus and Millicent French were not exactly chums. Millicent's idea of civic betterment was to stage Shakespeare for school children at the Palladium. Evey, who had a show-biz side to her, trumped with opera. Opera was on TV. People had seen Beverly Sills on Ed Sullivan. In yet another editorial, Sarah pointed out that if the Palladium was given back its old orchestra pit, the city could enjoy not just opera but musical comedy. When the pit was restored, Sarah was as astonished as anyone. Her stock went up with her editor. "Stay with the story," he said. And she did. Eventually, she was able to announce, not just on Page One but on Page One "above the fold," a "first," a "premiere," the first-ever performance in Pallas of grand opera. It would be "Tosca" and it would be performed by the Grand Opera Touring Company. Shuffled into the wings, Millicent French took up that new thing in medical care, the "regional" or general hospital. And pretty soon, Sarah was writing about efforts to merge St Luke's, which is where the Catholic mill workers went, with the House of Mercy, which had been founded by Protestant Palladians, though, of course, the tactful Sarah called this latter group, "an older generation of townspeople."

So "Tosca" it would be, and the production would, moreover, "showcase"—Sarah's verbal inspiration—the talents of countless local citizens. Music students who qualified would play in the opera orchestra. Sets and costumes would be built at the community college. There would be instructors to teach the necessary scenic arts. A backstage crew would be trained.

Othmar, in New York City where he was living, read Sarah's reports with fascination. "She must be smoking pot," he joked to Gilly and Liz. "Why does she keeping running things together. She's got me down for stage manager as well as director." Gilly said it would save a salary if he did both.

Best of all, Sarah wrote, people who sang in the city's church choirs would swell the opera chorus. A Catholic church in the next county agreed to lend its boychoir and Holy Name in Pallas agreed to find parish families to board them for the performances. That, in fact, was true. The first act finale of this "Tosca" would have real boy sopranos, not girls and women with their hat piled under their choirboy caps so you couldn't help but notice the bobby pins. Sarah wrote a funny piece about "Tosca" without bobby pins that was really Othmar being funny. She had her uses, as they both knew.

To annoy her, Sarah's editor would call Othmar "Mister Tosca." Which was not all that inaccurate: As well as the stage director and producer, he was nominally the set designer and the costumer. It was he who had named it the Grand Opera Touring Company and he who designed the poster. The words Grand Opera and Company were printed in curly gilt letters. "Riverboat baroque," Othmar told Sarah. "Touring" was in a faint Italic. "So the eye skims over it."

"But why?" To Sarah, touring was romantic, exotic, running away with the circus.

Othmar changed the subject.

He was not easy to know, Sarah thought. She found him prickly and remote, but maybe with theatrical people—she pegged him as "theatrical"—he was more relaxed. Theatrical people would talk the same language, and she was aware that as a reporter she asked a lot of dumb questions, and that irritated people. "Why are playgrounds unsafe?" she'd asked Millicent French.

So it was understandable that Othmar had a short fuse.

But he was "great fun, too," Sarah insisted to herself. He phoned often from New York and she was beginning to feel she could joke around with him. He would answer any question she had. (Moron! he breathed at the phone. Hadn't she ever been in a theater!) He suggested stories (and bagged her bad ideas). She would have "an exclusive," he promised, when he was ready to announce the cast.

He was always interesting. She loved his account of the opening night of "Tosca" in January 1900 and what the conductor was told to do if a bomb was thrown at the Queen of Rome. In the opera itself, which takes place exactly one hundred years earlier, the Queen is the Queen of Naples.

"You know who her sister was?—None other than Marie Antoinette," said Othmar grandly.

"Oooh," breathed Sarah. "Marie Antoinette! You don't think of famous people having a sister."

"I know exactly what she means," protested Liz. "You don't think of famous people having families."

"But Marie Antoinette, she daid by then."

"So what," and Liz reached over Othmar and speared the last shrimp.

But in person, on his quickie business trips to Pallas, Othmar did have a way of withdrawing, Sarah noticed. He closes in on himself, she thought. It sort-of went with his posture, which was ramrod straight, almost too military. Other people leaned toward you more, or you leaned toward them so you became sort-of one person. Sometimes Othmar seemed to be holding his breath. "He's clenched," Sarah said out loud, glad she'd finally found the right word. One moment, they'd both be talking away a mile a minute, and then hers would be the only voice, "leaving me high and dry." He'd be there, but not there. She called it his disappearing act. It didn't seem polite. From Aunt Evey, she'd learned how to edge away from bores. You said, concern in your voice, that you "mustn't keep" the person you wanted to get rid of. Othmar was different. Off in another world. She'd learned then to pack up her reporter's pad and go back to the office.

So Othmar was just as unhappy as Sarah when Sarah's editor assigned her to do a profile of "Mister Tosca." Her little essays on Puccini as a composer of *verismo* opera, with their plots about common people, were all very well, the editor said, and a credit to Sarah, but there was nothing like a personality piece to grab the reader. Just remember, he said to Sarah, that ninety-nine percent of Pallas has never been to the Palladium let alone seen an opera.

"You hear opera," she said.

"Whatever. Well, find out about him. What his interests are. Hobbies. Family. Jeez, I don't have to tell you this."

"Just as long as I don't have to ask if he sleeps in the nude."

"We're not the New York Times." That sheet, in an effort to be punchy and with-it, had started tabulating data about its profile subjects. Jaded New Yorkers were startled by the "pajama" category and agog about who admitted to wearing no nightclothes.

The last thing Sarah wanted to ask Othmar about was hobbies. That seemed prying. He thought so, too. Why did they have to know anything about him, apart from his professional credentials?

"Do you think it explains my approach to 'Tosca' if I tell you I hate cabbage but love Ping Pong?"

She wrote both down.

"Well, tell me how you spend a typical working day in New York." That should get him going. Such a neutral subject, and he could work in stuff about "Tosca."

"So, you walk out of your apartment. Which is where?"

"I live in Manhattan," he said loftily.

To say that Othmar lived in Manhattan was true in the sense that he always had a roof over his head. It was seldom his own. On and off for months, he slept on a sofa-bed in Gilly's den till Liz threw him out.

"I'm sick and tired of his complaining you don't do enough for him."

It wasn't that Liz didn't relish music shoptalk but Othmar didn't know when to stop. "That's the third time you've told that story," she'd say to Othmar. "Like talking to a wall," she complained to Gilly.

They were a tight couple. She was tall and willowy, but all steel wire underneath, and she drove the car, bought his underwear, decided where they would go for dinner—and how often to include Othmar. Othmar called her The Whip and sometimes, Stiletto. Their kind of marriage he didn't understand, which really was very simple: Liz was Gilly's manager so he could manage others. With a cat slung across his lap, Gilly could look sleepy. On his feet, he was all bustle. He walked to work. He dictated letters standing up. He worked the intermission crowds at Carnegie Hall, the Met. He loved to go dancing. He was short, a good few inches shorter than Liz in heels, but he was not the kind of short man who slopes forward to seem tall. They'd met in Boston at a Waltz Evening. He kept cutting in and pushed off around the floor till she was breathless. "I'm going to have to marry this tugboat," she thought, but it was also his fiery touch on her spine, much further down her back than they allowed in dancing class, that persuaded when her insides gave a pleased little twitch. "She's an armful," he smiled into her breasts. Now approaching forty, he still looked boyish, his cowlicks and bushy eyebrows disarming people as they had when he was Gurdon Gillespie's cute little son. In the rough world of classical music, Gilly's word was his bond but he cut many a sharp deal. The true son of a lawyer who had made his family a comfortable living in Boston by hiding the assets of husbands in divorce cases, Gilly had been invited into his father's firm. "This nearly was mine," sang Gilly ("Kismet" was new). Instead, he married his radiant Liz and moved her to New York. He still dressed Boston, though, affecting a battered old felt fedora, the "State Street" hat of his father. He was one of the few who called Othmar "Johnny."

When Liz told Othmar to start looking for a new bed, Gilly had gone to Houston to shepherd a pouty Danish soprano through her American debut. She had come to Gilly named Inger Engstrom Fengstrom. This Scandinavian mouthful Liz pruned to Inga Engstrom, Inga on the grounds that Americans would think Inger a man and Engstrom for brevity. The soprano was not happy.

"How was I to know she was the great granddaughter of 'Denmark's Grieg'?" Liz protested.

Gilly laughed. "A Nilsson she'll never be. But I'll have her for a while. She'll make her name. She'll love me and leave me. They always do."

Houston went very well. On his return, Gilly told Othmar he was just as sorry as he could be about Liz. "Nothing personal," he said. "She really does like your company."

Left unsaid was the irritation that wouldn't go away, Othmar's whining that Gilly wasn't doing all he could to advance Othmar's career. "The final blow," said Liz, "was his saying you didn't tell him whozits in Chicago was looking for an assistant. Everyone else knew about that job. He just didn't go after it. So how can he blame you! You've been a real friend."

"That may be the problem. He expects more from me."

"Wouldn't matter who. The great Mister Othmar always acts like he's entitled. And that all the world's against him."

"I suppose he could sleep in the office."

"Noooo!" said Liz.

"You know women, Gilly said to Othmar. "They get it in their head to redecorate." Othmar said he understood, and moved in with George, who played for Broadway rehearsals. When George moved to L.A., Gilly put "ol' pal Johnny" onto a tenor he'd once managed who wanted someone to look after his Pekes while he sang in Europe.

Soon after that, luck began showering down on Othmar. Gilly, who had all the better gossip, tipped him off to a project to bring opera to the 'boonies. "Just think of all that arts council money there for the taking," said Gilly, jumping the line for his share.

At first Othmar didn't see anything in it for him. "Why not you?" Gilly reasoned. "Better than Chicago, if you ask me. You'll be the boss."

Othmar did not like being reminded of Chicago.

"You've got to start somewhere," said Gilly. "Make your mistakes where no one knows any better."

"Mistakes?"

"Touchy, touchy. We all make mistakes."

Thus began the "wilderness years" in upper New York State and western Pennsylvania of a venture called "John Austin Othmar Presents Grand Opera." On the posters the word "grand" was a starburst. "As in, 'Ain't life grand!'" said Gilly. What Othmar actually presented was an evening of opera scenes. He and Gilly cast them from Gilly's roster of young singers, and a friend of Gilly's who booked small venues got them dates. Othmar directed. The singers, along with Othmar and the pianist, crammed into a VW bus, and the scenery, such as it was, and the costumes followed in a VW van. They did one-night stands, till fortune again smiled and Gilly's friend got Othmar and the little troupe booked into a small college for a two-week "residency." The singers made themselves useful in the music department and Othmar gave little talks on opera and the singers he had known (from afar). When he borrowed anecdotes from the Saturday matinee radio talks given by the Met's great Francis Robinson, he was the first to admit the source. "Francis Robinson has done more for opera than anyone I know." This modesty got Othmar a raft of invitations for cocktails and dinner. People could not get enough of life backstage. Othmar retailed stories he promised they would never read in Opera News. He would smile knowingly. "Opera News?" he would say. "It's like Holiday magazine: No flies in Eden. Need I say more?" Like Francis Robinson, he knew just when to pull the blinds.

Othmar was a success with the opera scenes. He toured for several years, then managed to specialize in college residencies. The college term called "inter-session"—those weeks between Christmas and February when students are encouraged to explore the further reaches of the curriculum— might well have been invented for the perpetual care and maintenance of John Austin Othmar. He was also seeing a part of the world that as an Army brat he had not known. Tucked around these campuses were small cities full of people well pleased with their lot in life. They saw the latest Broadway shows. They traveled to Europe. They were always glad to get back home and knuckle down, make a few more bucks. "Plenty of *pengos* out here!" Othmar reported to Gilly from "somewhere near Elmira," which was their code for the 'boonies.

And so Othmar began inching toward producing what he considered his first full-length grand opera, the Pallas "Tosca."

There had been a full-length "Hansel and Gretel," but in English, and "way back when," and that need not count, Othmar thought. To begin with, it wasn't his production, merely a revival he had been called in to refurbish. And he'd had no say in the casting. When he spoke of it at all he would only say that it was a "learning experience" and roll his eyes in a way that invited, that begged for, tales told out of school. "I wasn't the only babe in Mister Humperdinck's woods," he'd say. Which only made people want more. "Another time," said he shucking it like snakeskin. But if they persisted, he told them the problem with "Hansel" was it was a student production "and you know students." True enough. Never again, he told Gilly (who was "responsible" for the "Hansel" job) would he work "below conservatory level." College kids, said Othmar, don't know the first thing about basic stage craft. That "Hansel" was "all remedial reading."

That settled in his mind, Othmar put "Hansel" behind him. "Hansel" was not so easily dislodged from Gilly's mind. He thought of the beloved voice teacher who had sung the Witch and Othmar's staging that ended her career.

Othmar decided to change repertory and work in a range of operas ever so slightly off the beaten track. He was still an apprentice, that much he'd admit, and it would be wiser to make his mistakes on works little known by his chosen public. He had a flair for devising stage pictures. He could clarify character without stooping to the vulgar. He liked working with conductors and most liked working with him. If he was a perfectionist, if he bullied his cast, most singers were grateful for making them go the extra mile. "Goddam, they do learn a lot from me!" he told Gilly. By the time of the Pallas "Tosca" Othmar had staged Douglas Moore's "The Ballad of Baby Doe" and "The Apothecary" by Haydn. When Gilly's roster suddenly had a surfeit of "girl singers," Othmar obliged and did a double bill of Wolf-Ferrari's "The Secret of Susanna" and Puccini's "Suor Angelica." Two of those singers vowed never again to work with Othmar. One soprano "resented being practiced on." Gilly laughed that away. "I told her that was the living end coming from someone who was the second-cast Tatiana at Juilliard." The other story carried a black shadow. Gilly kept his own counsel, not even telling Liz. "How could he humiliate her like that? Like 'Hansel' all over again," mused

Gilly, who knew more about that production than Othmar thought he did. "Lucky I wasn't sued."

The Pallas "Tosca" looked safe, Gilly thought. A professionally-equipped theater. Four young, but well-schooled, Americans in the small roles. A conductor whom Othmar respected, nay, worshipped. "Wait till he hears I got Pompelli!" Gilly crowed to Liz. An audience that would be pleased to see anything, and, Gilly's ace in the hole, Evey Titus, to smoothe Othmar's path in the community.

So when Sarah Smythe in faraway Pallas observed to her pillow that Othmar was difficult to know, she came as close to the bone as any of his friends. He had been fairly candid to her about his dashed hopes for a career as a singer. He had a nice enough voice, a sturdy, flexible baritone. If he caught on, he could eke a living out of the secondary roles. Plus concert and church jobs. If it came to that. Gilly spelled it out for him and refused to take his cut.

"But I was found wanting," Othmar told Sarah. He did not invite inquiries.

In his heart of hearts he had known the stage was not for him. All his life he had withdrawn into himself. "Someone has to look out for little Johnny." He was gifted, better still, cursed with extraordinary distance vision. This made him a watcher. He was a noticer. He saw dandruff. Dust sprang to his eye, and a single leaf on the lawn. He could spot a dangling button, creases the iron had missed. He pointed out fingerprints on knives in diners, butter pats that had gone soft, bread he was sure was yesterday's, and assessed blame accordingly. Energy that could have been put to fruitful uses found itself dead-ended in disgust, in resentment and disappointment. He was doomed to insist on perfection. A part of him knew this. Another part knew he was right.

There was more. The great stage personalities, he believed, went deep into themselves but came out on the other side. The audience side. They could meet this mass of people they didn't know and make it believe, make it love them, and laugh with them, and cry, and connive, for what is performance but mutual complicity? I believe I am Tosca, or Figaro, and you agree I am. But suppose you offered yourself and they didn't accept? That was Othmar's tragedy, as he saw it. His tragedy was to run afoul, the very first time he was on stage in a major production, of a member of the audience who was not worthy of his trust.

It was entirely thanks to Gilly that Johnny O. was included in Gilly's package of three bright young American singers for an Oper Wupperthal "Bohème," Othmar singing the Schaunard, not that it matters because he never got the chance to show what he could do. It was his first trip out of the country. Only his second in an airplane, and it took days for the propeller drone to work out of his ears. But, oh! the excitement of the rehearsals! Finding out, after all, that his voice was nothing to be ashamed of. And working on his character so the audience could tell him from the other Bohemians. Making his Schaunard a musician.

"OK if I wear boots with heels?" he asked the director.

"You are not exactly a midget. I don't want you towering over Rodolfo." Fat chance of upstaging that ham!

The boots, as Othmar didn't want to have to explain, made him buoyant, dancy, full of rhythm, and that was the key, because unlike Rodolfo with his quill pen and sheaf of poems and Colline with his paint brushes, Schaunard has no props to identify his character as a musician till the horn thing in the Christmas scene and by then it's too late.

Furthermore, as he and the director agreed, when it came to the part about the dead parrot he was to let the audience in on the joke. His mistake, his awful mistake, was to break through that fourth wall and play cute. Young singers are prone to do this. "To let the make-up do the acting," as the expression goes. Othmar was instantly punished. He had let his eye fall on a center seat, on a buxom Frau or Fräulein. This was at a time in Germany when young American singers were just being allowed in, a few at a time. He had stood in Berlin to watch Annabelle Bernard's first Aida, and Annabelle not just an American but she was a Negro. Though, in the murk of Wieland Wagner's production, who could tell? And now here he was actually in Wupperthal singing Puccini, the Italian going pretty good, not that the krauts would know, and he was more or less enjoying himself, in rehearsal getting really into the ensemble, and the horseplay, and now was his big chance to lay his Schaunard on the attentive audience, and perhaps a critic or two.

From those center seats came a flash of metal, of gold, and eagle-eyed Othmar followed it to the seat next to the woman, the Frau. The man was obviously her husband. He was busy in his mouth with a large gold toothpick. Light glanced off the gold. His eyes were fastened on the stage, with those upside-down eyes some Germans have, and part of him was loving the music. Othmar could see him sway with the music. Swaying and carving away at his gums. It never occurred to Othmar that the audience would not appreciate his efforts, would not be caught up in his enthusiasm, would not give him the same concentrated attention while watching as he gave them in performing. Othmar looked and was unmanned in a way he could never explain. He ducked behind his fellow Bohemians, thus confusing the ensemble.

He managed to finish the performance, and the run. That awful night he took his revenge. Waiting to be presented to the German couple, he swiped makeup off his neck, and then stepped smartly forward, the nice young American so honored to sing in Wuppertal, and insisted on shaking hands in the American way with the German lady, who of course got the bonus of "Schaunard" greasepaint on her dress. The opera house intendant persuaded the "industrialist" to see the handshake as an accident. "These Americans!" The theater would pay for her dry-cleaning. No need to tell the "industrialist" he did not have an understudy for Othmar.

Othmar never told Gilly the whole story. Shame at going out of character weighed just about even with revenge. He never again set foot on stage—in a singing role.

4.

"All they know is *'Vissi d'arte.'* You'd think they would invest more of themselves in the audition. Learn the goddam opera." Othmar intended his disgust to invite sympathy from a fellow professional but instead Gilly gave a yip of laughter.

"'Invest themselves!' You should have been a guidance counselor. Come on, Johnny, how long have we been in this business?" For Gilly, it was not quite ten years ago that he started managing singers. "They only learn the opera if they think they've going to perform it on stage."

They were sitting in the office of Gillespie & Associates, which consisted of Gilly and the girl who did the typing. For someone who looked like a fox terrier in a three-piece suit, Gilly was actually a cat person and across his lap stretched a tiger named Archie. People beyond counting had reminded Gilly that Mehitabel was the cat's name in the book. He simply cocked a bushy eyebrow and smiled. Several times a mother was Archie. "I keep her for roach patrol. You don't want to know what goes on next door." By which he meant a club where flower children writhed in clouds of herbs and incense to unspeakable music. "God knows what else they put in their mouths," he said as Archie turned a blind eye to commuting silverfish. The building had once been a church, "defrocked," as Liz put it, when its congregation died off. Gilly acquired the parish house. He used the Sunday School rooms for his office and "lent" the parish hall as rehearsal space for multiples of a ten dollar bill. When the stack of tens fattened sufficiently, Gilly took Liz to dinner at La Caravelle. In New York you had to eat Chinese to keep up but long ago he'd given his heart to France. Knowing to a penny the sorry state of ol' pal Johnny's finances, Gilly did not charge him for the use of the hall. And, good soul that he was, he put the word out that John Austin Othmar was auditioning for "Tosca."

It had been Othmar's intention that the auditioning sopranos come prepared to sing the one stretch of music in "Tosca" he loathed. New voices, new approaches, might help him as stage director to find his way through the passages beginning *"È luna piena,"* the moon is full.

The Toscas arrived with their music, and the tape cassettes that showed them off in a variety of roles, some recorded in this very room, and their bottles of water, bottled spring water having just replaced thermos bottles. They all wore high heels. One or two hopefuls wore shawls, as though a shawl was halfway to a costume. They had their war paint on and their hair was piled high, and one candidate had thoughtfully positioned a large hairpin to loosen so that in the throes of love or lust a ringlet would fall with becoming drama. Every single one of them had nailed *"Vissi d'arte,"* Tosca's big number— just about her only number. They'd sung it for years, ever since their voice teacher had said, yes, really and truly, you are a dramatic soprano and one day you'll be singing at the Met. "There isn't a recording of 'Tosca,'" Othmar observed to Gilly "that *'Vissi'* doesn't sound like it arrived silver-plated on a platter. Even in the live recordings—especially the live recordings! I want *'Vissi'* to surprise. I want it to be ripped from her."

Not that the young, modern Toscas didn't agree. But their solution was physical, for they were of the generation who had studied stage movement. They were prepared to sing *"Vissi d'arte"* flung down any which way on the Act II sofa, their limbs exposed and bosoms heaving, just as long as the director understood they wanted to sing it "beautifully."

Under no illusion the auditioning Toscas would be much different, Othmar put *"Vissi d'arte"* off till later. "We'll get to it, we'll get to it," he promised each Tosca. "For now, I want to hear your entrance in act one."

That, in perhaps the most famous entrance in opera, was the cue to carol Cavaradossi's name. *"Ma-ri-o Ma-ri-o Ma-ri-o!"* each Tosca sang, and all the old associations, the doubts and the pleasures, that Othmar brought to staging opera came flooding in on him. He had seen "Tosca" on stage only five times.

"Don't you think it's a great opera?" Gilly had asked, when having proposed it as the initial Pallas production, he was encountering resistance on Othmar's part.

"Great? No. I mean I like it. But it doesn't get to me the way Mozart does. Or Wagner, and Verdi, for different reasons. There is such sadness in Mozart, so many points where you shiver. You know he has looked at people and seen our failings. No! not failings but he knows the dilemmas in life. You are always going to wonder at the end of 'Così' if the masquerade hasn't somehow damaged the lovers. After the curtain comes down in 'Figaro,' will the Count be faithful to the Countess? Will it matter? She's a different woman. She has shamed the Count—embarrassed him. He's not so thick he doesn't know it. And there will always be a flirt like Barbarina. And isn't her little aria just about the most frightening thing you ever heard! It's in F-minor. Pompelli says it's in a key Mozart almost never used in opera. She's the one character who won't ever change and seems to know it's her doom. But about the rest, you can wonder and wonder, and hear Mozart again and again, and hope, and every time it will be different. But what's there to know in 'Tosca'? That's the problem. They all die, bang, bang, bang, and you know why. It's all plot. But I have to say it's a goddam effective opera, and I have been known to cry at the end. And I think Puccini is a more interesting composer than people give him credit for."

Gilly, who had mentally cast the small parts from his stable of singers, searched for an encouraging note. "Always go with effective!" he said cheerily. "It will be your first full length production." He'd listened with half an ear, passing the time puzzling out anagrams. Tosca was "ascot." Cavaradossi contained "avocados."

Othmar nodded. "I might discover a few things. The journey not the arrival, that sort of thing."

"Is he always so pompous?" Liz asked later. "Fasten your seat belts."

For the auditions, Othmar did what he could to suggest scenery. That block of folding chairs was the Attavanti chapel. A dais with lectern was Cavaradossi's painting stand, and Othmar would hum Cavaradossi where necessary to cue Tosca. He wore his working uniform of jeans and black turtleneck. He began the audition by taking his seat next to the upright piano. "I'm the kind of director," he liked to tell a ladies club audience, "who prefers to hear the singer first and start staging later."

The first Tosca to audition had heard this kind of palaver before. She was at least Othmar's age and this production would probably be her last Tosca. Four or five years ago, Thekla Dalton or her agent would have considered so public an audition "beneath her." But time had not been kind to her voice and a well-known opera company declined to renew her contract. Gilly had phoned her personally.

"I wouldn't ordinarily ask you to sing for Johnny Othmar but it's his first 'Tosca' and, between thee and me, he might welcome someone with your experience," he said, and Thekla Dalton was graciousness itself.

"She's worth hearing," Gilly told Othmar. "So what if she is dropping in class"—Gilly was known to frequent the race track—"but in a small house she still can out sing most. And you'll be getting someone who knows her way around the stage."

"That's not the point," protested Othmar. "And you know it. The point is, I want—as you and I have agreed—I want someone who'll look at Tosca in a fresh way. Tell a first-time audience who this Tosca is."

Invited by Othmar so to do, Thekla Dalton declined to look at Tosca afresh.

With her clarion *"Ma-ri-o!"* she announced herself as Tosca the diva, Tosca the star. Her voice had the metallic lustre that Othmar associated with vocal wear. He heard her through *"È luna piena,"* wincing as always at the sentimentality of the cavatina. "The moon is full and the night's aroma of flowers will bewitch our hearts." Thekla Dalton sang it as a meditation.

"Very nice," said Othmar. "Really lovely. I wonder if you'd mind telling me who you think Tosca is at this point. What is she trying to say to her lover?"

Thekla Dalton appeared to consider. Her beehive towered and confidence was her armor. She took a dance step forward and smiled down at Othmar. She would have thought it obvious, she said, that Tosca was setting up a rendez-vous for the evening.

"Yes," said Othmar. "Anything else about her?"

" '*È luna piena*' begins double-P," she said. "But more than a *pianissimo.*"

"Yes, I do hear that."

"It's the first quiet moment in the opera. We've had nothing but noise and running around the stage. Angelotti has escaped from prison and Cavaradossi is trying to help him, and the Sacristan is poking his nose in. I think with *'È luna piena'* Puccini is opening a window. On Tosca's soul, if that's not too corny. So I don't do anything. I'm not one to climb all over Cavaradossi. Not at this point." She laughed so roguishly that Othmar shut his eyes. "I just stand there and sing it as simply as I can. And there's something else. There has been a lot on stage to take in. It has been my experience that up until this point the audience has been very busy just watching. Then Puccini makes it suddenly quiet. This *pianissimo* is Puccini's way of getting them to listen."

"Granted. But for the sake of argument...Can't we think of a revealing gesture by Tosca that..."

Who was this man, Thekla Dalton wondered, to question what had worked so well in San Francisco, in Chicago, on the Met's spring tour. The rumors were true: His way or not at all, and look what happened in "Hansel." She heard him ask for *"Vissi d'arte,"* and heard the coyness in his voice.

Who was she, Othmar snorted, to pull Puccini on him. What was wrong with the idea you could have both, the music and the stage picture? She was over the hill. He could see dimples in her face, to his mind, the sort of dimples that betrayed over-strained muscles. The worse thing was she reminded him of someone else who wouldn't take direction. He was glad her *"Vissi d'arte"* sounded so rote.

In parting, both observed the formalities: "Wonderful finally to meet you," said John Austin Othmar, making her a bow. "It would be wonderful to work with you," said Thekla Dalton, but did not extend a hand. A few weeks later, she accepted an invitation to head the voice department at a state university eager to cash in on opera.

The second Tosca was a pert redhead. "Tosca, the spit fire," Othmar told her. "Tosca as Gwen Verdon." He warmed to the idea.

"I want you to tell me what is going on here," he said, setting the scene. "Tosca has come to the church and what is she carrying? She is carrying a bouquet of flowers from her triumph last night. And she is going to lay them at the foot of the statue of the Madonna. Don't you love it! a prima donna, the toast of Rome, and she's got religion. And not any old church but the church where she knows her lover is painting a holy picture. And she asks him for a date. So to speak. 'Now listen to me,' she says. 'Tonight I am singing in a concert but the piece is short. Wait for me at the stage door and we'll go off all alone to your pad, your villa.' That catches Cavaradossi by surprise. 'Tonight?' he asks. We know his mind is on helping his friend Angelotti who has just escaped from prison. Cavaradossi needs Tosca like a hole in the head."

At this, the second Tosca giggled. She had come to the audition on a dare. She had a big voice but her inclination was for comic opera.

Othmar pressed on. "Now I want to tell me what comes next. What sort of a woman is Tosca?"

To a woman, the auditioning Toscas agreed Tosca loved Cavaradossi.

"Just remember, Cavaradossi's never going to marry her!" said Liz when Othmar was trying to unwind that evening at the newest Hunan place.

"Now, why did you tell him that!" Gilly said to Liz still later that night.

"Well, it's true. Marry an actress? A singer's no different. It's the only thing that makes you cry. The fallen woman with the heart of gold."

"Let Johnny discover that for himself."

"There are other Toscas in captivity, *mon vieux*," said Gilly to cheer Othmar up. "When did you ever know an opera to go without a hitch? You used to be full of tales about costumes that didn't clear customs till opening night and the time a rain storm flooded the Tanglewood pit."

Othmar's wintery smile indicated those were other people's problems. In the corner of Gilly's office that he had appropriated as his own, he went back to perfecting the lists for his production.

"Nuns with wimples," he wrote in tiny script on the file card marked Costumes. He underlined "wimples." This would be a "Tosca" set well before Vatican II took nuns out of habits worth looking at. He wasn't Catholic, in fact was not much of anything, the sort of generalized Christian who believed in good works and "live and let live" but didn't go out of his way. But he did like ceremony, and ritual, and in that, he was his father's son. Drill wasn't meaningless at all, but the way to discipline and from discipline came order. When he lived in Chicago, he occasionally lucked into church jobs, which had the added thrill of dressing up in choir robes and becoming, in the Processional and Recessional, part of liturgy's grand choreography of worship.

"I will have just two nuns because three or four nuns," he argued to himself, "would make you think the scene was about them, and their wimples will be pure white and starched, and bell out like sails, and I will have them bring on the choir boys, shoo them on, and then try to keep order, so the nuns toss like ships on all the confusion going on. That's the kind of costume detail"—he was now lecturing to an imaginary audience—"that delivers an image that doesn't need an explanation. Costume as metaphor, you might say."

So there would be wimples. "Even if I have to have them made."

On the card marked Props, he wrote "collapsing knife" and added "muskets." Under these, he put "blood." Upon reflection, he added a question mark. Stage blood was sometimes more trouble than it was worth. It certainly added to the bills for dry-cleaning. He wrote down "pistol."

Othmar liked propping his own shows. Ever since he was a kid he had loved making things. Special-effect props were big boys's toys. The wine glass that shattered when the soprano hit the high note. The wonderful birdcage he saw for Papageno with the birds on swings (or their little legs attached to springy coils) so that all was aflutter when the bird catcher walked. Yes! some day he would do Mozart! "Hansel" had been his first chance to indulge himself. Goddam! The gingerbread house had been good! He believed that a prop would be beautiful, appropriate, authentic. The Russian maps for "Boris Godunov" should be a feast for the Tsar's eye. Othmar took care with the script for letters and documents. (And took care to lock them away between performances lest some joker slip in an obscenity to throw the singer off.) "Tosca" required little in the way of illusion. He wrote down "A's fan," for The Attavanti's fan.

That reminded him he must give some thought to The Attavanti's portrait as the Magdalene. Even if the canvas was positioned on stage so that the audience never saw it, the painting should be more than a daub. And if it was a portrait worthy of the name? So it would be something of value down the line. Should he, he wondered,—did he have the time to commission a painting, not just of the Magdalene…but of himself as The Attavanti who's the model…for Caravadossi's portrait…of the Magdalene. Make it a souvenir he could keep of his first "Tosca." How would it work? He was getting confused. Should he be painted as the Magdalene herself, that is, with the suggestion of his face in hers? But not as she is dressed: he didn't mind costumes or disguise but drag scared him. Better to make it a family resemblance and pass the portrait off as his sister (except to his mother who would know better) as the Magdalene. He would have to look up her up in the library. See how the Old Masters painted her…and what she wore. When "Tosca" was over, he would…

"What kind of knife will you use on Scarpia?"

"Knife?" Othmar blinked at Gilly from the hood of The Attavanti's cape.

"I've never understood how Tosca is supposed to do him in with a fruit knife." Gilly had a way of asking the basic question.

"A fruit knife?"

"Isn't he sitting at dinner peeling an apple?"

"It takes place in June."

"All right, a peach. And he has stabbed the peach on his fork, the way they did then, and is taking the skin off with the fruit knife. The heartless bastard! Doesn't he have any redeeming feature."

"Whadda ya mean?" Othmar was back with both feet firmly on Broadway. "Our Scarpia is all heart!"

"That's the other thing. How can she stab him in the heart? Isn't it behind your ribs?" Gilly felt around under his waistcoat.

"Other side, Gilly. Your heart is on the other side. And the libretto doesn't say heart. Puccini says *'in pieno petto,'* deep in the chest. Scarpia has lunged for her. God knows where the knife goes in. The convention is, it's the heart. One lucky cut. He's down on the floor, groaning and writhing. Lots of blood, she tells Cavaradossi. She could have gotten him in the gut."

Gilly made a face. "Good old suspension of disbelief for me."

"No, it's true. Lots of blood. He dies from shock. I asked a doctor about it once."

"I believe you, I do, I do." Gilly thought that was more research than he would have done.

Liz would know who did portraits, Othmar was sure, but he wouldn't give her the satisfaction of asking.

5.

Thanksgiving was fast approaching. In sandboxes in many a first grade classroom, tee-pees sprouted and little children made Indians from pipe-cleaners and Pilgrim hats from construction paper. Liz was on the phone about plans to spend the weekend with their families in Boston. Othmar let his mother know he was too busy to join her in Chicago. Although word never reached Manhattan, the Clarion Voice reported that the Pallas Rod & Gun's turkey shoot had been won by Abraham Lincoln (Linc) King for the third time in four years, thus disqualifying him from further competition. Linc King did the right thing, everybody thought, and gave the turkey to the Salvation Army. That he had medals for sharp shooting, as well as a fine record in Korea, allowed for two opinions to co-exist peacefully about his command of something called The Pride of Fairstead. Either this was guys dressing up as toy soldiers, and Linc King was the biggest dope of all, or The Pride "does our county proud," as the Clarion Voice editorialized, "to bring our Colonial history alive in parades and battle enactments."

From his little lists, Othmar had progressed to plotting, on a big grid calendar, the events that would lead to opening "Tosca" on a Thursday in late March. Then would follow a Saturday matinee—"At Popular Prices." Then another Thursday evening. Then the "brought back by popular demand" grand finale that Saturday. Say what you want about the right singers for the right parts, the curtain doesn't go up without the right stage manager. And Othmar finally found him. He spent most of one day trying to track down Bill Potter, who was his first choice, and when he got him on the phone, sweated and sweated while Potter, a laconic Yankee, listened and listened, before saying Yes, but only if he could bring a student interne as assistant stage manager.
"But only if she is pretty," said Gilly.

With the stage manager in place, Gilly sprang his surprise.
"Good news," he announced the Monday of Thanksgiving week. "Victor Pompelli is available."

48

"I don't believe you."

"Upon my word."

Victor Pompelli was the greatest teacher Othmar had known, and the conductor above all others he longed to work with.

"For a 'Tosca'...like this?" Othmar sputtered, not daring to hope. Pompelli's reputation was such that his opera repertory classes were oversubscribed and Othmar had chased all over the East Coast feeling lucky to attend three as an auditor. When they could lure him their way, it was cities like Akron and Portland and Miami that gave the maestro a production of his choosing. "Worked with Victor Pompelli" was a credit to envy.

"He remembers you from Detroit," said Gilly, watching to see how this went over, for what he had actually said to Pompelli was that he might remember John Othmar from Detroit when Othmar helped out on that "Butterfly." Pompelli agreed that was so.

"One other thing," said Gilly. "I have to tell you that Pompelli comes with his missus. His missus does Tosca or he don't."

Othmar sat so still for so long a time that Gilly began to worry. "I have his phone number in Italy," he said to break the spell.

Othmar did not move. Impulses crowded thought. "He can't remember me." His heart raced. "Well, it was my idea about the football..." Expectation beat on him like the sun, and fear darkened it. "Why would he conduct for me?" He could hear but not understand what Gilly was saying about the phone. His mouth went dry. He longed to suck an ice cube.

"Call him tomorrow and talk it over. Too late now."

Othmar nodded. "Too late." Then like the first fat raindrop of a storm, another thought intruded.

So Pompelli would conduct for him, and he blushed. That was the good news, the wonderful news, the certification—beyond all expectation—that he, John Austin Othmar, had arrived. And there was more: In far off Pallas, where there would be little else to do, he'd have Pompelli to himself. He would bring his scores, even if they were pocket scores or piano vocals, and he could borrow more. The tenor would never miss...He would appeal to the maestro for help. In later years, he would be able to say he had studied privately with Pompelli. "Staging always begins with the music," he'd say (as he always said). Pallas, he would say, when Pallas was famous, "Pallas was my conservatory." Yes! Pompelli! But who was this other person, this intrusion? He shook it off—then said so quietly that Gilly almost didn't hear: "...news to me Pompelli has a wife."

Gilly believed her name was Margarita Dettori.

"Sounds Italian," Othmar said heavily. "Has anyone heard her?"

The Toast of Trieste, Gilly understood.

Othmar had to think where Trieste was.

Gilly said he would make "guarded inquiries" about her career. There might be a tape. Better he, Gilly, ask Pompelli for it than Othmar. He could say Othmar wanted it merely for casting purposes. "I will say you need it to have an idea of her vocal color when considering other voices." Gilly's fabled tack was his other stock in trade.

Gilly arranged for Othmar to telephone Pompelli on Thanksgiving morning which would be just another Thursday afternoon in Trieste. "That way, we'll pay for the call and you'll have the office to yourself. Record it if you want." Not strictly legal, as Gilly knew, but useful to have on tape. He rummaged for a blank cassette. "You stick the suction cup on the receiver and…" he started explaining. But Othmar had tuned out.

When they had last met, it was at someone's apartment in New York and Pompelli was at the piano, ringed in laughter as he volunteered to fuse music from one opera with another. Smarty-pants Othmar, in recent proud possession of two recordings he could ill afford—the Colin Davis "Troyens" and the Solti "Rhinegold—yelled those out, and Pompelli made Berlioz's lovesick Didon fall for Wagner's loveless Alberich. For an encore, he made Melisande go down and dirty as Pirate Jenny. It was a party trick but beguiling because by then Pompelli was everyone's picture of a maestro with his aquiline nose and aureole of greying hair. "Karajan with charisma," joked Gilly. "And warmth." Othmar thought Pompelli would understand the "Bohème" fiasco as Gilly would not.

That Pompelli was also lame added a piquancy. He got around on an ornate walking stick and sat to conduct. He was *simpatico* but no saint: If people hovered, they would find themselves skewered on the stick. *"Basta!"* he would roar, and laugh. Enough! The Italian, the good-humored Italian, the Pompelli that people loved. In contrast, his "bye, bye" meant a sharp shove with the stick. The physical pain this might cause bothered Othmar less than the maestro's lapse into American.

Now, on Thanksgiving Day, in an empty office and deprived by the phone of the vibrant picture of his hero, Othmar was struck by the deep melancholy of Pompelli's voice. He sounded more "Italian" than he remembered.

"Gianni, Gianni," Pompelli breathed down the line. "I learn from Ghee-lee about your 'Tosca.' I tell him I will be glad, I will be honored to conduct, to help how I can. I remember 'Butterfly.' You are the big man now. That is good."

Othmar watched the office clock tick. Static pecked at Pompelli's voice. "Hello, hello," Othmar appealed. "Hello."

"…propose to you Margarita Dettori as the Tosca. My wife. I do not think you know her. Her career mostly, no, entirely in Europe. She say farewell for her house in Trieste. Teatro Verdi you know of, but the…" More static.

"…she was house soprano. It is a disgrace how they treat her. No respect, no respect after twenty-seven years devoting to them her art. They only give her an evening. Not an opera. An evening! They make her speeches and a purse. She will sing her arias and make a pretty speech to them. Inside, she hurts. I wish to comfort her. To give her triumph in America. Where she has never been. So she can leave Trieste behind. Gianni, you understand the human heart. I notice this about you."

Othmar winced. "Maestro," he began.

"Now I explain how I help you. I and my Rita will come to you in your city. We will live with you. I work with the orchestra. She coach the Italian. Such diction. The old school. She will place the vowels. You will hear the difference."

Othmar began to listen.

"Now I will tell you something else about my Rita. She is the Tosca of the old tradition. You will like to see this style. It is authentic. But perhaps you will think it is antique? I will help you understand. Her voice is still good. The legato! I marry my Rita for her legato. We will think about inviting critics to hear her."

Critics? Othmar inhaled. Things were moving too fast. Yes, she would want…it would be her American debut. But did he, Othmar, want the critics? Pompelli's voice came at him as though from a faucet on full.

"Now Gianni, also important. I want to propose to you Bruno Cappetto as her Scarpia. A colleague. Many times they have done 'Tosca' together. What this man knows! He understand her. And for the Cavaradossi, I think Luigi Luongo who is well regarded. Not known to you."

None of this was making any sense. He and Gilly had agreed on an American cast, Tom Boylston, whom he liked, would be the Scarpia, and a tenor they were taking a chance on, Stefan Weld, would be Cavaradossi. The contracts would go out next week. As far as he knew, Gilly was still in negotiation with a Tosca they both heard in Washington who would be free after a Verdi Requiem in Cleveland. Did Gilly know what Pompelli had in mind?

"Luigi is young. Tosca play him off Scarpia in a way the audience understand. Not politics, which is difficult to understand. Napoleon! Napoli! Ha! But youth. 'Sex-y.'" Pompelli's American was perfect.

"Luigi is Cappetto's last pupil, so it will be nice for Bruno to introduce this talent to America. We all come together, yes?

"Now I tell you one other thing. This Tosca, my Rita, she lip!"

Othmar thought he could not have heard right. "Say again."

"She lip, she jomp, Gianni, she jomp. This Tosca is not afraid. She does not climb down stairs. She does not walk into wing. We know names who do. When Puccini want her to lip from Castel Sant'Angelo to death, she jomp. You will like this. So it is settled, Gianni? I thank you from my heart. Rita thank you but she shop. *Così fan tutte,* heh, Gianni? Little joke."

After a second wave of expressions of gratitude and respect, Pompelli hung up.

When he could no longer bear the office clock and the tinsel in his ears, Othmar shivered and got up. He badly needed to swim, to thrash away his confusion, and made for the Y. But it was not an ordinary day on West Side sidewalks, when he might slip and dart like every other fish in the stream. The Macy's Thanksgiving Parade had just passed and tourists stood uncertain where to turn and what to do, and like a good New Yorker, Othmar made sly use of his elbows. When he finally achieved the Y, one sniff told him the place was given over to a vast turkey dinner for God's unwashed. He trudged to the nearest movie house and let the Beatles pummel him (it was "A Hard Day's Night" which he had seen).

"Not your usual Thanksgiving," said Othmar, trying for lightness, when summoned by Liz and Gilly for sushi at Irimiru Karabrao that Sunday night.

"You and all those little girls wetting their pants over Ringo."

Othmar was shocked. He did not like coarseness in women. "I was almost the only one there."

"Didn't you talk to Pompelli?" Gilly wanted the bad news out of the way before he faced Othmar alone in the office.

"If you mean, did the call go through, Yes. If you mean, did we talk like colleagues, No." Othmar was doing his best to stay calm.

Gilly laughed.

"I suppose he told you she 'lip' to death."

"You knew all the time?"

Gilly knew about Bruno Cappetto as the Scarpia but he did not know the full extent of the Italian invasion. "The old fox," he said when Othmar told him they were bringing their own Cavaradossi.

"Cappetto's last pupil."

It would be useful now, Gilly thought, to be outrageous. "I bet we'll find out he's his boyfriend."

"He seems awfully reasonable about the Italians," Liz said later. "Wasn't the whole idea this was his 'Tosca'? Or is he so in love with Pompelli?"

The least of my problems, Gilly thought.

But the following morning Othmar was all smiles. He arrived at Gilly's office bearing coffee and Danish for all, and a potted plant for the windowsill. The girl who did the typing asked what kind it was.

"It's…" began Othmar. "…red," said Gilly. "Chinese red," insisted Othmar, "for good luck."

"Poinsettia," said Gilly, "old Chinese custom." He laughed so hard the cat went away and stood in the corner.

And when the mail came, it contained a fat manila envelope with foreign stamps and a customs chit.

"Handsome devil, isn't he!" Gilly said as he and Othmar looked at the publicity stills for Luigi Luongo. Dark of eye and high of brow, he wore an open white shirt that plunged almost to the waist, tenor togs for almost anything in the romantic repertory. The few reviews were in Italian but in one Othmar spotted the word "Tosca."

"So he has sung it."

"Would appear so," said Gilly. "And lookee here. His very own tape cassette." This Othmar grabbed, and grabbed the cassette player and earphones, and pretty soon Gilly could hear pleased murmurs.

"He'll do," Othmar said, tossing the cassette on Gilly's desk. "Got some phoning to do."

If the truth be known, Othmar's designation as a set designer meant only that he was borrowing the scenery. Thanks to an arts grant, a clearing house called Opera in Storage was in the process of being formed to record the whereabouts of old sets and props and costumes that might still have some useful life in them. Still at the inventory stage, this venture could be of no help for the Pallas "Tosca," but command central was glad to tell Othmar what they knew. Rumor had it there was a "Tosca" in Seattle, a "Tosca" that had originated in Toronto, and was "historically accurate"—not "concept opera" with four chairs and a step ladder and "they point their fingers to shoot Cavaradossi."

So Othmar sat on the phone and waited for the West Coast to wake up. Besides, there was nothing like a schmooze on the phone to exchange gossip. Thus it was that Gilly overheard him break into the boasting stage and talk rather grandly about the sheer luck of securing Margarita Dettori as the Tosca.

"No, I don't know how old she is, but after all Madga Olivero is still doing it, and she's seventy if she's a day, and a little bird tells me she will do it for Sarah Caldwell. And here's the other thing about Dettori. I didn't have to ask her to place the vowels for the Americans—she volunteered."

6.

He could sneak into Pallas, or he could strut, and either had its attractions, as he reviewed them in the overnight train to Chicago for Christmas. Taking the train "to save money," as he told his mother, had the advantage also of cutting short his visit. He loved his mother, perhaps less than he used to, but there were pithy observations of hers he still liked to quote, such as the one (so applicable now) that air in trains stifled the nose "like dry cleaning." He would arrive early on Christmas morning and he would leave late the next afternoon. That would leave the better part of his departure day for the project so dear to his heart. His mother was a gifted seamstress. There wasn't anything she couldn't "run up" from the crudest sketch. He had gone one better and brought along an Old Masters postcard from the Metropolitan Museum of the kind of hooded cape he wanted to wear as The Attavanti. God knows what this would cost to have made in New York, and was not exactly cheap to rent from a costumer like Brooks.

"It will be your best present to me!" he would tell her. And what fun they would have discussing the exact shade of blue. Othmar called it "Madonna blue," envisioning, as he did, The Attavanti as virgin being painted as harlot. He would leave the choice of material to his mother. She might even have a good word for one of the synthetics, for she was bound to know what marvel of textile chemistry mimicked silk or a light wool. "Tosca," he must remember to tell her, took place in June. The old Roman churches are cool places even on the hottest of days, he would say, and she would believe him. There was a time when she had been involved in everything he did. It couldn't last, he knew, and why should it? There had been weeks, maybe two months, without a word from her after the Christmas he told her the circumstances of his father's death.

"We'll never know, dear, will we?" was her comfortable reply.

"We do know he was going there. It was in the log."

"For a German lesson, dear, so he could move up. I knew all about it."

That would have been five Christmases ago. By the next Christmas she was all over it and he was still her darling boy.

He certainly could tell her about Pompelli. And that he had a real Italian for the Tosca. A list-maker, as we have seen, he always made mental lists of things to talk about. Oh, and scenery that promised an authentic picture of the three historic sites in the opera. He was pretty sure the Farnese palace was designed by Michelangelo. "I've got a line on some Renaissance furniture to go in it," he would tell her. She liked old things.

With his one suitcase, he was out of the train and onto the platform and sprinting for a taxi well head of the other passengers with their misshapen bundles of Christmas expiation. His gifts to his mother were wrapped by the stores where he bought them, and it would be a topic of conversation that glazed paper was giving way to printed foil, and wasn't Midnight Blue and silver "just elegant." There was a new perfume from Saks and three of the latest murder mysteries, one each from Doubleday's and the British Bookshop and Davis & Bannister, which accounted for their different ribbons and papers. The red cyclamen he had ordered through a New York florist was already on the television console in his mother's little apartment. A perky little Christmas tree stood on the card table, which she had skirted in red plaid taffeta and tied with green bows.

She was sure he was "hungry from the train," but both knew that was just a way of luring him to the breakfast nook where his old Christmas stocking lay beside his plate. The bulge in the toe would be a tangerine and she never forgot the Life Savers or a new Scripto pencil—he was still her little boy. Later, when they "attacked the tree," she pulled up the table skirt to reveal her presents to him. They came in a cacaphony of wrapping papers and the unworkable bows she learned from women's magazines. There were spills of crinkled ribbon that pulled away to release a fine, black wool turtleneck. "Cashmere!" he exclaimed. "Kissing cousin," she laughed, and he leaned over and kissed her soft fat cheek. There were broad ribbons fashioned like neckties which ordinarily might give away what was in the three necktie boxes. And neckties they were, but one in Op Art circles that wearied the eye and another of psychedelic persuasion. They could have been worse, and so he said jovially, "Why is it I can never find these in New York?"

A round tin box held her own sugared walnuts—no surprises there. Christmas wouldn't be Christmas without one novelty, and surely that was the scarf-like length of tweed, each end turned up so it made a deep pocket, and she had sewed it herself.

"You wear it around your neck to keep things in."

There was one more gift.

It was, Othmar thought as the train ground back to New York, a present as only his mother could come up with. It was lavish for one on her budget, and useful, for she had a practical streak he had inherited. There had been other presents like it, a Swiss Army knife the Christmas after his father died, and she was trying to make up for the loss. In truth, he did not love his father.

"She totally misunderstands what I do," he thought. And yet she had been patient, and generous (a five dollar bill weekly in the mail) when he was a voice student uncertain of his future. She liked to hear him tell about singing in opera choruses, a topic that bored anyone else, but come to think of it, what she really liked was hearing about his costumes (she loved historical movies). One Christmas dinner, when he was scathing about a chintzy "Aida" production that cheated by putting Nubian limbs in dark tights, she saw the very point he chose to ignore.

"Well," she said mildly, "if you don't wear make-up all over you, it saves on dry-cleaning, and they must have been thinking of that."

She loved thinking of him in costume, and he used to send her news clippings of the Coronation Scene in "Boris," say, or the ball in "Traviata," with an arrow pointing, sometimes truthfully, at "Yours truly." But the further he drifted from performing himself, the vaguer her responses.

"You tell them what to do? Up on the stage?" And when he said, yes, that's what directors did, she said with considerable surprise, "Well, imagine that! I thought they acted the words like the movies."

Just as he was gathering up his Christmas "haul," she stopped his hand. "Shut your eyes."

He did, and could feel something join them on the sofa.

It was tall and oval, and Othmar did not immediately recognize it as a wastepaper basket, for it had a big sheet of music pasted around it, medieval of some sort, liturgical, with black diamonds for notes and red squiggles.

His mother beamed up at him. "It's for 'Tosca,'" she said. "I read the story at the library and there was a picture of Scarpia writing at his desk. This is to go under his desk."

In the end, Othmar strutted out of New York. Gilly was not exactly sorry to see him go. Othmar was in the way, and for once he knew it. The usual delights of the city palled. Did he have to eat ethnic one more time? See another movie? Swimming bored him. He'd heard all he cared to at the Met and City Opera. New York was beginning to look grey, and small. He had offered to help Gilly with his other clients. "Good for me to learn, from a pro, about the music biz," he cajoled. "Another time," said Gilly.

All that could be done in advance of the "Tosca" rehearsals had been done. Weeks ago now, Gilly dealt expertly (by telex) with the Italians' management—"such as it is." He checked on their visas. When they arrived in New York, he would march them right over to the bank to open checking accounts from which to pay the IRS on their American earnings. Pompelli and the Tosca and the Scarpia were asking surprisingly little for their services but they wanted more for the Cavaradossi than Gilly hoped to pay.

"When it comes to money," said Othmar loftily, "I bow to your better judgment."

"Thanks, pal," said Gilly. He would get rid of "tenor fat" by offering to find him a gig or two in New York. "You aren't going to need him for rehearsals every single day."

"How do you know?—when I don't know myself. And won't know," Othmar thundered, "till the first go-through."

Tetchy-tetchy, thought Gilly.

So it was with considerable relief, on both sides, that one morning in late February, Gilly helped Othmar load the old Rash Rambler he had bought "for peanuts." There were two garment bags, one containing his tux. "I expect I'll have to do a curtain speech or two, and I think I will organize a gala," he said grandly to Gilly. "Grand opera should have its glamorous side and if I don't do it, who will?" A sturdy Pepsi carton served as a traveling bookcase for Othmar's opera scores. He also made quite a show, Gilly thought, over stowing a tiny bottle of perfume before deciding it would best ride in one of his shoes.

"He was acting so coy about it I didn't want to give him the satisfaction of asking who it was for," Gilly reported to Liz. "For the Divine Sarah?"

Liz wasn't sure. "Do you think he screws?" she asked once again, for Othmar's sex life was an absorbing topic of conversation.

"What else was there?"

"Cut-rate Scotch—quite a lot of it," said Gilly.

"Ah," said Liz, "that is for the Divine Pompelli."

The Othmar who swanked out of the city slipped into Pallas, and that was by design. "First, know your territory," he quoted his father. He would announce his residency in good time. Stopping at the theater, he let himself in and hung up his tux. Through a classified ad in the Clarion Voice he had already found a room on the edge of town, and this he now made for, following driving directions till the subdivisions with their blinding-white cement sidewalks gave way to older houses and old trees. The address was an old farmhouse, its clapboards painted white until an enterprising vinyl-siding salesman hustled his rainbow of samples and promises of easy financing and easier maintenance. Othmar's mother would approve of the siding. "Makes an old house look so neat and tidy," she used to say on their Sunday drives in the countryside. And neat and tidy this one was, sky blue with white shutters and a wishing well in the side yard.

His landlords were a Mr. and Mrs. Keohane, an elderly couple who took in lodgers. He was a retired machinist, slightly deaf. She was a seamstress who did alterations for dress shops in Pallas. Her sewing machine was humming when her husband opened the door to Othmar. The room they offered was in the ell off the back and had its own entrance. No kitchen but there was a hot plate and a tiny fridge. It would be no trouble to do his laundry, Mrs. Keohane said in her motherly way. "You have to run the wash anyway, right?" said Othmar trying for light and cosy as the adored son.

The less he had to do with the old man the better. Keohane was heavy-set and slow of speech. And slow of mind, Othmar was sure. He had the high soft voice of men going deaf, and to hear him, Othmar found he was bending toward him more than he liked. That caused Keohane to back away and his wife to tap her ear. Othmar now raised his voice and heard the tinkle of little glass animals on glass shelves.

"Show him the garage," said Mrs. Keohane. "Plenty of space for storage."

Out they went, following a cinder path from the kitchen, Keohane shuffling along and silent. He unlocked a side door. One wall was hung with rakes and hoes.

"You must have a garden," boomed Othmar.

"I can hear without you shouting."

Othmar decided to ignore this, and noticing the sacks of fertilizer, said: "It must be a big garden."

Keohane mulled this over. "Have to plant enough for the rabbits, and the moles. But not for the rats—I lay poison for the rats."

Othmar shivered. New York seemed far away.

"The poison eats their guts out," said Keohane laughing in his throat.

"I wouldn't know about rats," said Othmar briskly. "I'm a city boy."

"That is where you are wrong. Rats are everywhere."

Still and all, it was the perfect accommodation, and the best thing to Othmar's mind was that the Keohanes were wonderfully incurious about his reason for coming to Pallas. "The wife used to like the Firestone Hour on the radio."

That was Thursday. That evening, Mrs. Keohane phoned her sister-in-law Katherine, the waitress at Kulda's Koffee, and they exchanged notes.

On Friday Othmar spent several profitable hours in the public library availing himself of newspaper microfilms and the scrapbooks maintained by the county historical society. He was prepared to be chummy to get the information he needed. But no need—the librarian was very helpful. Miss Poirier was not a gossip, which made things easier for him, for he had nothing—yet—to gossip back with, and he must remember about "eternal vigilance." But she was able to explain relationships among the major families of Pallas. Sarah Smythe, as he might have guessed, was plugged in pretty near the top. Her aunt, Mrs. Titus, was the town's mover and shaker, as the librarian managed to say without actually saying so. "Mrs. Titus was a Carruthers, you know," she said, glancing away from Othmar as if breaking a confidence.

"Of course," he said gently.

But she would not be drawn and turned to talk of "Tosca." She was quite sure she had heard it many times on the Met broadcasts. Othmar said he would send her a pair for opening night.

"He says he will give me tickets," Miss Poirier said on the phone to Evey Titus.

On Saturday Othmar drove around outlying Pallas. The "Greater Pallas" he saw through his windshield was surprisingly big. He was glad. He liked the idea of putting distance between his room at the Keohanes and the theater downtown. Letting the car find its own way, he took inventory of the places he would need, marking in his mind the hardware stores, the dry cleaners, a lube shop for his poor old Rambler. Not much in the way of entertainment. The cinema in the mall was showing last year's movies. If it came to that, on the outskirts of town, there was candlepin bowling at the Main Line Lanes which shared a parking lot with Broyle's Roller-Dome. Further on out was the sign for the Pallas Rod & Gun Club with its sodden poster for a turkey shoot. He rejoiced in his own company.

On Sunday he went about finding an execution squad for Act III.

This chore had not been high up on his list of things to do. There were, what? four or five soldiers, and their captain. All non-singing roles, and he supposed that most productions used extras, or possibly chorus people who don't sing in the last act anyway but have to hang around for the final curtain call. He liked the story that Covent Garden used guardsmen on duty in London. But in browsing through the historical society scrapbooks he had seen countless articles on something called the Pride of Fairstead. Way back when, it had been the local musket company. If the Clarion Voice were to be believed, and Othmar came across an all-too familiar byline, the Pride of Fairstead in full costume would provide "historical re-enactments" for any and all patriotic occasions. "Spare me that nonsense," muttered Othmar. Consulting the phone book he found a listing for Old County Road, Fairstead.

February, in these parts, was still deep winter, despite the teasing thaws, and the day, though sunny, was hard and cold. Othmar drove along fields that even he could see begrudged farmers a living. "Poor saps," he muttered. He was thinking more of the poor saps in "Tosca," of Cavaradossi and how Scarpia tricks Tosca into being present at her lover's death, both having been promised it's a sham execution. Not so, of course.

"Come facemmo del conte Palmieri," as we did with Count Palmieri, sang Othmar (as Scarpia) as he bumped along Old County Road. For, just as the Count Palmieri, a liberal whom Scarpia wanted out of the way, died surprised by a volley of very real bullets, so too would perish another liberal aristocrat, *il cavaliere Cavaradossi.*

"Si. Come Palmieri," Othmar sang, this time as Spoletta, the henchman who arranges the dastardly deed. And Tosca, betrayed, would leap to her death. "My Tosca lip," he mimicked Pompelli, and giggled. "She'd better. Or I'll see that she does." And thinking ahead to the climactic moment of moments of his first grand opera, he overshot the driveway he was looking for. It was marked by a mailbox painted to look like an early American flag.

Down a dirt lane he careened. To the left and right were old apple trees and at the edge of both fields the sun glanced off metal pails. The maple sugaring season was about to begin, though Othmar would not have known, or cared. He slid to a stop at a very old farmhouse with sagging roof. Smoke streamed from a chimney. There was no doorbell so he knocked. Nothing. As he turned on his heel, he heard a low roar. Looking back, he caught a slide of snow full in his face.

"Rufff!"

A goddam dog! Othmar staggered, hugging himself small. Dogs scared him.

"Roof," said the voice. "It lets go at this time of year."

When he could clear his eyes of wet, Othmar saw, in the doorway, a pink and white man in an old brown bathrobe.

"I'm having a sun bath," said the man. "Purging my tin. Isaiah, chapter one, verse fifteen. Care to wait?"

Against his better judgment, Othmar stepped through the door.

"Bathroom off through there," said his host. Othmar thought it was just about one step up from a privy. But the towel on a nail was clean.

In the low-ceilinged parlor, under the bleaching glow of a sun lamp, lay a man naked except for a jock strap. There were black plastic ovals over his eyes. "My wife went to church," said the man. "Pull up a pew."

Othmar decided on silence. A timer ticked for long minutes. The room was hot and his damp self began to steam. "How was I to know about snow?" He wondered if he could simply leave. "Leave!—he doesn't know my name. Get out of here, and deal—as I should have, with the gun club I saw. What the hell do I need history for? All the audience needs to see is gun barrels, and they can be dummies for all I care. Why does this always, always happen to me?"

The body turned over, revealing as hairy a back as Othmar ever could recall seeing. He shut his eyes against the greying tufts, and the fat cheeks. He hated nakeness, hated hairiness. Had been shocked how hairy women actually were, and how their pubic hair smelled breathless—dead. Your hair grew after you died. Hair, he often thought, was the story of our life. Too much, too little, always in the wrong places. Why should men have to shave? Dogs were hairy, cats not. We know we are old by our hair. But it outlives us. He had seen his mother's locket of her mother's dead hair. Death and decay! Death saddened him but failure disgusted him. It was wrong for a living person, the human being, to fail. Wouldn't it be better to be cut off at our peak, well, not all of us, because that would mean him too, but get rid of the failures before they embarrassed everyone, including the person. He kept his eyes shut tight and, certain that a smell went with the body baking before him, tried not to breathe in through his nose.

The dinger went off, sending a shock through him. He bolted upright.

"Gun shy!" laughed the man. "I don't believe we've met. I'm the Pride, if I may say so, of the Pride of Fairstead. Abraham Lincoln King."

Othmar was a long time comprehending the name. He decided it had to be a joke. Of course, it wore a beard, and big eyebrows, and was now saying in a basso profundo that verged on static:

"Founder, commanding officer, and, my wife says, if I'm not more careful driving, I will end up someone else's hood ornament.

That usually got a laugh. Hearing none, the bright eyes narrowed. "You must be the opera fella."

"Linc" King, as he told Othmar to call him, taught social studies—"what you and I knew as American history"—at the regional high school. About as popular with the kids as Hygiene, which was also required. In an attempt to engage their interest, and because he also loved history, he persuaded his senior class to stage the battle that Fairstead's Pride marched off to fight in 1775 in Vermont. They did it in a field, and charged admission—"we called it a 'contribution'"—to park. The considerable proceeds went to defray the costs of the Senior Prom. "I got girls as well as boys to fight. The girls liked that. I was way ahead of my time."

And from little acorns, big oaks grow, as he was sure Othmar knew. Linc King was in on the start of the historical re-enactment. It was a nice little business, too.

"History is big just now. Not here in Chatham County, which was named for William Pitt, Earl of Chatham, "Friend of the American Colonies," or so they say. Really, all you need to know about us is the railroads made the difference. Though today's economy is tourism, and Nature. Oh, God, around here, we're riddled with beauty spots! But if you follow the money, it was railroads. The county seat used to be Fairstead, where you're sitting in the fourth oldest house. Then it became Pallas, which was Titusville originally. Named for them, because of their mills, on both branches of the Nubanusett. You know how geography seems to favor the fortunate? Well, the tracks from New York and the tracks from Boston crossed at Titusville but the railroad bridges for each were on Titus land. And it was nothing to run a freight spur to each mill. Know what they made? Wool shoddy. Shoddy is a secondary product, used wool that's then processed to make blankets and uniforms. Every time there was a war, the Tituses prospered. They were shoddy millionaires. A contradiction in terms, you might think"

Othmar managed a smile. He liked hearing about money.

It was the Carruthers family that made the Tituses spend it, said King. "The Tituses were glad to keep it in the bank—their bank. The Carrutherses had better ideas. They aren't from around here—arrived just after the Civil War. One Carruthers taught school. Another bought the weekly Clarion and lived off the job printing. Another was a lawyer. The Carruthers boys went away to college but always came back. They made themselves useful to the Tituses. They told the Tituses to invest in the town. I don't think the Tituses were mean people, or unduly grasping—for the times. But, remember, the century was a time of financial Panics. Then there was the Flood '78. It took one Titus dam and breached the other. They rebuilt. And saved jobs. But it has to be said the Tituses were without civic vision."

Othmar yawned. Too much history.

"It was the Carrutherses who changed the name to Pallas."

"Now that is interesting," said Othmar.

"For Pallas Athene—who is the godddess of wisdom."

"I did know that," Othmar almost snapped. "But why change the name?" he asked. "Why did the Tituses give their name up? Did they have to? Was it blackmail?"

"You've got a vivid imagination!" said Linc King, and laughing in such a way that Othmar thought he Othmar must be on to something, which pleased him. "You'll have to ask Evey Titus when you meet her. She was a Carruthers, you know. I almost married into that family. I used to buzz Sarah Smythe around. Isn't Sarah something! Tells you almost more about your 'Tosca' than you want to know. You're here because you need soldiers."

He led the way out of the house, Othmar slipping and sliding down a path of sheer ice.

"Salt is bad for pussy," Othmar thought he heard, and blushed.

Working open a thick wooden door, King helped Othmar up over the high threshold. Cold rank air rose to meet them, and Othmar gagged.

"Used to be a cow barn. You'll get used to it." King's breath was white.

Ahead, as far as the eye could see, were racks of military uniforms.

"I got the idea from those catalogue companies that sell clothes. Very instructive, their warehouse. Everything organized on clothes racks so you can find it. Usually by style, then size, then color. Here, I do it by time period, then by rank, officers where you see the gold braid, then by size. I've read up on 'Tosca.' Can't help it—it's in the paper everyday, or so it seems. Sarah is still a friend, and of my wife's, which makes it easier in a small town, I can tell you. Rome 1800. They think Napoleon has been licked by Melas at Marengo. Ha! That was cute of Sarah to dig up the recipe. Boney! There is a man I would like to meet. We won't see his like again."

And more, much more, as Othmar's head throbbed and cold stabbed his feet.

"I will undertake," said Linc King, "to provide your execution squad. Uniformed, and drilled, and commanded by myself. I am very careful about my men, about the men I ask. I always ask if they have any reservations. About war. About whose side they will be fighting on. I try to let them choose. I try to be accommodating. If I'm short enough men for the unpopular side, I do a lottery. Fair's fair. Don't think there will be a problem here."

Othmar said he was glad to hear it.

"No, America didn't have a dog in that fight. Although of course the Napoleonic wars were the European theater of what was going on over here. But a death squad, an execution squad, is different. I'll ask if they have feelings on that."

"Good idea, Linc." Othmar tried not to laugh.

"No capital punishment in this state, you'll be glad to hear. But you can always get an argument on the subject."

Led by Abraham Lincoln King, Othmar supposed.

"I'll send you an estimate."

Before he knew it, Othmar was back in his car. He turned up the heat till it was all he could hear. He was seething.

"Who the Christ asked you?" he said to the absent Abraham Lincoln King. "Who asked you to un-der-take to provide my death squad?"

The continuing cold, for the old Rambler's heater did not cut far into a Pallas February, made Othmar even angrier. "That jerk, that utter jerk," he shrilled, "sunbathing that way, all flabby. What right has he to expose himself to a perfect stranger? No one I know would do that to me! What is it about these people? They tell you things you don't want to know, don't need to know. Abraham Lincoln King who knows everything about history. Fine! But he should leave it for the classroom. Goddam fucking Keohane and his revolting talk about rats as though he was delivering a goddam sermon."

In the city, thought Othmar fondly, you could always tell the loonies. Mostly harmless, and they didn't expect your full attention. Panhandlers is what they were, and satisfied with money, but here you were expected to take an interest, to join in.

His stomach spoke. He was sure there wasn't anything open on a Sunday, not even a greasy spoon. (He had much to learn about Pallas.) He drove back to his little apartment and heated up a can of minestrone the thoughtful Mrs. Keohane had provided. He went to bed with the taste of tin and carrots in his craw.

7.

As readers of the Clarion Voice could not escape learning during the Washington's Birthday car sales, the world-famous opera composer Giacomo Puccini himself owned eight automobiles, and the fair city of Pallas would be privileged to hear his incomparable, etc., at the Palladium on etc. And now the producer of that very opera, John Austin Othmar, found himself very much against his will, bucketing through the winter's landscape with the author of that latest Puccini advisory, Sarah Smythe, at the wheel of her late husband's very old Mercedes and listening to her explain that "on the job," she always used one of the newspaper's two American cars—a Chevy and a Ford—because local dealers thought people in Pallas should "Drive Detroit."

"You'll find people have their own ideas around here," said Sarah Smythe.

"How so?" Othmar was trying to steer the conversation back from its unhappy detour at lunch. They had gone to Kulda's, where else? he promising her an exclusive when it came time to announce the cast for "Tosca."

"Yer usual?" Katherine asked Sarah after Othmar ordered a BLT.

"No, today, I think I'll try his."

When the sandwiches came, it was apparent the short-order cook practiced economies with the bacon. Each BLT had one half-slice and Othmar could see Sarah got the longer. To make things worse, Sarah didn't seem to be able to send the waitress away when she lurked.

"I've been meaning to ask you," Othmar began, his questions about Sarah's aunt, Mrs. Titus, rehearsed and formed in his mind.

"Yes!" said Sarah brightly. "I'm sure you have, and I've just come up with a wonderful idea. You can ask while I drive you around the county and show you the important things about us. There is more to us than Pallas."

It hadn't been Othmar's intention to go anywhere with Sarah, let alone be driven. In the best of circumstances, he hated being a passenger, and now he was captive in a car that obeyed all the traffic rules, such as signaling for a turn, but not all the safety laws, such speed limits and stop signs, and when he showily "put on the brakes" as she ran the third-such sign, she laughed and said county people knew which were important and which useless. The further Sarah took Othmar away from downtown Pallas and the safety of his theater, the more the phrase "county people" seemed to figure in a conversation— turned-monologue on the natural beauties and cultural importance of her little part of the world, the village of Fairstead.

"They couldn't pay me to live here," Othmar thought gloomily, when invited to view the exact vista—but not, apologized Sarah, not in moonlight on new fallen snow—as painted by a noted American Luminist, R.Clark Shaw, to represent Winter in his magisterial series of the Four Seasons. So popular was this sequence of Nature's beauties that "county people" had the very good idea to have it reproduced in chromolithograph. "That meant," Sarah explained, "even very modest people could afford to hang a Shaw over their sofa." And Othmar was shown the path to—but not visit, no, not in this weather—the never-melting Ice Glen itself. Another of Nature's wonders, it had inspired the lyric poet H.A. Kenny to write his sonnet on the lesson of Winter's blear Kingdom resisting Summer's warming Empire. "County people" saw to it that school children memorized "The Glacial Heart" when they studied local history as part of fourth grade Geography. Did "county people," Othmar wondered, really like Nature or did their fascination have more to do with the profit they could make from it? For that matter, did they like people? He longed for the city.

Finally they came to what Othmar took to be the object of Sarah's pilgrimage. It was the village center of Fairstead, and Sarah was saying that Fairstead was everything Pallas was not. Fairstead was eons earlier and smaller, purer, self-sufficient.

"I'd invite you in but they are re-doing the floors," said Sarah, pausing before a small, plain stone building. "It's the second-oldest house in Fairstead. It's called Pound Cottage, from the time when the town's green was the pound for stray cattle. And then it was a smithy and then a warehouse. There was always some use for it, which is why I think it got preserved. They were going to tear it down and I bought it when I moved back home. I am so lucky to have a place of my own. And my aunt to stay with during the renovations."

"And your aunt would be Mrs. Titus?" Othmar leaped at his cue.

"Aunt Evey?" Sarah was astonished Othmar should know her name.

"I would very much like to meet her. I understand she's what makes Pallas tick."

Sarah appeared to consider this. On the one hand, no one did more for the community than Aunt Evey. It was entirely to Evey Titus's credit that the

Palladium should have opera at all. And it was agreed between aunt and niece, though not spelled out in so many words, that Sarah would be "helpful" about "Tosca" in the Clarion Voice. On the other hand, to involve Aunt Evey in the production raised all sorts of, well, questions, especially given that she didn't like her name in the paper and Othmar, as Sarah well knew, was not at all adverse to publicity.

"I'll have to ask her."

"Oh, would you? You'd be a living doll! I can't just phone her myself. But coming from you, that would be the right sort of introduction."

No response.

"Your aunt can be soooo helpful with 'Tosca.' Not the money, because we've got most of that, though all contributions will be gratefully received, but the leadership. You 'county people' must know all about leadership," he said, descending to basest flattery. "I hear your aunt was a Carruthers."

Sarah stiffened. That old thing! Never far from the surface. Though Denny's family could have cared less! How did Othmar know Aunt Evey was a Carruthers? Just when things were going so nicely—though the detour to the Ice Glen was perhaps a mistake in winter. She frowned. "It's time I should be getting back to the office."

Othmar put a hand on the steering wheel.

"Seriously, Sarah, I want her advice on organizing things like local ticket committees. We've got four houses to sell. She's done her share of that."

Well, yes, but how did he know? By his tone, she was sure he "knew" Aunty Evey had organized Bond drives in the War. (Which he did, having read about it on microfilm.) That she founded the committee that got Community Concerts to bring classical music to Pallas and the county. (Ditto.) Did he know as well that hospitals and social work were projects Aunt Evey stayed away from? (Given more time at the library, he might have observed the absence of her name at hospital benefits.) What never made print was her remark to Sarah's mother that she must leave something for the "new people" to do. Music was Evey Titus's great love. She played the piano and she sang show tunes in her wispy soprano. The year it was new Sarah's father gave her "Kiss Me Kate." On 78s.

Still no response from Sarah.

"You've done all you could in the paper for 'Tosca.' Really, it has been the kind of publicity you can't buy. And interesting too! People in Pallas already know more about 'Tosca' than they do in New York. I've certainly learned a lot. And I'm sure there's more you can do, especially when the cast is ready to be announced. Interviews—that sort of thing." Othmar felt he was running short of blandishments. His stomach growled.

"You should have had the tuna melt with bacon."

In truth, as Sarah came to realize, she was loath to lose Othmar to her aunt. Since September, he had been her property, so to speak, the source not just of stories for the Clarion Voice but the beginning of a new interest. She hadn't gotten to the point of day-dreaming about a new life but the possibility was there, like the crinkle-plastic boots in Bossidy's window that she meant to try on.

In the end, it was Aunt Evey who forced her hand.

"What did Mr. Oddwine think of our beauty spots?"

"Othmar," Sarah corrected her crisply, and spelled it out. "His name is John Austin Othmar. But Fairstead—how did you know I took him there?"

Evey Titus lived in Pallas, in the Titus homestead. It was at the top of a hill and looked over the Nubanusett curling below. High above the noisome fumes of commerce and industry but close enough to keep an eye on things, she liked to say. And: "Pallas looks up to us and we look down." The house was built of the same brick and brownstone as the Titus mills and the Titus Trust, the family bank. Sarah thought it ugly beyond belief. Copper beeches flanked it, which only seemed to add darkness to bulk. There was a piazza on which no one ever sat. Those were its doubtful features. What Sarah didn't see, in love as she was with the easy symmetries of colonial Fairstead, was its amplitude and thrust. The windows were tall and deep, causing shadows to form and define the facade. The roof was steep and sprightly. Bays stacked two stories high vied for attention with a massive tower. If Fairstead's tiny-eyed windows looked inward, the Titus pile reached out (to a select list of Pallas worthies). The approach was ceremony clothing the practical: the gravel driveway curled gradually upward and fell slowly downward, for nineteenth century Tituses were as mindful as any farmer of the harmful effects of hills on horses's legs. Upon reaching the house, carriages paused under the porte-cochère to let passengers alight. For riders, there was a mounting block. Evey's own mother had caused raised eyebrows when she rode astride. Unbecoming in a young woman and known to be dangerous for a young wife in her child-bearing years. So much for received wisdom! Evey's mother produced a healthy brood of which Evey was the youngest after a spate of boys. "I was the caboose and I was thoroughly spoiled, I'm glad to say."

Sarah liked Aunt Evey. Her aunt dealt from the shoulder and that was a comfort. But she had learned not to confide in her. "We aren't that sort of family," Aunt Evey reminded Sarah after Sarah had unburdened herself of the gory details of her failed love affair with Linc King. (And married "darling Denny" on the rebound.)

"There is a good deal I don't need to know, don't want to know. Edit, as you might edit a story, and you'll be the happier for it." And less of a bore, but Aunt Evey kept that to herself.

"I know about your little jaunt because Katherine told her sister and her sister told me when she came to fit my spring coat."

"Well, I thought he should see something of the county."

They were sitting in the library, Aunt Evey reclining as usual on the big chaise longue. From a dark corner came a fetid smell.

"Poor Maida," said Sarah. Maida was Aunt Evey's ancient Irish water spaniel.

"Not long before she goes to Dr. Brielman's for the last time."

Sarah thought Aunty Evey was heartless for saying this in Maida's hearing.

"Let's have a drink, my dear. Very brown for me."

They sat with their bourbon, Sarah's with a good deal of water, "coasting," because she knew Aunt Evey as always wanted the latest gossip and dinner could go hang till she got it. She was a connoisseur of variations of the same sad tale. She rather than Sarah should be working at the Clarion Voice, Sarah oft times felt. "What is reporting but hearsay?" Aunt Evey liked getting a rise from Sarah's editor. But in Evey Titus's day ladies did not work. They did good works and they brought up families. Not that Aunt Evey cared much for children. Till they grew up. Her own three seemed to have thrived on benign neglect, raised devotedly by their nurse Helen. "About the only thing I remember about my mother," said one of Sarah's cousins, "was that she liked to take us out in her convertible for ice cream cones."

Maida made another smell. Sarah could also smell onions from the kitchen.

"You've found a cook?

"That remains to be seen."

Sarah freshened their drinks.

"Tell me about this Othmar you keep writing about."

"He wants to come to see you," said Sarah. "He thinks you could get 'em into the tent.' I'm quoting." Aunt Evey said she'd guessed.

70

"You'll like him. Lots of fun. Very bright." Sarah could feel her face flush. "He's going to do The Attavanti in drag." There! she'd said it, "drag," not knowing how Aunt Evey felt about men that did that.

"I don't believe the Attavanti has come my way. Is it something like the Frug?"

Sarah explained in some detail who The Attavanti was and how the opera would begin with her in the Attavanti Chapel and her praying. "Then he rises and crosses herself." Sarah swept hand to shoulder and up and down, as she'd seen Othmar do it.

"The gesture has to be large so it 'reads' to the audience," Sarah was saying. All she could hear was Aunt Evey hooting with laughter.

"The Catolicos will love it," she finally said. "Bring him to see me."

And so it happened a few evenings later that, toward the appointed hour, two cars ground up Evey Titus's hill, Othmar in his Rambler so as not to appear to be Sarah's "date," or under her auspices. Tonight was strictly business. A time to size things up. Pick her brain. What Evey Titus didn't know about Pallas wasn't worth knowing. Pallas could lead to something. Make up for "Hansel" and those losers. After drinks he would slip back to his office.

Sarah sped through the porte-cochère, spewing gravel as she braked. He followed, then was made to back his car back till she was satisfied he was correctly placed to enter the front door. "You're company!"

Othmar preferred to take his time, and making toward the side lawn, affected taking in the view. City lights twinkled below. "Magnificent," he murmured. He turned toward the house. "Such a grand place must have a name."

And Sarah, suddenly hostessy, said it was called Spring Side, for its laurels and was prettiest then. The drifts of daffodils on the lawns were quite fine, too. Planted in clumps, as they are in London parks. She gave him a push toward the big front door.

They made their way to the library. Aunt Evey had the fire going. She announced Othmar could make her a martini.

"Not too dry," she said. "I like to know there's something more than gin in it. The trouble with Eleanor Roosevelt was she never learned to make F.D.R. a martini and no wonder he looked elsewhere."

Maida shuffled in and sniffed at Othmar's shoes. He stroked her gently. Sarah thought she might have to change her opinion he was probably a cat person. After days of agony worrying if Aunt Evey would take to Othmar, she now had high hopes for this visit. She longed to know more about Othmar—and her aunt was a demon interviewer. "Nothing is so seductive, my dear, as the direct question. Forget that at your peril." Sarah had heard her ask people what they paid for their house and if it was true they had been stopped for drunk driving. Of course, Aunt Evey was only rude at parties; and Othmar, it occurred to Sarah, had come dressed for business. He might as well have been in the theater. He wore his usual dark turtleneck. How light his hair seemed. And his usual jeans. If not tight, Sarah thought, then snug. Well-polished loafers, rather than tennis shoes, were his only concession to what was also a social occasion. When Aunt Evey admired his Irish tweed jacket, he told her about a shop in Manhattan where you could get the most wonderful cast-offs. Called "Back of the Closet." Maida removed her head from his knee and walked away. In silence, Aunt Evey and Sarah and Othmar listened to her toenails click on the hall floor.

"How old is she?"

"Nearly fifteen. I got her the Christmas my husband died."

There was a rumble and whir and, with a dull bong, the grandfather clock launched the half hour.

"You've been stalking me," said Aunt Evey pleasantly. "Asking questions at the Historical Society." Sarah was mortified. How could he!

"No harm in walking the course." Othmar took the offensive. "I need your advice," Mrs. Titus."

A lesser woman would have said tush but Evey Titus smiled.

"Sarah tells me you think, and I quote, 'I can get 'em into the tent.' Where I lead, they follow. I'm flattered." She looked it, too, Sarah reflected. Her aunt lay back in the chaise longue obviously "receiving." Lamplight played on her silvery hair. This particular "At Home" costume was new to Sarah. She knew the caftan. And the velvet tea gowns in burgundy, in sapphire, and the black-widow with the old lace. She recognized the Turkish mules with the turned-up toes. From Mr. Neary at Saks. But this was a new Aunt Evey, lean in black silk pants cut like jeans and a purple silk "poor boy" jersey. She was not one for the distraction of little scarves and bracelets. Her only ring was a large emerald in an old-fashioned setting. Othmar thought the stone too cloudy to be of great value.

"As you can imagine, four performances is a lot of tickets to sell."

Evey Titus nodded. She could guess Othmar's drift.

Nine hundred thirty-eight times four," Sarah chirped.

"Less house seats and whatever," said Evey. "And partial view seats." She already had a seating chart for the Palladium.

Othmar thought it was not yet the time to reveal he had consulted Sam Adler about scaling the house. The grand old man of box offices, the much-courted doyen of the old Boston Opera House and the Colonial Theater, the genial Adler had scaled the Palladium tickets twice for Othmar. The second, or higher range of prices, would fatten the gross. Adler, moreover, had found Othmar a seasoned box office manager who would come out to Pallas for the final three weeks. For these and other professional courtesies, Othmar put Adler high up on his comp list, allotting him two pairs for each show. "It will be a pleasure to see you in my theater." And Adler, who liked a bit of swagger, beamed. "My pleasure."

Opening night will nearly sell out, Othmar told Evey Titus.

"Go clean," she said. She had once read an issue of Variety.

"We have this whole county to draw on. And," said Othmar, "just possibly the Albany area. What do you think?"

The second Thursday would be the hard sell, they both agreed. Everybody who's anybody wants to go opening night, he said.

So true, said Evey Titus.

Evey Titus loved a project. In the months leading up to Othmar's arrival in Pallas, she had, she thought, pretty nearly addressed every want the production of "Tosca" might have. She wasn't going to tell him how, lying abed nights, she had dealt mentally with piano rentals, intermission refreshments, the printing firm for the program book, the bus posters, free advertisements, parking and a police detail. Titus & Titus would do the legal work pro bono. Unlike her niece, she had a more realistic view of what the community could contribute in the way of services and what was off limits. She was an old hand at persuading people to buy tickets. It was a bit like fund-raising. You said what you were going to give, and then you said you expected them to do the same. Everyone understood. And understood they could always give their tickets away.

What about reduced prices for the Saturday matinee, he asked. He was thinking of making it a performance for schools. There was money for an educational program tied to "Tosca."

Sarah giggled. "They'll love it. A murder a minute."

Othmar was glad she was off Nature.

"Stabbing. Firing squad. Suicide."

"Two suicides," said her aunt. "Everybody forgets Angelotti."

"Gelati," squealed Sarah. Her face was red.

No head for liquor, her aunt knew.

Othmar pressed on. "What do you think about free tickets for the schools?"

"Absolutely not," said Evey Titus. "People must learn the arts are a commodity, not a frill, and like everything else, have value. Every child who went to a Community Concert paid something. Even if we underwrote it." She also warned Othmar away from advertising tickets at half price or reduced price. "That makes the public think you don't trust your product. Couldn't you say popular prices?"

Othmar smiled to himself. "Score one for me."

Sarah slipped out to get more ice. Things were going so well! Murder and mayhem. Unspeakable things offstage with a vice. Or was it a vise?

Things were going smoothly, but to Evey Titus that was not the same as going well. Othmar seemed perfectly pleasant. Presentable looking. Someone she could introduce around. People liked meeting the man in charge. He had a singer's speaking voice, a projected resonance, but it didn't seem affected. She could wish he didn't insist on this new thing, "making eye contact." She did not trust people who stared. The odd thing was they didn't really see you. He certainly was well organized. For that she was glad. But where was the fun in him? She had sat on committees all her life. The life of committees was not the agenda, and the minutes, and Robert's Rules, but the brainstorming. Though a bit different from the election committee of the Golf & Tennis, the nearest thing in Pallas to a country club. Evey used to lie in bed with her husband regaling him with details of the latest "malice break." Everybody on the committee would say everything bad they had ever heard about the candidate, especially if it was one of the "new people" in town, and then, having done their duty, elect them anyway. She had the feeling Othmar was too fastidious for committees, not one for the rough and tumble. Unable to give a little to get more back. No! It was worse than that. She bet he wouldn't take a chance on being wrong. Too bad! Being wrong had its uses. Well, the last thing she wanted was to dictate to him. She wouldn't pry into the artistic end. Not her territory. But, by God, she wasn't going to chase him. She could wait.

Othmar could play that game too. The way he read her, Evey Titus was dying to manage things. The way she never met his eye—shifty. So superior, with all her New York talk. A horrible woman! He would throw her a scrap. She wasn't like the committee ladies in the college towns where he had done the opera residencies. They came and went at his bidding, women still girlish and armed with clipboards, birds of passage in their station wagons, chattering of children and husbands and other committees. He was just another one of their projects, which meant they were too busy to get in his way. All he asked of them was to find accommodation for the cast. All they asked in return was the "great privilege" of giving the "après opera" reception. "Our small way of saying thanks," they gushed. Othmar's rule was that everyone, cast and techies, attend for one drink—or for twenty minutes if they only got punch. "Your reward is dinner on me." That dinner was in the budget, hidden under hospitality.

Pallas would be different from the college towns. He knew that from driving the length of the main street. It was a dump at both ends, like a banana going bad. One block in the center had gone "modern," as if in desperation. This town was going nowhere fast. Evey Titus, and he supposed she knew this, was the last of a breed. He bet she was lonely in her big house on the hill. It could do with a clean, God knows. His mother had taught him how. He liked things clean. He wondered if Evey Titus's library would ever be truly clean. It was dark from the paneling of the bookcases, and there was something repellent on the walls, a sort of leather wallpaper. How would there be so many light fixtures and so little light? That accounted for the big lamp standing behind her couch. How else could she see to read? He'd never seen such stacks of books and magazines.

"'Tosca' was the first opera I ever saw." Evey Titus cast a fly toward Othmar. Like her niece she wondered what his tastes were. It was no use asking him who he knew, what friends they might have in common, for he would have "played the game" and told her by now. She was not going to tell him her "Tosca" was in Paris and she was sixteen. Paris would be rubbing it in. But "Tosca"! Everyone must have had a first "Tosca," and she was trying to be friendly. Othmar sipped at his drink.

"'Otello' was the second." Then, with a satiric wave at her piles of books: "I've just been reading learned commentary which says there's something of Iago in Scarpia."

Othmar took another sip. "I've read that too," he said dryly. Really, she was meddling. "I don't want to spoil your fun but you'll just have to wait till opening night to see how we do it."

He met her eye. Who was she to tell him about opera? Had she ever sung on stage? He doubted she could even read music. Did she know the first thing about producing opera? Directing it? Working with casts which were always of unequal talent and experience? Sacrificing your best directorial ideas in order to get anything on stage?

Othmar looked so fierce that Evey Titus felt obliged to offer another olive branch. "You certainly have led an interesting life. And it can't have been easy, dealing with all those egos! And all the things that can go wrong. I marvel they can remember their notes." She laughed encouragingly. "What was your worst experience?

Another man might have seen this for a peace offering as well as a delightful invitation to brag. Another man would have said, Oh, I can laugh at it now but my first "Bohème" (or whatever) was a complete disaster. Picking their goddam teeth with the biggest, shiniest goddam toothpicks you ever saw. Othmar set his glass on the table. Why tell her, or anybody, when they couldn't possibly fathom how it destroyed him? She was asking him to trivialize himself and his profession.

"I've heard such tales!" she began, only to be cut off by another glare. Now he was worried. What did she know?

"Not about me," he said icily, "and not from me."

That was intended not merely to snub but to crush, and Evey Titus knew it. By the time Sarah returned with more ice, she was all business, telling Othmar about the time she organized town committees to sell tickets for a music festival. "I'll dig those subscriber lists up, if you like." Othmar had his file cards out and was taking notes. She wanted to be clear on one thing, to level with him. Volunteer committees can be a bother. The last thing she wanted to do was to get in the way of professional management. "Sam Adler tells me he is sending you one of his good young people."

Othmar breathed in.

"I have my spies," she said.

Just like Scarpia, he thought.

Then, to draw Sarah into the conversation, she began suggesting other committees and names for those committees. "The old settlers," she told Othmar. "Sarah knows them all. She covers Society for Clarion Voice."

"Whatever that is these days," said Sarah. The gin made her daring.

"You'll find Chatham County likes a party," said Evey. "I'll come up with a patrons' list. And you"—this to Sarah—"will get the young marrieds, and find out who the new people are." Othmar could hear Liz saying "Quel snob!" He wished he could leave.

"Anneandmark and emmaandtodd and simonanka…" Sarah babbled on. Othmar made as if to rise. Why did women always, always have to personalize?

"…michaelandnancy and" This just might be the time, thought Sarah, to do something for her new friend, and she ventured a name. By Aunt Evey's standards, her friend was one of the "new people" in Pallas. "She'd be terrific to head the young patrons. She adores music," said Sarah. With interest, Othmar saw Evey Titus frown. That one adores the sound of her own voice, thought Evey. That one has designs to become Mrs. Titus. I am the Mrs. Titus.

The grandfather clock insisted it was only eight.

"I'm hungry," said Evey Titus.

"If only this were New York," said Othmar coming on buttery, "I'd take you out for Chinese." Enough of Pallas! High time, he felt, to take back his own, rise up on his hinders (as Gilly would say) and remind Pallas who he was and where he came from. He was the New Yorker here, not Aunty Evey Titus.

"Couldn't we get the China Clipper to deliver?" Sarah begged. "Mugo guy poo."

"Stop sucking your thumb," her aunt said sharply.

"With lots of almonds."

Suddenly, she was off the chaise longue and standing. Othmar was surprised how tall she was: she almost looked him in the eye. "I expect we'll find something in the kitchen."

They made their way into the dark hall. Sarah danced ahead. "Whee!" she whinnied and snapping on lights set Spring Side's reception rooms ablaze. In the drawing room, Othmar took in heavy furniture, dim mosaics, inglenooks, violently patterned carpets, sagging cord fringe on sun-rotted silk curtains, marble plaques, carved screens, gaudy landscapes, bronze utensils of indeterminable use. Swathed in a paisley shawl, a piano stood on the heavily carved legs that Othmar associated with pool tables. Sarah ran a finger over the lid. "Mummy always told me, if you dust people won't notice you haven't vacuumed."

Evey Titus strolled once around the room. "Its time will come again."

Sarah shepherded them through the butler's pantry. "Party! party!"

In the gloomy, varnished kitchen, her aunt stopped and blinked. "I'm a stranger here myself," she said to Othmar.

And to Sarah, crossly: "I need something right away."

Sarah scattered. She located Saltines and a bar of scabbed cheddar. She found a knife. She got Othmar busy assembling toasted cheeses, then, forgetting to watch the broiler, she incinerated them. No loss, thought Othmar—he had tasted the crackers and they were stale. From the pantry Sarah emerged with cans of baked beans. From the refrigerator came two hot dogs. "Cut each one in three," Aunt Evey instructed Othmar, "and we can each have two pieces." There was toast, too, once he had sliced mold from the crust. They drank beer, Othmar having tipped a decidedly brown jug-wine down the drain.

"We save the jugs," said Aunt Evey. "Do you do much entertaining, Austin?"

Othmar shook his head.

"Yes! Austin," she insisted, smiling at him. "I will call you Austin.

Sarah almost said, like Bompa Titus's last chauffeur.

"Yes! 'Austin Othmar Presents.' It has the right degree of mystery. The 'Austin' will keep people guessing. Some people will think 'Othmar' is too foreign."

"My name is Othmar."

"The 'Austin' will reassure."

Othmar felt a great fatigue. He was being stripped of purpose. He felt reduced. The kitchen filth pressed in on him. How could people live like this? Her with her shopping trips to Bendel's and Bergdorf's. That loon, Sarah. Why hadn't Sam Adler warned him? He knew the answer to that: Sam was in her camp. He needed Gilly. Terrible thought! Whose side was Gilly on? He'd had too much to drink. They all had. He could hear Aunt Evey set Sarah straight on something.

"It was not blackmail, as Austin seems to think."

Austin! His new name! He raised his head obediently.

"Not blackmail," Aunt Evey was saying. "The Tituses were entirely without civic vision. But my family, the Carrutherses, changed all that. They persuaded the Tituses they would lose everything if they didn't move with the times. But for us, the Tituses would still be putting it in the mattress. Invest, build, control, share, delegate. Run it yourself but hire your weaknesses. My family understood about money."

Sarah laid her head on the table.

"We put Pallas on the map. My grandfather chose the name. You won't be surprised to hear we commissioned your theater. I won't have you fail. My grandfather walked the length of Main Street every morning. He spoke to every merchant. You'll be wise to do the same. You'll find you have to sell opera here just like anything else."

Othmar was now aware of bile rising. He was going to be sick. He heaved to his feet. Evey Titus slapped him hard.

"Never fails." She took his arm and steered him out into the hall. The halls have halls, he thought. She opened the big front door. Cold air rushed in. Othmar saw the sickly lights of Pallas below. It was an effort to be gracious but he knew he must.

"Thank you so much," he muttered. "So generous. Very valuable."

"I have your phone numbers," said Evey Titus. "I will be in touch. You will want to come back to look at furniture for 'Tosca.' I have a monstrance."

"Monster?" That's what she was, a monster.

"Safe home," she said, edging him into the porte-cochère. She banged the door shut and snapped off the lights. Othmar was left in the dark.

8.

Othmar woke with a terrible head. Squinting into the mirror while shaving he tried out his new name.

"Austin Othmar. Austin Othmar." It began to sound big, and affirmative. It had authority. He drove to the theater and let himself in. On cue, the phone rang.

There was a barking laugh on the other end. It was Gilly.

"Johnny, Johnny, is it you?"

Gilly to Liz that evening as they dug into polenta at the newest northern Italian place: "Our friend sounds absurdly happy." Liz took the bait: "We'll just have to drive up there and spoil his fun."

Othmar was indeed absurdly, wonderfully, happy. Happy as he never thought he could be. A happiness that had him smiling to himself, and smiling as he caught himself at it. It was not so much his new name as a new identity he could feel bullying its way up over the old. He minded not a little that his new self was the creation of the monstrous Evey Titus. "Auntie" Evey!—let the diminutive fit. Just wait! He'd cut her down to size. As the Car. Carruthers sowed, so shall they reap.

All those years ago, and in the name of civic virtue, the Carruthers had commissioned a theater. This was the Palladium, their Palladium, as she made sure to tell him, was now Austin Othmar's. It was his temple, his lair, his sword and buckler. "They will have to carry me out feet first."

Othmar sat in his office. For the pure pleasure of not answering, he let the phone ring. And ring again.

When Joseph McArthur Vance designed the Palladium in the last year of the nineteenth century, he was a young architect just starting a practice. Every building was his first, and the Palladium his first theater. To ascertain what would be desirable in a theater he took the train to Boston and called at several stock companies. Actor-managers were glad of his attention and delighted at the prospect of a theater to fill the booking gap between Springfield (or Hartford) and Albany.

In a week's time, Vance became acquainted with the necessities and the options. He absorbed averages, and medians, and standards, whether they applied to the height of the flies, the width of the stage, angle of rake, number of traps, depth of wings and distance between blacks, capacity of pit. Managers explained the need for a props closet that would lock. Vance learned how to configure the seating and where to place the aisles. He was told the number of boxes his theater would support. He was made aware of the effects of climate on the box office. Because of the summer heat, most theaters were "shuttered"—theater talk for closed down—in July and August; and June and September, those months on the cusp of hot weather, tended to draw poorly. If you can, Vance was advised, contrive a "mushroom" cellar for your theater. This was a fully excavated area below the basement running under the stage and auditorium. By opening vents the cool subterranean air flowed upward. Or so the public believed.

"And do you grow mushrooms there?" Vance was a solemn young man. There was general laughter.

"If you've no bookings and no prospects," joshed John Deedy, who managed the Commonweal. Besides extending the season a week or two, all agreed a mushroom cellar was useful for storing scenery and sections of the raked stage.

About lighting, the managers were of two minds. They would all of them miss the genial glow of gaslight foots. But to a man they appreciated the hazard of fire. Jerrold Hickey of the Bostonia remembered the time a dancing girl's tulle skirt caught on fire and the devastating effect it had on ticket sales for the rest of the run. Vance was already convinced electricity was here to stay. He also believed in indoor plumbing. And because he liked the actor-managers, enjoyed their hospitality (lobsters at the Parker House) and their lavishness with free tickets (in one week he saw four shows) Vance was determined to endow the Palladium with a suite of offices fit for these impresario kings. He did, and Austin Othmar had now fallen heir to it.

On the train back, Vance sketched and refined plans for the office. As he worked he hummed "A Bicycle Built for Two." There was a Miss Titus he had his eye on. Something of the perceived nature of actresses and showgirls informed part of Vance's plan for the office. He would be considered prescient a few years later when "Stanny" White was shot for defiling Evelyn Thaw. Of course, that was in New York, and in a private club of sorts, and White was a society architect, and a red velvet swing was involved. But Vance supposed there were times when actor-managers took their ease with compliant young things. Accordingly, he equipped the office with a recessed couch. It was like a Breton bed, or a captain's berth. Vance set it into the wall and framed it with an arch. The finishing touch was a pair of velvet curtains which could be pulled shut. This he explained away by saying that managers might well like to catch forty winks between shows.

From the office a tiny spiral staircase led upwards to the manager's box, the first box after the proscenium arch. When Vance married his Miss Titus, the Palladium manager of the day lent the young couple his box for "Romeo and Juliet." The new Mrs. Vance was pretty for a Titus, and knew it, and liked sitting where the audience would inspect her looking so handsome and attending with such rapture to Shakespeare's art. It was to be hers and dear Joseph's little secret that one did not see the stage very well from such a box. There was a whole section hidden by the proscenium arch and she had to take it on faith that Juliet stabbed herself.

Nor did Vance skimp on the practical aspects of a manager's office. He had observed that managers needed the quickest possible access to many different parts of the theater. Especially back stage and the box office. What was needed was an internal corridor linking these. Perhaps it was the train on which he was riding but it occurred to Vance that something like the concentrated space of the Pullman car might answer. He roughed in a suite running the length of the theater from stage to lobby. At the box office end he inserted a stout door with metal grille and nearly he specified a big iron safe. On the stage side of the proscenium, at the first black, he drew in a lavatory. A manager who also acted would like having a private spot that could double as his dressing room. From this, a tiny hall led to the office proper. Having laid in the recessed couch with its arch (and doodled a head of Pallas Athene for the keystone) Vance turned to more mundane matters. He established egress with a door giving out onto the alley. He considered, then rejected, a window or windows. He turned his attention to furnishings. He placed a roll top desk along one wall. In one corner he put a miniscule fireplace with coal grate. The office was spacious enough for a library table and around this Vance set six chairs. He was sure that managers had meetings, and some managers, perhaps, had reading rehearsals. He made the whole room as elegant as he knew how—without resorting to pilasters and columns, architectural elements best left for public display in the lobbies and auditorium. The office walls would be paneled in fine wood. One large panel gave Vance particular pleasure to design: push it in a certain way and it was a door opening into the auditorium. Other wall panels were cunningly hinged, and behind were shelves. When Prohibition came, a manager or two had cause to thank Vance for providing a means of concealing their tipple.

Vance's plans for the Palladium were well received. His Miss Titus put it over with her family, or so she liked to think. Vance did not tell her of visitations from one or more Carrutherses to inspect his drawings. But Vance also knew the value of distributing credit where credit was due. His report to the building committee, too detailed to quote here, carried the day with its appended letters from Boston's leading managers stating that no finer theater could be envisioned.

And mindful of Pallas's place in worlds ancient and modern, Vance commissioned the great mural by T. Vrettos that to this day enriches the theater lobby. Pallas Athene is shown condescending to the populace. In fact, in the year Joseph Vance spent designing and overseeing theater construction, he had only one sticky moment. His darling girl thought it would be simply wonderful if the mural could be made a group portrait of Pallas worthies. Vance had to take her little hand in his and speak a bit firmly.

"Art, my dear," he said, "is not a photograph."

Right on schedule, the Palladium opened in 1900 with the audience dressed in their best bib and tucker to see "Robin Hood." A month later, Mr. and Mrs. Vance—"she was a Titus, you know"—took the train to attend at a far grander theater opening. Boston's Colonial staged "Ben Hur" with a cast of thousands (350 by rough count) and a dozen live horses hitched to chariots galloped on a treadmill. No wonder such local events eclipsed a third theatrical marvel of that year, the premiere in far-away Rome on the fourteenth of January, of an opera that would bring a certain notoriety to the fair city of Pallas. This was Puccini's "Tosca." Out of that happy coincidence Sarah Smythe got a story for the Clarion Voice.

Othmar lay on the office couch, legs crossed, right heel resting on left toe. Still the phone rang. And still he didn't answer. It could only be one of them, Sarah or her Auntie Evey. This place was his: He placed the calls.

He had always loved theaters. Not all theaters. Not, for example, the many modern theaters whose dry acoustics favored articulation over vibrating space, the speaking voice over breathing, the teeth over the lungs (as he thought of it). It was the woodiness of old theaters that gave them life. The stage was wood. The seats rose on a wooden amphitheater. The first evening in Pallas he had let himself in and sat high up in the second balcony—the "gods"—and listened to the theater creak as wood contracted in the chill of night. He could hear wind whistle in the flies, and the metal cables rubbing and twanging. He loved the hiss and ping of stage lighting. Theaters even had their own dust—and quantities of it. His first-ever job was sweeping the stage before curtain time so singers would not inhale throat-drying motes. He had read theatrical memoirs which called the audience the "beast" and critics, "vipers," and there was something to that.

As well as something animal. "Like a Greek myth that explained where we got willows or butterflies or constellations, and the myth about the creation of theaters could begin with a muse—unrecorded by history—whom the gods transformed for the purpose of giving audience to human utterance." This idea, too personal for his opera talks, was bound up with a boyhood memory of sitting around a campfire with the Scout master telling ghost stories, and there was this one kid who wanted to know if it was true if a tree fell down in the woods and there was no one around to hear it, would it make a noise, and thinking about that, Othmar still thought, was as spooky as anything about ghosts. People talked about theaters being inhabited by the ghosts of great performers. Othmar couldn't go that far. But he was sure theaters had a purpose deeper than entertainment. Religious, almost. So he never entered an old theater with less than reverence. There was something else. One thrill of this theater, apart from what he, Austin Othmar, might be able to create on stage, was he could call the Palladium his home.

The theater manager's office was the first place in his life Othmar could truly call his own. Boyhood bedrooms scarcely counted. As an Army brat, he had been moved around. His father, career Army, was an irritable man, ramrod straight, a nitpicker who saw conspiracies everywhere. What else could explain his always getting the wrong end of the stick? And bad posts? And staff who weren't worthy of their commissions? The less said about the quality of recruits the better! When angry, veins bulged and his mouth hollowed. Little Johnny watched the transformation with awe but teenager John with silent laughter. In compensation, Othmar's mother was round and cheerful, "always doing." As he grew up, Othmar came to see her cheerfulness had a frayed quality about it, this despite her favorite utterance, "It will all turn out all right." They would arrive at yet another military base and find the housing assigned them. The previous family had just decamped. If Othmar's mother was lucky, they had left it "broom clean." His father would send a squad of soldiers over to wash the walls and the floors. As he rose in rank, the soldiers painted the rooms. Othmar's first memory of home was of damp plaster.

He made few friends. His father—Captain, then Major Austin (for that was the family name)—had decided ideas about associates for his son. Young John was middling at school. He did well in math. He loved taking Shop.

"There is nothing that boy can't build, Father." The Austins were Father and Mother to each other. John, named for his father, was their only child. There had been a baby girl, stillborn, "with the angels." Her headstone, a baby lamb in marble, moved post to post with the family.

In Shop, John built a bird house and a box that could be used for sewing (his mother saw that at once!) and was working on a pipe rack for his father when they moved again. He would miss the orderly disorder of Shop. And the smells!—the sappy wood and dank metal. He loved how metal filings shimmered like a silver thread—and thrilled how they broke at the touch. It wasn't making the birdhouse or the sewing box that so absorbed John as the tasks involved and the bond with the Shop teacher as they worked together. Only in music, when he came to study clarinet later, did the teacher work along side you. Not in English, where the teacher already knew the grammar and how to spell, or in math, where they knew all the answers. In Shop, the usually quiet John chattered away. He did odd jobs. He helped clean up. He could not hear enough about tools and technique. When they moved yet again, he was learning about the different kinds of wood and would have learned cabinetry. In Shop, one could feel close without it being personal. John felt safer with the Shop teacher, Mr. Cosel, than with his own father. "Stop examining the boy," Mother would protest when Father "got on" John about his marks or his friends. As long as there was Shop he was happy, and Mr. Cosel's creed was his creed. "Measure twice, cut once" he'd sing out as he dashed his bike through a gap in the fence.

Major Austin's next base was very large. If he did well he might reasonably expect a foreign posting. His heart was set on Germany. Except for Hitler, Germans knew how to do things right. *Ordnung*, order. It might look well if he learned German (he knew a GI bride). This Man's Army was all about public relations. He cast around the base for projects that would bring him to the attention of his superiors. He had noticed the number of boys John's age. There were enough for a Scout troop. Major Austin determined they should learn how to shoot.

"Guns?" John inhaled.

His father winced. "Rifles."

John was beside himself with excitement. His father soared in his estimation. He longed to be tall like him. He tried on several of his father's expressions: "Sweet Jesus" and "Dammitalltohell." He loved the Scout uniform. The sharp crease in the pants, his mother's doing, made him his father in miniature.

And he was good at rifle practice. Fire as you let your breath out, Sergeant Teale told the boys. John was the first to get this, and Ben Teale was quick to praise John to his father. Major Austin's only reaction was to remind his son how he had secured free ammo for the Scout troop. Unlimited free ammo, emphasis on free. Any other rifle club would charge a quarter for a hundred bullets. John was impressed (his allowance was fifty cents a week).

So he saved his paper targets and hung them over his bed. It got so that most were bull's eyes, whether he shot in the prone position, or kneeling, or standing. His father glanced without comment at this evidence of his son's marksmanship. Another father might have boasted his kid outshot his old man and joshed Sergeant Teale for making this happen, and the growing display of paper targets with their furry black holes would have vanished as the son, as boys will, moved on to baseball cards and comic books. Johnny collected those too, and he sent box tops away for decoder rings and cowboy spurs with rowels that glowed in the dark (but never all night, no matter how long you had exposed them to a light bulb).

The summer before John would enter high school was a summer of odd, furtive looks from his father. "Almost as if he was seeing me for the first time." Just before Labor Day, the scrutiny stopped. "As if he had made his mind up about me, and I was no longer there."

One afternoon, John came home to find his room stripped bare of his precious bull's eyes. That evening at supper, Major Austin announced he had enrolled John in a military academy. A scholarship for the son of a career officer "was going begging."

"Molders of Men" the academy liked to boast. It proved John Austin's salvation. At Commencement, he got the prize for physics. He discovered an affinity for engineering. One day he was volunteered for the chapel choir. Not his idea! But he took suddenly to singing. At first it was the sheer noise he relished. Then the sheer physicality of holding your part against another. He started clarinet and played in the band. Jazz he never really took to but he played for dances. He was bashful with girls. The dance band meant he didn't have to dance.

Above all else the academy taught John the value of uniformity. In uniformity John found freedom. He was careful never to be tops, or showy, or creative. Second string all the way, though his marksmanship scores were such that he could have made the rifle team. He liked drill: He marched with the others, matching his shadow and his stride to the norm. He was punctual. He "did his share." He "kept his nose clean." He was busted just often enough to keep the sympathy of his few friends. He kept his equipment immaculate.

His uniform was always in order. The great thing about all this, John Austin came to realize, was that uniformity let you hide in plain sight. If we were to look in now at Austin Othmar stretched out on his couch of sin- at the Palladium, we might wonder what he was dressed for. An artistic calling, or academic, at any rate, a job at which men didn't have to wear neckties and jeans were tolerated. If we looked in the closet of his rented room we would see his clothes constituted a uniform. There must have been six pairs of jeans, all washed and pressed, on individual hangers. In the bureau drawers, neatly folded turtlenecks in dark colors.

John Austin was within two months of graduation when the commandant summoned him to his office. Lieutenant Colonel Austin had died. An accident. Deepest regrets. A fine officer. John could be proud of his service to the country. Only later did John learn that his father, on duty but in civilian clothes, was hit by a car. "In a part of the town I don't think I was ever in," John's mother said, perplexed. Interment was private, and took place some weeks after the funeral, when the remains of "infant girl Austin" could be retrieved and finally buried under her lamb.

Then began the years of migration. His father would not have been surprised that the Army he served so faithfully had euchred his widow and son out of what he would have considered their due. Mrs. Austin, ever resilient, said never to mind. She did not mind leaving Army life, not one bit, she assured her son. Why, she would go out to work, something Father would never hear of her doing. It would be a new life. They would move wherever Johnny wanted. He was eighteen, and already a strategist, already a list maker. He chose a city with a state university that offered engineering and music. If he lived at home they could afford the extra money for voice lessons. And so it happened.

Othmar yawned. Had he dozed off? The couch was very comfortable. He admired the view of his office through the dark green velvet curtains. He had been in apartments far smaller and less well equipped. I could certainly spend the odd night here, he thought. More than that if there were a shower. He supposed he could use one of the dressing rooms backstage. Better still!—and he bounded up and made for the lavatory. Yes! There was just room for a stall shower. He would get that put in for next season.

Again the phone ran.

"Austin Othmar," he answered.

"It's Evey Titus." He thought she might call herself Mrs. Titus to him

"When do the artistes arrive?" she asked.

9.

In the normal course of events, Gilly—as their management—would have escorted the "Trieste talent" to far-off Pallas and installed them for their engagement. He did the same for all his talent. He settled them in their accommodations. He met the Press on their behalf. He lingered to see that all was going well in rehearsal. If the talent was a piano soloist, he hoped they liked the instrument. And if they didn't, perhaps something could be done. If the hall displeased? Well, there was nothing he could do about the acoustic. He was there to trouble shoot. For a man who was indifferent about his own belongings, he was something to behold when he had to track down a client's mislaid flute or find a brand new pair of high heels, in her size and to her taste, for the soprano who had neglected to pack same. Not on his watch but shepherded by other management was the English conductor who forgot his infant in its Moses basket while coming through Immigration at Boston.

"Bad news, old chum," said Gilly to the man who now answered the phone as Austin Othmar. "I myself cannot bring your crew to Pallas."

As management, Gilly was catching on. The latest to sign with him was a young American-born Chinese conductor. He was to make his debut in Detroit and Gilly must needs be there. "His first Mahler One," said Gilly, hoping that explained a lot. Liz thought it worth her while to go along. The right kind of management wife, as she didn't tell her husband, would be favorably received. Othmar could hardly protest.

"I'm not the only kid on the block?" he asked mournfully.

"I will be in constant touch," promised Gilly. "In telephonic communication, if you'll answer your damned phone."

So those had been the calls as Othmar lay communing with fame in his office.

Gilly and Othmar compared calendars. The "Trieste talent" would take the train from Grand Central to Albany. "They're Italians—they like trains," Gilly averred. Othmar would meet them at Albany.

Othmar had taken Evey Titus's advice to heart and paid court to the merchants along Main Street. There were actually two Main Streets, north and south, stretched over ten blocks. Once upon a time, when the trolley ran down the center on its way to its northern conclusion at Five Towns, it bustled with foot and wheeled traffic but nowadays the thoroughfare was overly broad for conviviality and too long to walk for the shopper in a hurry. Hence, the growing attraction of driving out to a shopping strip and catching a bite. Did Evey Titus in her heart of hearts think a restored Palladium would revive downtown? "We can but hope."

Adding to the general gloom were the public buildings, among them the Titus Block, where Titus & Titus had their law offices, and Titus Trust. The Titus Memorial Library, built of the same hard, dark stone, seemed to discourage visits. "Titus Town need not detain us," said Sarah Smythe attempting a funny. She was his guide, rather more business-like than when showing off the beauty spots of Fairstead. She introduced him around. She at least was tolerated, a familiar figure who trawled the ten blocks weekly in search of stories. Under her escort, Othmar did his little number, drumming up trade.

He saw to it that every store had a poster for "Tosca." Rosenfeld's, the leading men's store, took several for their windows. Othmar modified his impresario act for local consumption, getting so he could kid grand opera a bit. He promised them they'd like "Tosca." Blood and gore, and plenty of tunes. He told them one critic had called it a "shabby little shocker." This was not the happiest of recommendations, and Othmar was forced to conclude that, in Pallas, merchants took "shabby" as bad for business and "shocker" as bad for civic order, which came to the same thing. Othmar went to bed hating himself for debasing "Tosca."

Worse was to come when he was interviewed, "grilled" was more the word, on WPAL, the Voice of Pallas. The real Pallas Athene wouldn't be caught dead here, Othmar thought sourly when it was all over. A crome-voiced announcer introduced the show, crooning the theme song, "We're Pals, Radio with a Heart." These two afternoon hours occupied the tiny fragment of Pallas not watching the soaps. The "hostess," as she styled herself, was Mary Ellen Adams. The first hour was the mail bag, even if, increasingly, she wrote those cards and letters herself. Promptly at four, and thanks to the magic of radio, the sound of spoon clinking on saucer was heard. "I'm going to make myself a cup of tea." Mary Ellen's voice soothed like lilac talcum powder. "Won't you join me?" It was part of local lore that the gas and electric companies reported a power surge as hundreds of water kettles hotted on hundreds of stoves. Her tea cup was Wedgwood and her tea spoon, silver—and so was Othmar's. "We try to make it just like home." She was a hand-patter and had the plain woman's faith in "interesting" scarves.

"No cookies, I'm afraid," she apologized to Othmar. "I don't have to tell another professional what crumbs in the mouth do to one's diction."

Events in the greater world might come knocking at Mary Ellen's door but not all were admitted. Television was not her only rival. She had been grievously hurt by a barrage of letters from Chatham County's three or four feminists feeling their oats. "Who has done more for women than I," she would say, "than by keeping them company and giving them comfort." Her hands worked at her scarf and her voice trembled, for she liked to think her two hours were more than the conventional recipe-swap and chat show. Once a week she reviewed a book and she had decidedly conservative views on movies. By broadcast conventions that still applied in places like Pallas, the old medium of radio pretended the new medium of television did not exist. Mary Ellen Adams also had a profound distrust of newspapers. "They twist your words," she'd say. On my 'Pals' you hear what people have to say for themselves." Then, with emphasis: "In their own words." Needless to say, she loathed Sarah Smythe. Needless to say, the hour—one whole hour, less two commercials—she set aside for "Tosca" rather implied that nothing whatsoever about the opera itself or the production had been made known to the people of Pallas. So much for the Clarion Voice and what Gilly, eagerly awaiting them, called "Sarah's daily rushes."

"To give her credit," Othmar told Gilly later, "the old bag had done her homework and she got a recording so I could play excerpts. The new Caballé and Carreras with Colin Davis. But, oh, God, she hummed along."

Othmar had been afraid Tosca's morals might not find favor with the high-minded Miss Adams. But she dismissed her as "no worse than any other opera heroine," and she knew them all—as a "regular listener" to the Saturday broadcasts of the Met. She "loved" Boris Goldovsky's talks with piano. She was "addicted" to the intermission quiz, had even sent in a question "to stump the panel of experts." But for a commercial break, praising yet another margarine that tasted like butter, Othmar might have learned what her panel stumper was. Animals in opera? Baritones who get the girl?

"As I was saying, when we were so rudely interrupted," she twinkled at Othmar, "radio was made for opera. If you can't be there in person, our god-given gift of imagination lets us people the stage. They can be the lovers of your dreams." Here, she expertly cued Cavaradossi's farewell to life and added her breathy voice to his. "Who is more villainous?" she asked rhetorically, "than the Scarpia of the mind? Or more frightening than deaths we can't see?" This interview was a piece of cake, Othmar was beginning to think. He could see the studio clock gain on five.

"Murder most foul!" crowed his hostess.

"Most foul indeed," Othmar agreed. He realized he hadn't yet made his pitch for the Saturday matinee for students.

"Now I have a little confession to make."

"And we all know confession is good for the soul," said Othmar jollying her along till he could pounce.

"I love murder mysteries and I wonder…oh, I am wicked to ask you this but I wonder if anyone has ever murdered Scarpia. Actually killed him."

Othmar saw his chance. "Only a critic or two, but we mustn't dwell on that. You're such a positive person and I just want to thank you for having me on the show. And to all the mothers out there listening, I just want to say that the Saturday matinee of 'Tosca' will introduce your children to one of the greatest operas ever written. And student tickets cost only…"

But here Othmar's luck did run out and there had to be a station break.

"Bundle up," Mary Ellen Adams fluted as he crept out of the studio.

In this windowless hell of acoustic tile there was no one to ask the way out. Othmar walked first into a closet and then into a closet-like studio where a man was busy at a recording console.

"Most people on her show get asked their favorite recipe," said the man turning to chat. Othmar saw he had a wall eye and stiffened.

"Pretty interesting," said the man. "Done with a collapsing knife?"

"When they work," Othmar allowed.

The man laughed and nursed a lever upward. "How do you do the gun shots?"

"Glad you asked," said Othmar. This was not a lost afternoon after all.

Still and all, when he thought about it, the engineer's questions rankled, a techie's fascination with the mechanics of blood and gore. Nor did he like it one little bit the implications of that self-described opera lover, Miss Mary Ellen Adams, taking Scarpia beyond the stage character Puccini delineated. Is there anyone in Pallas who takes opera seriously? Who even knows what it is? Othmar, used to solitude, felt lonely.

It would be years, he knew, before he could afford the luxury of declaring his love for Mozart above all composers. Puccini was there to learn on, as the "Hansel and Gretel" had been. So what if "Tosca" was melodrama? You couldn't learn if you didn't take each of those composers at face value: to fulfill their expectations for their work. You could, of course, protect a composer from himself. "Tosca" was by no means perfect and not every director has allowed the Sacristan the full range of comedic tics that Puccini wrote into his music. Othmar would have to see how it went into rehearsal. As for the music itself, that he would leave to the maestro. As an Italian, Pompelli had grown up on Puccini, knew the tradition—may even have heard him conduct. He was a link to the past. What he said about authentic performance was worth listening to. But if we could go back to the first performance in 1900, would we believe what we saw on stage? Not even the French revive the Sardou play, which was the original of Puccini's "Tosca." Yet the opera has never been out of the repertory. Over the years, certain details of staging have changed. Tosca's first act costume is no longer Diva Goes to Church. (Well, less so. Or if so, ironically so.)

"Now why don't you tell our listeners the approach you intend to take with your 'Tosca.'" Mary Ellen Adams had said, issuing the invitation with a brisk hand-pat.

Othmar sat back as far as he could. "It isn't *my* 'Tosca' but Puccini's and I tend to agree with the great Tito Gobbi, who sang Scarpia more than eight hundred times and who staged some famous productions, and who should know a thing or two, that opera works on its own terms. Enlightened fidelity to the text and absolute belief in the music will always keep 'Tosca' on the boards."

"I know a direct quote when I hear one," beamed his hostess.

Why was it, Othmar wondered, that they were all out to question his credibility, put him on the defensive? Sure, there was nothing wrong with the Gobbi approach that a stellar cast would not enrich. "So it isn't the Met or La Scala! My goal is loftier, if I may say so," Othmar told his own best audience. "For most people in the fair city of Pallas, it will be their first, and only 'Tosca.' I will set the standard."

Gilly's defection to Detroit meant Othmar would have to lay on transportation. No limo purring up Route 22 from New York. He would telephone the Volkswagen place and try to con them into lending a van to fetch the artistes at Albany. In exchange, they would get a nice credit, even a free ad in the program book. "Transportation for the production generously provided by Bedell's Volkswagen."

"It's Evey Titus calling," said a familiar voice.

Othmar told her he was about to arrange for a VW bus. There will be a lot of baggage, he explained.

She would not hear of it.

"Let me call Wellington's and see if they won't have let you have one of the funeral cars. I know Roger very well. A fine tenor voice. He sings Stainer's 'Crucifixion' at funerals. His father was the last sheriff to preside at a hanging. He laid out Andrew Carnegie. A story for another time."

So it was that Austin Othmar set out for Albany in a Cadillac limousine so old it had vestigial running boards. No one thought to tell Othmar it had first belonged to old Titus, whose grandchildren called him "Bompa." But a limo it was, boxy and black; and it was fitted out with black silk shades that drew down on black silk cords to shield mourners from public view. Othmar, who would have much preferred to sit with the driver, lounged in back with the two huge black umbrellas and the box of Kleenex that Wellington's provided for the bereaved. Many years had passed since this Cadillac had been out of a trot. The driver knew, moreover, that by going over through the Canaan Flats he could avoid Lebanon Mountain. The country roads grew narrow, and Othmar grew bored, then mischievous. He pulled down the shades. Othmar the Bandito. "Take that...and that." He shot his way to freedom. There was a whine like an insect. Someone cued the siren.

"Everything all awright here?" It was a local cop.

The long and short of it was that Othmar was late at Albany to meet the train.

Of the Trieste trio, Othmar was sure he would recognize Pompelli, and Pompelli, him; and there would be an embrace and Pompelli would introduce him to the others. But no one resembling Pompelli was visible in the station. Othmar was about to look for the ticket window when his eye was caught by the heads of three men sitting facing away from him. That aureole of silver hair must be the maestro's. Othmar advanced. He was nearly knocked down by a small figure in fur and high-heeled boots. She wore enormous sun glasses. Then he was nearly knocked down by a man who sprang after the woman. This man was totally bald. Not Pompelli. Then came the familiar voice of Pompelli. He rapped with his walking stick. "We wait one hour."

The figure in fur and shades could be none other than Margarita Dettori. Othmar stumbled after her. "Signora," he called, intending to declare himself at her feet. She marched right past him. "Rita, Rita," the bald man soothed, and took her arm.

Stunned by her hauteur, Othmar turned back to Pompelli. "Maestro," he pleaded.

Pompelli rapped again. "My Rita," he said lovingly to Othmar. "Ha! She is Tosca. You will see." He pointed his stick. "Your Scarpia." The bald man bowed.

To complete the introductions, Pompelli waved his stick in an arc. "Luigi watches the bags."

Othmar blenched, and hoped it didn't show, when he saw the mountain that was their luggage. The bags were so foreign, so grotesque in their strangeness, and yet so familiar from the train stations in Europe that he wondered where he was. This was America. And yet telling him different was this mound. There were at least three very large bags, whole hides of leather, and as soft as bellows, with great straps, and there were a number of smaller cases, square and sharp, and bound in metal. His heart sank when he saw pointy shoes on the bald man. Even Pompelli looked more foreign than Othmar remembered and it put distance between them. There were sure to be difficulties with language. But Pompelli would translate. There were sure to be differences of opinion about staging but Othmar was willing to mediate. Who was he to tell them their business? If it had only been Pompelli and one other foreigner, preferably a wife whom Pompelli would control—Othmar thought he could deal with. But here he had an invasion of Italians.

There was another reason he felt the one against the many. It was their age. These were old people and Othmar looked away in shock. All the years he had known Pompelli he had known the maestro was older, a vintage wine—but not "getting on." He had known the Tosca was retired from her opera house, else why would they all be standing exiled and shivering in the Albany train station. He who had joked about the advanced age of Magda Olivero as the Boston Tosca was now face to face with the elderly fact of his. Her hair was thinning, her top lip deeply furrowed, her rouge too red, and she hid behind those ridiculous glasses. It wasn't youth she was concealing, he thought bitterly. Othmar had no experience of grandparents; as a grown man, he was acquainted with few people much older than himself. Maestros, he knew, still conducted well into their 80s. But did they attempt new music, or music new to them? Pompelli, he was sure, would not have chanced exposing his Tosca and their Scarpia if they could not produce. That was not to say they would not tire. What could he expect of them at rehearsal? He wanted to make his name on ensemble opera, not on star turns who "stand and deliver." Could they still learn? Would they have the stamina? He now saw the bald man in intimate conference with Pompelli, and saw Pompelli send him off toward the waiting room in the company of the younger man.

"*Momento, Gianni,*" smiled Pompelli. "They return in a minute for the journey."

And when they did, Othmar, slowly as one might lead royalty or the impaired, guided them to the waiting car. "Maestro," he murmured to Pompelli, "there will be a slight delay while we load your things."

"*Momento, Gianni!*" *And Pompelli limped off.*

On his return, Pompelli conducted with his walking stick the orderly placement of their many and strange bags. One was a small trunk with hinges running down the middle of the back. "Vigs," Othmar thought he heard the bald man say. There was a large valise that the Dettori had a decided opinion about. It must rest on the very top.

"My Tosca bring her costumes," said Pompelli. "You will like."

What with getting the bags and boxed stowed, Othmar had not considered the placement of passengers in the limousine. The back seat would hold three. There were pull-down seats for two, who would have to ride facing backwards. It was clear to Othmar he must endure one of these—and the young Italian the other. Pompelli thought otherwise. With a grip of the arm that brooked no argument, the maestro placed Othmar in the back seat on his left and his wife on his right.

"We talk," said Pompelli.

The Dettori sat well forward of her seat. To balance herself when the limo lumbered through a turn, she placed her hands on the knees of Bruno Cappetto facing her. Othmar wondered if this was some kind of Italian footsie. He was having his own problem keeping his legs free of the other men's. Pompelli, oblivious, droned on about the disappointments of New York. Dealing with Gilly's girl was no substitute for dealing with Gilly. Othmar could understand. No? The Dettori's fur cascaded to one side. Othmar could see it was no longer in its first youth. If Evey Titus had been there she would have understood the Dettori's forward crouch for what it was: a woman taking care not to "sit out" her fur.

The limousine crept on. In no season was this countryside much to look at. Scrub woods alternated with scrubby fields. Perhaps when it had been aggressively farmed it might have had a pleasing tidiness of purpose. The

Italians may be pardoned for wondering where they were being taken. New York had surprised by disappointing. They looked up and the buildings looked down. It was big and noisy and dirty; it was not big but noisy all the same, and dirty. People pushed. Where were the elegant clothes? It was not like the movies. The train trip was better, the river magnificent, but Rita Dettori would not hear that it was more beautiful than the Po. Bruno Cappetto reasoned with her: "In America, it is beautiful." And now this, what they called the country. A billboard was a welcome event. Cappetto read one aloud and the Dettori echoed: RASS WHA. "Race way," Othmar corrected her gently, glad to see she spoke some English. "Vroom! Vroom!" he added helpfully. She considered this and let out a long sigh.

Othmar had long since ceased listening to Pompelli. Nor could he mange to look fully at the two singers in the pull-down seats. The older man, the Scarpia, smiled a lot. A worse set of capped teeth he'd never seen! How could the man look at himself in the mirror? Another smile. Any minute, Othmar was sure, the Scarpia would try to engage him in conversation. Would ask him a favor he was not prepared to grant. The Cavaradossi, Luigi Something, wore jeans that Othmar guessed were right off the rack. And why not? Jeans were America, and Othmar imagined the tenor rushing out to buy them, a first souvenir of the New World. Jeans would give him something that wasn't music to talk to him about. There was something else about the tenor. Also familiar. His hair was very curly. Extremely curly. Othmar could not quite place the style. Then, with a sinking feeling, it came to him. "He's had a perm." Men's perms were still something of a novelty in New York. "What will Main Street say?"

"Goff!"

"Beg pardon!"

"Goff!" The Scarpia gestured at a driving range he could see out the back window. "Eeers Jawnie." Then: "High goff." He patted the Cavaradossi's knee. "Ee coddy."

"No respect," Pompelli was saying.

The Dettori reached across her husband to pound Othmar's knee.

The Scarpia demonstrated a chip shot for the Cavaradossi.

This too will end! Othmar was near prayer. He who knew everything there was to know about the stage characters of *la cantore* Floria Tosca and *il barone* Vitellio Scarpia and *il pittore* Mario Cavaradossi was suddenly struck by the awful thought he knew absolutely nothing about the performers who were to inhabit them. A Scarpia who played golf might be a nice touch in a modern-dress production. It would add the menace of normality to the torture scene. Othmar had read of a "Tosca" set in Mussolini's Rome with Black Shirts crowding into the church in the act-one finale. That Tosca, he recalled from the photos, was wonderfully svelte, a woman made for slinky satin cut on the bias. In the Attavanti chapel scene she made much of heaving a white fox stole around. The Pallas Tosca, his Tosca, had all the charm of a potato sack. What was with those glasses! Did she think she was Sophia Loren? She was muttering to her husband.

"She don't slip too well," Pompelli told Othmar. "She like to slip now. Beauty slip. Look her best."

Othmar lowered the black silk shades.

In the gloaming he smelled things he might not have noticed in the distractions of daylight. The Dettori's fur gave off a taint of camphor that was not unpleasant. The Cavaradossi reeked of, what?—perm? Pompelli was the onions. Othmar realized he had missed lunch. His own damn fault. No! Goddammit. The damn driver for taking back roads. Where the hell were they? He needed to pee. To shift his legs. Pompelli's stick was in the way. One foot prickled. Going to sleep. Someone broke wind. Othmar considered trumping. Gas 'em all! The Dettori snuffled: she had found the cheek of Morpheus in a silk shade. There was the scent of damp powder. Othmar shut his eyes.

Then there was nothing. Then, a banging. Why were people shouting? Othmar became aware of Evey Titus's high voice. "They're locked in, Austin." Obedient to a familiar family voice, the chauffeur touched his cap and freed his passengers.

In the slanting shaft of a lowering sun, the principals of "Tosca" and their esteemed director staggered from the limousine. On bandy legs, Othmar crept forward, only to be waved aside by Evey Titus. With her straight back and arrogant head, she stood waiting till the artistes regained composure. A step or two behind was the manager of the Hotel Olympus, for it was here that the funeral car had fetched up. Behind the manager, two strapping youths in hotel livery to take the luggage.

When, at last, the artistes spied someone to receive them, they formed into a group with the Dettori at the center.

Evey Titus advanced, hand on heart and bowing her head along the phalanx. She took the soprano's hand in hers.

"Come sta lei, signora." This was how-de-do at its most formal.

Continuing in Italian, she said: "Welcome to the city of Pallas, which is soon to be adorned by your voice and your art."

Those were the last complete sentences in Italian that Evey Titus would utter. It had come to her after watching the subtitles on foreign films that one did not have to say much to be understood. Gesture was all: the silent movies had known that. Conversation, indeed much communication, she observed, was by shards of speech. Evey Titus became the master of the pleased (or displeased) exclamation. The fragment of a compliment. The descriptive scrap. The sympathetic word. She knew these in several languages, her ragbag Italian mostly recently acquired for the events attendant on "Tosca." This cornucopia of hospitable welcome she now emptied on the artistes. By process of elimination, she gathered that the tall young man with the strange hair must be the tenor who would sing Cavaradossi. She gave him a sweet smile. Addressing them all, she pronounced the weather chilly. She indicated she recognized their fatigue. She promised them all the comforts of the hotel. Lashing them with kindness, she marched the artistes into the lobby. The bellhops plunged ahead to open the elevator doors. Registration could wait, she informed the hotel manager. (He had guessed as much.) Long moments later they arrived at an upper floor. The bellhops sped to open big double doors.

"The Sears Suite. It is named for a dear friend—the Governor." Evey Titus said to Pompelli.

It was the hotel's grandest accommodation, the only suite worth the name. Large windows gave on Pallas's Park Square. The steam heat was on full. Europeans, Evey told the manager, like it warmer than we do.

The suite would be theirs for the length of the engagement, Evey conveyed to Pompelli and his wife. The two others would have rooms nearby. All this she had negotiated with the hotel manager. She had some idea of the opera budget if the only principals they could hire came from one of the remoter Italian provinces. She was equally sure artistes of this level would find America expensive. She did not see why money should get in the way of their well-being. If they stayed at one of the new motels, where would they eat? Her mind made up, she arranged with the hotel to give them reduced rates for their month's stay. She had thought it out. In case the manager didn't get her point, she dangled the possibility, no, the probability (by the time she hung up) of the hotel as a site for several parties in connection with the opera. He saw it her way and agreed to discount their total bill as a due bill exchanged for a full-page advertisement in the "Tosca" program books. The artistes were not to know that the Hotel Olympus was seldom full: salesmen preferred to stay at motels on the bypass.

And there was more: Evey stocked the suite with a small bar. She piled a basket with fruit and a glass dish with bonbons. There were flowering plants. The towels were hotel issue but new. Much more to disguise the faded splendor of the Olympus she could not do. Pompelli gave the signora to understand that after their New York hotel this was *paradiso*.

Even so, the diva needed reassurance.

"Elegante, " said Evey Titus, gesturing the length of the Dettori's fur coat.

The Dettori felt a little better. Her fur had not looked its best in New York City. Here, it looked quite fine. She thought she might like this woman, so obviously a lady, who took the trouble to speak Italian. Of a sort.

Evey Titus was about to say her farewells when in burst Sarah Smythe breathless with apologies. Deadlines. And so on. Othmar, watching, cringed.

Sarah now took both the Dettori's hands in hers and to her pronounced slowly and phonetically the most famous lines from "Tosca."

"Vissi d'arte, vissi d'amore…"

Tosca's great aria. One of the treasured moments in all opera. That art must not be profaned. The Dettori shuddered and tried to pull away.

"…non feci mai male ad anima viva!"

Dazed, her hands crushed and her freedom in doubt, the Dettori could only wonder what this woman wanted. Was it a request for the Dettori to sing? Was the woman asking to sing for her? An audition? Was she deranged? Those blue eyes? Rather too blue! Or merely stupid.

The Dettori wrenched herself loose.

"Cretina!" she commented to the company at large.

"Precisamente!" said Aunt Evey.

10.

The Cavaradossi (Luigi Luongo) was not the boyfriend of the Scarpia (Bruno Cappetto), as Liz had wickedly suggested, but his nephew. He was also his last pupil, and unquestionably the best. The rasher critics were calling him "the next Pavarotti." It was the boy's own idea to learn pop ballads. He liked Sinatra, and Cappetto could see where that might lead. An attractive mix of classical and popular. Like Pavarotti with his Neapolitan songs, but for today's young people. And, thanks be to God, the boy was good to look at. Tall, dark haired and warmly dark-eyed, "Italian," as the world understood that to mean, not the other Italian, with the chilly grey eyes of the north, Bruno Cappetto thought with satisfaction. Dark eyes carry a face on stage. In his declining years, Luigi Luongo would be his pension plan. But first the boy must work on his instrument. He must perfect his art. Cappetto would work daily with him during the month they had together in America. He had considered asking for a piano in their sitting room at the hotel. But, after dinner at the palazzo of la Signora Titus, Cappetto formed another plan.

Evey Titus was not sentimental or even good-hearted. She would have long since dispatched poor stinky Maida to Dog Heaven but that meant another bill from Brielman and she had other bills ahead of that. Maida would go when she could. She was, however, a connoisseur of life's disappointments and, for her own reasons, dearly wished to hold death and decay at arm's length. It did not take her many minutes that afternoon at the Hotel Olympus to see that fame had bypassed the artistes from Trieste. She was also increasingly doubtful of Austin Othmar's capacities.

Word from the musical world confirmed he was all he said he was. Still, she wondered. Sam Adler had asked around Boston for her. Othmar had indeed worked on two operas for Sarah Caldwell and had sung in the opera chorus. Newspaper accounts of "John Austin Othmar Presents Scenes from Great Operas" attested to success with their audiences. When other inquiries also panned out, the Grand Opera Touring Company—as Othmar had named his newest venture—was invited to Pallas and Evey Titus had every confidence the curtain would go up on a respectable production of "Tosca."

Of Othmar the man she was less sure. She thought it odd he did not have an assistant. In the right circumstances, two can do the work of three. The opera budget, moreover, would seem to allow for an extra hand. She worried that Othmar could not leave well enough alone. In that respect, he was like poor dear Sarah. She over-reported. His obsession with detail was deadening. She'd taken him around Pallas to meet merchants who could be useful in promoting "Tosca." Sammy Vincent and Alan Blau had been perfect dears to put up with his finicky questions about how things would work out. They knew their business and he ought to know that and to trust them.

And he seemed what? Angry in a way she couldn't quite fathom. And impersonal. She wondered if he were a homo. The few she knew fawned all over her, calling her "Mrs. T" in their booming voices and inventing instant little traditions. Tiresome after an hour. She judged Othmar to be in his late thirties. (He was forty-one.) She would like to be able to break through to him. Loosen him up, make him relax. He needed a local pal. She doubted it would be Sarah, and that was probably a good thing. It didn't have to be her, and, really, it shouldn't be. She could do more for him by pulling strings. She had already had a word with the VW people—they would donate a van. She had an idea about restaurants. But, she supposed, she couldn't teach an old dog new tricks. It hadn't worked with Sarah. And now there was this new mess.

What Evey Titus and very few others knew was how close her niece was to the edge. In *"Vissi d'arte,"* Tosca may claim she "never hurt a living soul," but Sarah was sweating out the threat of a libel suit for misquotation.

A patron of the arts, to give a name to Evey Titus"s position in Pallas society, is reputed to have deep pockets, if not unlimited funds, but she had far less money than Pallas thought she had. Her mother had known how to make one dime do the work of two, and Evey was her mother's daughter. Not for nothing was she also a Carruthers. Carrutherses tended to put a bright face on adversity. Evey decided to give a party. She consulted her checkbook. She believed in paying local merchants first. She ignored the dunning phone calls of American Express till it suited.

She saw her way clear. And laughing at the connection to "Tosca," she trilled "Mario...Mario!" and picked up the phone to call Mario, chef at the Golf and Tennis Club. He knew all about the opera. The artistes, she told him, were far away from home and needed something to cheer them up. When could he come cook for her—and she would issue the invitations accordingly?

"For you, Mrs. Titus, this Saturday." He was always glad of an excuse not to cook dinner on a night when the club lived up to its nickname of G & T—for gin and tonic.

He heard her smile. "Oh, goody! Oysters with drinks."

"With a mignonette," said Mario, knowing her dislike of catsupy sauces. "And clams casino?" She succumbed to temptation.

"And your lamb." She loved Mario's lamb, loved that he served it pink, loved knowing he bought it from a Boston poet who fattened spring lambs on salt hay and finished them on windfall pears. They were slaughtered at Blood's, a name that never failed to amuse her. But do Italians like lamb? They agreed that, to start, there would be a clear soup with mushrooms. Instead of the lamb, he might do his rabbit.

"Even better," she said. "With polenta. You choose the wines. Surprise us for dessert."

Next, she found people to clean. Her weekly woman she put onto polishing the silver. She decided against a tablecloth. Too formal. People would serve themselves at the sideboard, and Mario would hover, as he liked doing, to see to the wine and urge another helping. He wore what he cooked in, a white chef's apron and a red sleeveless sweater over a white shirt rolled to the elbows.

The guest list wrote itself. Besides Mario, she must ask someone else who spoke Italian and that could only be Father Luca Fioravanti, pastor of Saint Francis of Assisi, Pallas's "Italian" church. For the Bluestockings, a ladies club with intellectual aspirations, Father Luca had read parts of "The Inferno" while a member showed slides of the Gustave Doré illustrations. The dinner would also be a chance for Evey to meet the new professor of music history at the community college. His wife was said to be charming. With Sarah and Othmar and the academics and the priest and the four artistes they would be ten. Eleven if Mario could be persuaded to sit down.

The Italian artistes had settled into Pallas each in their own way. Of the four Americans, scheduled to arrive by late afternoon of the Titus dinner party, only Johnson Jones seemed to pose a problem, and a minor one at that. He was the Angelotti, the liberal hunted by Scarpia. For the right singer, the role is a theatrical plum, and hardly taxing as the character is on stage only for the first act, but Gilly had found it hard to cast. "The kids hate to be away from Big City action," Gilly explained. Then Jonce Jones became available.

"You'll love him," Gilly had promised. "Probably the best of the four. Has a big, bright nimble voice and he should have a big career as a *basso buffo*. There is just one thing…"

Othmar waited to hear what it was. Can't act. Shoots up.

"I've got him two auditions he absolutely must do and you'll have to rehearse around him."

"I can live with that."

And because it seemed so minor a thing, Othmar put it out of his mind and rejoiced in the phenomenal luck of having Victor Pompelli as his maestro.

Pompelli started in immediately with orchestra rehearsals. Sarah Smythe in her enthusiasm to make "Tosca" a community event had rather overestimated the ability of the Chatham Philharmonic to tackle the complexities of Puccini. They had rehearsed for three months with their own conductor and they promised to put aside every night until the final curtain of the fourth "Tosca." They were determined to do themselves proud.

"Such hard work already," Pompelli beamed at the thirty players assembled before him. "You work hard with me and we make a recording." The orchestra liked hearing that. The strings tapped their bows on their music stands and the winds stamped their feet. The whistle came from a kid scarcely bigger than his drums.

All during the first rehearsal Pompelli was full of compliments. "We all speak the language of music." He had nice things to say about the horns. He praised the strings. It was not so much what Pompelli said, Othmar decided, as how he appeared to the orchestra. Although he sat to rehearse, he was obviously a maestro. But also wonderfully Italian, lyric and warm. There was yearning in his Italian inflexions. He had a beguiling way of slipping in the translation. "Puccini is not easy. He demand we play with great expression, *con grande espressione.* But he is so precise what he wants. The orchestra we sing, *col canto*, with the singing; we act, *incalzando sempre*, always pressing, persuing Angelotti, 'ounding him. We are the bad guys. It is tone poem."

Moments after the first rehearsal, Pompelli and the ChatPhil conductor, Mac Gilson, sat down with Othmar in Othmar's office and together they drew up of list of the additional players Pompelli would need. The orchestra pit, Gilson thought, would seat forty. It was Othmar's first exposure to Gilson. The ruddy face and greying crewcut said veteran band leader, and yes, Gilson was a trumpet player (but a student of Roger Voisin's) who had parlayed the job that brought him to Pallas—head of music at the high school—into conducting local orchestras. He harbored no illusions about the quality of the ChatPhil (for years he had hired professionals to sit in as ringers) and as he also conducted a chamber orchestra in Albany he was well placed to suggest names. Othmar listened patiently: His time with Pompelli would come.

"They not too bad," Pompelli said of his new orchestra.

Gilson shrugged. "They can't count. Anything not in four is a challenge. And Puccini! He's diabolical! The whole thing is a waltz. And the constant *rubato!* Difficult even for me."

Pompelli smiled.

Conductor and maestro drew up rehearsal schedules. Gilson volunteered to do the sectionals with the locals. Pompelli's fame as a teacher had preceded him. "An honor to work with you, maestro."

Pompelli bowed graciously.

This first week the other artistes clung together. Pallas puzzled them it looked so vacant, so flat. Where were the markets? The little streets? Where were the people? They missed the Adriatic and the smells the wind brought from the water. They missed the damp. Especially they missed their own coffee, thundery and strong, coffee that layered the tongue like a rough red wine.

"Cornflakes?" The waiter set a bowl in front of Rita Dettori.

Bruno Cappetto laughed at the face she pulled. "When in Roma…"

It was an adventure, he told them. Over in a month…and they'd spent worse weeks on tour. His was a laugher's face, creased at eyes and mouth, and his eyes were gentle. He spoke some English, the accident of war when the British occupied Trieste, and a little French and German, all learned in preparation for the international career that never came. The America he knew came from the movies. So, cornflakes with breakfast. In Pallas, it didn't work that way: Cornflakes was breakfast. As pasta was dinner, when they ventured out to the three "Italian" restaurants. But there were compensations, such as American cocktails, and Cappetto vowed to drink his way through the cocktail list. He began with a Boxcar. The next night he had a Ward Eight. The closest he came to seeing golf was Johnny Carson's swing on the TV.

On their third day arrived Evey Titus's hand-written invitation for dinner that Saturday. Lest her wardrobe not be up to the occasion, the Dettori thought she might have a look at the shops, whose brightly lit windows she scrutinized when they dined out. She returned to the hotel a happy woman. There was nothing to buy.

Came Saturday evening and Othmar fetched the artistes at the hotel in a VW van emblazoned "Courtesy car for Grand Opera's "Tosca." This time he, rather than Evey Titus, "had a word with" the dealership, or so he was led to believe. He had to admit he could not have promoted the production without her, and advance sales were beginning to show her powers of persuasion. She had walked him along Main Street with an authority that poor Sarah lacked. At Sammy Vincent's Music, the boss came out from the back room to shoot the breeze—and to agree to devote a window to the recordings of "Tosca."

"Do you know, Sammy, I bought my very first LP here. Serkin and Ormandy playing the 'Emperor' and it was on sale."

"For $4.19." They both laughed. An old story.

At England's, they took the elevator to the fourth floor where the department store offices were. Evey marched right in on Alan Blau. And wafted out, thirty minutes later, with the assurance that "darling Alan" would set up a ticket bureau at which England's charge customers could put their "Tosca" tickets on their bill. He'd done this for the music festival she'd organized.

"Now, Alan," said Evey, "I want you to take two boxes. I will have one for all four performances. We didn't tell you about the fourth? The 'Tosca' we are bringing back 'by popular demand.' May I put you down for a box for opening night? A box seats, what is it? Austin, six? Though between you, me and the lampost, you don't see very well in the back row. The second box is for Thursday night, and Thursday, frankly, is our hard-sell night. Might you not just give that box to people in the store? As a reward. Well, I don't have to tell you your business. I'm thinking, for example, of Miss Jaeger on the Main Floor. Always such a help when I come in the store, and such an ornament, so handsome." Alan Blau, short, balding and dapper, and "married to an England, you know," knew a salesman when he saw one. He loved music and he loved Evey Titus.

And so Austin Othmar the impresario allowed himself to be paraded around Pallas. Let "The Titus" think she was running the show! He thought of it as laying the ground work for future seasons. Pallas could be his base. Next year, he would do a comic opera. If all went well, he would expand and rename the company. He was thinking of calling it "Opera Prima." It was catchy, yet dignified. It said opera, that is, the work, came first—not stars, and not the kind of staging that is more about the director than the music. Ensemble opera. He would get young singers on their way up. But not neglect worthy old timers, who still had much to offer. (And would be grateful.) Opera Prima avoided the tag, the curse, of "regional" opera. The way "Metropolitan" promised the greater world of opera. "I heard it at the Met."

"I heard the Prima do it (and it was better)!" He would take the Prima on the road. A small company like The Prima would go places the Met couldn't, or wouldn't.

"Oh, to have been a fly on the wall when Othmar spoke at Rotary," Gilly to Liz.

"Into every life some rain must fall! How does he sound? Still sappy happy?

"OK." But Gilly wasn't sure.

"The first time I saw 'Tosca' I was sixteen, and it was Paris," Evey Titus was saying. Mario was about to produce salad and cheeses. The wine smiled. Bruno Cappetto had began the evening with one of la Signora Titus's whiskey sours. *"Encora?"* she invited. *"Prego, Signora!"*

"I was scandalized." Evey reached for one of her own candelabras. "I simply couldn't get over Tosca doing what she did with the crucifix and the candles. It seemed so, how shall I say? so sacriligious?" There was a murmur of Italian around the table as the priest and Pompelli interpreted for the others. They all spoke some English but this was a party and they looked to their hostess to set the pace.

It hadn't occurred to Luca Fioravanti that Tosca was doing anything more than laying out her victim in a most theatrical way. But sacriligious? The priest was amused. He supposed it was sacriligious—to a Protestant. "I am always touched, dear lady, when you fight our battles for us."

That compliment deserved one in return.

"Austin! Austin!" Evey broke in on Othmar's reverie. He had absented himself, knowing something the others did not. Yet.

"Look at Father Luca's noble profile. Why don't you offer him the role of the Cardinal?" To the priest: "Please say yes! The Cardinal's hat. Nothing to sing. You would lend us authority."

"Dear lady, at the risk to my mortal soul of committing the sin of simony!"

The mention of Paris had ignited reaction among the Italians.

"The 'Tosca' at Paris was sung in French' no?" Cappetto snorted. "Is not *possibile* to sing Puccini in French!"

"Possibile? Of course, *possibile!"* said Pompelli. "But it is no longer *lirico."*

"Capisco!" said Evey. "I've always thought speaking French ages women terribly. Do you know I once saw Princess Grace talking in French and it simply added years."

When this was explained to the Dettori she smiled broadly. She had been right about la Signora Titus. *Molto simpatica!* And rich! Look at her table. A different pattern of plate for every course. She must have dozens to choose from. Othmar saw only that the wine glasses didn't match. Six of one and five of another, which meant she didn't have a dozen of either. Evey Titus wasn't as grand as she'd like you to think. And everybody sucking up to her! The evening was getting to him. And there was this other problem—these other problems.

Othmar could hear Cappetto talking golf with Mario but not what they were saying. The professor's wife, pretty and animated, was talking to the Cavaradossi about Frank Sinatra. Sarah Smythe, sensing that Othmar was being left out of the general conversation, took the occasion of a lull to ask:

"What does your father, the general, have to say about Vietnam?" Vietnam was always on the evening news.

"He's dead."

"Miss Mouth."

Othmar's face tightened. "What did you say?"

"My big mouth," said Sarah brightly. But inside she felt awful. She could not get anything right these days. Wandering into a feud between two brothers was bad luck. That she attributed the quotes of one to the other was carelessness. The lawyers were busy on it. The Carruthers instinct to put a cheerful face came to her rescue.

"Wasn't Mario's rabbit wonderful!" she exclaimed.

Evey Titus watched to see who at the table had thought it was chicken.

Mario brought in the dolce: strawberries with a sabayon he had whisked together moments before and he trailed fumes of marsala as he dished it up.

There were toasts.

"Signora! Grazie sentitamente per questa serata speciale ed indimenticabile." Pompelli spoke on behalf of the artistes, Italian culture, world friendship.

Evey Titus bowed her head modestly but her smile was seraphic: she couldn't sing a note but she could make an atmosphere.

"E complimenti vivissimi al signor capocuoco per la preparazione del coniglio con rosmarino." Thus Cappetto's compliments to chef Mario on his rabbit with rosemary. Cappetto now had hopes of "winter golf" at Mario's club if the winter stayed open.

The music professor raised his glass to Evey Titus: "May she have music wherever she goes."

"My nephew will sing," Cappetto announced.

The party moved into what Evey was now calling the music room.

Abandon hope, Othmar said to himself. He was truly in the camp of the enemy. This goddam house. Still dirty! Rabbit! He wanted to barf—and rub their superior faces in it. And Sarah. Sarah was everywhere. "Miss Mouth" was no accident. Sarah knew something she shouldn't, couldn't possibly, unless...It had to be one of the American singers she got it from. They had only just arrived but Sarah was obviously already on to them for a "story." The Americans had brought their own surprise, which he would have to deal with tomorrow. He began to sweat thinking Sarah knew about "Miss Mouth." It was with enormous difficulty that Othmar turned his attention to Luigi Luongo's recital.

Houses find their destiny and the lively acoustic of the Titus drawing room was to favor music. Velvet portières and animal skins could not dampen the sound-enhancement of mirrors and mosaics, parquet and veneers. The artistes, appalled by the newness of New York, felt right at home. It was obvious to them that by the way she lived *la signora* Titus was a patron of the arts. Patrons were as much a part of their musical life as opera house *intendanti* and agents, and when they could afford it, publicists. As though into a second skin Luigi Luongo slid into the piano well and sang for his supper.

This he did also for his own pleasure. He liked singing. He liked the effect of his voice on his listeners. Sometimes he saw tears. He'd cried at concerts, over old records—and Tio Bruno cried too. For a tenor, he was tall, and well built. For that, he thanked God. The suit he wore tonight, expensive but worth every penny. It would pay off in the end to look a success from the start. Tio Bruno's words. So the Pallas Cavaradossi would be his first on stage— though Tio Bruno was for keeping that intelligence from Othmar. Uncle and nephew had not discussed strategy, Cappetto simply assuring he would teach him the role and how it was to be played. The little recital tonight was for another audience. Cappetto took his place at the piano. Maestro Pompelli sat next to him to turn pages.

As a singer Luigi Luongo was doubly blessed. He was musical and he had also the gift of simplicity. His "Ave Maria" could melt the heart but it was also instantly recognizable as Schubert's, occupying a land beyond tears. In the Neapolitan songs he was sunny and he had a way of flirting that let everyone in on the joke. Cappetto had worked long and hard with his nephew on *legato*, on *mezza di voce*, and much else in the treasury of Italian lyric singing. Cappetto knew also when to stand back and let the boy's natural instincts flower. The older man was a good editor as well. There were many things in the Italian stage tradition that would not play true in a world that put a premium on realism. What was stylized but understood as true-to-life, when Rita Dettori was a coming soprano forty years ago, would be laughed off the stage in today's opera houses. Her Tosca and his nephew's Cavaradossi were indeed a generation apart.

He was now singing Cavaradossi's farewell to life, *"È lucevan le stelle."*

"And the stars shone…" Sarah Smythe was awash in tears.

The Dettori watched as much as she listened. She had not heard Luigi in almost a year. This was talent! She might wish it was not "Tosca" they were to sing, for she longed to add her voice to this—and this Puccini is virtually without duets. As a stage lover, he was everything she could want. The *pittore romantico*. And an aristocrat. True, he was but a boy. He was youth. She would still play youth—her Mimì had held up well. Tosca, happily, is about temperament. Artistic, emotional. A woman of experience. Age did not matter, only art.

Like the musicians they were, Cappetto and Pompelli communicated by breathing a silent singing. Pianist, page turner and tenor were one. Every once in a while, Luigi caught one of them humming. Things were going well. He was happy.

Othmar finally succumbed to the tenor. The Schubert wasn't a fair test. "Not a dry seat in the house," he could hear Gilly say. And he'd never cared for Neapolitan songs. He was fascinated, and not a little envious, at the way Luongo drew listeners to him. "He is very quiet, he does not come after you," Othmar thought. "He makes you come to him."

Evey Titus passed a hankie to her niece. How well everything was going! She liked this young man. He had been charming at dinner, eager to please, boyish, laughing at his English, not afraid to correct her Italian. Obviously gifted. He needed a different tailor, she thought. His suit was shiny in the Italian way. But who was she to criticize? A very "Italian" Italian might just amuse her friends in New York. She would have a word.

When Evey Titus rose to thank dear Luigi for his art, she was inspired also "to propitiate Athene," as she called it. Raising both arms, but speaking slowly (enough) for the running translation she knew would follow from Father Luca, she declaimed:

"Benisons to our patron goddess and her theater. May the Palladium once again be a temple to art and music and opera."

There was a ruffle of applause, in which Othmar half joined. He had no objection to Athene. But Evey Titus's assumption it was the Titus temple profaned the whole endeavor. "Me—Sampson," he said with a wicked laugh, and, feeling instantly better, he made ready to fetch the "Tosca" van.

Evey Titus was further inspired. She would like to extend an invitation, she said. Would the artistes consider using her music room for their private rehearsals? She would be greatly honored. Cappetto breathed a sigh of relief at not having to beg. Here, in this beautiful room, he could continue working with his nephew. Here, in privacy, he could coach him far from the presence of Othmar. "That's settled," said their patron.

Othmar, organizing the artistes for their departure, had not paid much attention. When rehearsals started in the coming week he knew he had first call on their time. With patient impatience he herded them toward the van.

"Uno momento, Gianni," said Pompelli. "For Bruno." Off stage, the mighty Titus toilet roared, and Cappetto, patting himself, strolled forward.

"Chop-chop," said Sarah winking at Othmar. He caught his breath— There was no question about it, she knew! He breathed out. She would have to go! But first he must put another fire out. He drove the artistes to the Olympus and heard their fulsome thanks. He drove to the theater and let himself in. He needed most urgently to talk with Gilly.

110

11.

"But you never told me he was black! Don't you think you might have? Don't you think I have enough problems in this goddam place." Othmar's voice was shrill with self-pity. "You sprung it on me!"

Gilly, from the safety of New York, let Othmar blow. Yes, yes, he didn't tell him. Yes, the basso he had engaged to sing Sciarrone was black—he didn't think it was all that important. "But wait till you hear him! I think you'll see why." And going on the offensive, he said: "Johnny, you're going to thank me for Alex Avery."

That got Gilly past the embarrassing truth of why the other Sciarrone, upon further consideration, had returned his contract unsigned. "Conflict of dates," Gilly told Othmar. The real reason was that Othmar, when staging "Suor Angelica," had almost destroyed the career of the basso's girl friend (now wife).

"Black is beautiful," said Liz who was listening on the other phone. "Actually, he's not black-black, more tan, and with make-up…"

Othmar moaned.

"No, you gotta hear him," Gilly declared. "A real dark voice. He will go far. The Grand Inquisitor. Pizarro possibly. Already does The Commendatore. He's covering a Boris. Not exactly an unknown. Just happened to be free and knows the others. They come as a package. They have it down cold. Like you in the old days."

Goddam Gilly to remind him of the Wupperthal "Bohème."

"Just out of idle." This was Liz asking out of idle curiosity. "Where's he living."

Pallas had few black families. He, along with the Angelotti, the Spoletta and the Sacristan, were boarding with a Baptist minister who was white.

"Won't Sarah do the honors? Interview him for her rag?"

"Oh, God!" said Othmar.

And Sarah did, after worrying one whole night abut how to describe him. "Colored" was out, she knew. "Negro" was polite. "Black" she knew offended the older Negroes in Pallas (who had said as much to her editor). Nor had she been prepared for his not being the normal black color. Nor for his Afro, which was shaggy to a degree.

"My nigger curls alarm?"

Alexander Avery, known as Alex, and Sarah became instant friends.

A white mother explained much. And from his accent, or rather his accents, Sarah inferred the same sort of schools her family had gone to. Yes, indeedy, Andover and then Yale. He had never met a Baptist before, let alone a Baptist preacher man. Sarah didn't think he ought to say that, and she certainly didn't put it in her story. She was grateful to him for providing a quote that said he was black. She had wondered how she was going to say he was black in print. It seemed awkward to mention color if you were supposed to ignore race.

"I was a fucking gent," Alex Avery told the others at breakfast. "I handed it to her on a plate. I said, and I quote from this morning's Clerical Vice: 'I'm very grateful to Johnny Othmar to take a chance on me. As a young black singer I have all kinds of things blocking my career in opera. They don't want me kissing the girl. I can be Mister Funny Pants. I can be the villain. But not the romantic hero. The Sciarrone is pretty close to slime—he's Scarpia's tame policeman. He does have one big moment but you'll have to buy a ticket to see.' End of quote."

Othmar called the first rehearsal for Monday morning. He arrived well before ten and stood in the lobby to welcome them to his theater. The artistes walked over from the Olympus, a tight band of strolling players. Othmar watched their stately progress. The Dettori parading on the arm of the bald man, the Scarpia. Pompelli, limp, limp, impaling the sidewalk with his cane, and lugging a briefcase. It held scores and batons, as Othmar correctly guessed. The Cavaradossi was the pack animal: he was slung with all sorts of bags and under each arm was an old plaid steamer rug. A man's pocketbook bobbed. The Scarpia had charge of an old brown leather case about which he took great care. It would prove to contain two enormous thermos bottles of hot tea. The Tosca carried only her handbag. She was wearing stylish high-heeled red leather boots. Othmar noticed they were weather-stained at the toes.

"*Buon giorno*, Johnny!"

Othmar wished for an audience to hear this intimacy.

He led the artistes down through the auditorium to the stage. He had turned on all the house lights. The old Palladium glowed silvery gilt and pink. It was feminine, delicate, well-mannered, architect Joseph McArthur Vance's assurance to the good people of Pallas that their womenfolk could be seen in a theater which caused no blemish to their reputations. There was just enough rococo for men to dream of assignations with actresses. The artistes gave Othmar's worldly kingdom nary a glance.

Up on stage the Tosca fussed around the Cavaradossi making the young tenor drape the steamer rugs "just so" over and along the folding chairs. Another chair became a table for the tea things. Still other chairs were for vocal scores. "She's moving in, she's setting up house," Othmar marveled. "On my turf." The day was not starting well.

But Pompelli's reaction to the rehearsal pianist was all Othmar could have hoped. A large chunk of his budget had gone for musical prep, and he and Gilly combed New York for a repetiteur who might know Pompelli or work in classic opera house style. Their find was a Viennese named Franz Ludwig. He was short and plump, and dour. Whoever thought the Viennese were dumplings had seen too many movies with S.Z. (Cuddles) Sakall. "Who was actually Hungarian," said Liz.

Ludwig now kissed the Dettori's hand and pronounced himself honored to be working with her. It transpired he knew Trieste. In the years before the war, he had heard the very young Dettori. But not as Tosca, of course. Not at Teatro Verdi.

"Teatro All'Altro," said Pompelli and looked full at Othmar. "A little joke in Trieste," he said. The Other Theater. "Macy don't tell Gimbel." He translated for the Cavaradossi.

Cappetto, having overseen the housekeeping, pressed forward to present his nephew to the pianist. Their fast and furious Italian excluded Othmar. He would not learn until the break for lunch that Cappetto had reserved the afternoons to work with his nephew in Evey Titus's music room.

In trouped the Americans. In their wake was Sarah Smythe, notebook in hand. Her first impression was, the men all had loud voices. She wrote down "loud." They looked fairly ordinary. In fact, they looked a little "common." She decided not to get into that. Most of Pallas was "common." It was what you made of yourself. She reconsidered "loud" and wrote "carrying" and thought better of that and wrote "projecting."

Othmar made the introductions. "Ed Nelson is our Sagrestano." He was very tall. Sarah, as an aid to memory, wrote down "tall." She would get the names later. "Johnson Jones, known as Jonce, who will sing Angelotti." He had thick dark hair he tied in the back. Sarah wrote down "pig" for pigtail. "Rollo Shaw, who will sing Spoletta." Sarah wrote down "blue" for his eyes. "And last but not least, Alexander Avery, who will sing Sciarrone." There was deep silence.

Sarah thought it was brave of Othmar to have a black singer. She didn't know if she would have taken the chance. She did not like to think she was prejudiced but had she ever gone out of her way in college, say, to strike up an acquaintance with the two colored girls in her class? (One was Filipino, she now remembered.) It made her nervous even to talk about differences of race and religion and "position" with people just like her, white and Episcopalian, and, well, she didn't like to say upper. If she had to say one of those qualifying words, she could feel herself pause and gird for the jump. "They're...Methodist." "He works in...the mill." People were... "Jewish," though not the Jew sisters who were Chinese,Chow misheard at Immigration, the only Chinese in Pallas, whose family ran the China Clipper. Alex Avery made it easy for her to write her story by coming right out and saying he was black. She wondered if he would like to come by for a drink. She was frankly dying to know what he knew about those twins in his class and why they were expelled. She had known their sister but not well enough to ask. So, for Alex Avery, she wrote down "Alex" with a big question mark just so she wouldn't forget to ask the spelling of his character's name. The way the rehearsal was starting was not at all what she expected. The dead silence. Was there going to be a signal, like the off-stage thumps of old she had heard about, for the curtain to go up, so to speak, for things to begin?

Was it the black man that so offended, for Othmar heard the silence as rebuke, as disapproval? Or was it the way the Americans dressed, as though chinos and sweatshirts suggested behavior that did not comport with the seriousness of art implicit in Pompelli's suit and the Dettori's string of pearls. This silence, this stand-off as Othmar understood it, was at last broken by the pianist playing arpeggiated scales up and down the piano. On cue, the singers began to hum, and, finding their notes, to vocalize. Sarah wiggled with anticipation. She had already decided she would free-associate, write down whatever came to mind, and see if that made a "mood piece," as she called her essays. "Confusing" was the first word. And "buzz" and, once again, "loud." And "spit."

After some time, Pompelli judged the warm-up complete, and, at a nod, the pianist trumped out grand chords and fell silent. These first rehearsals would be a run-though, Othmar reminded all. Singers, if they chose, could move around, but the sessions this first morning and afternoon were for Pompelli to get an idea of what his cast sounded like, Othmar told them. He and the Americans arranged a semi-circle of folding chairs half way back on the stage. They helped Ludwig wheel the rehearsal spinet so he faced the singers. Othmar lowered a music stand so Pompelli could conduct seated. Then he took himself off to the auditorium. These rehearsals were the maestro's.

Othmar sat on the center aisle. He scrunched himself back in his seat and fastened his gaze on the proscenium arch. He waited for Puccini to tell him what to do.

That, of course, was naïve and Othmar knew as much. "First the words, then the music," Or vice versa. Salieri, who was supposed to have murdered Mozart, got a whole opera out of the question. On stage, where there are words, there is sure to be a director lurking.

Johnson Jones, the Angelotti, began.

"Ah! Finalmente! Nel terror mio stolto…" Thus, Angelotti, liberal aristocrat, on the run from Scarpia. Not just on the run but having just escaped from the fastness of the Castel Sant'Angelo to, one must imagine, the acute embarrassment of Baron Scarpia, *capo di polizia,* chief of police (to give his title) and proto-fascist (if you're updating), the man "before whom all Rome trembles."

"…vedea ceffi di birro in ogni volto."

Jonce Jones was tending to rush, to make rushing stand for terror. Pompelli stopped him, and smiling reassuringly, made him begin again. "It will be more terrible when you let terror take its time."

"…vedea ceffi di birro in ogni volto."

"In my blind terror I saw an informer's snout on every face," as one rather antique English translation has it.

Othmar smiled at "snout." Worse was to come in the same translation when the Sacristan likens Cavaradossi's filthy paint brushes to a "shabby priest's collar." There was talk of subtitles for opera, as there were subtitles for foreign films, but so far it was only talk, and Othmar was glad. Endless repetitions of opera's often empty phrases—who wanted that? And who could be certain that people wouldn't fasten on them and fail to listen or watch? Nor was he totally convinced that opera should always be sung in the language of the country in which it was being performed. He had heard a terrible story of "Così fan tutte" sung in German for Austrians which had the unforeseen result of the cast mugging their way through Mozart's bittersweet tale till it became crudest farce and, with the audience egging them on, mugging became the performance of "tradition."

"Tosca" was melodrama. Puccini used the word on the title page. With his first step on stage the Angelotti must alert the audience to a society ruled by fear. Pompelli was right: the politics don't matter. ("Who is for Napoleon and who is for Kingdom of Rome? The audience read the program book for that.") Costume and makeup will explain much. Angelotti must seem to sweat. If Jonce Jones didn't powder his makeup, would that do? If he applied lines of Vaseline with a CueTip? He should look worked over, bruised. There must be desperation in every move. Also fatigue. In his mind, Othmar saw the figure of Angelotti splayed out along the chapel walls. His panic as his fingers scramble around the pillar for the key that his sister, the Attavanti, has left for his escape though the crypt. His whole body trembling as he tries to make the key turn. His disappearance into the crypt. Jonce Jones should play this as broadly as possible. Othmar wondered if Jonce would agree to introduce a suggestion of exhaustion and hoarseness into his voice.

Othmar now heard Puccini wipe the slate clean. Hurdy-gurdy time. Sweetness and light. One of Puccini's charming time changes from the busyness of narrative to coloration for character. No dialogue, no figure on stage, just the orchestra in an intermezzo, a rolling 6/8 marked *allegretto grazioso.*

Here comes trouble, Othmar groaned as the Sacristan scuttled forward. Ed Nelson's was a nimble voice. This role could be his for life. Othmar could see that Pompelli was merely marking.

Every director has to suffer the Sacristan. The comic priest. Audiences eat him up. Othmar doubted the great majority of the Pallas audience could tell the Sacristan's place in the church hierarchy. Some sort of lay brother that did the parish's scut work. The "Tosca" Sacristans whom Othmar could recall were well-padded and waddled. Their fixation on the fat hen in the painter's dinner basket was all you needed to know both for character and the plot. Swept forward in more 6/8, "Tosca" Sacristans dipped and swelled. Ed Nelson, however, was tall and very thin. He was a crow, a crane, a—the vision came to Othmar—a Uriah Heep, Mister Meachy himself. This would play wonderfully against the flowing sweetness that accompanies his first stage business. The body tics that Puccini specifies in the score with a little circle pierced by a dot would play out along his string bean of a figure. He must seem to be genuinely pious when he falls to his knees for the Angelus. But loving his piety. Othmar had giggled at the Italianate sob that the Sacristan in the Callas recording gave to the plainsong chant. The Sacristan at prayer should be a tiny bit stagey, as though he had a sense of being watched, of being spied on. Everyone is nervous in Scarpia's police state. The Sacristan spies for Scarpia even as he is spied on. This will be a "Tosca," Othmar thought to himself, with every action a turn of the screw. It must be unrelenting, inexorable, implacable. My way, or not at all. Tito Gobbi saw the opera as Scarpia's. Othmar would be his instrument of torture. "For that, I'm you boy, your everlovin' blue-eyed boy."

The Cavaradossi simply sang. Once again, he made Othmar come to him. "Damn him." Nor did the young tenor move around but simply stood by his chair. On this morning Othmar would look in vain for the traits of movement he could make into character. A big hunk of nothing, so far as he was concerned. Mister Curly Locks. That left the Sacristan without a Cavaradossi to play to. Jonce Jones skidded to a halt, stood stock still.

For the tenor had begun.

"Recondita armonica di bellizze diverse!" Sweet and quiet, another 6/8 meditation. As though it were an idea new to the world, Cavaradossi sang of paradox, of the mysterious harmonies of contrasting beauties.

The Scarpia, piano-vocal at rest on his knees, gazed out into the auditorium. Yes, yes. It was all there in his nephew's voice. The *legato* that so few young singers had these days. *Legato*, the voice gliding on the breath as a swan on water. The words are there but sung through and the rhythm of music and words obeyed, for *legato* is also about propulsion. You see the swan, and you see the swan's reflection and the wake that disturbs the reflection. They are both the swan but the reflection is echo, science, mechanical, nothing the swan creates, only obedient to it. The *legato* of the singer is not the *legato* of the orchestra. You are not a clarinet, he told his students, not just a column of air. Not a violin vibrating the length of the bowing arm. Such are mechanical. And the piano is worst of all. We singers are our instrument. Our gift to music is we are human.

When the tenor finished, there was a rustle of applause, and the approving tap of Pompelli's stick. Although his nephew seemed slightly embarrassed by the bravos, Cappetto frowned. The boy was young, impressionable, eager to please. He must be armored against the cheapening of his art. "I have so little time."

Then the first of the waltzes. These will grow corrupt and hellish.

Pompelli nodded as the Sacristan ever so slightly embellished *"tanto d'inferno"* as though hinting at worse to come. The Americans were intelligent. Prepared. Musical. Not without possibilities. It will come better when Rita has worked on their Italian.

Then: "Mario!"

Tosca offstage.

"Mario!"

The oldest trick in the book! and Othmar giggled. How many Broadway plays had he seen with the leading lady caroling dialogue from the wings and—wait for it, wait for it—stepping through French doors into the expected adulation. And hadn't he laughed and clapped, too, glad to contribute to her fame.

"Mario!"

Oh! the cunning of Puccini. The clockwork. On stage, Angelotti to get rid of.

"Grazie!" from the exhausted Angelotti.

"Presto!" from Cavaradossi as Angelotti slips into the Attavanti crypt.

Mario Cavaradossi to Floria Tosca: *"Son qui,"* I am here. And Puccini calming us, playing with us—the pause between lightning and thunderbolt.

"Mario! Mario! Mario!" Tosca brooking no delay. *Stizzita* Puccini calls her, the "quick-tempered" one. In she sweeps, voice thrilling. La Tosca!

At last! Diva time! Othmar hugged himself.

Hidden as she was by the rehearsal piano, he did not see her knitting lime green baby booties.

But Othmar was to be disappointed. Diva time was over before it began.

The Dettori did rehearse. She stood, piano-vocal behind her on a chair. She did better than mark, she sang out. The Americans fell into rapt silence, scarcely breathing, awed at the way she created an ensemble with Cavaradossi. He did little, singing his way into the part. He didn't have much to do. After Scarpia, it is Tosca's opera. But for the little he did there was always her swift reaction helping him, willing his character's response. There were the expected human reactions, and the cameos of all the things Tosca is, the jealous woman, the flirt, the diva. She is totally without introspection. Possessive to a degree that is almost shameful to watch. "In his pants," thought Ed Nelson, the Sacristan. When the Americans talked later about this first rehearsal, to a man they said it was one of the most incredible things they had ever heard. The Dettori seemed to breathe as one with her young lover.

Othmar, listening in the auditorium, thought the Dettori brought no more to Tosca's first extended piece of music than Callas, say, or Caballé. The vocal line is oddly strung out, he thought, prosy for all the poetry the lyrics promise, as though Puccini didn't like Tosca and was exposing her for the manipulator she is. *"Non la sospiri la nostra casetta?"* she demands of Cavaradossi. "Do you not yearn for our little house?" Then some godawful nature stuff: silent starlit woods, parched grasses, ruined tombs, night whispers, starry vaults. Who's she trying to kid? Then *"Arde a Tosca nel sangue il folle amor!"* In Tosca's blood burns the madness of love. "Actressy," Othmar thought.

So actressy it will be fun to stage the next bit. Cavaradossi has said, OK, siren, you've caught me in your snare. Enough already, I've got to get back to work. Work is something she ought to understand. You sing, as you are always telling me. I paint. If you bother to notice. We're both professonals, right? Would this young Cavaradossi be up to playing the suave gent, the aristo?

Then, of course, Tosca catches sight of the picture he's working on. She would have had to be blind not to notice but that's our Tosca. *"Nostra casetta,"* meaning our love nest. First things first, get the boy into bed.

"Aspetta...aspetta," sang Tosca. Wait...wait! Not exactly racking her brains—she's seen those blue eyes somewhere—but hoping to catch Cavaradossi out. "It's the Attanvanti!"

Bravo! says Cavaradossi. Amused? Dripping with irony? Sarcasm would surely be wrong. Playful? He's got nothing to hide.

And so on, and so on. Seductive, childish, grasping. Not a little desperate. She knows no one important marries the Toscas of this world.

"Di me, beffarda, ride." The Attavanti mocks me and laughs at me.

"Follia!" Your imagination!

Building and building.

"Diro sempre," he promises. "I will always say, 'Floria, I love you.'"

This Cavaradossi did love her. "From the bottom of his little old heart," thought Othmar.

Climax. She gets what she wants.

"This is sinful in church," she says. As if butter wouldn't melt.

Still she won't leave. They smooch: the big clinch.

"In front of the Madonna?" Cavaradossi teases.

That was pretty much it that morning. The Angelotti comes back on stage from his hiding place in the Attavani crypt. It is revealed who his sister is, the blue-eyed Attavanti. That she has hidden a disguise for his escape. Women's clothes, a veil, a fan, the *ventaglio* we will hear so much about. "Iago used a handkerchief," Scarpia muses about the instruments of jealously. *"Ed io un ventaglio!"*—and I a fan.

Cavaradossi has a better plan for Angelotti. Then comes the boom of a cannon. The signal someone has escaped from the Castel Sant'Angelo. Cavaradossi throws his lot in with Angelotti. Another reason for Scarpia to hate him. The two liberals make a quick exit.

Enter the Sacristan, *gridando,* breathless, too winded to sing. "Great rejoicing, Excellency," he gasps, expecting to find Cavaradossi busy painting.

"I think we stop here," said Pompelli.

12.

"AT-water 9-6020," said Gilly's Liz. "Ex-Members Room." Her ruse in case of obscene phone calls.

It was Othmar on the other end and he had to speak to Gilly. Ever on the prowl for clients, Gilly had gone to hear a Hungarian basso.

"Anything I can do?"

No, nothing.

"He sounded pretty strung out," Liz reported.

It began with an innocent question from the stage manager.

"How did you do the gingerbread house?"

Bill Potter, "Potts" to most people," had been sitting in Othmar's office while Othmar showed off the stage model for "Tosca" he had built. "It's just corrugated cardboard and white glue," Othmar said modestly.

"Very fine," said Potts.

"Now I want you to see the scrim," said Othmar. With hands delicately splayed, he upended a black frame about the size of a cigar box and inserted it downstage. "I didn't put the netting in the frame."

"Umm," said Potts.

Othmar came around to the front of the model and knelt before it. "You see how the scrim enhances the scene. Focuses the attention."

"Yes," said Potts, who had seen a scrim or two in his time.

"The real scrim will fly. I didn't make a fly loft for the model. So my little scrim runs up and down in these grooves here." But the cardboard jammed and Othmar was some time getting it to travel freely.

"It doesn't like being watched," said Potts to jolly him along.

"It will be in the down position for the beginning of each act and you'll fly it on a music cue, which I'll be there to give you."

Potts was sure he'd be there. Word had spread, theater to theater, that Othmar liked to be his own stage manager. Potts would proceed cautiously. "So you're not going to pull a Met and sing the whole show behind it," he said to kid Othmar.

"Pallas isn't ready for that 'Walküre,'" said Othmar beginning to relax.

Stage managers can make or break a production, and Othmar thanked his lucky stars that Bill Potter had been free for "Tosca." He was a lean, wiry man with a trim mustache and a flat voice. He never looked directly at you, which Othmar liked, and he always wore a suit and white shirt, which set him apart from the technical crews under his command, and this, too, Othmar admired. One story had it that Potts had escaped from the rural poverty of a Maine chicken farm, and another that his father had been a railroad conductor. Arriving at the theater, he would hang up his jacket and tie and pull on a sleeveless sweater. He would wind his pocket watch. Work could begin. He was famous for running a tight ship, and famous for his kindnesses to young people. Othmar wasn't quite sure where that put him, and sometimes affected a facetious formality: "Mister Potter, sir, I'm yours to command."

Of the real scrim, Potter needed only to know three things. But so absorbed was Othmar in his toy theater that the stage manager thought he had better get his questions in now.

"No projections on the scrim?"

"No, nothing, no images. Just the tableau you see through the scrim."

"Does it come down at the end of each act?"

"Like a freeze-frame?" Othmar appeared to consider this. He liked his productions to seem a joint effort of all involved. Then, crisply: "No."

"Bow curtain at the end of each act?"

"Don't think so," Othmar said as mildly as he could. Taking their bows was a perk not lightly ceded by singers, and he knew it, and Potter knew it. "My goal is seamless drama. We'll do the bows at the end, not between. Make things easier for you backstage. If I had me druthers, I'd play it as one long act. Like a movie. You know, 'Tosca' takes place in just one day."

"Yep," said the stage manager. Then, as Othmar appeared not to hear, again he asked:

"How did you do the gingerbread house?"

With his mind taken up by "Tosca" and the potential problem of the curtain calls, Othmar had not expected to be plunged back into what he regarded as ancient history—his "Hansel and Gretel" production. Three years is a long time and there was a long moment as he gathered his thoughts. What had Potter heard? he wondered. Best to find out now. He decided to appeal to the Potts who loved the tricks of the trade, and all manner of stage illusion. Not much to intrigue Potts in the real-life sets and ordinary people in a verismo opera like "Tosca."

As though imparting a great mystery, Othmar whispered "Sty-ro-foam," then laughed. "Pretty goddam wonderful, if I may say so myself."

"Ah, Styrofoam," agreed Potts. "Where would we be without it!"

"Cut it, carve it, gouge it, even burn and melt it, paint it, antique it. You can do the most amazing things with it. You remember Boris Goldovsky?"

Potts did, and the Goldovsky Opera Theater which toured America with casts of young singers.

"And Boris's experiments with fiberglass scenery?—and how heavy it was, and the awful colors. Boris would have loved Styrofoam. Well, you should have seen me—seen us." Othmar thought it prudent to correct himself. "Seen us carve the gingerbread oven. The gingerbread house wasn't nearly as much fun. All we really did with the house was decorate. But the oven has to explode."

"Yep," said Potts and settled back to be told.

"So we had these giant slabs of Styrofoam. For the Witch's oven, I thought of a beehive-type oven, essentially like an igloo, except with a tall, tall chimney, and terrific smoke. So we sawed the slabs into blocks, and fitted and stacked them, and built the oven; and here's the beauty part. You know how when you pull a foundation out from under, the rest falls? In a real theater, you'd build your foundation on a wagon and winch it back. The college didn't allow anything like that. Stage machinery was against the 'rules' for a student production. So I thought of a sled. Like a giant Flexible Flyer but really just one big Styrofoam slab and a rope running upstage to a pully, sort of a come-along. Oh, God, it was funny. Gretel pushes her into the oven, and the Witch flops belly down on the slab, and she is kicking with those crazy lace-up witch's boots, and the lighting guy, this eighteen-year-old kid, has got the flames licking. Remind me to tell you about the flames! Something like Christmas tree lights. Anyway, inside the oven the Witch grabs the handholds I made, and we yank the slab upstage with her on it, and the whole thing collapses. Not just collapses! The stuff bounces and bounces, and bounces and bounces. The lighting guy has got the strobes on the chimney as it comes apart, so your eye's distracted from the Witch. You know where the strobes come from? From a rock band! Oh, Potts, I wish you'd been there."

Othmar was flushed from the telling, and happy, and it was some reluctance that Potts then asked:

"And you flew the Witch?"

"They did, the kids did, and it was sen-sa-tional."

"Hard for kids to do," Potts observed.

"Well, they did, they did. Can't take any credit."

So there had been those unsettling questions from Ed Potter. Nothing he could bother Gilly about. Gilly would only say "Hansel" was behind them.

Far worse was the attitude of the Italian singers. And that stinker, Mister Johnson Jones. For Othmar had lost control of the production.

The Italians refused to rehearse. Or rehearse very much. They showed up well in time for rehearsals. They poured themselves tea. They listened to Othmar's plans for staging their respective scenes. They let him walk them though his ideas. *"Si, si,"* yes, yes, they said. And *"bene,"* good. Then they drifted away. Othmar didn't know how they did it. One minute they were on stage, and after the rehearsal break, they had gone. He had taken Pompelli aside and complained.

"Gianni, Gianni." Pompelli was placating. "My Rita is already Tosca! Bruno's Scarpia already very fine, classic. It would not be showing respect for you to make so many rehearsals for them. You must understand. She keep her bargain. She coach the Italian, she place the vowels, and already I hear it in the Americans. I almost mistake them for Italians! Be patient, Gianni. You will see!"

Othmar had to agree about the Italian. The Dettori took over the upright in the lobby and Rollo Shaw or Ed Nelson took turns playing. Only the Sacristan had more than a few lines, so the others brought piano-vocals for roles they sang or hoped to sing. Othmar could kill Jonce Jones for monopolizing the language coaching but the others didn't seem to mind, and Sarah Smythe got quite a good article about banishing the all-purpose American vowel that so many singers used to sing Italian. "Take just the sounds for the letter A," she wrote. "Depending where it is placed in the mouth," and here she resorted to phonetics, "the vowel becomes 'ah' or aah,' even 'aye.' This basic vowel is the alpha of alphas, a whole alphabet of sound in itself. Vowels are the building blocks of sung language."

And about Pompelli's musical preparation Othmar had only praise. The man was tireless. He loved working with the orchestra. He sat in on the sectionals, as Mac Gilson drilled now the violins, now the clarinets, of the Chatham Philharmonic "and friends," the ringers from Albany. Gilson took to bringing other music to Pompelli for advice.

But one big happy family it was not, dashing Othmar's hopes for more than ensemble opera on stage.

"I want us all to be involved in as many aspects of the production as possible," he said one morning to the "Americanos," as he playfully began to call them. "We will all learn useful things about the craft of opera."

Jonce Jones snickered into his chest.

"Take the chorus," said Othmar.

"Take it, please," the Americanos shot back.

"Hunt Smith says he would be grateful for someone to take section rehearsals. Especially the tenors."

"What tenors?" joshed Rollo Shaw, who was one.

"Come on, guys. They just need confidence, and you only get that from rehearsals. The good news is, we'll eventually have three more tenors from an Albany church."

And so the Sacristan and the Spoletta and the Sciarrone allowed themselves to be pressed—"press-ganged!" said the Angelotti—into odd musical jobs. Othmar was relieved. If they were in the theater, all present and accounted for, they were not "out there" talking against him. He had seen how quickly they befriended the Cavaradossi. The Italian was eager to practice his English and, in exchange, he taught them quite a few Italian expressions not in "Tosca." Othmar suspected Jonce Jones was behind this. "Just building his vocabulary," winked Ed Nelson. Why did they all stand up for Jonce? Othmar's one stab at making friends had been a disaster. Whatever Othmar said about the Cavaradossi's new jeans had been misinterpreted, something about Levi's being for men and Wranglers for girls.

"What did he goddam think, that I wanted to get in his goddam pants?" Othmar exploded to Gilly. Liz, listening in, thought to herself that Othmar really didn't know how to swear.

When Othmar blew up about Evey Titus and her bad influence on the Italians, Gilly knew it was "manager time."

"Gotta storm the gates of Pallas," he told Liz.

"I'm already packed."

She drove fast and expertly. Gilly lay back in his seat, fedora pulled over his eyes. He had a lot riding on "Tosca." The two Italian "stars" figured least in his plans. When it was all over he expected to put them on a plane back home. Rita Dettori would have her American triumph and could retire to look after her grandchildren. Victor Pompelli would come and go, as he always had, teaching and conducting. Bruno Cappetto was an appendage of Luigi Luongo, and Gill's had plans only for the young tenor. Cappetto was a problem for the future. The four young Americans were all solid. Too soon to tell if they would have important careers but they would always get work. Gilly's stable was expanding nicely. The music business was booming generally but he was making his name for aggressive management. Well concealed, as Liz put it, under a layer of good manners. "Your secret weapon." He was doing so well he was thinking of taking on an associate. This trip was to straighten out Johnny Othmar. What was going wrong? He had set Othmar up, seen him succeed as "John Austin Othmar Presents Scenes from Great Operas." Got him through that "Hansel and Gretel," a mess that was not entirely Othmar's fault. Delivered him into the safe hands of Evey Titus, though Othmar was not to be told she was behind his getting the Pallas job. "Tosca" was to launch Luigi Luongo and if it made the fame and fortune of John Austin Othmar, well, then, everybody's happy. "They won't rehearse," Othmar had complained on the phone. "Isn't it in the goddam contract they've got to rehearse?" Gilly supposed it was, and supposed that in a real opera house, the powers that would be would see to that, but Othmar was not Rudolf Bing.

"Problem is," Gilly chortled, "Johnny thinks he's running the Met."

"The Met?" said Liz crossly. Her darling husband had interrupted quite a nice daydream about the Chinese conductor.

They arrived in Pallas in light snow. Liz followed black ribbons of pavement into the town center and after only one wrong turn delivered them to the Olympus. The hotel manager himself took them to their room. "Mrs. Titus says to phone her when you get in." They did, and she proposed dinner. They should come to her for drinks and they'd take them out. Our friend, she said, is in a bad way. "It may be my fault."

Gilly made for the theater. Liz said she was going to tour the main drag.

Othmar was in his office. Here he felt in charge, and he wanted Gilly to see that. There were seating charts spread out on the table. Each had great red blocks representing tickets sold—"and paid for," Othmar said pointedly. It was not quite two weeks to opening night.

"Permit me a dumb question," said Gilly, "but why are you so worried? It will be standing room only, *mon vieux*, and there won't be a dry seat in the house. They'll love every minute."

"This lousy town," Othmar began, and there was a lot more along the lines of not knowing their ass from the their elbow. Gilly had seen Johnny Othmar through some sticky times and the Othmar of those days had been outrageously funny when things went wrong. Even Liz didn't mind his tale of the community bake-off for "Hansel." Othmar was a good enough judge of singers for Gilly to know when Gilly must reluctantly replace one who wasn't working out. As far as Gilly could tell the Pallas "Tosca" was going well musically. "Rita Dettori up to the vast sum we are paying her?" he asked cautiously.

"When the diva deigns to set her dainty foot on our humble boards."

The cliches flowed nicely, Gilly noted. A good sign. One drunken evening in the 'boonies "somewhere near Elmira" he and Johnny had founded the Society for the Preservation and Improvement of the Cliché, known as SPIC. Othmar's bitterness was new. Gilly said he'd never seen the Palladium and please to show him around.

Othmar marched him right up to the back row of the second balcony.

"Great sight lines," Gilly enthused. "You ought to get top dollar from Palladians for sitting in the Gods."

"If any of them knew what that meant." Back to sarcasm.

"I come up hear a lot. To think."

"Perchance to scream?" Othmar ignored him.

"I've never had to stage for the second balcony. The college theaters didn't have them. But the Palladium takes me back my Boston days and how much Sarah Caldwell had going on high up on her sets."

"Nosebleed time, I've heard."

"She had the chorus all over the scenery, or the supers, and there was always something to look at, if you had a cheap seat. Otherwise, you're just looking down on wigs and traps and stand lights in the pit."

Othmar was leaning forward, arms folded on the seat in front. From this vantage, the Palladium was like a toy theater and he could move things around at will.

"The last act is the easiest. The fortress silhouetted against the sky and the angel high above that. The second act plays like drawing room comedy. As far as the slobs in the second balcony are concerned, it's all about doors opening and closing."

"Well, isn't it? Scarpia banging the windows shut to shut out the cantata," said Gilly. "Like he's killing something. Tosca or music—which mustn't get in his way. And isn't it worse not to see Cavaradossi tortured?"

"Yeah, and wait till you see how I'm staging the procession of Roberti the torturer, and the Judge, and the Judge's' scribe with quill pen. To take down his confession. *Ordnung*, rules. Cops are the same the world over. Puccini specifies three *sbirri*, three police agents. Which I guess means undercover cops. So they'll be costumed like the average Roman."

"Who isn't a cardinal."

Othmar swatted at Gilly.

The first act was spectacle. A great church. "And churchy things going on," said Othmar. "That may be a novelty for the people here who go to the First Congo. I had a time bagging the idea that we would auction the role of the Cardinal. It was hard getting across the idea you shouldn't recognize people, that acting is disguise. By the way, Alex Avery understood perfectly about making up white as Sciarrone. Did I tell you, he is doubling as the Jailer rather than Jonce. We had hoped to get someone from the chorus but there simply wasn't a good enough voice. Alex will make up white for that, too. Well, swarthy white. You know what we're going to call him in the program? 'Giorgio Spelvino.'"

"Bravo, Gianni."

"Actually it was my idea, Italian for George Spelvin. A funny thing. Ed Potter who knows everything, didn't know that 'George Spelvin' is how they list a ringer in a cast list. I tell you, Gilly, the master has not lost his tou-chay."

The sets would come in on Monday. Othmar had found a local carpenter to copy the artist's platform that Cavaradossi uses to paint the Attavanti Magdalene. "Geez, it was like being back in Shop," Othmar laughed. "I showed the guy a couple of production photos and explained the action, and how I wanted the painter to be up where people could see him and he could sing out. And I hope to God Luigi Luongo goes along with that. I could kill Bruno Cappetto. He won't let me move him around very much. So the carpenter really gets right into the act. He asks me, do I want real wheels so the platform can move? We worked it out so the wooden wheels—rounds from planking he braced—will conceal the working wheels. And do you know what those are? Hospital bed wheels—that lock. We roll the goddam thing on and we roll it off. I might have the Sacristan play around with it. It's tall. You can stand inside."

This sounded like the old Othmar, Gilly thought. It wasn't exactly the heart-to-heart he had intended but there would be time later.

"More to see," said Othmar, taking the stairs two at a time.

The Palladium was not only a very pretty little theater, and wonderfully restored, but it was awesomely equipped. There was a computerized light board, when such things were by no means to be found in every theater. There were motors to fly scenery. The stage was well trapped. Another season, Othmar told Gilly, he would see if funds could be raised for a hydraulic lift. He would also dearly love to have a revolving stage. Again, the old Othmar talking, the Othmar of a million plans. Othmar showed off the prop closet. They looked into the dressing rooms, small perhaps, but three located conveniently on stage level. Othmar had a passkey for the Dettori's. Oddly unused, Gilly thought.

"She still hasn't let me see her costumes."

"There's always tomorrow." Gilly was soothing.

When they got back to Othmar's office, Liz was stretched out on the banquette. Othmar was not pleased.

"Your posters are all over town. Good work!" She laughed. "A red tide has taken over Pallas," she said holding a handful of candy hearts. "Be my valentine!"

Othmar stiffened. In Liz's company he did not seem disposed to talk. Without waiting for an invitation, he announced he couldn't have dinner that evening and he couldn't have Sunday brunch either. "Have a grab a bite before tonight's chorus rehearsal," he said ushering them out.

"Here's your hat, etc." said Liz outside the theater.

Valentine's Day was occupying Sarah Smythe. Othmar, she thought, needed a little boost. He was definitely not her type, she had long ago decided (with a confirming eyebrow from Aunty Evey) but there was something forlorn about him that was new, and that appealed. She would make him a valentine, and was in her kitchen busily pasting letters she shut out from the Clarion Voice to spell "Guess Who? On a big red construction paper heart. (She got most of the Guess from an Esso ad.) A beautiful box of store-bought chocolates seemed a little, well, heartless. Or, possibly, "romantic," which she didn't want either. She giggled and sought out an old cookie tin. There were two gingerbread people left over from Christmas. The gingerbread girl's skirt was broken but the boy was good and brave and true and needed only a candy heart to make him Raggedy Andy.

"'Bewitched, bothered and bewildered,'" sang Sarah as she sped to the theater. From the lobby she could hear the chorus rehearsing on stage. She slipped into Othmar's office, left her valentine, and sped off to pick Alex Avery up for dinner.

"I suppose it was selfish of them," admitted Evey Titus. Gilly had made her a martini, which she said was perfection. Wind howled as they sat in the library. Winter couldn't get enough of Pallas. Gilly fussed with the fire.

They had brought their hostess as generous wedge of Brie.

"You'd have thought we'd given her the moon," Liz said later. (The Brie was her idea.)

"Johnny was right about the stale crackers."

"He's bound to be right about some things."

"She hasn't given up on him."

In retrospect, Evey Titus said, she probably should not have offered her music room to the artistes for rehearsals.

"I just couldn't resist the idea Luigi Luongo might turn into a star in my house."

"Happens all the time," said Gilly.

"I told them if they could get themselves here in the afternoons I would drive them back to the hotel."

Bruno Cappetto and Luigi would arrive by taxi and go directly to the piano. She would excuse herself and go curl up on the window seat on the stairs with her needlepoint.

"I've had piano lessons. I ought to have known it's not interesting to listen to. But it was kind of fascinating to hear Bruno's corrections and hear Luigi try it again."

Sometimes, in the late afternoon, another taxi would arrive with Victor Pompelli and Rita Dettori. Evey served tea. "Or something stronger." She got out whiskies for Bruno to compare. Maryland rye and Tennessee sour-mash bourbon were new. She promised to find Irish for him.

"It was quite a squeeze in the car getting them back to the hotel. But by then we were laughing our heads off. They're awfully nice people. Modest. Grateful for anything you do for them. I wish my husband could hear them on Italy. He loved it so. They're from Fruili-Venezia Julia, an area new to me, but up beyond Venice, which explains Trieste, I suppose. Life hasn't been easy for them. The war coming at the wrong time for their careers. It was held against her she started off in operetta. Is there a theater called The Other? Bruno tried to explain there are two. I kept wondering why his accent is Cockney. Seems somewhere along the line he fetched up with the British Army. You've got to hear him sing army songs. Very funny."

Gilly made another round and Liz let herself be admired.

Evey to Liz: "You must have some idea why things have gone sour for Austin, as I call him."

"Yes, I do."

"Holy toledo, you didn't quite come out and tell her it was her fault!" Gilly was not so much angry as nervous.

"Because it is not all her fault. She wants to help and she can't help being who she is. Evangeline Titus—'All Pallas trembles before her.'"

"Great line! I'll have to try it out on Johnny."

"After the final, final curtain. But I think she'd got it figured out—just didn't know what to do about it. Her other idea was brilliant."

Gilly was not so sure.

The way Liz saw it, she told Evey Titus, was that Othmar felt excluded at every turn. Bruno was keeping Luigi under wraps. The Dettori wouldn't rehearse for reasons not yet known. (Evey had made a shrewd guess and it troubled.) Pompelli was busy building the orchestra. He was now working with the chorus as well. The Americans weren't very pally.

"I don't think the Italians bear him any ill will," Evey said. "They don't gossip about him to me, which I think is a good sign. They could so easily put him down, the superior Europeans. European friends have done that to me! But, no question, they go their own way. I think…I think what I will do is limit, yes, limit, the afternoons. I will say I mustn't be selfish. I will say they are needed at the theater."

Gilly said that would certainly help.

"I hadn't realized about the rehearsals," Evey went on. "Are they so important? They know the opera. Don't they just have to know their way around the sets? And how Tosca jumps." She laughed. "Little things like that."

Gilly whacked the last knot of log till it spurted flame. The room was cold. Evey seemed not to notice.

"I suppose I could have a word with them. I might suggest that Othmar isn't as sure about the opera as he pretends. It's his first 'Tosca,' and they, how should I put this? They could teach it to him. Without them telling him that, of course."

"Without him knowing?" Gilly was dubious.

"It would get them back into the theater," said Liz. "Maybe if you didn't say teach it to him but correct or steer him, when they felt it was going wrong. That would let him try his own ideas. It's his production."

Evey smiled. "I knew you would have the answer. Who should this come from? Should Rita be the mother-hen? Does he work better with men? Bruno, perhaps? To be continued over dinner."

But it wasn't. They shot down the Titus driveway and slipped along country roads, Evey's driving directions interspersed with her rather candid comments about Pallas and environs.

"I hope you've written this down for future generations," said Liz and negotiated them out of a skid, for it was suddenly icy.

"I do love my native health," protested the former Evangeline Carruthers.

"As a lioness her cub," Liz said later.

Dinner was at the G & T. Depending on your point of view, this was either Sarah Smythe's idea of "great fun" or something less than a treat. Mario, the chef, was expecting Mrs. Titus.

"I have a nice surprise for you, Mario. This is Gurdon Gillespie's son, who now lives in New York." When he cooked in Boston, Mario ran something called Bonelli's. It was the club of Boston clubs, just a lunch table on one of the wharves. Gilly's father had been a regular.

Mario gave Gilly a little poke. "We miss him." Liz thought he had the saddest eyes she'd ever seen.

It was also one of the best dinners she could remember. Nothing fancy, just classic cooking, the lamb pink, the roast potatoes superbly crusty, the spinach—or was it chard?—in black butter, the salad very lightly dressed in good oil. Gilly couldn't remember all the wines they had to drink. Mario had wheeled a little table up to theirs. It held six or seven opened bottles, none without a full glass left, some with two, and he decided what and when to pour.

Dinner had begun with raw oysters, which Mario got sent by bus from Cotuit. As he set Mrs. Titus's plate down, he nodded in the direction of a booth at the far corner. She could see (and hear) her niece but not her guest.

"One of the opera singers," Mario prompted.

Gilly saw a dark hand. "Alex Avery," he breathed.

Mario asked after the Italians. Snow, he regretted, had kept *i due signori* from playing golf.

"She has been seeing quite a lot of him," Evey murmured. "It's easier if they come here. Pallas talk, you know!"

"I wouldn't worry about it," said Liz. "He has his own sticky bun in New York."

Gilly coughed into his napkin. "What Liz means is..."
Evey Titus's peals of laughter produced Sarah's head from the booth.

"What possessed you?" Gilly asked as they lay in their airless hotel room. "And where did you get 'sticky bun' from?"

"Rather not say," said Liz, wickedly. "But it was something she needed to hear."

The rest of their stay was uneventful. Liz went by herself to see Evey. Othmar was still on their minds. "Men are hard to read," said Evey. "One man trying to read another?" asked Liz. "Oh, especially so. Men are so hidden about things." Each knew it was true. After a long silence, they plunged into gossip, very little of it about "Tosca," which was a relief to both.

Gilly spent an hour with Othmar at the theater. He was preoccupied with minutiae. Could they substitute a bass drum for the cannon booms in the Act One finale? Would a tape recording work. Could that link into the PA system?"

"God, 'Tosca' in Cinema-Scope! I love it!"

Othmar was not amused.

Liz drove them back to New York. "He has let his hair grow."
"Who hasn't?"
"He's not as blond as he was."

13.

"It's not as if anyone was killed!" he reminded himself, punching out the words. And, along with that thought: "She went behind my back!"

Othmar had come back from the chorus rehearsal to find a candy box with big red bow on his office table. Liz's teasing him with candy hearts still rankled but there was something about the shabbiness of this box that beguiled. As he undid the ribbon he could see it had been used before. A Christmas leftover, he supposed; his mother's cupboards were full of them: "Too nice to throw out." The box itself was elegant, one of Louis Sherry's embossed gilt coffins for chocolates; and to give it away was a sacrifice for Sarah who used it for grocery coupons and Green Stamps. Othmar lifted the lid. He read "GuESS wHo" on the paper heart. He pulled it away to reveal the gingerbread man. On his candy heart Othmar read "bewitched."

A blush of rage came over Othmar. He dashed box and gingerbread to the floor. The gingerbread man bounced and came to rest heart-side up, grimacing its candy smile. Othmar stomped on it. A foot came off. He stomped again. The icing used to affix the heart oozed and stuck to Othmar's shoe. He howled.

When had had collected himself, Othmar got into his car and drove aimlessly. If he were in the city he could swim laps and thrash it away. He made for the bowling alley. Nothing doing: Saturday nights were league play only. He crossed the parking lot to Broyle's and rented skates. Round and round he went, keeping to the outside, stroking long strides, head low and battening on the rink's damp sweet fug of floor varnish and bubble bath from the teenaged girls shrieking in the center.

The valentine was obviously Sarah's work. Pathetic! He could see her putting it together from scraps. But who was there watching her? Who suggested the gingerbread? Who was in on the joke and laughing. He didn't think it could be Ed Potter—though Potts' questions indicated he knew something. It had to be one of the singers. What had they heard?

Into his path veered a pack of girls towing a red-headed boy. Othmar almost mowed them down. "Beat it!," he screamed back at them.

He must remember it was not his fault. Gilly knew that, and the college knew that. He had finally made Kay Seelye see it his way.

By way of introducing Kay Seelye, Gilly had said to Othmar: "You will never again meet someone who was in 'The Firebrand of Florence.'"

"Only in the chorus," she protested when they finally met. Othmar had seen her at work before he knew who she was. He had opened a door marked "Rehearsals" and come upon a blur of activity. A small, fast human figure was pushing hulking students around as if they were little chairs. As it pushed, it punched. Othmar, wincing in sympathy, closed the door and continued along the corridor to find Miss Francis, the head of Tate College's performing arts department.

Tate was a small, private liberal arts college, and co-ed. As it happened, that year Kay Steele had more good female voices among her voice students than she knew what to do with and so she made the case for dusting off their old production of "Hansel and Gretel." She would double-cast the leads but sing the Witch herself. The man who usually staged the opera workshops, as Tate billed student productions, was on sabbatical. His temporary replacement was a modern dancer, whom Kay Seelye considered this side of tone deaf. Otherwise, the two women got on like a house on fire. Between them, they decided to spend a bit of the college's money and hire a director. Inquiries were made, inquiries that reached Gilly at a time when Othmar was "at liberty" and on Gilly's nerves.

"A piece of cake," said Gilly explaining what Tate wanted. "They've got the sets and costumes, and they'll do it with piano as it's too much for the student orchestra. They sing it in English. Kay Seelye is big on opera in English. She's the real thing, everybody says. A terrific teacher who really gets involved with the kids and campus life. If I were you, mon vieux, I would invest in six bottles of good wine to take her. Tate is strictly Mountain Red. It's the back of beyond—for your jollies you'll probably want to go on up to Montreal."

And it was pretty much as Gilly promised. He hadn't foreseen the modern dance teacher would wear her dark hair loosed over her shoulders and play twelve-string guitar in the local coffee shop. "Fleur"—for that was the dancer's name—"is the faculty flower child," said an amused Kay Seelye, pouring Othmar some of his Beaujolais. "A little thin, don't you think, this year's nouveau, but we can hope for the Villages and the Saint Amour." Kay herself was robust, with bright brown eyes and high color. It wasn't long before she called Othmar "Johnny." When she taught she wore a rakish beret and high heels. "Singing is theater," she said. He told her some but not all of his troubles with the Wupperthal "Bohème." She was sure there was more to it but didn't press.

The problem with "Hansel," as Kay saw it, was how to refresh a production that was "way down South with Disney" in cuteness without wasting Othmar's time or the college's money. Moreover, they had exactly three weeks to pull things together. She was direct, a good listener, and Othmar thought he would like working with her. "I warn you, the only way we can survive on our budget is to horse trade. It's my year for opera. Fleur will choreograph the Angels. Next year, when it's the dance department's turn, I will supervise the music if she can be persuaded to involve singers. Really, I just don't know about modern dancers. They might as well be born with out ears. 'Hansel' is lovely, Humperdinck's way with Wagner, isn't it, but folkish, not mythic, if you get the difference. Did you know Humperdinck copied out 'Parsifal' and was the first stage manager for it? You won't be surprised I have to explain who Humperdinck is. The kids think he's the pop singer. That's another thing. The cast wants to be miked. All their little friends in bands are miked. Johnny, you'll have to back me up but good. Crikey, I'm in the business of teaching singing not broadcasting."

The old "Hansel" sets, upon inspection, proved salvageable. They consisted of painted flats and cut-outs, framed by leafy panels; and Kay dragooned a stage crew to brace the major pieces so Othmar could get the general effect and make notes. The Witch's Oven was missing: Kay had a vague recollection she had lent it for a Halloween party. "Halloween is big here."

A pair of students now positioned a long ground-row about five feet high, a cut-out of spectral branches rising above gnarled oaks and inky hemlocks. "What's that?" Othmar asked.

"That? Oh, that, that's how I fly—how the Witch flies. Actually, I don't leave the ground at all. I get up on a sort of pedestal and they drag it stage left as the tree stuff is dragged stage right, and as I am glimpsed behind the trees I appear to rise. It's illusion."

"We might be able to rig something to fly you."

Kay chortled. "No, you won't! I have no head for heights."

Tate College was an old school, founded in the 1830s for the education of local youth by local worthies—for whom the first buildings were named. Thus, ranged around the college green, were what Kay lightly described for Othmar as "Brewer Brown's Conscience," which was the math and science building, and "Lawyer Jones's Lien," which was the history building, and the "Widow Williams's Lending Library," which also housed the literature and language departments. When four Tate graduates fell in the Civil War, the chapel became their memorial. Tate itself was named for Downing Tate, builder and amateur architect, whose granite quarries were a bottomless source of funds for the new college. The old college buildings were all of a piece, none without pediment and column: the American view of the glory that was Greece and the grandeur that was Rome, but rendered in brick and Tate granite, and all a mite misshapen, so that they were too broad for their height, and, when deeply cushioned in snow, looked oddly like Quonset huts. Classic "champagne glass" elms ringed the Green, though disease was fast thinning these. It being January, snow stretched as far as the eye could see, deep and white, and renewed every few days; and Othmar's first purchases were a heavy turtleneck and a ski cap. Kay recommended boots and heavy wool socks.

"Yes, it is always this cold," she assured him. The air tore at Othmar's throat as they walked though the Green to the new campus and the Guy R. Strutt Student Center, known as Strutt. Othmar was about to ask who Strutt was when a snowball whizzed by.

"Pay no attention. They'll never actually hit you. You've noticed the snow forts on the Green? Not much else to do around here."

Perhaps for that reason, and because it was the inter-session between semesters, Kay had more students than she need to put on "Hansel."

"I sometimes feel they will do anything but study."

Othmar had already pegged Tate as a cow college.

"How could you do this to me?" he whined on the phone to Gilly.

"You're there to bring civilization. 'Johann Othmar Hoppleseed Presents 'Hansel unt Gretel,'" said Gilly in his comic German.

Within the week, Othmar had a student crew repainting the sets in a palette of earth colors he found in the Tate library's book of Grimm fairy tales. He found a kid who knew something about lighting to organize that. Where there were boys, there were girls, and visa versa; and when Othmar could get everybody's attention, the areas that Kay called the "tech arts" went swimming. The level of student acting was as abysmal as he expected.

"Well, what do they know?" said Kay to comfort him. "And if they did have an inkling what it was like to be a German peasant it's not everybody who can project it on stage. You think you've got it hard? It has taken me since September to get my little cast this far musically."

They did know their parts—Othmar gave Kay that—but they were apt to forget details when he asked them to move in character. Getting them to move freely was his greatest challenge, and Othmar could now understand why his first glimpse of Kay Seelye was that rat-terrier of a teacher yanking singers around the stage. He despaired particularly of the two girls cast as Gretel.

"Mister Othmar," said the Gretel who thought Othmar was kinda good-looking, "it's like I run out of music or I run out of Gretel things to do."

The two mezzos singing Hansel were better as boys.

"Well, you've given Hansel more to do," Kay observed during a break in the forest scene.

"Look at me! Copy me!" he pleaded with the Gretels. "I want it simple, I want it innocent, Gretel is the little sister. I want impulse, trust, fear, doubt, belief. It's there in the music." And, as the thought had just occurred to him: "In this opera it's Gretel who grows up, who saves the day. I want to see the seeds of this in you. Begin by putting Gretel on you."

Beaming faces from the Gretels. "Put Gretel on like a costume?" This was a novel idea. Far more interesting, they thought than what Othmar had told the Hansels.

The Gretels warmed first to Othmar's demand for childish impulse and had a fine old time racing their respective Hansels into the woods. Othmar figured he could edit some of this into winsome hide-and-seek around a berry bush. "Not very original," he confessed to Kay.

"Originality is not the point, is it? They're here to learn the basics."

The Gretels' attempt at fear was wide-eyed gothic. "Would that every girl was her own Gish," said Kay when Othmar was unwinding over more of the Beaujolais nouveau. "They get the eyes but not the body. This is the first generation to think everything important comes from the face, because of movies and television. That's all you can see on a small screen: face and boobs."

Bringing out shadings more interior was beyond them, and, as Kay thought it would come to, Othmar was reduced to staging gesture by gesture and step by step. Tate was his first experience with teaching. To Kay he justified his every move. I suppose I was like that once, she thought, but it seems to me I was freer—I certainly had more fun. For Tate, he was a novelty. "Doesn't he just smell of New York," Kay had said to Fleur, who expressed puzzlement (she was from California). "His stage talk, the people he has worked with. The kids eat it up. We oughta to think about an Artist in Residence for every inter-session." And yet, and yet. To be truthful, she

138

herself did not have one original idea about staging "Hansel and Gretel," nothing more that what she could glean from libretto and recordings. But neither did Othmar. When she asked if "Hansel" was more a fairy tale than a folk opera, his blue-eyed stare was faintly supercilious. Dammit, shouldn't he have an opinion? Shouldn't he at least talk about, it chew it over, jolly her along! "What about a 'Hansel' that's one big bad dream?" she had asked. "A kid's nightmare. Two spoiled brats, a girl and a boy, and what happens is each their worse dream?" Othmar had merely rolled his eyes. "Not possible in three weeks," he said. But get him on the do-able and you couldn't shut him up!

"I'm aiming for stylized movement and hope it won't come out mannered," he informed her. She hid a smile. "One more glass?"

Then, one afternoon, Fleur Francis arrived to work on her choreography for the principal singers and the girls in the gingerbread chorus. She carried a pail of water and several students followed with big cartons. The first box she tipped forward, spilling footwear out onto the floor. "Clogs for the girls," she said, "but not in all sizes. For you playing boys, take these," and she held up a pair of long, leather-soled socks, "which you will put on over your sneakers and bind around the legs with this," and she held up a long leather thong. "Then you will wet, but not soak, the soles." Out of another carton came stiff leather shorts for the Hansels and wide dirndls for the Gretels. "Time, children, to learn how to walk."

The first week of his residency, Othmar had caught Fleur before the dance studio mirror trying out some unfoldy dance thing with flailing arms. "And fraught with meaning," finished Kay. Fleur was tall and willowly, and while Othmar would be the first to admit he didn't know much about dance, he thought she was too languid to excite the eye. Kay, in the kindest way, suggested that Fleur was without humor. "They are the worst, aren't they, because they are apt not to see things except their way."

Their feet deadened and their legs muddled by costume, the students stepped back in time. They were to skip as they danced, Fleur told them. "Running or jumping is about the only way you can move on grass. Hands up, if you know how to waltz?" A few admitted to "ballroom dancing."

"Well, the waltz originally was a bouncy peasant dance done on the village green. It was not until it was brought indoors and danced on smooth floors in nice shoes that it became gliding." Fleur grabbed Othmar. "May I have this waltz?"

Of course, he had to dance with her and he had to put a smiling face on it. He never forgot the surprise and the horror, the revulsion at being embraced, and pulled along, as Fleur loudly counted the steps. Fleur was wrong to do it, wrong to embarrass him before students he was there to teach, wrong to interfere. Her sense of possession! Like a cat that won't leave your lap. And Kay was wrong not to take his side. At first, Kay was indifferent, merely grimacing and saying "Fleur has a tendency to lead, doesn't she." When he persisted, Kay grew annoyed. "Drop it, will you?" she snapped. "You'd think you'd been raped!" And, then, fatally, something else happened. Kay, who liked to say she prided herself on her cooperative nature, began to compete with Fleur.

The first confrontation was over the staging of the Angels in the second act pantomime. Shy eight of the fourteen guardians that Humperdinck specified, Fleur had borrowed the more limber of Kay's voice students.

"It will never work for my singers," Kay informed Othmar when Fleur ventured for idea for what she called interpretive dancing. "I know their limitations," said Kay. "They can't strike poses going down a ramp in the dark and waving their arms."

"Well, why not?" asked Othmar, beginning to take sides. "Ever seen how they move to rock!"

"Writhing is more like it."

"But I've watched you teach and your kids are exceptional the way you've freed them to move and sing. Do you know how long it took me to learn I had a body? I wish I'd had you."

"It's distracting, what Kay intends. Artsy. No! I want them coming serenely down the ramp two by two till they circle the children. That's the way it's always done. That way, the music is allowed to build. Nice and simple."

Othmar was at a loss. Fleur's way accomplished the same effect musically but visually it could be stunning. Until this week at Tate, he felt everything had been going his way. His "investment" of wine—Gilly groaned that it was cheap stuff—had assured him of Kay Seelye's welcome. She was "a happily married lady," she announced early on, and her husband was a "snow-hating" archeologist named Lawrence Casper (Cal) Cornog who used the Tate inter-sessions to shepherd his seniors to Arizona to dig "and he to delve," said Kay. Kay was fun, a "new ear," as she reminded Othmar, for his tales for the greater musical world beyond Tate. "How did you wind up in this dump?" he had asked, and she sang thrillingly "Where thou goest I follow," and, looking sharply away from Othmar, said that a career on the stage was not for her, and upon meeting Cal in Chicago—where she was on tour with "May Time"— she had fallen "headlong" not so much for him but the implied promise in marriage to him that "slow and steady wins the race," and that took them to Tate. In the event, they were childless and Tate gave them all the children they needed. A popular couple, she and Cal lived in one of the faculty bungalows across College Avenue from the old campus. Cal had built his department into a specialty of sufficient importance to justify him time away from Tate. "And anything musical I have a hand in." All this came out in dribs and drabs over the wine, Othmar listening intently, hungry for more gossip— there was little else to do at Tate—and she rationing her "war stories," and giggling, when, alone and she was making ready for bed, that the range of her particular voice could just about squeak through "Sheherazade." Othmar was not for her; and as she was not sure what sort of cat she had hired to stage "Hansel," she was glad she warned him earlier about Tate, town and gown. "If you do drugs," she said, hoping that was the current lingo, "don't. The cops here are pretty understanding about booze and girls, but then it gets tricky, and I'm sure you'll get the hang of it."

Fleur was very different. Nothing came easily, and she was apt to defend her smallest victories. Watching her play guitar one evening when rehearsals ended too late for dorm dinner and the Gretels dragged him to the coffee shop, Othmar watched Fleur with fascination. She frowned as she played, and her anxiety only increased when she had to accompany a singer. She was in many ways a "solo act," as he put it to himself, and he wondered what pleasure performing gave her. Kay still missed the stage, he was sure. But for marriage to her precious Cal she would be out there somewhere, in operetta, in summer stock, touring in bus-and-truck packages of Broadway shows, everybody's friend and confessor, "Miss Congeniality." On the other hand, "Miss Gloom and Doom," as Othmar thought of Fleur, was lucky to have washed up at Tate.

So he was ill-prepared for the Fleur who presented him with a stunning way to stage the Angelic host. She had sent a student to fetch him to her studio and he went warily, thinking of the waltz. Shutting the door against the student, she sat him down. On an easel stood a spiral-bound pad of artist paper, and by flipping the sheets rapidly she contrived a crude but effective way of animating the flow of dancers. They would wear simple, sleeveless columns of jersey down to the floor. Fleur flipped on the tape recorder. In a low voice she counted steps and marked them, as dancers do, with hand flops. As the Angels came down the ramp (and she began to mime) they were to swoop low and stretch high as though fluttering to alight. Their wings were designed to do two things, she said. When spread wide, they looked like the conventional feathers of an Angelic host. But as the Angels circled Hansel and Gretel, they gently drew their wings across themselves (more miming) and the reverse of the wings was not more feathers but a lacy tangle of leaves and vines.

"My way, this way," said Fleur breathily as though she might cry, "the Angels become one with the woods and they make a bower to protect the children."

There was a long hush.

"Slow curtain," said Othmar nodding intently. "Beautiful."

That Kay "got" the Angel staging a little too quickly might have raised a warning signal but Othmar, eager to get on with the last act and his ideas for the Witch's Oven, was relieved and distracted when, not a moment too soon, the Stryofoam arrived.

"Come and get it," Othmar cried, tossing big white cubes in the air. As a plaything, the crusty slabs and blocks were new to the students and the boys immediately built a clumsy fort which the girls not very seriously attempted to demolish. Cutting and dressing the "stone" for the Witch's Oven absorbed all. As for the Witch's House, the old flat, newly repainted, needed only a light application of Styrofoam "candies" and these the girls conjured up from memories of the gingerbread houses that their mothers built every Christmas from instructions in women's magazines. This led to excited talk about making gingerbread men for the cast party after the opera. "We'll have a bake-off and please will you be the judge," said a Hansel appealing to Othmar.

There remained to design what the opera libretto described as a "hedge" of gingerbread figures between house and oven. When the Witch meets her just desserts, the hedge comes alive to reveal the real boys and girls the Witch has baked into gingerbreads.

"Any ideas for the hedge?" asked Othmar secure in the knowledge he had his own plan.

A boy put his hand up. "Oreos. Or sandwiches. Hoagies. The stretchy stuff, Spandex."

"Whoa there!" said Othmar.

The boy persisted. "So you see them trapped inside the gingerbread, and it's like cookies out of the oven, and they haven't hardened, and Gretel is just in time."

The girls cheered at this. The boy, a lanky kid with bad acne, was sort of their pet, and if you had to come up with a neat idea, you asked him, you asked Tommy.

"The hedge," Tommy finished triumphantly, is like the Witch's clothes line."

"Take that man's name," said Othmar and they laughed.

Tommy, when not festooned with girls, hung about with a boy called Pete who led Othmar to a boy called Joe who was the lighting whiz. The idea that rocks groups had to have light shows had percolated to Tate, but as Tate and environs could field only three bands and Joe had bedazzled all with strobes, he was looking for pastures new. Othmar would look back on the couple of intense days he spent with Tommy and Pete and Joe as his best at Tate. "If she had just kept out of it!" Othmar would remind himself. His sadness was his age. It bothered him he was never able to buy his "kids" a beer. He was then well into his thirties and they were, not quite, the age of a son, if he had married, but, even so, of a whole different generation. They called him Mister Othmar and said "See you around" and for the first time in his life he felt old.

But he had felt in on the dawn of the new when he listened to Tommy explain how to make the gingerbread people work. They were to be clothed, head to foot, in stretchy brown nylon or whatever Spandex was.

"See, it stretches," Tommy began. "The more it stretches, the more you see what is inside. Like when you put your hand in pantyhose. So you see the real people, the kids the Witch has baked. There are ways to light them so the Spandex is opaque."

"You light from the front," said Joe.

"In other words," said Othmar, "you can make it so the audience sees some gingerbread people all finished, the ones in the brown Spandex, front-lit, and some gingerbread people right out of the oven and drying, the translucent Spandex, back-lit, and that tips the audience to what'll happen if Gretel doesn't act."

Tommy had another suggestion. The figures would have to stand still for most of the third act, with their arms out—like gingerbread people. That was tiring, and the kids might get dizzy or get prickles in their arms. "Their arms go to sleep," Othmar put in. If the hedge had a low fence, said Tommy, they could grasp hold of the top railing, and that would also help them stand still.

"Could be expensive," said Tommy. Neither he nor Othmar had the vaguest notion of what Spandex cost or where it could be procured. "Tell you what," said Othmar, "Miss Francis will know about stuff for costumes. She's doing the Angel wings. Deal with her."

Then Joe slid his ideas forward about a lighting plan. He could do fire (for the oven). In fact, he could wire the oven so you thought you saw red embers. He would save the strobes for when the Witch flew.

"She's going to fly, isn't she?"

"Tell me more," said Othmar.

Pete took up the plot. He—they—whoever (Othmar was never sure and didn't care) flew this kid across the stage for a rock concert and one time they flew two kids at once. "They're suspended on wire from the scenery pipes and you travel them across, left to right or right to left, like they're a window curtain, and if you want to bring them forward it back you pull on their harness. All it is," said Pete, "is a swing like you put babies in."

"Good morning, Miss Mouth," caroled Othmar to Kay the next morning when he brought coffee to her voice studio. Rosina Dainty Mouth was the name given the Witch in an ancient G. Schirmer libretto and Kay loved to compare translations of the original German, *Knusperhexe*. "It means 'Nibblewitch' and I've seen it given as 'Candychops' which stresses her teeth. I blacken one or two mine to make it look like she chaws. The French call her *Rosine la gourmandine* which tells you right away she's piggy. But there is something revoltingly genteel about Dainty Mouth that I love. Can't you just see her flourishing a 'serviette'!" This was the Kay Seelye who lightened Othmar's heart and inspired. If he ever staged "Hansel" again, if he ever had to, he would remember her ways of teasing aspects of character out of the merest textual reference.

"Good morning, Mister Wind." This was Kay's and his joke about the possible reference to farting in the third act, a reference they decided not to share with the students.

"Good news! I've thought of how to make the Witch fly without you."

"But I do fly! I gallop around on my broomstick and I fly."

"You don't. Not in the air, and anyway you couldn't and still sing. We'll use a double." As if that settled matters, Othmar opened the piano-vocal to the place where the Witch vanishes for a time behind her cottage. "Thirty bars of music to fly your double. Then back he goes behind your Witch's House, and out you come hobbling, and you cross to Hansel and poke him to see if he has fattened up any."

144

Kay was furious. "Don't you think you might have consulted me?"

"It really is the director's call, Kay."

"And who's my double?"

"The kid named Pete. He's flown kids for a rock concert. Nothing to it, he says. Says it's nothing more than a swing. He has volunteered to do it. Hell, if he says it's safe, then it must be. Like packing your own parachute."

Kay looked away. He thought she said something like that not being the point.

A student knocked on the door. Usually Kay invited Othmar to watch her teach.

"Another time," she said. "We have work to do."

Three days later, Pete came to Othmar. "Miss Seelye has solo'd."

Miss Seelye had indeed solo'd. She had gone right to Pete, stated that she intended to fly and he should teach her. In no time at all, he told her about the stunts he staged for rock concerts and the trapeze act he was "skulling out." Kay was not surprised to hear he was an engineering major. "I'm in safe hands," she told him. Between them they designed a padded harness that would carry her without unduly pressing on her rib cage. The flying wire would attach to a swivel concealed in her witch's hump. "No self-respecting witch is without a hump," she joked.

To prevent her twisting in the air, Pete attached guy wires to each end of her broomstick. "Twisting is what makes you dizzy. That, plus we've got to maneuver you around the Oven and back behind the Witch's House," he said.

"Let's keep this to ourselves till we see if it works."

Late one night, Kay "suited up," as Pete put it, and was hoisted up little by little. The broomstick was a problem. Riding astride was holy hell (more than that she was not going to tell young men). It was also tippy. Down they lowered her. "We'll try sidesaddle," said Pete. That was at least bearable, and Pete had her grip—with both hands—the nag's head end of the broomstick. "We'll guy that end up higher than the tail end. Lean forward, and think of it as riding up a hill." When she found that her hands sweated and slipped, he gave her a pair of leather driving gloves to wear. She was impressed and touched by his concern. He was a "mothering" kind of boy, she thought, the kind who taught you as he went along, droning instructions, tugging and testing the wires, patting her the way she remembered her grandfather had dealt with cows or her father his small sailboat. She wanted to kiss Pete when he said, not quite looking at her, that she might want a hot shower later. "Awful lot of muscle strain when you fly."

"Mind you, I wouldn't choose flying for a living," Kay said when she filled Othmar in on her "adventure in space."

"I don't get you." Othmar's sigh was admonishing. "You—you who criticized Fleur for distracting from the pantomime music."

"May I remind you," said Kay tartly, "it was your idea to fly the Witch. We can go back to the old way. Illusion works just as well."

But something in Othmar would not let him disappoint his boys. "I forbid you to fly."

"Just try to stop me!"

And fly she did. News that Miss Seelye was going to fly undoubtedly helped fill the auditorium for the dress rehearsal. As Othmar knew it would be, the "dress" was the usual mess of missed cues and incoherent movement. He could tell which of Fleur's Angels were her dancers and which were Kay's singers, but it added to the home-spun air of the old tale. The costumes worked and he smiled as he heard applause when the audience saw the wings turn from angelic feathers into guardian greenery. Another time, he mused, he would play this behind a scrim and onto the scrim, just before the curtain, he would project an image of the whole sheltering forest. The Witch flew— "More or less," he muttered. The Witch's Oven blew up, just as he'd planned. Tomorrow, he would have another session with the Gingerbread people: They weren't quite quick enough getting out of the stretchy stuff. He would tell them they had to "slither." The less he said about the musical performance the better. The voices were slight and sweet and wobbly, even the young baritone as the Father, the only male role sung by a man. It was up to Kay to encourage her conductor-fixated cast to sing their way into character.

The things that could be fixed went much better on opening night. This performance had an early curtain so parents could bring young children, and, with satisfaction, Othmar looked out over a sea of shining heads and not a few little kids standing in the main aisle eyes riveted on the stage. When the Witch got her hands on Hansel, there was a wail like a siren and a small child had to be hurried out. "As it should be," Othmar said to himself.

The second performance had the air of a party. The cast invented an instant tradition: Everyone had to autograph the scenery.

Only Kay was out of sorts. "If God had meant us to fly," she moaned to Pete as he strapped on the harness and pulled her witch's costume neatly over it.

"You're doing fine."

It wasn't as scary as she thought. She had soon learned to keep her eyes open and focussed on where she was going. "Like driving a car," Pete told her. If the tension made her hoarse, it was only temporary, and perfectly in keeping for the sounds people expect from a witch. "You must never sing ugly," she babbled to Pete. "You must sing in the character of a terrible person."

"Right! Miss Seelye. All comfortable below?"

"Do you know the most interesting thing about the Witch? She's deaf. I suppose she has to be deaf for the plot, so she doesn't hear Hansel escape. But it's a clue for the sound I give her. On the sharp side of 'in tune' and I make it hollow, the way some deaf people talk because they can't center their tones. But the singing has to be precise. It's all pattersong. Wonderful, wonderful German tongue twisters all the way though the opera. We do try in English! And then the sheer surprise of the waltz, so pretty, and that other folksy dance."

Kay was conscious Pete had taken her hand and was stroking it. "Show time," he said. "You'll do just fine."

Together, they watched the women's chorus take their places along the hedge, arms resting on the hidden fence rail, and stiffen into gingerbread figures. Othmar'' instructions had been to look "blindly"out over the audience. "Preferably with your eyes shut but if that's disorienting, you can look out but down though your eyelashes."

When Kay appeared silently at the dutch door of her Witch's House, she could hear the audience quicken and the feather of applause as they realized it was "Miss Seelye." Oh! how she made her voice strip the Witch's candied manners. Oh! how she galloped around on her broomstick, the overture to her barnstorming act. She was manic, and the whole cast seemed infected, loose, daring. She heard her students crash thought the shell of timid competence and sing with one another. They rode the music. Grinning madly, she gave a thumb's up as she took to the air. Up she rocketed, Pete hauling on the wire that flew her. Up she soared, too quickly for the boy who guyed the broom end. With that wire slack, she began to twist and veer off course. To compensate, the boy on the handle end yanked his wire, which pulled the broom handle down and her with it. She was moving fast, plummeting as she swung out, and she screamed (the audience roared back). Pete played out his wire to bring her down but not in time. The broom was now a weapon and it scythed through the row of Gingerbread children, scattering all and sweeping two over the stage apron and onto the piano. Back she swung, still fast but lower, both guy wires now free and whipping lazily, and as she passed over the stage she smacked the fleeing Hansel who fell under the stage crew rushing in to tackle her.

Othmar ran for the stage. It was a tangle of bodies and fallen scenery. The foam plastic blocks of Witch's Oven batted at him. Wires grabbed at his ankles, and, snatching one up, he followed it to the heap on the floor that was Kay Seelye. She was wimpering and bled from the neck. Pete was trying to free the flying wire from her harness.

"You wouldn't listen to me," Othmar shrilled down at Kay. "It's all your own fault." There would have been more: He needed to get it said. But there came Pete's roar and his lunge. Othmar went down. Someone—later discovered to be Fleur—raced forward with a pail of water and dowsed them. Someone dumped the pail over Othmar's head and he fainted.

The blood on Kay Seelye's neck was from a shallow abrasion and that soon healed. But in her swoop across the stage, she had hit her windpipe severely injuring it. She never sang again.

14.

The rink lights were blinking at Broyle's. Time to go home. His anger nearly spent, Othmar felt physically calm again. Mindless exercise did it every time. By preference, he swam. He would look for a pool. A city the size of Pallas must have a Y, and if Pallas didn't, Albany would. He had only to smell chlorine for his shoulders to loosen. Swimming was private, and cleansing. In the rhythmic flow of water and the sputter of breath and spit, he worked his rage down and calmed his bitterness till it was far, far away, till it was the bright crest on long, low rollers. Roller skating wasn't swimming, but, as though one possessed, Othmar slept the sleep of the righteous.

On Tuesday morning, Othmar could look at himself in the shaving mirror and feel he had come through the worst. He was not a spiritual man, nor emotional. There was a good deal of his father's "seeing it through" and none of his mother's conviction that "every will turn out all right." He had not learned much from the people he hung around with. He could have used Gilly's suppleness in adversity—but who was Gilly to emulate? Gilly with money that would always bail him out. And his la-di-da manners. And his dangerous wife. There was no one in Pallas he cared if he ever saw again. He was frankly tired of Sarah Smythe and her pathetic stories in the Clarion Voice. Poor hapless Sarah, always trying to do good. Othmar wondered if it was laziness. Her Aunt Evey was another matter. Always around your legs, willful as a cat. Next year, when he came back to the Palladium, he would do things differently. The best Othmar wanted said of him was that he had grit.

"Here's looking at you, Kid Carson," he said to Tuesday's face in the mirror.

The breakthrough had come on Monday. It had been like no other day in the miserable weeks he had spent in Pallas. The good times began as soon as he got to the theater. Within minutes, a tractor trailer pulled up with the borrowed "Tosca" scenery in the box. Exactly on schedule. Moreover, whoever organized the loading was a man after Othmar's own heart. Drops and flats were placed in some sort of logical order. And each was properly labeled, so that when they came off the truck they could go directly to their appointed pipe to be strung and flown.

Best of all, in the very back of the trailer was the figure of the angel that Othmar had commissioned for the Roman landmark that crowns the Act III set. Under sculptor Anton Verschaffelt's great sky-parting bronze of the warrior angel Michael sheathing his sword to mark the end of the Plague in sixth-century Rome, Tosca's lover Cavaradossi will stare down death on the ramparts of the Castel Sant'Angelo and Tosca will leap to hers. From the wonderful bronze patina of the angel no one would guess that designers Herb Senn and Helen Pond had carved him from plastic foam, and Othmar joined in the fun as the biggest clown among the stage hands pretended he couldn't budge the statue, then one-armed it to the wings. Fun and games aside, the stage crew worked with dispatch. Othmar loved the concentration and chatter of techies hanging sets. Give them something to do and they did it. Singers, you had to persuade. Never in his life had Othmar seen a show go up so fast.

There was more to come. A pick-up truck backed up to the loading ramp. In it was the painter's platform for Act One—and the carpenter who built it. This was not due for two days. Together, Othmar and carpenter inserted the working wheels and pushed it up the ramp and into the wings. The carpenter had something else to show him. Three rustic ladders of various lengths. The carpenter said he remembered seeing them at a farm museum. The two longest were roofer's ladders, he thought. Awful lot of camber, but safe all right, and still used. Not for him: he had no head for heights. On loan: he knew the museum's staff carpenter and the museum was closed for the winter. Not exact copies but a good deal like the ladders in the photo of the painter's platform—and wood dowels of course. "Well, you wouldn't want aluminum, would you." If you lashed the two tall ladders to the platform and ran planks along through on the rungs, you'd get sort of an upper scaffolding like in the photo. Like painters still use to do ceilings, the carpenter said. Things don't change, do they. The smaller ladder was the ladder up to this upper platform. So they can climb up to paint the picture. The carpenter gazed around the stage. Opera?—was it like the operettas the high school put on? Othmar said he send him some free passes for the dress rehearsal. Everyone who helped on the production would get to see "Tosca." It would give Othmar his first audience.

All this while, Othmar was aware of Bill Potter, the stage manager, watching how he did things. Potts had just one question that day.

"Your Tosca will jump?"

"She swears on a stack of Bibles."

Potts appeared to think. "A murphy should do it."

And so it came to pass that at the next rehearsal Othmar had sets to work with. There was still considerable furnishing and set-dressing to be done. But things were taking shape. More than once he stood humbled that a production, his production, was springing to life. It put him in such a good mood that he decided he would, after all, take Evey Titus up on a table for Scarpia's room at the Palazzo Farnese. Throw her a bone, the bitch. Put it in the program book: Table courtesy of Evangeline Carruthers Titus. Because of all the work on stage, Othmar had postponed Monday's piano rehearsal to Tuesday. At the appointed hour, his entire cast stood assembled and was looking at him expectantly. Another miracle.

This too was owing to the fine Italian hand of Evey Titus. It need not concern us what exactly she said to dislodge the Scarpia and the Cavaradossi from her music room. Suffice it to say, she had a word with the hotel manager who hurried in a piano tuner to tune the upright in the hotel ballroom. A humidifier was rented. The room was at their disposal whenever they liked. Just an elevator ride away! So much more convenient, didn't they think? She may also have had a word with the Dettori, as one woman to another, as votive to priestess, as patron to performer. In the event, there they all were, the Italians and the Americanos.

"Da capo?" asked Ludwig from his piano bench.

"From the top!" said Othmar.

Yet another miracle. The Cavaradossi did not have to be persuaded to sing from the painter's platform. Up the ladder he bounded like a regular Tony Curtis. He'd come to the rehearsal wearing scraps of what Othmar guessed were costume. Black leather boots that swept up the calf. Tight dark pants. No jacket but a white shirt open at the neck and the sleeves rolled below the elbow. Sufficient to sketch in the romantic hero. Even better, Othmar saw a tremendous energy he could use in the staging. This would be a physical Cavaradossi to play off a static Scarpia. The one sexy and life affirming, the other the kiss of death.

With the utmost diplomacy, the Scarpia asked Othmar's permission to watch from the balcony. Another set of eyes, Bruno Cappetto suggested, would help Othmar spot what movement and gesture of the young tenor needed to be sharpened. For which offer, Othmar was grateful. It kept Cappetto at a distance.

"I need to look," Cappetto said to himself as he climbed to his vantage. And he was not disappointed: He was finally seeing for himself what he had suspected and prayed God was true, for in addition to a young glorious voice, the boy gave audiences a man to love. Some singers you believe in, mused Cappetto, and that quality has prolonged many a career after voice and looks have faded. Other singers attracted a following because they were difficult and there was the thrill of potential disaster. Every opera house buzzed with reports of Franco Corelli on his own particular calvary. There is more to opera than singing, as Capetto well knew. In his many years he had known singers who couldn't act and singers who got by on their acting. A singer that people loved—that was God's gift. That evening he toasted Luigi with a Rob Roy. "You may turn out to be more than a church singer," he teased. And to himself: *Grazie addio.*

The Dettori, too, was watching. She, too, liked what she saw. The audience will care for him, and care for me, because I care. She was under no delusion that Tosca was a very complex or every a very interesting character. But, and she thought she would take dear Bruno aside and have a little talk, it seemed to her that Luigi lacked a bit the finish of a true aristocrat. The audience must always sense that Cavaradossi is of high birth, a *cavaliere.* And that Scarpia, baron though he may be, is a cop. Poor Tosca, a peasant girl saved by the nuns and God's gift of a voice. Marriage? Impossible with *il cavaliere* Cavaradossi. Rita considered herself lucky to have found Victor. She remembered Francesca who swept off with a man she thought was a count and ended up singing in clubs. She would love making love to Luigi. Her last Cavaradossi was like wet felt. So long ago now! But the boy needed direction. Lover in the voice, aristo in the figure. She would say to Bruno, as a way of introducing the subject, that she was sure that the husband, *il marito della Signora Titus,* was of the cavalier class. Evey Titus was a never-ending source of speculation for the Italians. Rita Dettori had spent Monday with her. This, as the Dettori was not supposed to know, was as a reward for agreeing to rehearse. But, also, as the Dettori was not supposed to know, because *la signora* was frankly curious about the Italians. And, also, just a bit, because the great Mrs. Titus was lonely on her hill.

Evey's excuse was she was going to Albany to get her hair cut and wondered if *la signora* Dettori would like to see the city shops. The appeal was two-fold. The Dettori's name might not be known much beyond Trieste but neither had she ever performed in a city as small as Pallas, not even when, like Tosca offering the Madonna her bouquets and jewels, she gave her services if a Verdi Requiem, say, was a benefit for a provincial church's organ fund. So she was quite looking forward to the bustle and excitement of a great capitol, as Evey Titus gave her to believe this Albany was. Then, too, her mirror told her she needed her hair color refreshed. When Signora Titus appointed the hour of nine to meet at her house, the Dettori's taxi arrived before the grandfather clock had lurched into silence.

The two women drank their coffee in the library. Smiles and good-will and intuition got them over the language barrier: the Italian's archaic English was rather more comprehensive than the Titus Italian which lacked verbs to carry the nouns much distance. But words are seldom needed to enjoy a house. There isn't a woman alive who doesn't want to see how another woman accomplishes things. As audience, the Dettori was everything *la signora* could have desired; or so the Dettori felt. The butler's pantry was exclaimed over. She was right to have supposed on the evidence of the dinner party that there were a great many dinner services, if not all very complete. The linens in the linen closets—there were two, imagine!—were inspected and the Dettori allowed to stroke. It was to the photos in the Titus bedroom that Rita Dettori gave her most profound attention. She had known that Signora Titus was *una vedova*, a widow. Here were pictures of her beloved Samuel, Sam, Sammy. Army lieutenant Samuel Titus in uniform. Sam Titus in waders fly fishing. With Evey riding with the Carroll Hounds. Sammy holding their first baby. Sammy with many little children (all cousins) swimming in a pond. Sammy at bat at a picnic. He was angular and knobby, with a comically long, square jaw, not at all handsome in Rita Dettori's estimation, but she saw he was that other thing, a man above other men. What Rita Dettori read in the photos as icy disdain Evey Titus knew as shyness. Her eyes misted and she felt an arm slip into hers.

At five, the two returned from Albany. Pleasure first: they had their hair done. At the beauty salon, Evey Titus insisted all the hairdressers meet the Dettori and the place was soon an uproar, Salvatore, who was trimming la signora's thick silver crop, braying Italian across to the next cubicle where Arthur was doing the Dettori's color. She was Arthur's first diva. Word would spread. Then to business. They lunched at la signora's club. The Dettori was on show and Evey introduced her to this potential opera patron and that. Not yet announced, she confided, but there would be a gala dinner before the final, Saturday performance, and they would simply walk across the street from the hotel ballroom to the opera. It would be the most marvelous fun, and of course Gracie and Felicia (who ran Albany) and Kitty and Fran and Persis and Misha (who watched from the bridge table) would not want to miss it. To each and every lady the Dettori indicated she was deeply honored to be in their presence and in their country. "Ah! America!" she sighed. After the sixth or seventh rendition of these sentiments, Evey thought she detected a simper which distressed. Not easy to be "on" all the time, she thought charitably. Well, she had done her duty, and even enjoyed it. When she caught the Dettori giving an admiring glance in the mirror to her beehive newly restored to dark beet red, both women laughed. The Dettori giggled to her new friend: "Tosca has black vig."

Also in this week of weeks, Gilly began phoning Othmar every day, sometimes twice a day, and sometimes with actual news. That Hunan had really replaced Szechwan was worth knowing, no? And what did Othmar want Gilly to do about inviting the critics? Late in the game though it was? Gilly thought that at the very least he would sound out Mary Campbell of the Associated Press and see if he could get her to come up from New York. The nice thing about Mary was that her reviews were as much news stories as criticism, Gilly said. "She really reports. Unlike some of the music fraternity who write for each other. Though it would be terrific to have one or two squeal over Luigi baby."

Later in the week, Gilly was pleased to report Mary Campbell was "free, willing and able baker." There might be an AP photographer. Regional opera was suddenly hot. The Boston Globe also sounded interested. The Springfield, Hartford and Albany papers had it on their calendars. "Tosca" would of course be front page in the Clarion Voice.

"Linc King here." Well, the week was not without its irritating moments, and the Pride of Fairstead topped the list. How could a grown man still play goddam soldiers? Bet he didn't know one end of a gun from the other. Bet he never served. Othmar shied away from that: it would not do to have to talk about his particular exemption. This compulsion to dress up! How could he have exposed himself like that to a total stranger, lay goddam naked under a goddam sunlamp, if that's what it was. Got to have a screw loose.

"Rome, am I right? 1800."

"Yes, Linc. Rome 1800."

"Wanna know what I've found out?"

As if I had a choice.

"Two kingdoms."

Double the trouble.

"Think I can undertake to provide you with correctly uniformed officers for the big crowd scene. Bound to have been officers attending the church service for Melas's victory. Also Swiss Guards attending the cardinal. That'll really dress it up. 'Course, Melas is really beaten. By Bonaparte. But they don't know that yet."

Othmar was withering. "But you know that and I know that."

"Just wanted to get the story straight."

Lincoln King was not a man you could insult, Othmar thought.

"Wouldn't do to have the wrong uniforms. Parade-dress, I think, for church. The men will uncover."

"Just as long as they don't moon."

"Beg pardon?"

By week's end Othmar could permit himself to daydream about next year. He lay in his office "cogitating," as his mother would say. After the dress rehearsal and opening night he would have a better idea how the good people of Pallas took to opera. Certainly the box office response was enthusiastic. Could be simple curiosity about the theater. Not a lot else went on here in the winter except youth hockey. Geez! Could he stick it out, the two months it would take to put on another opera? He would budget for an assistant. He needed another body to run interference, to put distance between him and Evey Titus and the rest. He would insist on weekends off, he would get to the city, keep his sanity.

What should follow "Tosca"? He longed to do Mozart but he didn't think he was ready. A romantic comedy would be best. Tuneful. He remembered an "Elixir" from Chicago. A million years ago. One of the first operas he saw on stage. "L'Elisir d'amore." He relished each syllable. The elixir of love was, what? A glass of wine. It had a mercifully small cast. The girl was Adina, the soprano. Nemorino was the tenor. They'd swoon over Nemorino's *"una furtiva lagrima,"* the women would. Interesting that it was the women who bought the tickets. He would get the old bag on the radio to plug it with the Di Stefano recording. There was a comic basso: the quack doctor. He bet Alex Avery had a comic underside. Nemorino's rival for Adina's hand was a soldier, probably a baritone. Rollo Shaw would look the part. He didn't remember much about the sets. Rural Italy. Could be very pretty. There was a dance number for peasants. Was it a wedding dance? There must be a ballet school around here, or in Albany. Even if was a "toe and tap" studio. He'd have to look at the music. It might be that the chorus could double as the dancers. Much less of a "production" than "Tosca" but with great charm. Gilly could certainly find him a soprano. He would offer Nemorino to Luongo and hope that Pompelli would conduct. Nothing in the opera for the Dettori, who was a dramatic soprano, or for Cappetto. Othmar smiled a mad smile.

This week also Bruno Cappetto finally got to the golf course. The snows had not so much melted as dried and blown away. The day was sunny but soft, holding the promise of spring. Mario had rummaged around the Golf & Tennis and produced a set of clubs. Luigi Luongo would have to caddy. If they played the beginning of the back nine, they would be out of sight of the clubhouse but not too far from the hospitality of the kitchen.

So the two trudged off, the older man in his good, his only, black overcoat, which the younger man helped him in and out of for each shot. It was just as well they had their privacy. Cappetto had played half a dozen times in his life. We need not concern ourselves with his stabs at the game. They spoke in Italian and that will be translated here without any attempt to give the flavor of the language, for they spoke as they did back home in Trieste, in a Venetian gutteral that gave Mario pause.

Nor is it important to know at which hole Bruno thought it time to deliver Rita Dettori's message. Very fine, and very musical, his Cavaradossi, she had said. And so handsome! How well he looked on stage! A credit to his teacher! *Ma*, but. At this point perhaps more the *giovanotto*, the charming young man, than the *aristicratico*. Did he know the young Caruso desperately wanted to sing their first Cavaradossi? The voice was not yet secure and, worse, Caruso looked like a peasant on stage. No, Puccini wrote it for an aristo. You do see why that must be so? It is because Scarpia needs someone to despise. He, Bruno, would work on that with Luigi. It was nothing that Othmar would truly understand.

Suffice it to say that the golfers came upon a hole that reminded Bruno of a tiny stage. The back of the green was dark with bushy pines. Bunkers rose like amphitheater seats. The wind had died away: Luigi could sing without drying the voice. The time was ripe. Bruno unscrewed the tea thermos. Our last holiday, he said. Dress rehearsal was now set, one week away.

Then, to the point.

Your Cavaradossi, said Bruno, needs no help from me with our Tosca. She loves singing with your voice, and she can make love with you. She also loves how you make Cavaradossi tease her. Teasing is flirting. Tosca has no sense of humor. Always the diva. The leading singer at court. But she is human, and you understand that, you indulge her caprices. It is very attractive to watch. You like her, I think. She is old for a Tosca. She knows this. It will work. The famous singer, the younger man. I have seen the other way around. Our way has pathos. Time is running out for her. And for Scarpia, too. When Cavaradossi cries out *"Vittoria! Vittoria!* It isn't just tyrants who will be overthrown but youth will triumph over age. I feel this. My poor Scarpia is running to keep ahead.

And what he didn't say out loud: I, too, am running. It was never easy. I had a modest gift. Not one that interests a patron. My father's ambition for me was church singer. Steady work, he said. Learn the organ (he could just afford the choirmaster's fee) and succeed your teacher. I was lucky Victor liked me. Lucky it worked out with Rita. I must say I am simpatico. People like me. La signora Titus, yes, she will help. And this young Gilly. Beyond that, Bruno Cappetto's interior monologue stopped. Words would not form because he could not see the faces of his future, but well composed in his mind was the grand plan. Luigi would…would audition in New York. In Chicago, for the Lyric. In other American cities. And I, Bruno, will be his management. I will be there to watch out for his interests. It will be a living. Better to keep the money in the family. Invest for him. We have so little time.

Have you noticed (this aloud to Luigi) that the opera takes place in less than a single day? The noon Angelus to the next sunrise. The Sacristan starts the clock when he says the Angelus prayer. It is almost the first thing he sings. He begins with the filthy paint brushes of Cavaradossi. Then comes the Angelus bell. On his knees. What for? asks Cavaradossi. Your entrance and right away the two frictions. All we need to know. An artist! Bad enough! But, says the Sacristan, not to recognize the Angelus! Worse, to ignore it. One of those *volteriani*. A freethinker, like Voltaire. An intellectual. Yes, the Church is right to warn us of them. The Church still says that, and Bruno laughed. There is something to what Scarpia says. And I will tell you. I will tell you by asking who is this Cavaradossi who is such a threat to the Sacristan and his wretched life?

What we need to work on, you and me, is who this Cavaradossi is. I have watched Othmar. He tries. Othmar tries. But what can an American know about aristocrats? La signora Titus, perhaps. And you! Ha! For you, aristos are all fast cars. You will have a fast car one day. I know it! Today, we must make you Cavaradossi. Long cloak. The white shirt of the artist. Open at the neck, of course. Your height. The picture of the man. The way you take possession of the chapel. It's yours the way you toss the cloak at the painter's platform. Fast. Othmar understands this speed. Speed is sexy, he told me.

Now I will explain how to make the aristocrat. It is how you behave with two men, and then with Scarpia. Tosca has nothing to do with this. If you are not *cavaliere* by the time she comes on the stage it is too late.

Primo, first, the Sacristan.

It would be easier if the Sacristan was short and fat. I prefer that. We have no choice. You must disdain him for several reasons. He is a lay brother and you are a Deist, voltarian. He is a nosy pig. Undoubtedly a spy. Some Cavaradossis sweep the Sacristan out of their way, like a dust ball. I knew one who held a handkerchief to his nose. The Sacristan we have is too tall, almost as tall as you, a thin stick, a crane. With him I think you must play the gentleman. Your manners must be exquisite. But not sarcastic. You sing that you have painted the unknown lady at her prayers. Isn't she lovely! Include him, appeal to him, man to man. Be generous! Then, you sing: *"Dammi i colori!"* Give me the colors, the paints, my palette. Not as to a servant but as to a lover of beauty. Then comes the matter of the food basket. Fat or thin, the Sacristan is always hungry. Do you remember our old Collini? A crust after the morning Angelus, another at midday. Cavaradossi is always well fed. Dismiss the idea of food. But again, not meanly. Wave it away. Show me! For God's sake, don't make it limp. That's better. To show him you want to get on with the painting.

Now, the Angelotti.

The shock! Who would not be shocked. First, it is unexpected that someone is in the Attavanti chapel. Then, that this man is obviously in terror. All your reactions are the human reactions. Then, you think you recognize him. I do not envy you having to sing the only unmusical line in the opera. *"Angelotti! Il Console della spenta Republica Romana!"* *Spenta*, ill-fated; extinct like a volcano. Yes, yes, all right, but then Roman republic! Spare the poor singers the politics!

It is not yet revealed that Angelotti is the brother of the unknown beauty. But you know him for a liberal, like yourself, and for a gentleman. He is at least equal to you. Perhaps he is of noble family: His sister is married to a marchese, though we do not know that till later. He is older than you. He held the office of consul. You admire him. Your greeting must be heart-felt but with deference. I suggest you present yourself. Let him clasp you. Let us try it. I will be the Angelotti.

"Fuggi pur ora da Castel Sant'Angelo," Bruno Cappetto sang softly. I have escaped from Castel Sant'Angelo.

"Disponete di me." Luigi Luongo, in fuller voice, responded. Count on me. Yes, yes, try again.

Try again, and this time, spread the gesture out. You can't see yourself, but you are hiding your obeisance with your body. Cheat it, open it up. Think of the two of us as a shallow triangle, your hand on my arm lifting me up…and into…your promise. *"Disponete di me."*

About Cavaradossi's scenes with Scarpia, Bruno Cappetto had little quarrel with Othmar's staging. It is convention by now, he said, to follow the great Tito Gobbi and make Scarpia always the focus of everyone's attention. That Cavaradossi refuses even to glance his way deepens the conflict.

My Scarpia will try to engage you, to make you look. You must avoid. You will not have much room. The stage is crowded. Roberti, the torturer, is there. The judge who will year your "confession" is there, with his scribe to write it down. Three police agents. Scarpia's two henchmen. Tosca, who is beside herself and vying for his attention—and taking up twice as much space. The way a woman always will, thinking if she can just get you to listen. He feigns not to hear. I have not seen all of Othmar's set for this. He is to borrow tables from la Signora Titus for Scarpia's grand room at the Palazzo Farnese. Just where the tables are in relation to the door of the torture chamber we had better see before rehearsing.

But you and I will waltz, will we not, this dance of death!

15.

One evening Othmar came back to his rented room to find a large package propped against the door. It was addressed in his mother's handwriting and it contained the cloak she had made to his specifications for The Attavanti. She had followed every particular: the hood that tied with a flowing bow and, more important, the capelet that circled the shoulders and fell well below the elbows. The garment was good and full. The less that could be seen of the figure of a man the better. The bow would cover his adam's apple. By clutching the folds of the cloak from the inside his hands would not show. Underneath he would wear a dark turtleneck and dark pants. He had thought about shoes and decided upon plain black ballet slippers, which he now brought out from a Freed's box in the closet. Late as the hour was he practiced walks. To go on tippy toes gave lightness but also height and a sway, and the last thing he wanted people to think of was Jack Lemmon in drag. But a light speedy shuffle conveyed the idea of a woman hurrying in the hope of not being seen. From another box he drew out a tangle of blonde curls. In the morning, in better light, he would pin these in under the hood.

There was a note from his mother. She sent him "oceans of love with a kiss on each wave." She hoped all was going well. She knew he was too busy to write. Not having heard from him for a month she imagined he didn't expect her to come to Pallas for the opera. She assumed he wouldn't mind she had made plans for a bus trip to Florida with her bridge club. There were two possible reactions to such a letter. Othmar could have played the loving son to the hilt, could have immediately phoned her in Chicago, promised a plane ticket to Albany (or a compartment on the Lake Shore Limited that stopped at Pallas on its way to Boston). Such a son would have told her to buy a snazzy new dress for the opening and ordered a corsage. Othmar chose instead to credit his mother with knowing her own mind. He looked again at the cloak and wondered if he had told her what it was for.

The next morning he knocked on his landlady's door. His own closet, he said, could not accommodate the cloak. Could she keep it for him? She had recognized the package as a dress box but it would not have done to ask. Discretion was as much a seamstress's stock in trade as her tape measure and straight pins. Long before most people in Pallas, Mrs. Keohane always knew who was "in the family way" or had gained weight (no one ever got thin) or who was "making do." Mrs. Titus was one of those she sewed for, for whom new buttons and a new collar made an old coat new. Her lodger, she had learned through the Keohane family grapevine, had some connection to Mrs. Titus. Mrs. Keohane knew this to be so from her husband's sister Catherine, the waitress at Kulda's, and it was confirmed by their sister Helen who was the Titus children's old nurse. That mere servants would have a network as entangling as the social circle of the tyrant Titus and silly Sarah was beyond Othmar's ken.

Mrs. Keohane stroked the fine wool of the cloak and fingered the seams. Such fine work, she said.

"Put it on for me," she said. "I want to see how it moves. Go on! No one will see you." Her enthusiasm was so like his mother's.

"It's a costume for the opera."

"She must be tall."

"She wears spike heels. For the stage everything has to be large-scale and exaggerated to be seen."

Mrs. Keohane walked around Othmar squinting and tugging here and there. By any chance would he let her copy it? She could think of several of her ladies who might like such a cloak. One was an expectant mother. The bridal shop might be interested. Not necessarily in white but a color that would be good as an evening wrap. Had he noticed that so many people were having evening weddings? No? With sit-down dinners that followed the service. She wondered how families could afford it!

Othmar was not listening.

"How long do you think this took to make?"

She considered. Would there have been material to shop for? An existing paper pattern to follow? She seized the day. "Well, I could copy this in a week," she assured Othmar, knowing it would take her four days.

A handyman, by the look of him, answered the door when Othmar rang the bell.

"Missus Titus says yer to wait in the liberry."

Except for a far-off whine, which Othmar identified as a power drill, the house was silent. In daylight the library was far larger than it appeared in the evening gloom with Evey Titus reclining on her chaise longue and guests clustered around the fireplace. The room smelled of dead ashes and dog. He inspected shelf after shelf of uniform editions. Dickens and Thackeray and Trollope (of whom he had not heard) and two-volume sets of "Lives and Letters" (of more people he had not heard of). The books could use a good dusting. He poked a finger into a potted tree. Needed watering. It was cold and he shivered. As long as he lived he would never understand the Yankee indifference to warm houses. Gilly and Liz were always throwing windows wide open in their apartment high above West End Avenue. He longed for the city.

"It really is a night room." He had not heard Evey Titus enter. "The dark hides the high-mindedness. Though, mind you, I'm not sure how many of these books were read. None of the pages of Trollope were cut when my husband and I first read him.:

She presented Othmar with a large cardboard box. Its shiny white paper had yellowed and there were smuts she hadn't succeeded in rubbing off with her sweatered arm.

"They are old Mrs. Titus's fans from Paris. My husband's grandmother. I thought you might like to see if one would work for the Attavanti."

There were fans with feathers and fans with painted scenes. In its own leather case was a black lace fan with gilt handles and a jeweled clasp. The oldest one, Evey thought, was late eighteenth century and bought from an antiques dealer.

"They would be right for the period, I suppose, though I'll bet fan styles changed in the blink of an eye. Like hats and hair-dos. Tell me again: the Attavanti's fan is the one she drops, or forgets, not the one she may have left with the clothes to disguise what's his name as a woman."

"Angelotti," Othmar said a bit sarcastically (she ought to know the story by now). Did which fan make a difference? She was wasting his time. He had come to look at tables for Act II.

"Feathered fans were for evening galas. For day I think the Attavanti would have carried a light, pretty paper fan. Women did, of all classes. Cheap and colorful. Like this." Evey flipped open one in blue, banded with pink and yellow.

"But it had her crest on it."

"May well have had. Perhaps an embossed paper decal, or painted on. Anyway, it won't show from the stage. Or rather Bruno will make you think you see the crest."

Othmar found it interesting she was on first-name terms.

He picked up the antique fan. He knew nothing about fans. But the exquisite work of this one—painted scene of flirtatious couples dancing, pierced ivory vanes, gold ring and gilt tassel—and the charm of its fine leather box, excited his eye. "Would Tosca have carried this," he asked as casually as he could.

"It would be more fun to have her make a grand entrance with the feathered fan. Sweeping in. Can't you see her accosting Bruno, Scarpia, with the feathers!" Evey chortled. "Such a sweet man."

The feathers were of no interest to Othmar. He dismissed them. "For a gala, as you say. But as you know," he said heavily, "she is coming from the performance of a cantata."

"Something more severe? Like the black lace. Rita might like that, unless she has brought her own."

First names again. It annoyed him.

"The signora has yet to let me see her costumes."

Evey gathered that was a sore point. "I could have a word," she said without thinking. Her first mistake.

Othmar stiffened. "I am perfectly capable of asking to see them before the costume parade. It is my right as director."

"Why don't you take the lace fan along and see if that gets her moving."

"If you think so." Othmar didn't want to seem to be pushing. He let her hand him the black lace fan with its box.

"How is your own costume coming?" The question was Evey's second mistake. Othmar made his face a mask. He was about to lose his temper. He took a deep breath. To his knowledge only his landlady (and mother) knew the cloak had arrived.

"Nice of you to ask."

"Nice?" There was challenge in her voice. "Nice?" She appeared to muse on the word. She gave a steely laugh. "People who should know tell me the defense of libel is the truth."

What exactly that meant Othmar didn't know but he felt soft at the knees. He listened to the far-off power drill for a long moment. He became aware of the leather fan case in his fist. He gripped it harder, received its message, then relaxed. "Well, you are nice. Everybody knows it."

"Shall we look at the tables?"

The second act of "Tosca" takes place in a grand room in the Palazzo Farnese. To call it Scarpia's office is to put it in modern dress. It is his lair, the setting in which he operates as the power behind the throne. Rooms off it are for unspeakable activities magnified by our imagination. Through windows giving on to the courtyard we hear Tosca in her prime as court singer performing in a victory cantata. Scarpia's is a beautiful room, as beautiful as the set designer can make it. From production pictures of the scenery that Othmar was borrowing for the Pallas "Tosca" he knew it would impress the eye and reinforce Scarpia's opinion of himself as baron, chief of police and lover. Power is the greatest aphrodisiac of all. The most crucial pieces of furniture were two tables. Oh, there's a sofa onto which Tosca will sink and audience will marvel how beautifully she sings when recumbent and wrung out with despair. Many in the audience will admire her heaving cleavage. Legend insists, and history confirms, that in rehearsal the great Jeritza fell from the sofa and sang *"Vissi d'arte"* with everything showing. Puccini knew how to make a virtue from a fault and kept it in the staging. Compared to the tables, however, the sofa plays no part in the drama. The larger table serves Scarpia as desk and it is from here he will do the dirty. But as the act begins, he is seated at the smaller table partaking of dinner. So elegantly is he cutting his food and sipping the wine and patting his mouth with flowing napkin that you want to shake him. Evey Titus proposed to lend tables that would stand in for either, or both.

The table she suggested for Scarpia's desk was a heavily carved console. In style, the Victorian view of the Italian Renaissance, she thought. Othmar liked it for its bulk. It was ugly as sin, he thought. If he had only said that aloud, then he and Evey could have had a fine old time. She had to persuade him about the other table. "I know it doesn't look like much. It's eighteenth century, probably a card table. But it's the kind of useful table that Scarpia would have known and used. Servants would have brought it from wherever it was parked and they would open it up." Here, she splayed the leaves and set them to rest on supports. "Voila! Dinner for one, supper for two. Servants hovering with serving dishes. Pouring the wine—though of course Scarpia pours a glass for Tosca. The old letch."

Othmar, scowling, turned away from her setting of the scene. Of the many irritating things about The Titus, almost the worst was how much she had come to know about "Tosca." In an unguarded moment she would have said it gave her something to talk with her niece about, something friendly but neutral. Sarah Smythe's "going around" with the black singer was the talk of Pallas. Were they "dating"—horrible word!—she imagined people wanted to know. The answer to that, she had to admit, was, she didn't know. Sarah couldn't stop talking about him. And about the "gang," as she called the other American singers. They had all gone to Albany one afternoon to shoot pool. It was all a blur to Evey Titus which one was "Jonce" and why "Rolly Shaw" was probably related to the Fairstead painter. Sarah's slang was new. She "schlepped" places and things. Someone was a "schmuck," someone else a "schlemiel." Show biz slang, Evey guessed. Evey had no particular opinion about Alex Avery. He seemed nice enough. She couldn't imagine he had room in his life for her niece. That he was black was certainly not his fault but it did present potential for scandal. Not the same thing as Howard Titus who'd helped himself to other people's money at Titus Bank & Trust and mercifully, the family could cover the defalcation, but which, together with staking him to a citrus ranch just about wiped the family out. The true story about Howard was never known. Else there would have been a run on the bank. Evey Titus blamed her husband's early death—he was not yet sixty—on his worries over his younger brother. Pallas never guessed why the great Mrs. Titus pinched pennies. She used to say she had grown up as a Carruthers living "close to the bone" and that old excuse carried her through the worst of the Titus debacle. Sarah's fling, if that is what it was, was public. It was Evey's belief that girls in love ought to look radiant. Sarah looked reckless.

Sarah's "gang" at that very moment was finishing the ample breakfast cooked for them every morning by their landlord, the Baptist minister. His name was J. Weston Macadoo and he was divorced. His wife alleged he beat her. He had hit her, but just the once. Off she went with one of his deacons, and the kids, and his reputation. He was of an age when he should have been called to a major church in a large southern city. Instead, here he was, freezing his nuts off in Pallas and frozen out by the city's establishment. He had not been asked to join the Thursday Evening Club at which men dined and read learned papers. The G & T, even if his church countenanced membership, was for the country club set, for the Tituses who went to the "First Congo," never mind it was now the United Church of Christ, and the Carrutherses, who were Episcopalians. He had never lived in a city in which his church was of so little account. Pallas had separate Catholic parishes for Irish, Italian, and Polish; there was even Old German. It had two Orthodox churches, Greek as well as Russian. And two Jewish congregations. It was too far north for Presbyterians but there were Methodists and Lutherans. The Mormons were sniffing around. There were already two "fundamentalist" churches; but they never came to Rotary. He supposed he shouldn't complain: his church was well-attended and from time to time someone from the newspaper would interview him on ecumenical issues. But he was lonely. There were pastors who had to beat women off. Not here in Pallas, and he beginning to entertain shaming thoughts of "going over to Albany." More than that he would not allow his mind to put flesh to. He was in the full vigor of life, a good-looking man with a long strong nose and a high forehead over which fell a dark lock he would dramatically toss back. Alas for his career, teleministry was still in the future.

The mornings that Macadoo didn't flip flapjacks he did eggs "anyway you like" with hash-browns. There was always a pound of bacon, which he baked, and endless cups of strong coffee. The maple syrup was local, sap from the trees of Linc King. Had he but known, Othmar would have said "sap from the sap." But just as he avoided dining with the Italians, Othmar did not seek an invitation to the Macadoo breakfast table. His reasoning was impeccable: If you socialize, you get friendly, and if you get friendly, people take advantage and what you to do it there way. He was pretty sure, anyway, that the Americanos were a tight bunch. Performers tended to be.

On this particular morning, Jonce Jones was asking the breakfast table the difference between "schmuck" and "gonif." Yiddish was an acquired tongue for the four singers and it was virgin territory for their landlord.

"The *lingua franca* of the theater," Alex Avery said in his polished way.

"You pick it up more around musicians," Ed Nelson insisted.

The four young men had little in common except Gilly as their manager. Gilly's statement to Othmar that they had worked together was a fib. If it hadn't been for breakfast they would not have been so pally offstage. Bent on their careers, they were busy learning new roles for other productions and music for concert gigs; and two had steady girl friends who visited on the weekends. They all talked shop. Jonce Jones had two important auditions coming up and they all got into the spirit. Macadoo gave him the key for the church's choir room, and Ed Nelson, who was a better than average pianist, played for him on the upright. To while away the "longeurs" (Alex Avery's word) and purely for their own amusement they had adopted Sarah Smythe. In part, it was to help Alex out: he was finding her constant attentions wearying. Jonce especially found her irresistible to tease. She had ten years on him and a bit less on the others. Still and all, she was so gullible that they treated her like the little sister you taught bad words to and would then parade in front of the grown-ups. Jonce thought he would try "putz" on her. The Rev. Macadoo was uneasy.

A car honked, Sarah's signal, and she was soon at the breakfast table drinking coffee and distributing doughnuts.

"Guess what!" And not waiting for an answer: "Othmar is going to let me be the Attavanti for the matinee."

"He's not such a putz after all," said Jonce, and Macadoo said to shush that.

Sarah would wear Othmar's costume and she would wear as high a pair of high heels as she could manage. "So we don't have to shorten the cloak."

"You will get to take a curtain call," said the Rev. Macadoo, enjoying her enthusiasm.

Celebrity made her generous and she dimpled at him: You ought to play the cardinal. A piece of cake."

The singers thought this was a fabulous idea. All costume and nothing to sing, though he would have to mouth the chant in the processional. The Rev. Macadoo demurred. He was he wasn't sure theatricals were…"Appropriate?" Rollo Shaw finished for him. That, too, but he also had no knowledge of how a cardinal behaved, never having seen one.

"There must be a priest you can take Catholic lessons from," said Ed Nelson who was singing the Sacristan and wouldn't mind a tip or two.

"Father Fioravanti," said Sarah. "He turned the cardinal down. Said it put his mortal soul in danger of something Simon said."

"I expect I said simony." The two clerics, Fioravanti and Macadoo, laughed. The priest had come to the rehearsal to help Othmar stage the great processional that concludes the first act. In the Titus way, Sarah had "had a word" with Othmar, and Othmar, now strangely open to suggestion, had picked up the phone and called Macadoo "to ask a favor." When Othmar said that Sarah Smythe should be given full credit for the idea, Macadoo felt relief flood over him. "What a wonderful girl!" he said to himself, and the notion of "going over to Albany" was put back in its box and the lid snapped shut. The opera would be over soon, and distractions like Alex Avery gone. He had watched Sarah with Alex. He sensed Alex's discomfort.

Elevation to cardinal had one other positive result: he gained a nickname. His boarders had not known what to call him. He was "The Rev" when he was out of earshot. The problem was when he was slinging hash. If "Mister Macadoo" was too formal, his given name of Weston was worse. Rollo Shaw came up with "Padre" and it stuck.

Came his first rehearsal and Weston Cardinal Macadoo, as Fioravanti called him, waited to make his entrance, a grand figure in a blast of scarlet, the color one with the office.

"Cardinal," called Othmar from mid-auditorium where he was studying the stage picture. Macadoo peered forward. "I can't see your face."

Othmar to Fioravanti who was sitting next to him: "I want the cardinal looking like one of those Spanish saints. I want him in religious ecstasy. I want it spiritual. The contrast with Scarpia, our villain, who goes on his knees for all the wrong reasons. Don't you see?" Fioravanti's experience with cardinals was limited to one chilly administrator.

Fioravanti to Macadoo later: "Tilt your head upward, like this, as though you were gazing at heaven."

Fioravanti, very much later at the dress rehearsal, felt a poke in the ribs. He had asked Father O'Grady from one of the Irish parishes to be his guest. "Do you see what I see?" Before them was a very Protestant, the Reverend Dr. James Weston Macadoo, as an unnamed Italian cardinal unknowingly aping a certain Portuguese prelate who lolled his head to one side.

"What was the Vatican thinking to give him Boston!" exclaimed O'Grady as he sat over a beer with Fioravanti. "Our good cardinal was a Christian Brothers boy, like myself, and the first English he was exposed to was their brogue. 'Course, it came across like stage Irish. They would think about his sainted predecessor and fall about laughing. And his Eminence so, well, I won't say black, but dark. And that head tilt! 'From looking at too many holy pictures,' even the priests joked. And here he's on stage to the life."

"Bless me Father for I have sinned."

But that is to anticipate.

Within minutes of Othmar settling with Evey Titus about the two tables, she sprang yet another surprise.

"You will remember I promised to lend our monstrance for the processional."

Monstrance was not a word Othmar knew; in a drunken stupor, he had heard it as "monster."

"What is it?" he now asked. She was about to tell him it was used to display the Host when in rushed Sarah Smythe, overnight bag in one hand.

"My floors are being refinished," she said as if Othmar had asked. He rejoiced he couldn't even remember where she lived—some dog kennel.

"Uncle Sam schlepped that home from the war," said Sarah dismissing the monstrance.

Schlepped? Othmar wondered where Sarah got that from. He looked at Evey Titus and caught her face stiffen. Ha! thought Othmar, the only Jews this family knows are Chinese, so it can't be that. His scalp tightened as his mind raced ahead. Words like that could only come from New York, from the theater, from the Americanos that Gilly had hired for him. So Sarah had heard about "Hansel" from one of them. But which one? Jonce Jones who had been at Eastman about that time, and Eastman was near Tate? Ed Nelson? Juilliard, where nobody's reputation was safe. As he tried to work it out, there came an explosion of laughter.

"The story gets better," said Sarah. "He won it in a crap game."

"Not quite." Evey Titus was annoyed. "Tosca" could not be over too soon. "My husband won it playing poker. There was terrible looting. By us as well as the Germans. He was afraid if he didn't play for it and win, it would disappear."

"And Lady Luck smiled," said Othmar, momentarily distracted from his new worry by the monstrance's seductive golden glow.

When the war was over Sam and Evey Titus went to Italy and retraced, as best they could, the route of battle. The courier they hired as interpreter told them the monstrance would have come from anywhere, but Sam Titus, remembering the night of the poker game, and the circumstances, thought the other office had found or "acquired" it that day. He had made a map marking all the towns within a fifty-mile radius. It was spring as they drove and the new green softened the rubble. Sam had good sharp pictures of the monstrance, professionally photographed to show detail. If this monstrance was a familiar part of his altar, a priest would know. But no one claimed it then, or later when Sam had a friend write about it for an art journal that took an interest in war loot.

"The supposition was, it came from a church bombed to smithereens. We saw two or three of those in towns where he had trouble even finding the priest. It didn't have to be an important church for a monstrance of this quality. They were often gifts from the local grandee. Or a memorial for a bishop who had been born there in humble circumstances."

"So romantic," said the old Sarah.

Sam Titus had not been much of a church-goer. The carol service on Christmas Eve was about the extent of it, and, as he got older, the funerals of friends of his father's at which he ushered. But he believed in belief and in those who believed, and he maintained a reverence for the rituals of faith. When his eye first fell on the monstrance he had to think hard what it even was. It was implausibly shiny, which told him it was gold. It was not that it was beautiful (he thought it too heavy for that) but he responded to its bravura. This monstrance, and perhaps they were all like that, was an engine, the bringing of truth to the faithful. Around the little chamber securing the Host was a plain gold ring. "Like a simple halo," Sam told Evey. The came a broad circular band composed of pointed staves pointing outward. "I think of this as a nimbus casting light." Then a third circle, wildly flaming, "an aureole, the wind, the word of God in the world."

In the years just after the war, the monstrance stood tall on a shelf in Sam Titus's den and was the subject of occasional meditation. Sam Titus had liked the thingness of things. He made up little stories about how the monstrance was made. In one of his fantasies the great Benvenuto Cellini was a consultant at the casting. But his art-history friend said it was nowhere near old enough to be sixteenth century. More likely, nineteenth, and probably late. Then his father died and he inherited Spring Side with its belief in another, a worldly power, and he put the monstrance on a console in the main reception room and thought "it fit right in." When Sam Titus died fifteen years ago, plans to repatriate the monstrance died with him. If Spring Side didn't become a historic house museum, which was one scheme, Evey Titus was going to leave the monstrance to Father Fioravanti.

"Don't go by me but ask Father Fioravanti where the monstrance comes in the procession. All I can remember is, it's held high so people can see and bow their heads."

Othmar wasn't listening. He still clutched the box with the black lace fan but that paled next to the possibilities of "liberating" the monstrance. There were dealers, he was pretty sure, who bought church decorations, for he thought of it as such. Would he do better selling it for the gold? The money would give him a cushion. So fixated on this scheme was Othmar that he really didn't hear Evey Titus say she would keep the monstrance for now and he could fetch it later.

"The finishing touch, don't you think!" Sarah almost had to shake Othmar to get his attention.

Like one crashing awake he gave a great luxurious stretch. "It's so beautiful," he murmured. "You are so good." This was said to Evey Titus, and for once he meant it. He felt he ought to do something nice for her. There was nothing in the opera at his disposal beyond a credit in the program.

"Have to schlep off now," said the new Sarah.

That word again! There had to be a connection. If she were handled delicately, if he tried friendship (perish the thought!) she might gossip, spill the beans. He didn't need to know how they knew, only who knew.

"Wait, Sarah, wait!" Othmar called, and offered her the part of the Attavanti at the Saturday matinee.

"A piece of cake," he promised. "You got the dress rehearsal and opening night to see how I do it."

16.

The Wednesday which Othmar awoke to was grey and bleak. By the time he parked at the theater, it was coming on to snow. Just his luck! he groused. The weather, he could feel in his shoulders, would play holy hell with today's schedule. The chorus, he just knew, would show up late for the costume parade. So would the others. It would be another long day. He already worked most nights till midnight, and on other nights he rollerskated. Opening night of "Tosca" could not come soon enough. There was more grey in his hair when he looked in the shaving mirror. "Boring!" he said to his face. "You're boring me. Boring, boring, boring." The razor bit back and tears came.

In the six weeks that Othmar had made the manager's office his own, it had taken on the properties of a working theater. With the greatest satisfaction he could gaze at seat charts for the four performances and know that "Tosca" would sell out. For someone preternaturally neat and tidy, he relished a certain professional clutter, oddments like the pile of gels left behind by the lighting crew, an orphaned piano-vocal, his stopwatch on a a day-glo lanyard. And always, his lists. Ready for posting in the chorus dressing room were costume sketches with lists of who wore what and who would dress when. Another list concerned wigs and still another, makeup. When he pressed open the little door in the office wall which concealed the secret shelves, he reveled in the buttery smell from the sticks of grease paint he had stashed there. She, the Attavanti, would have pink cheeks. Pink was pretty. Tosca was not. One whole wall was devoted to rehearsal calendars. He charted choral rehearsals, and boychoir rehearsals, full orchestra and section rehearsals, cast rehearsals. There was one rehearsal (in Fairstead) of the colonial militia company, The Pride of Fairstead, Abraham Lincoln King commanding. The Pride of The Pride phoned almost daily.

"Linc King here." To which Othmar longed to reply. "Why, hello, Hayseed!"

"The men are unhappy."

That's a crying shame.

"That they cannot wear what they perceive as proper uniforms."

Tough shit.

"I've researched it. Rome in 1800."

"So you've said."

Othmar, who only wanted the company for their muskets, tried to paint the picture. "If they were soldiers on parade, Linc, I'd say yes. Uniforms are fine for the church scene. As we agreed, if you remember. But in this scene, in the grand finale, if you will, they are an execution squad. Bang, bang, bang. And I wouldn't be surprised if they were hired guns. Nothing Scarpia wants to advertise, if you follow." And draping Abraham Lincoln King in the old Red, White & Blue, Othmar added: "It's not like here in the good old U.S. of A., where there would have been a public trial."

"Stop me if I've got it wrong," said Linc who still wasn't hearing, "but shouldn't they look like soldiers?"

To the extent of the costume budget, as Othmar didn't tell him. "Could they wear the equivalent of fatigues? And those strap things?"

"Bandoleers."

"Right," as Othmar well knew but didn't care to let on. "And, Linc, you carry a sword to give the signal to fire. And the pistol for the coup de grace, which, as you know, you don't fire."

"I don't finish him off so Tosca thinks it's all going to plan."

"Ri-i-ght, Linc."

"'Course, I do have those dark jackets with frogging. Nondescript as to period, but soldier-like."

I'll soldier you, Nature Boy.

And when the housekeeping details for "Tosca" began to wear on him, as increasingly they did, he took an intermission and turned to the delights of planning for "Elixir."

"Maestro," he said to Pompelli while waiting for a rehearsal to start, "would you conduct if Luigi does Nemorino?"

A charming opera, Pompelli agreed. He laughed merrily. "Everbody in America discover Donizetti. *Bel canto*, everybody want *bel canto*! 'Lucia.' 'Stuarda.' A long time ago your friend in Boston do 'L'Elisir.' Nice for young singers."

That was lead Othmar was looking for.

"I was thinking about next season. As a contrast to 'Tosca' to do a romantic comedy. With Luigi as the Nemorino. Alex as the Doctor. Ed as Belcore." As soon as he said those names he realized he had not yet "investigated" what they knew about "Hansel." He hurried on: "Gilly tells me he has a couple of sopranos I should hear for the Adina." That would come as news to Gilly.

"Don't forget the Giannetta."

"Her, too. It's not a big cast. We might be able to tour it, Maestro. Take it to one or two colleges. We avoid having to deal with unions that way. Two acts but four scenes, but I have an idea about sets that would travel OK."

Pompelli then asked such specific questions about preparing the orchestra and chorus that Othmar got his notebook out. "Elixir" could just happen! Othmar welled with happiness.

"Don't say anything just yet. I have to present the idea..."

"To la signora."

"Among others," Othmar said sharply.

"It's Evey Titus calling." As if he didn't know the voice.

"I have the monstrance if you'd like to come by this morning for it."

He was about to tell her there was no need for the monstrance in the costume parade but she rang off. No peace for the wicked, he murmured and made for his car. But there were constant interruptions, not least of which was Sarah Smythe "popping in" on her way to the paper. She just had to thank him again for letting her play the Attavanti. No good deed goes unpunished, Othmar said to himself when she "schlepped off." And: She knows who knows.

But then came almost welcome distractions. The fire department's safety officer phoned about stationing a man backstage during performances. The box office manager let himself in: Time, he said, to bestow the tickets that Othmar was holding back as comps and press seats. He and the box office guy debated over where to seat the critics. In a theater like the Palladium with a decent rake to the auditorium, Othmar himself preferred sitting further back. "Back of the cross aisle, I think the sound comes together better, also the stage picture."

So it was late morning when he arrived at Evey Titus's. As if she had been watching for his car, she opened the door. She was wearing a heavy coat and Othmar's first thought was that finally her goddam barn of a house had gotten too cold for her. On a bench inside the front door was an old tweed jacket covering something.

"It's Maida," she said, stroking the jacket. "I wonder if you could take her to Brielman's for me. He's expecting her." Othmar made the mistake of meeting her gaze. It was cool, untroubled, unnerving, merely the request to a servant to run an errand. She held the car door open. "Don't bother to bring the jacket back."

The driving directions to the vet's were accurate as far as they went. He was to turn left off South Main and take the third right and go straight on that to three large brown barns, can't miss them, on the left. What Evey Titus neglected to say was how far Brielman's was from town. His was a country practice and he was the last of the old time veterinarians, farming his land when not worming dog or summoned to difficult calvings. "How is Little Mother?" he had asked tenderly of Evey Titus when she was in the House of Mercy nursing her first baby. Generations of Titus animals had gone to Brielman's in sickness and in health. All their carriage and riding horses ended their days there, some so long ago that he had put them down by standing the poor old nag in his gravel pit and shooting it between the eyes. A quick release by hypodermic needle awaited Maida. Othmar drove on and on. Miles and miles, it seemed, and was, an eternity with clouds lowering and snow whitening the open fields. He cranked the Rambler's heat up. Maida's shivering ceased.

On his left he passed what he took to be a golf course. It was the G & T— though there was no sign to mark it (and Evey Titus had not taken Othmar there for dinner). All his concentration was on the road, now narrow and slick. There was suddenly a foul smell and, when Othmar looked over at his passenger, he saw a brown puddle forming on the seat. He swerved off the road and stopped. He leaned out and retched, got out and retched again. He let the snow dance in his face. It was powerless against the stench, his and the dog's, but a comforting anger told Othmar what to do next. Serve her right! Goddam bitch.

"And you make two!" he roared at the bundle.

With a vicious heave he threw Maida and jacket into the ditch. He drove back to Pallas with all the windows open. He desperately needed a swim. At his rented room he took a long shower and gargled and gargled.

At four he went to the theater, grateful he had work to do. He had called the costume parade for six. Othmar was not unmindful this was dinner time in Pallas but he needed to rehearse the processional in costume. The extras began arriving at four-thirty, mostly women and many of them the wives of men in the chorus. A spring snow like today's would bring New Yorkers to their knees but it was nothing in the country, and, besides, having achieved the elevated status of costumed extras, the good people of Pallas felt a "dress parade" was a thrill not to be postponed. The lobbies were soon deep in piled coats and boots, and children roamed while their parents disappeared into the big dressing room below stage to be transformed into pious Romans on a hot day in June 1800.

Othmar knew that borrowed costumes, such as these were, could be a bargain or a headache. The purpose of the dress parade was to see what was missing and what would have to be contrived by skillful draping and pinning. Doubtless on this date in history the Sant'Andrea della Valle would have been crowded with people from every level of Roman society. For Othmar on a budget, there were only two kinds of women: those who did not require wigs and those (few) who did. The former would drape whatever they had over their heads, a neck scarf, say, or shawl, and draw it tight so that no hair showed. These women were either servants or wives of the "poor but honest" working classes. To give variety to this mass of humanity, Othmar liked to introduce the odd character or two. He had more than enough volunteers for the young wife far gone in pregnancy. "Does your husband know?" he kidded as he patted her belly, and a squeal of laughter went up. The role of "crone on a cane" was soon filled. To qualify as one of the "hats," as the costume people called them, you had to have long hair which you could wear up or gathered on a knot. Over this was tossed a light veil such as women of the prospering classes might chose to wear on the street. There were only two or three chapeaux at Othmar's disposal, each with ringlets attached. He grabbed one and placed it on the head of an older woman with (he blenched) the fine white skin of Evey Titus. "You'll play a proper young miss," he said, "and you'll be chaperoned by," and he reached for a "servant." There was a pleased demurral from the "young miss," and more laughter, and Othmar's ears should have buzzed that night with all of the talk of him at Pallas kitchen tables. He did the impresario bit very well, and he knew it.

The boychoir from Albany also thoroughly approved of Othmar. Six weeks ago he had told them that any boy who had his hair cut before the performances would not be allowed to sing. The same went for the singing men.

The male extras did not have nearly so much fun, defined as they were by which of them wore shoes and which, boots. As for their hair, nearly all were issued hairpieces. The Reverend Weston Macadoo was much relieved that his cardinal's cap came complete with wispy white locks. He was beginning to wonder if his stage debut as prelate was the harmless fun Sarah Smythe made it seem. As the spare Attavanti she would wear blonde tendrils that fell from the hood of her deep blue cloak.

Then Othmar seized a folding chair and stood on it. He clapped for attention. "Listen up!" That got a laugh from the men. He was going to explain how he wanted them to enter the church and process to the altar. They would all file up the stairs from their dressing room and enter from stage right. "I know it sounds confusing but that's from the left as you look at the stage. It's the point of view of the actor not the audience." So arcane a theatrical convention awed them and there was respectful silence. It was finally going to happen, this opera, and they pressed into a tight crescent around Othmar.

Altar boys come first, he said, then the crucifer, the cross-carrier, with the candle-carriers, then the boy choir and singing men, then the priests, one lofting the monstrance, and finally the cardinal. The first people in the procession were to walk toward the audience and made a shallow sweep to their left, "stage right, that is," as though going to the main altar. As this happened, parishioners were to crowd around to watch. "Remember to genuflect as the crucifix, the cross, passes you." He would explain later about the monstrance.

"You, the procession, are headed toward the high altar." He paused. "The audience," and here he gestured toward the auditorium, "can't see the high altar, and, in fact, we will not have a high altar in this production—the stage is too small. But the audience"—another gesture—"will assume that is where you are going. Why? because that is where choir boys and priests always go. The audience does not have to see the high altar to know it is there. But they do have to believe it is there. And that's where you come in. It's how you behave, how you walk. It's very, very important. You carry the audience with you. You complete the illusion of the stage picture."

Othmar's audience hung on every word. He did not think he should diminish their sense of importance by mentioning the theatrics of Puccini's curtain. With the candles flaming and the cardinal looming, Scarpia drops to his knees and makes a showy obeisance. The curtain falls like an axe.

"Let's see you do the processional," Othmar called. Down they trooped to the dressing room, reversed and lined up. Othmar walked backward ahead of them and then like a traffic cop shunted them on an oblique line across the stage. He clicked his stopwatch. They would need to rehearse this with piano to get up to tempo. It was only a few minutes of music. But at the first attempt, either they rushed, and then piled up at the sweeping turn, or—because the costumes were strange on their bodies—they felt constricted and dragged. Othmar knew to expect this. The chorus badly needed a focus and Othmar decided he would place their usual conductor, Hunt Smith, in the wing to direct them.

When the rehearsal broke, the usual number of busybodies present in any endeavor came forward with their suggestions. Othmar heard them out. One was the important little man who wanted the route of the processional marked in fluorescent tape ("like an airplane aisle"). Can do, said Othmar at his most reasonable. But think how it would look from the balcony! he said. Sort of distracting, wouldn't it? he added. And, crushingly, "as though you didn't know what you were doing." The little man took his importance away. He had tried.

It had been a draining day and when Othmar got into bed, he fully expected to toss and turn. He would plan more of "L'Elisir." To his surprise, he fell easily into a deep sleep. He was not one who liked to dream. Gilly and Liz adored dreams, as Othmar knew from the days he slept on their sofa. What the other dreamed was a favorite topic of breakfast conversation. The stranger the better. "Like foreign movie you don't quite get," Liz would say. Othmar had yawned thorough accounts of the missed-exam dream, and the throwing-water-at-people-you-hate dream, and the walking-naked-on-Madison dream. "And nobody ever notices." Gilly could be counted on to wonder if they really did not notice. After all, you knew you were naked or shoeless, or whatever, and they, the people watching you were you in a way, because they were your creation. So it was you watching you. And practical Liz would always say not-noticing was the fail-safe that kept you from waking up. Liz, but not Gilly, had the dream in which she discovered she had a whole different kitchen, or dining room, she never knew she had. "I had my house-dream last night," she'd say, and Othmar knew they were in for minutes of excruciating detail. She was a connoisseur of house-dreams. "Edith Sitwell's father dreamed he found a whole new wing on his Italian castle." Was it because Othmar had talked to Liz earlier in the day that he dreamed what he did? He had wanted to blow up about the dog to Gilly but Gilly was in Toronto with a girl clarinet player. "He disapproves of women sucking in public," Liz said. "But she's hot. She does a jazz number in the second half. Miss Crossover."

Othmar dreamed he was on the Palladium stage. It was not really the Palladium, and he could not exactly identify the theater. It was sort of like the old Donnelly in Boston and he expected to see Sarah Caldwell rehearse Beverly Sills in a death scene on the filthy lobby carpet, probably Violetta's in "Traviata" with a singer he couldn't remember as Flora, and he must be clear about this, when he confided in them his problems with his Tosca, that Tosca's name was Floria, not Flora. But the lobby was empty and he only knew the theater was his, because the stage was set up for "Tosca." There were lighting cables all over the place, and he had one hell of a time getting those out of the way so he could move the painter's platform down center stage. Damn, but the wheels didn't move. He was also aware that the set for the Palazzo Farnese lacked the windows that Scarpia would order slammed shut. There were windows but they were dinky little sash windows—not the grand casements of a grand apartment. He saw a light in the stage-right wing. Walking over to investigate he found, on the other side, another stage also set up for "Tosca." There was a splendid high altar worthy of the Met or Covent Garden and, for the congregation, there were dozens of the little rush-seated chairs you see in old churches. Othmar had a quick think: If his procession turned stage-right instead of stage-left, he could use this set. He was annoyed to see a VW Beetle parked further down the main aisle of the church. That would have to go. The asbestos fire curtain was hung the wrong way around: the huge black letters proclaiming it a SAFETY CURTAIN faced the performers. But these were all things that could be fixed if he got a crew in early tomorrow. He thought he had better have a look at the orchestra pit. It was boarded over. He peered into the auditorium. Where there should be ranks of empty seats, he made out a shallow room with tables set up for Bingo. His mother wouldn't stoop to Bingo. There were cobwebs all over. He turned away in disgust. If he had bothered listening to Liz's guide to dreams he would have noticed that the further he progressed in this theater the more it led him away from "Tosca." He found himself briefly in an airport. He got involved in winding a clock that wasn't his, and, when, at last, the clock became a watch, he was walking in a city he thought he knew and it was sunny. He awoke on Thursday to what Pallas's optimistic weather man like to call "brighter later."

When he got to his office, he found Rollo Shaw waiting. Of the four "Americanos," he was the man Othmar liked best, or, to put it another way, feared least. He could be droll but was gentle, a master raconteur whose anecdotes were excruciatingly funny but kind.

"A small thing to bother you with," Rollo began, "but Joey wonders when he is going to get a costume."

"Joey?"

"He sings the Shepherd." When there was no reaction from Othmar, Rollo amplified, "The little kid."

"Why does he need a costume? He's never on stage."

"He feels left out."

Othmar said he would think it over.

"Rollo, while your're here, I'm looking ahead to next season. I might do 'Elixir.' Do you know it?"

"It was the first opera chorus I sang in. You friend Sarah did it with a Nemorino who was so bad she hid him behind a column. It's a love of an opera."

"I was thinking of you for the Nemorino. Especially if I tour it," he added grandly. Othmar knew he was treading water. He had already mentally cast Luigi Luongo in the role, and said as much to Pompelli. Could he offer the cover to Rollo with the promise of singing a matinee or two? He looked at Rollo intently, and, he hoped, with genuine concern: "I don't know how Nemorino lies for your voice. But take a look sometime. It would be a nice change from Spoletta."

Rollo laughed. "This time I get the girl."

There was a knock at the door, for which Othmar was glad. It would put off the business about the kid.

"Don't say anything to the others just yet."

Evey Titus, barely managing a smile for Rollo, entered from the box office. But, of course, it would be the box office, Othmar thought sourly. The box office manager is one of Sam Adler's minions and Sam Adler is one of hers.

"I want to know what you did with my dog. Brielman's says she never..."

Othmar felt a gladness he did not fight. "You should have taken your precious dog yourself. If you want to know, she shat all over my car and I threw her in a ditch."

Evey gave a little moan. "I..."

"Serves you right. I am sick and tired of fetching and carrying for you. Why me?"

Because, she was going to say, she wasn't brave enough. Didn't have the heart. Knew it was best for poor old Maida. But it would be like killing a...It wasn't planned that way. Maida had been all right earlier. Then came the spasms. And sudden paralysis. She had watched her husband die. Not again. There was no one else in the house. When Othmar drove up to get the monstrance, she seized the opportunity.

"Why me! I'll tell you. You think you can simply give an order and this whole pathetic city will roll over and play dead. The great Missus Titus. I have had nothing but trouble since I came here. I've been spied on. My singers..."

That was interesting, she thought. "Spied on." And who started it? If she remembered, it was Austin Othmar who tried to get Miss Poirer at the historical society to gossip.

"My singers have been interfered with. I am the director of this opera, I'm the boss, not you. I decide when they rehearse. I lost one whole goddam week."

Not the way they saw it. She was beginning to enjoy this.

"Playing favorites. Opera is supposed to be an ensemble. You wouldn't understand that, would you! High on your hill. The great patron of the arts. Sure, they suck up to you. The big house. The music room. The fancy piano. I've heard better pianos in a bar. Your little soirées. Of course they would do it for you. You didn't think I knew? I saw them come back to the hotel. La signora this, la signora that. She is so nice. And while we're on the subject, let me..."

He doesn't really know, does he?—what really went on. About Bruno coaching Luigi. And the terribly, terribly sad thing about Rita. He doesn't know that yet. She wondered if Victor was right.

"Let me tell you. Talk about playing favorites. Do you know what your pathetic niece is up to? Do you know what they're saying! Ha! The talk of the town. You might be interested, you just might be interested to know Alex Avery is not impressed. Not one little bit snowed by you. She took him to your hoity-toity golf club and what does it turn out to be? A shack. That's what he called it. A shack with a short-order cook."

And lamb that Alex Avery couldn't eat because it wasn't properly cooked. It was pink. Sarah told her she wouldn't, she couldn't take him there anymore.

"You'll find your mutt on the golf course."

Maybe there was hope. She would bury her at Spring Side with the others.

"I didn't know it was the golf club. I'm glad. Poetic justice. By God, I've..."

Bad thinking. Hers was the sin. And that it had to be Maida, confidante since Sammy died. Heard all, said nothing. The least she could have done was to take her to Brielman's herself. I was found lacking.

"By God, I stood up to you. I am my own man in this theater. The stage is one place you can't have. You can have everything else. You've got it already.

The jerks on the main street. The pathetic newspaper. Nature Boy, that creep that runs the musket company. 'The men are unhappy...perceive'"

Evey hid a smile. Linc King was not her fault. He was a relic of Sarah's rebellion. Fortunately, there had been Denny Smythe, dull though he was.

"Lincoln King has his uses," she said, just to say something. A mistake. Coming from the great Evey Titus, that was no defense at all. Interesting, Othmar thought.

There was a flash of light as the box office manager shot the window shade up and squinted at Othmar.

"The box office manager is one of yours."

"Guilty as charged," she said. She was bored. He seemed to be winding down. She made as though to rise. She had a busy morning ahead, working out details for feeding the singers after the curtain. She had arranged for four restaurants to stay open late, one each, after the performances. The singers could eat. People could have a drink. Buffets would be best. There would be something for everyone—and not expensive: A prix fixe. It would be good publicity for all, the restaurants, the theater, and good for downtown. She wanted opera to be an annual event. Whether Austin Othmar was the man...she would have a word with Gilly.

"I brought you this," she said. It was the monstrance, forgotten because of Maida. She set it on the table. "The little..."

Othmar stared and blinked. The gold stared back. How could she? How could she come here and think she could buy him off?

"The little chamber is rock crystal. It held the Host, the Eucharist, the wafer, the bread for Communion." She realized she was stumbling, filling the silence. She felt afraid. Othmar in a rage was one thing, a wordless Othmar another. "It opens here." She pressed and the crystal door swung forward.

Othmar lunged at it and swept the monstrance to the floor. The crystal shattered. Her eyes filled with tears, clouding the proud sparkle of glass at her feet. She thought of her husband. "How could I have done this to you," she murmured. Eyes still closed, she shook her head to still herself. Breathe in, she advised herself, and did, but with the resolve of breathing in, she inhaled Othmar's dreadful perfume. Her emotions went beyond pity. She hoped her smile wouldn't show.

"You might give some thought," she said finally, "to a lighter cologne."

17.

Smothering in rage, Othmar got in his car and drove to Albany. He must swim, he must find a pool. As he punished the old Rambler over Lebanon mountain, he recited what he had said to Evey Titus. He embellished. He wrote dialogue for their next encounter, for he was sure it wasn't over yet. Goddam! Dogs did have their uses. He could never have one growing up. His father couldn't stand the shedding. His mother tried to console by saying they moved around too much for a dog to be happy. For a while he had a pet turtle. "Boring!" Othmar yelled at the road. "Boring!"

There was an awful lot of Albany, he discovered. Where was Downtown? He couldn't remember, couldn't even find the train station. He drove aimlessly till conscious of enormous hunger. Must eat, he said, and parked. It looked to be the main drag of a working class neighborhood, and Irish by the names of the bars and taverns. One had possibilities. He hunkered down on a barstool. The bowl of chili was good and hot, and he drank two beers. Not a poster for "Tosca" in sight. He began to feel better. The bartender, absorbed with another man over the racing form, let him alone. A cop came in. The bartender and his pal made a great pretense of pretending they were doing the crossword. Evidently their little joke. The cop had a Coke. Othmar thought he saw the bartender splash something into it. A sandwich with fries appeared from the kitchen. Then, pie and coffee. Othmar made a bet with himself the cop wouldn't pay for any of this. The cop stood to eat. He wore one of those new police parkas, the stiff ballistic nylon that rustled, and he was draped, he was caparisoned, with gear. The least was his billy club, though nowadays billy clubs were short black truncheons. A cosh, Othmar thought. Nothing Scarpia would stoop to carrying, but one of the *sbirri*, perhaps. The service revolver lay deep in a stout leather holster. What they never show you in the movies, thought Othmar, is the cop getting it out of the holster. The bartender caught him looking at the cop. "Anything else?" he asked. Othmar paid up.

He decided to walk for a while. The longer he walked the better the stores got. Nothing like the city but better than Pallas. How could people put up with Pallas? New movies took a month to get there. The TV reception was a joke. If it wasn't snow it was multiple images no matter the channel. In baseball season (spring training had started) Pallas was content to watch two pitchers throwing to two batters. "Ghosting," Sarah Smythe had called it, caused by the signal bouncing around the mountains. Doubtless, she had "done a story on it." God, he was tired of extraneous information—and Sarah never shut up. How was he going to "grill" her on what she knew? He found himself looking in the window of a hair salon. Posters of flirty male models with perms. Who were they trying to fool! Unisex, the salon said. He still wanted to go really blonde for the Attavanti and debated when to do it. God, there was another unisex joint! Albany was the place to come. He turned back to find his car. Across the street he now noticed a rod and gun store. On impulse he strode over to the show window. He could feel a rifle butt into his shoulder. "Both eyes open, boys." That was Sergeant Teale. "Sight down the barrel. Breathe out and pull." Damn, but he had been good! He loved the smell of shot. Loved the smell of metal. The oil for cleaning guns. Oil was the one thing he let stay on his hands. He recited something else from his past: "Men, prepare to assemble your personal weapon." That was the academy instructor. When snickered over in the dorms, "personal weapon" took on another meaning that frightened the young and naïve John Austin. He could laugh now. He tried the door and was buzzed in.

Just looking, he said, as a peppy little man came forward and tailed him rack to rack. "Just looking," Othmar insisted.

"I saw you come out of the tavern."

Christ! Spies here too. Would it ever end! "It's a free country," Othmar said evenly.

"The cop was in there."

What if he was?

"Thick as a plank." The little man spat. "One hell of a shot. I give him that. You are not from around here, I think."

"Over the line." Othmar decided to go rural. "Chatham County."

"Now they had a game warden," said the little man and named him. "Your father would have known him. This Fred Russell always let them get two deer, one legal and one for the meat locker for the rest of the winter. Three, if they were hard up. It kept the herd thinned, you understand. These days to get deer meat you have to know a state cop. Used to be the prison that got the road kill. The state hospital gets it now. And complains. Your new game warden—strictly by the book. I myself am that, for birds. You want the hens for nesting in the spring. That's hard for them to understand around here. The Eye-Ties like their quail. And the pheasant plumage. They traffic in feathers, the Eye-Ties do. Not so many hunt as used to. They've moved to the suburbs, Hooperstown, and Marshall, and that. And yourself, do you hunt?"

Othmar never had. When it came to guns, and much else, his father was totally without the sporting instinct.

"Rifle team," he said, stretching wish to fact.

The little man coughed and Othmar turned to sense a rifle coming his way. He lunged and caught it by the stock.

"A shooter!" The man gave a brilliant laugh. "You are who you say you are."

This was the most comforting thing Othmar had heard in days and weeks. For an hour or more he talked with Burke, whose first name he never did learn. Burke plied him with guns, urging him to try them for heft and balance. Burke had seen better times. An inch or two shorter and Othmar figured him for a retired jockey. He'd had his first gun at twelve, and only then because they were too poor for earlier. Boys weren't taught they way he was. They want the fancy sights. And there was much more along those lines. Burke's other complaint concerned the National bloody Rifle Association. All the money collected locally had to go to headquarters. That cop? The one in the tavern? Get him on gun control. The things you can pick up at gun shows. The cops sell their old revolvers. Imagine! No questions asked. But a hell of a shot was the cop. A pleasure to watch. How was "Jack" here—Othmar was John Austin on some driver's licenses—with a pistol?

Othmar told the truth and said he was rusty.

Easily remedied, said Burke. He turned the sign in the door to CLOSED and threw the lock. He beckoned to Othmar to follow. Down narrow stairs they went and around a furnace into a long basement. There, Othmar found a perfect little shooting gallery.

The architect of the Palladium had seen no reason to soundproof the manager's office. As a consequence, the box office manager had heard the shindy, seen Othmar storm out, seen Mrs. Titus pick things off the floor, and seen (but not heard) her on the telephone. Sam Adler's minion though the box officer manager may have been, he was also mindful of a visit paid him by "New York management." Accordingly, he dialed the number on Gilly's card.

184

Gilly later to Liz: "If I am not there for the dress rehearsal I may be sorry," she said she would come two days later for opening night.

Othmar returned from Albany about midnight. He and Burke had a pop at a tavern Burke favored. Othmar nursed the Ramble back over Lebanon mountain. That night he slept without dreaming. Well before he stirred, his landlady had telephoned Mrs. Titus to say he was back. Mrs. Keohane also told Mrs. Titus the Italian lady's costume was ready. It had been a pleasure and an honor to work on it. She was quite sure if the Italian lady did not have to raise her arms very often that the places where the bodice joined the sleeves would hold. She had rebuilt the interior. She was half way through doing the same to the second costume. She knew how to do that from the days when she refashioned antique wedding dresses. Mrs. Titus should remember Mrs. Lodge's wedding dress and the lace bertha? Mrs. Titus did indeed. Mrs. Titus had heard about it daily, ever since she thought of Othmar's landlady as the seamstress to help out poor Rita Dettori.

That afternoon there came a tap at Othmar's office door. It was Victor Pompelli.
"My Rita wish to show you her costume." They entered, he proudly leading her, and both giggling like lovers. She was wearing an enormous shawl of violet chiffon.
"*Eccola!*" Here she is! rasped Pompelli, his old man's baritone standing in for the cruelly expectant Scarpia of Act II. "*Eccola!*" was her cue. The Dettori threw back the shawl.
"*Mario, tu qui?*" she thrilled. "You are here?" Her voice stormed into Othmar's room. There was mettle in it, also sorrow. He would never again hear a life summed up in so short an utterance. He held his breath, protecting himself against the seductions of pure theater. She was pure diva from the flash of her eye to her impossible wig with its coils of hair rising like a civic monument. Her gown was of purple velvet and it was crude in the way of all costumes. Details shouted, such as the coarse lace that banded the cap sleeves and edged the overskirt. Stage lighting and distance would soften this, would also persuade you that a king's ransom in sapphires and diamonds lay on an alabaster bosom. Othmar saw this was really a kind of dickey of "illusion" netting on which was sewn an ugly paste necklace. There was matching paste at her ears and on each wrist.
Pompelli bent and kissed her hand. "*Carissima,*" he whispered. Then aloud: "Let me promenade you so Othmar sees how the dress moves." She

struck an attitude, head thrown back. Light glanced off the crystal chain filleted through her wig. She presented her right hand. Seizing a regal finger, Pompelli made the Dettori revolve, as one might a big doll on a music box. Her lace-edged train lapped at the carpet. Then, with her husband as cavalier, she glided about the room, her shapely court pumps of silver lame buckled in more paste. The little procession drew up before Othmar.

"The jewels are very fine," said Pompelli. "You see they are daisies, *uno gioco di parole,* a play of words, *margheritas* for my Rita. So beautiful." He squeezed her hand, then gave her a push forward.

"Now show Gianni the court curtsy. This is *autentico,* authentic, passed down to her. The curtsy to the royal box. This will be for her first solo curtain." The Dettori plunged forward until all Othmar could see was a mound of purple.

"Brava!" Now, *cara mia,* show the 'obeisance to art.' Gianni, this is for her next curtains—however many." The Dettori dipped slowly to one knee, hands clasped on the other, head prayfully inclined.

"The audience like this honesty, this truth, this…" Pompelli searched for the word triumphant. "…this humility. This, she hold forever. Nearly five minutes after her last Mimì. Flowers raining down. She give her flowers to hospitals. It was in the newspapers. Like Tosca bring her flowers to the Madonna. Life copies opera. We will do it here."

Deftly he righted his wife. "The final curtain we save to surprise you."

"Tosca, mi fai dimenticare Iddio!" he sang as he led her away. "Tosca, you make me forget God."

It was only long minutes later that Othmar realized he had not been given so much as a glimpse of her other two costumes. When he inquired about these at the next rehearsal he was told they would be ready by the dress.

What now faced Othmar as director was more worrying than costumes. He had not ever managed to get the Scarpia and the Tosca to show him how they planned to do their big Act II scene. In this, Pompelli seemed to connive, closing his score when Sciaronne and his henchmen drag Cavaradossi away for further torture. It was but two days to the dress rehearsal. The lighting people had asked pointedly when they might see the principals on stage. Come to that, no one had seen Tosca jump to her death.

"A word, if you please, Maestro," Othmar said meekly to Pompelli. The usual practice of rehearsing, he said he understood, did not apply to guest artists. They do not have to learn "Tosca," unlike the young Americans. Who, by the way, said Othmar, are a real credit to their teachers. "Your sainted Rita" (Othmar thought he could presume) "not to mention Bruno Cappetto have made them sound like Italians. At least to my ear."

Pompelli smiled. "They work hard."

Othmar sighed. "But the lighting people, the lighting people are driving me crazy. They tell me they've got to look at how the Tosca and the Scarpia move on stage." When this didn't seem to sink in, Othmar added: "I want her lit well. It is her American debut. The press will be here."

The message got thorough and Othmar was told he could have a private piano rehearsal of the Act II finale with the lighting designer present.

And it all went very well. There were no surprises. Why should there be surprises in "Tosca," a lead pipe cinch of an opera? For the rehearsal, Othmar had the stage fully set. The business with the French window was earlier in the scene, also the business with the torture of Cavaradossi. This was between just the two of them, Scarpia and his obscene desire to bring Tosca to her knees, and Tosca, flustered and frightened, grasping at hope. Othmar set the table for Scarpia's supper and lit the candles. Screw the fireman! He tested the collapsible knife and placed it on Scarpia's writing table. He withdrew to the third row, for he had promised they need not sing full voice.

But they did sing out, enjoying themselves, pros that they were. Pompelli had once praised his wife's voice as *"una voce di donna,"* a woman's voice. For the first time in Pallas, Othmar heard this, heard the luster and passion, also a musicianship that transformed Tosca from a brittle diva into a heroine worthy of our pity and regard.

As Scarpia, Bruno Cappetto chose to stalk his victim. Never once was he within an arm's reach of that heaving bosom. The lighting designer, sitting next to Othmar, grunted once or twice, stared fixedly at the candles on the two tables, and made a note to himself about pretending the candles were of sufficient power to throw Scarpia's sinister shadow across Tosca (who he thought a bit old for the love interest) and "rape T. that way," he wrote down.

The private rehearsal concluded, Othmar was all graciousness, profusely thanking the artists. To Tosca, he said he saw her "beautiful margheritas" glow like her voice. She took this as her due, then impulsively kissed him Italian style.

"It is so interesting," Othmar said later to Pompelli, "how this Scarpia by never touching her manages to suggest he is going to ravish her right before your eyes."

There was a quiet laugh from Pompelli. "Bruno, he need the role. He was never *prima classa.* Very good but never a Scarpia for Milano, Roma, the Met. My Rita was his pay check. He was quite a man for the ladies. It was understood: As you say on the television, 'Not with my wife you do it.' We work it out. She has fun, cat and mouse with him. It is theater. And, Gianni, I tell you again, it is all in the voice. You must listen more."

There was no stopping "Tosca" now. Like the cartoon avalanche that caroms through an Alpine village and becomes studded with bell towers and cow legs and fir trees and rubber boots as it rolls, the production gathered speed. Othmar, in the fastness of his office, checked off this errand or that rehearsal on his list of lists. He had overseen the training of ushers and usherettes. He had proof-read the program book. He had ordered bouquets for the opening night curtain calls. The radio engineer encountered when he was interviewed over WPAL would do the sound effects. The lighting people had come and made magic from their spaghetti of wires and murky gels. One afternoon they turned all the stage lights on, high and full, so the paint on the new light cans burned off. Better to have an empty theater fill with smoke than a full house in best-bib-and-tucker run for the exits in panic. The fireman assigned to the theater was firmly against open flame but Othmar still hoped for candles in the Attavanti chapel and on Scarpia's supper table. For all he cared, the jailer's lantern could be a flashlight bulb.

Very few tickets remained at the box office. High school girls, under the direction of the box office manager, mailed out big envelopes containing little envelopes containing the precious pasteboards. Citizens of Pallas who braved the box office could be observed studying the seating chart, and, as the little sign cautioned, examining their tickets before leaving the window. Pallas had much to learn about opera and it began at the ticket grille. Ticket buyers could, if they liked, step inside the theater to watch a few minutes of rehearsal. This might take place in the lobby where Margarita Dettori, Tosca herself, coached the young Americans. Sarah Smythe, caught short for a column topic, had tried to interview the Dettori on that other famous resident of Trieste, the tenor Gioccomo Joyce, who had finished third in a singing competition to the great John Sullivan. But the Dettori did not know il signor Joyce and Sarah had to resort to one of those what-if pieces that obscure more than illuminate. Gilly to Liz in New York: "James Joyce sang at the Trieste Opera? I didn't know that." Liz: "In a more perfect world."

That Sarah was actually going to appear on stage only increased her efforts. She who never wore makeup in the daytime was furred in eyeliner. Othmar, in contrast, sometimes chose not to shave to show how busy he was. His last haircut was well before he came to Pallas. In back, his hair frisked with his collar.

And when he needed a break from Puccini's Roman intrigue he took himself to the sunnier climes of Donizetti's Italian comedy. Except for the pleasant memories of that Chicago "Elixir" that built in his mind, it was not an opera he could say he knew. He would build from scratch. It would be his—as "Tosca" would never be. He would look in Schwann for a recording. The next time he went to the city he would get a piano-vocal. In the meantime, he would draw Pompelli out even further. He had to know realistically about the demands Donizetti made on an orchestra. He doubted the story itself had much literary or emotional significance. His "Elixir" would be an "entertainment" but of the highest order.

He was beginning to see it set up on stage. It would be played against an untroubled blue sky but one not without weather. Should it have a framing devise as he used scrims to focus "Tosca"? That has the advantage, he argued, of putting the action one remove from the audience, of giving the opera a narrative distance. A frame says: I am going to tell you a story of long ago and faraway. He thought of windows. Could each act begin with a "curtain" of jalousie windows, each of which would open—like an Advent calendar—to reveal part of the scene. They would open faster and faster, till there were only a few left, and that's when you'd fly the curtain and the stage would be alive with action. It worked for movie titles.

He could almost see the colors. Not the sugar-coated pastels of Jordan almonds in the Easter baskets his mother made but more like watercolor: slightly bleached by the sun, vinegary and a bit worn, and he would underscore this with dusty black and browns. There was a town square, he was sure, and he'd have his usual fun assembling a representative sample of village life. Would an organ grinder with monkey be too corny? A game of bocce ball? Another scene he thought he remembered took place at a farm or vineyard, anyway something rustic. He was pretty sure there was a house. But did he want a house-house—or a house that could be sketched, say, on flats, rather than built. Above all, he wanted a production that would travel easily. It was time to take Opera Prima on the road.

The dress rehearsal for "Tosca" was the Tuesday evening before the opening on Thursday. Of the many superstitions that enrich theatrical life, one is that a bad "dress" guarantees a good first night. Gilly reminded Othmar of this. It was the least he could do.

So much can go wrong in "Tosca." They tell of the poor soprano who fell out of her gown while singing *"Vissi d'arte."* Of the knife that didn't collapse, bruising the Scarpia. Of the knife that flew apart before the fatal stab. Once, in Boston, the dying Scarpia fell so far downstage that his feet sprawled on the stage apron and they had to page the Act II curtain across his legs. In another opera house, the trap door was too small for the girth of the famous Cavaradossi. Even lowly supers are not immune from miscalculation. Misunderstanding the instructions of a stage director, the execution squad to a man followed Tosca in her death leap from the Castel Sant'Angelo. So history tells us and Sarah Smythe was in the wings waiting for the worst to happen.

The house lights went down. Victor Pompelli, in a dark suit, tapped his baton and looked around at the audience. This was the signal for them to quiet. Several dozen people had been specifically invited to the dress rehearsal, people who, even in obscure ways, had worked on the production. Othmar's landlady was there, but also, as Othmar did not yet know, to keep an eye on the costumes she had salvaged for Tosca. The wife of the fireman assigned to backstage duty was there with her sister. Othmar had sent passes to the police station as well. Mechanics from the VW garage were encouraged to avail themselves, and one did, bringing his girlfriend. And there were others, Golden Agers on canes and in wheelchairs, for whom a public performance would be difficult. Every member of the orchestra and chorale, every crew member, could invite up to four people. "Won't the passes hurt ticket sales?" Sarah wanted to know. Othmar grandly informed her "Tosca" was as good as sold out. He needed bodies in the theater, for the dress was also an acoustic rehearsal. He had staked out one seat for himself just past the cross aisle and another in the balcony.

So Pompelli tapped, and tapped again, and the audience hushed, and Othmar who had been kneeling on a prie-dieu (stage right) in the posture of the pious Attavanti, slowly rose, made the sign of the cross, and muffled in blue cloak with blonde ringlets spilling from the hood, glided across, genuflected toward the unseen high altar (stage left) and vanished into the wing upstage. Pompelli raised his stick. With a sigh, the scrim rose and the orchestra brayed the music of menace that tells us "Tosca" will end badly.

Othmar threw off his disguise and sped to his seat. The one thing he couldn't judge, until Sarah Smythe took over the Attavanti, was how the first entrance of the Angelotti played to a real audience. As he suspected (and hoped) this audience knew so little about opera that they were willing to give it the benefit of the doubt. Othmar entered an auditorium absorbed in the stage scene. He heard a rustle of interest when the Sacristan entered and the first, so welcome, sounds of laughter. Damn, but Ed Nelson was good! Folded up in himself like a preying mantis and right on the button with the tics that Puccini wrote into the music but not so much you thought "spastic." And such nasal Italian! Where had that come from!

Another pleasurable rustle as Cavaradossi bid for their hearts. He cut a heroic figure in tall boots, flowing white shirt, and a cloak he let fly onto the painter's platform. Up he sprang on the ladders. Then, carefully, as though unveiling a masterpiece, he drew up the cloth that covered the painting of the Magdalene. Below, the Sacristan fussed and fumed. Othmar crunched into his seat, well pleased.

Angelotti again. Jonce Jones looking truly bruised and worked over, desperate, sweating. Great makeup! And the character all in the voice: a brightness that sliced through the orchestra, nimble yet rumbling, a man in fear for his life. Othmar could have kissed him. This was a great talent.

And now Cavaradossi peering at Angelotti. The recognition. The hand-to-heart, so universal a gesture, so natural, yet so illusive if the singer doesn't feel his body is one with his voice. Cavaradossi raising Angelotti up, and exploding, like the youth he was: *"Disponete di me!"* You can count on me!

And the shock of the offstage voice.

"Mario!" She is coming, Tosca comes. What are they to do?

"Mario!" And again *"Mario!"* Louder, nearer. Othmar wiggled with expectation. Oh, didn't Puccini just know the power of repetition, the fail-safe of repetition. A cough, a murmur, would blot out the most clarion-voiced of Toscas.

Margarita Dettori, in her American debut as Tosca, sailed forward and the audience broke into thunderous applause. There was a near collision with Cavaradossi, and Othmar could hear laughter begin. He was not sure what he saw. Had the stage lights dimmed? Was his eyesight failing? His scalp went wet. He squinted. The stage picture dame back into focus. For long minutes he could hear nothing that was sung. He could barely credit what he saw.

The apparition he resisted was a Tosca as she was dressed for Act I at the premiere in 1900. In place of the Dettori's impossible wig for Act II was an equally impossible hat. It rose like a galleon in choppy seas cresting the foam of three enormous ostrich feathers. The dress was a froth of ruching, tucks and gathers cascading down the sleeves and fanning out in a sunburst over the stomach. There was a silk stole draped over the arms. Tosca enters carrying flowers from last evening's triumph which, she tells us, she always places before the statue of the Virgin. Whether such a bouquet is, strictly speaking, a prop, and thus the director's responsibility, or an adjunct of costume, and thus the star's choice, Othmar had never decided. In fact, it had slipped his mind. This bouquet was this Tosca's and it was a tangle of velvet posies too old to hold their heads up. There was naturally a story about these flowers, which Othmar would hear later. This Tosca was dressed like any fashionable Roman in a fin-de-siècle version of an "afternoon" dress. Othmar now realized what Pompelli, so long ago had promised. *"Autentico,* authentic, Gianni, you will like!" Not for the Dettori the new and improved Tosca of a later twentieth-century *verismo,* the simple country girl in a dark gown who just happens to be a diva who might very well be confused with a modest woman of the quartier for whom Sant'Andrea della Valle was her parish church. No, this was the diva of divas, a Tosca for the masses, a Tosca presumed to have her own carriage waiting outside, a *donna* who frequented restaurants and dined with men in private rooms while their wives supped at home. In her left hand, this Tosca grasped a very tall walking stick festooned with a big silk bow. The Dettori now planted the stick stage center and from it she pivoted, turning this way and that.

Othmar was now afraid he knew less than he should.

The audience was eating it up. This was obviously the star. They have a raptuous reception to the confectioner's sugar of Tosca's aria about her life with Cavaradossi in their dear little villa. They were delighted, totally on her side, when she discovers the Magdalene her darling Cavaradossi is painting is blonde. To make this discovery, the Dettori actually uprooted her ferule and marched a few steps. The Cavaradossi then took her arm and soothed her back to center stage. He tries for a kiss. She tries, like any clever woman, to duck. "My hair is all ruffled," she wails. The sweet kid that he is, Cavaradossi playfully pushes her out of the chapel; and the Dettori simpered into the wing.

Then there was more with Angelotti, and Cavaradossi giving him the key to his villa, and laying plans for the consul's escape. Then a dull boom. *"Il cannon del castello!"* The fortress signal, Angelotti knows, for a missing prisoner. "Scarpia will unleash his human bloodhounds," Cavaradossi exclaims. He and Angelotti slip out and a blink later the Sacristan enters. Then comes the enjoyable confusion of the choirboys on their way to the vestry to robe for the victory Te Deum—and the audience straining to spot their little Mick and Matty and Con and Phil. And then, and then, goddam! Just as he had staged it! Like a whipcrack, total stillness fell—"Suck in your breath and hold it for a count of three," Othmar had told the boys—and in this slack, Scarpia materialized. In Othmar's mind was Yeats's lament for civilization, "the center will not hold." Into this center, as into a void, he had placed and isolated Scarpia. The evil that no man may conquer. But also Scarpia as vortex, the drain. Boys though they may be, the choir senses he is to be avoided. Othmar had them stream offstage, pushing but eerily quiet. "You must vanish!"

"Mario? Mario?" The audience listened forward. Tosca again, they knew. And disturbed she is, as she pivots uncertainly searching for Cavaradossi. Then, like a black shadow, the elegance of Scarpia offering her holy water. The only part in the opera that caused Othmar's heart to thump. *"Grazie, signor!"* Tosca thanking Scarpia and crossing herself with the holy water from his fingers. No! Don't do it! Don't take from him, don't give in, Othmar wants to scream, and is surprised at himself, and ashamed.

Then, the business with the Attavanti's fan. But still Tosca is stuck stage center. Othmar wonders at this. Step by step, though, Scarpia draws her his way. Yes, well, thought Othmar, that's one way to show her being lured. Tosca bursts into tears. Old pro Dettori had turned away from the audience, a protesting arm lifted to her brow testifying to her sobs. "God will forgive me: He sees I am weeping," she sings. Without touching her, very good! Scarpia escorts her, ushers her, sweeps her out of the church.

And now the robed procession of deacons and priests and choirboys, up to the number of costumes at Othmar's disposal, distracts the audience. Catholics are amazed to see themselves on stage, Protestants stare at popish pageant. And now deafening splinters of sound, like the tearing of paper, issued from every part of the theater so there was no escaping it, sound made terrifying by its regularity. It is the crash of cannon fire, a hundred times souped up, all thanks to the magic of radio engineering.

Othmar raced for backstage shouting "house lights up, house lights up!"

"But what if they had panicked?" Othmar kept moaning to Gilly. "What if the audience rioted?" Othmar, on the spot, had fired WPAL's sound effects man, and during what remained of the first intermission, was downing neat Scotch in his office.

Nothing like the same excitement in Acts II and III. Othmar thought, and Gilly had to agree, that everyone's timing was a little off. The Dettori kept bumping into things. Twice she plowed into Scarpia's writing table. Gilly got the impression that Scarpia rather than luring her to his sick desire was trying to run interference for her. But the knife went in clean. And the Dettori, in the opera's most famous scene, laid Scarpia out, crucifix on his chest and candelabrum at each side. She washed her hands of his blood, and so what if she tipped the water ewer over and so what if she couldn't quite to find which of his dead hands still gripped the paper promising safe-conduct. Wouldn't we in such circumstances be flustered too? The applause was ecstatic as the curtain fell on Act II.

The sound engineer was not going to go quietly. In the second intermission, he and Othmar had words, fueled in part by the sound engineer's certainty that Othmar was drunk. "You could smell it on him," he told WPAL's morning man.

Before the curtain went up on the final act, Gilly poured Othmar a double. "Courage, *mon vieux*."

As acts go, Act III of "Tosca" is short. For Othmar in his stew of Scotch and sweat, it was mercifully short. The shepherd boy sang (offstage) and first light came. Everybody got up and down through the trap door. Alex Avery, now swarthy as Giorgio Spelvino in the cast list, was unrecognizable as Cavaradossi's jailer (and masterfully affected his change back to the Scarionne in time for the curtain calls). Cavaradossi sang his farewell and Othmar could hear the audience snuffle. Tosca, wrapped for flight in a traveling cloak, gave her lover explicit lessons in how to act dead. In this, the Dettori seemed a bit tentative, Othmar thought. The stage was indeed a bit dark. She had trouble finding Cavaradossi's hands. She was clumsy when she withdraws as the officer marches on the execution squad. Blanks from the muskets shower sparks. Cavaradossi falls. The squad marches off and climbs back down the trap door. "Oh, Mario, don't move yet…they're going away, but still don't move." But "like Count Palmieri," that ill-fated republican, Cavaradossi is dead, though Tosca does not yet know it. Tosca should run to the edge of the parapet to make sure all is well. Tosca should bend over her lover telling him to rise and flee. But the Dettori seemed lost. Not until she fell over Cavaradossi's foot did she find him, and, even then, she faced away from him.

From below stage, a hubbub. Voices shout of Scarpia's death, Tosca's guilt. Lantern light glances upward. Sciaronne yells, there she is. Tosca stumbles up the parapet. Dawn reddens the sky. "Scarpia!" she cries. *"Avanti a Dio!"* We meet before God. Her cloak billowing behind her, she jumps into eternity.

18.

The Dettori was all smiles at her curtain calls. Audience approval of her several "obeisances to art" dictated, she felt, an unprecedented second royal curtsy. Othmar watched in disbelief.

"She jump! I tell you she jump!" Pompelli, after the final curtain, was thumping Othmar's back.

The oldest trick in the book, Othmar thought sourly.

"He says it's how they make the elephant disappear at the Moscow Circus," Gilly reported to Liz. "It's all a distraction. But that's not all I have to tell you, my sweet."

The Dettori was blind.

"No, Johnny, not blind. Not blind-blind," Gilly argued as he sat up till dawn with Othmar. "She just doesn't see very well. Maybe she has cataracts—something like that. Who knows?" Gilly was reluctant to play doctor. Then to put a bright face on things: "She's not nearly as bad as Alonso."

"Who's he?"

"Alicia Alonso, the ballerina. Dances in Cuba. One of the world's great Giselles."

"Castro gets all he deserves." Othmar was now quite drunk.

"My point is, she gets around the stage because everyone helps out. They all know about Rita."

"Well, they never told me! They never bothered, they never had the common decency to tell me-e-e-e." Othmar banged on the manager's table. "And just when, I'd like to know, when did you know? Whose side are you on?"

Gilly to Liz: "Of course, I lied, and said I figured it out at the dress."
Liz: "You'll go far."

"He won't leave well enough alone."

"But we've always known that about him."

Othmar spent that night, what remained of it, on the banquette in his office. He awoke not knowing where he was. He was parched, and smelly. Had he barfed? He washed as best he could. He was less hung-over than ravenous, and against his better judgment went across the street to Kulda's. Catherine the waitress gave him an icy smile. He ordered dry toast. Catherine brought stacks of it with pots of jam. She kept hotting up his coffee. Othmar was not to know till later that WPAL's morning man, in a snide and suggestive way, had alluded to merrymaking till the wee hours following the dress rehearsal of "Tosca."

"PALs o'mine," said this creep, "I hear there was fireworks at the Grand Old Opry last night."

His engineer gave him a broad smile.

"Well, you won't get me near anything I gotta put on my tiara and my tux and tails. Who-eeee! Let's spin your kinda music."

The engineer gave him thumbs up. Anything endorsed by Mary Margaret McGoon, as they called her, was not for them and theirs.

Catherine watched Othmar devour the toast and jam. She could now confirm their worst suspicions to Othmar's landlady, who had noticed he did not come home last night. "Yer could smell it on him," said Catherine over the phone.

Somewhat fortified, Othmar returned to the manager's office. He had summoned the artistes for a meeting a noon. He was going to have it out with them.

The Dettori, a corsage of purple orchids pinned to her fur, arrived on Victor Pompelli's arm. Othmar now understood the big eyeglasses. She beamed at him. She looked fresh as a daisy, as did they all, having gone to sleep well and truly satisfied after a small supper party given them by Evey Titus at the hotel. Mario had insisted on cooking. There were oysters to start, quail, a dessert with chestnuts. As it was near St. Patrick's Day, Evey had procured a bottle of Jameson's for Bruno Cappetto. *"Scarpia il mio favorito,"* she called him in her toast.

Luigi Luongo now eased the ratty old thermos bag onto Othmar's table and made as if to undo it.

The Dettori cooed at Othmar in Italian. She wanted him to know his theater was beautiful and a joy to sing in. The audience was everything a singer could want. The musical and stage preparation beggared anything she was accustomed to. She looked forward to working with him in future seasons.

"Last evening at supper we toast you," said Evey Titus's favorite Scarpia. "We think of 'Traviata.' We think you do 'Triaviata.' We think of Luigi. He sing his first Alfredo for you." To himself: And just maybe I, Bruno Cappetto, might one more time sing the Germont.

Othmar was lost for words. His head throbbed. This was not what he planned for next season. God damn them! And Pomelli knew that!

"For the Violetta," said Pompelli, and Othmar waited to hear him propose his wife. "For the Violetta, we introduce Rita's most promising student. Gianni, you will like her. She inherit my Rita's legato."

There was a shrill giggle from the Dettori. "He say he marry her for my legato."

Mirth ballooned and Othmar blinked furiously trying to gain control. A tiny cordial glass materialized before him and the newly anointed Alfredo was bending over him filling it with something clear and thick, and the others were raising their glasses, and Pompelli had stood and, wreathed in smiles, was saying "Gianni, Gianni, we…"

Othmar slapped the table. "Nooooo!" he cried and heaved himself up. His glass toppled over and the stink of liquorice was upon him. "Finished! *Finito!* No! No! No!"

"You lied to me," Othmar said to Pompelli, when Cappetto and Luongo had taken a shocked Dettori back to the hotel. "You all lied to me."

Pompelli's placating "Gianni, Gianni" Othmar heard as a whine. "No!" he bellowed. "You listen to me! You have let them undermine my authority at every step. Oh! no! they do not rehearse because they are stars, because they know 'Tosca' by heart. And what do I find out? This is his first Cavaradossi and he is still learning it."

"Gianni, no, he coach."

"And she can't see past her face without glasses. She is blind, I tell you, she is blind."

"And I tell you No! She don't see well but, Gianni, what does it matter? She see here," and Pompelli touched his heart, "and she see with her voice. The audience, what do they know, eh? eh? It is the story, the music, the voice.

They see her as Tosca, they don't see the old blind woman. So tragic. That is why, Gianni, they don't give her an opera for her farewell to her house. Only scenes and arias. The management, all cowards, *stronzi,* shitheads.

"And you, you did not know. Ha! You see Tosca. You, Gianni, are fooled! We all help her. You see she jump. You know she always close her eyes when she jump, even when she can see. We work it out. We position Rollo Shaw with flashlight in the last wing. She see light, she count the steps up, she throw her cape back. An old trick." Pompelli grinned. "Audience watches the cape fill the air and she slide down to the mattress. We practice this when you are away and don't know."

So they are all in on it, thought Othmar. I might be talking to a pillow. He was seething.

Pompelli thought it was time for a little joke.

"We have the expression in Italy: *"La situazione è gravissima ma non seria.'* Gianni, you know what it means? It means," and he gave a droll laugh.

Othmar wasn't going to play. "I know what it means. What I am telling you is, she is not being professional."

"Not professional? My Rita? Thirty years on the stage! Please tell me who is more the professional? Who? Who? Ha!"

That behind him, Pompelli got down to business.

"Now I tell you what we do about the cannon. It scare people. It scare me! With your permission," Pompelli bowed, "I engage a second bass drum. Skin on one side of the drum. Each player play with two sticks. Not quite in unison. Bo-om!! The audience hear, feel the vibration without knowing they feel. Much better than cannon. Theater is illusion. You know this, Gianni. Not your fault, the *professore* with the ear-phones and his *machina.* Crash! Crash! Oh, my God, Gianni, I think World War Three."

There was no reaction from Othmar.

"We must patch up your difficulties, Gianni. I speak man to man with you. You are good. Rita is full of praise for you. She tell you but I don't think you hear. We feel you are *simpatico.* You know opera from the performer's shoes because, because, Gianni, you were a singer." Yes, Pompelli thought, that should help. "Gianni, tell me, I am curious, why did you leave your career? Such promise. I see how you teach the Americans. I see how you tell Jonce where to breathe so the words come. I see you explain Spoletta's prayer to Rollo. You think I don't notice? So why you quit?"

"If you must know," Othmar was icy. "I over estimated the audience. I thought they cared." He began telling the story.

"'Bohème,' yes. Yes, good for you to begin with Schaunard," and Pompelli hummed the musician's little French march. "The boots. Very good. Rita tells her pupils they must project also with the body. She was trained by the great Delsarte. Did you know? Authentic movement by Delsarte."

Whose story is this? Othmar thought crossly. He told about fixing on the German frau.

"Ah, Gianni…"

"Let me finish, goddammit!"

"He has a toothpick? Oh! Gianni," and Pompelli began to laugh. "He dig his teeth. Ho ho ho-oo-oo!" Tears came. "Ha!" He gasped and rummaged for a handkerchief. "Ah, Gianni, why did you not tell me? The mistake of the beginner on stage. Never fix your eyes to their eyes. Keep your eyes over the heads. The gold toothpick! I will tell Bruno. He hate the Germans. He collect bad stories. Oh, ho ho ho ho! I don't laugh at you, Gianni. So sad you give up."

Go tell Bruno! Tell the world! You're as bad as the rest, you slimy bastard. Othmar felt he was being eaten away. Pompelli was just like the Titus: do it their way or not at all. He broke silence.

"Maestro, if you don't mind," he said elaborately. "I prefer to be called Austin Othmar."

Pompelli looked at him with puzzlement. Surely not Austin. Austin was la signora Titus's servant who drove them to the golf.

"Aw-stin," Pompelli said tentatively. He felt division between them and was sad. "Nooo, Gianni," he said softly. "Nooo, Awstin cannot be the name for you. Your name, I decide your name, it is Othmar Austin. Ot-mar, the Italian way, it is an Italian name, did you know? *Austino*, pronounced the Italian way, Ow-stee-no. You are one of us, Gianni."

Othmar rose in fury and thrust a shoulder into the secret door to open it. With sarcastic courtesy, he bowed Pompelli out of his office. He had been wrong about Pompelli. He would find another conductor for next season.

By mid afternoon on the day of the first performance, the population of Pallas had swelled by nine or ten: the music critics had arrived. They checked into the Hotel Pallas where a pressroom had been set up with a bar, and typewriters—and Mr. Bangs from Western Union to transmit their reviews. In his old fashioned way, he shook hands with Mary Campbell, the only woman of the group. The rest he was not so sure about, light on their feet, he thought, but as long as their copy was relatively clean and they worked to his deadlines, all would be well. The Hartford and Springfield critics would dictate their reviews to their respective copy desks. The Globe brought a machine that transmitted a typed story over the telephone wire.

The rooming arrangements were somewhat more complicated. The correspondent for Opera US was bunking with the New York Times as a sort of free-bee. Opera Queen seemed to have two friends with him, one of whom was not pleased to encounter the correspondent for the historically-minded Opera Then and Now. Opera Mondo was new on the scene; the Pallas "Tosca" might lead its second issue (if they could find the money for a second issue). Not every critic was in Pallas for the same reason. The Times covered opera as a civic event, art as a Good Thing. The opera mags were there for the sport. As music critics and writers, they left something to be desired. The light they cast seldom illuminated and never warmed. They were long on lore and fussy details. They followed agendas, promoted fights. The body heat was high. Opera Queen's exchange columns, in which autographs and costumes were bartered for rare and often illegal recordings, had a wide readership among drag artists. Opera US had the holy mission of promoting opera in every state of the union but carried a torch for many a diva. Opera Then and Now had a sugar daddy who paid the bills but so scatty a staff it appeared irregularly. Gilly called it Opera Now and Then.

His pitch to the opera mag critics was irresistible: Be in Pallas so you can say you heard the American debut of Luigi Luongo. Could be the next Pavarotti, the next Domingo. Be there in Pallas for Margarita Dettori's Tosca. And when they said they had never, or scarcely ever, heard of Dettori, he dropped the name of Ludmilla Kroll. There was a time in the not-so-recent past when they hadn't heard of Kroll either, had they? She whom the East Germans sent with a minder when she sang in Chicago. Who wore her Cherubini costume when she sought asylum at the local police precinct—and the cops thought she was just a kid on LSD. The Dettori was pretty special, Gilly told them. He hinted things about her autocratic nature, her refusal to record, the fame of her costumes, her retinue. "You won't see her like again."

The Dettori was a trouper.

There was nothing more she liked than performing. She was never sick, never nervous, never unprepared. On the day of her American debut, she rose as usual about eight. She had certain health rituals she followed, such as her daily stretching exercises. On an opera day, she had several small meals early on, *piccoli pranzi* or "snocks," as she learned they were called in America;

and she would have a big dinner after the performance. She did a thousand little tasks. At home she used to set this day aside to darn Victor's socks and turn his cuffs. And all the while she was getting ready inside. Without thinking about it. She had no reason to believe her Pallas "Tosca" would be any different.

Her darling Victor had gone off early to re-seat the pit to accommodate the second bass drum. He, too, liked the busy-ness of a performance day. After a large lunch with wine, he would have a "snooze," another American word that amused them both. He had told Rita something of yesterday's discussion with Othmar. Everything would go as they had planned. Nothing wrong with your hearing, he told her and they laughed. No, if anything it's more acute, she said to reassure him. She was famous in her old opera company for her hearing. And for her generosity in ensemble, for she would shade a tone if a colleague was drifting flat or sharp. Altogether the Dettori was a modest person, or as modest as her gift allowed. She had a following in Trieste and some music shops in Vienna carried her publicity photos. She was no plaster saint. If she had a fault, it was a tendency to play to the house. *Salami*, as the Italians say, hammy. Then her husband would signal to her by cupping his ear. Less *salami*, more *musica*.

Now as she wandered around the hotel suite, she would strike this pose or that from this or that scene, trying on Tosca a bit at a time. Her Tosca was less acted than it was a graphic creation, a profile, an outline, living sculpture. Sarah Smythe, interviewing her for the Clarion Voice, had asked what Tosca felt about Napoleon, a question which only reinforced the Dettori's opinion that Sarah was *cretina*.

"Tosca do not have opinion," she retorted. Sarah kindly paraphrased this as Tosca "was not a political animal."

That did not mean her Tosca failed to react to the news of Napoleon's presumed defeat and his eventual victory. She knew it meant a great deal to her lover Cavaradossi and the Dettori felt the situation was best played in human terms: He for Napoleon, she for Napoleon through him. But, of course, there was Tosca's own status at court to consider, for a victorious Napoleon might change that.

"Vittoria! Vittoria!" Cavaradossi rasps when he hears Napoleon has prevailed, triumph just managing to squeeze utterance from his tortured body. And like palpitations of the heart, Tosca is heard to sing over and over, *"Mario, taci, pieta di me!"* Mario, hush for my sake. Here, the Dettori will plunge a few steps forward, further maddening Scarpia. She will step back

and by the time of the third *pieta di me!* she will have raised her open palm to her brow, that brow now in noble profile, and Scarpia will of course notice her evident distress. Her *pieta di me!* has become "Take pity on me!" and Bruno Cappetto's Scarpia will mock her distraught Tosca by making her a slight bow.

Just thinking of Bruno's hauteur always makes Rita smile, for he is the sweetest of men, the least like a Scarpia. She remembers, as though it were yesterday, the first time his Scarpia made her that little bow and how it scared, yet thrilled her. He was acknowledging her Tosca as a character, giving her more life on the stage than the stage director had bothered to do. Was there more to the bow? More personal? She was the third-cast Tosca in those days, the insurance, one step up from the cover. In fact, people thought she had a nerve to try opera when she had already made her name in operetta. There would be no orchestra rehearsal for her but a piano run-though for her scenes with the pianist mouthing the other roles. And the briefest, most basic of instructions: Make your entrance here. Stand there till…Cross downstage when…Who was Tosca? Who indeed? Everybody knows Tosca.

But not Rita Dettori. She always says she did not begin to know Tosca until Bruno included her physically in this tiniest of scenes! The fight is really between the two men, the hero and the villain. Over and over, with what voice he has left, Cavaradossi flays Scarpia as *"carnefice!"* butcher, butcher. Scarpia sneers the full length of a sentence: "The gallows awaits—even half dead as you are!" A Tosca moaning "Pity me! Pity me!" now interests us: Which victory as she more to fear? Her lover's and his liberty? Or Scarpia's and the collapse of her world?

Then, Rita has to blush. What had possessed her on that long-ago night? Scarpia had bowed. This inspired her to pull herself up and step back. Yes, yes! Tosca's dignified response to his outrageous suggestion. But when Scarpia predicted the gallows for her lover, she made a little run at him, like a terrier at a rat, and tried to shake him. Well, she was young and this was a young Tosca—it was her Cavaradossi's farewell season—and dear Bruno had opened the door to all sorts of theatrical possibilities. How grateful she was to be encouraged to act!

Not a word from Bruno that night, or ever. Her Cavaradossi gave her the curtest of acknowledgments as they arranged themselves for the first curtain call. *"Ecco la Duse,"* he hissed as they smiled at the audience. She was being called actressy—and it would soon be all over town.

And was. The Cavaradossi held forth in the Caffè San Marco. For a tenor,

Tommaso Albi was only middling fat but even in jackboots he was short, shorter than his sopranos, and people still talk about his one innovation in the role: he sat to paint the Magdalene. Fans called it aristocratic.

The young Victor Pompelli ventured to comfort Rita Dettori.

"Albi! Ha! What does he know about acting? He is so lazy he takes a taxi between down stage and upstage. No, you continue with Delsarte, movement for clarity of character that doesn't get in the way of the music. Your sin was—forgive me speaking as a conductor—was to clutter the ensemble. You get your chance soon enough. You have the stage all to yourself with Scarpia and *"Vissi d'arte."* Just look out for Paolo Pacelli, when he is your Scarpia, and his *mani morti*, his 'dead hands' that wouldn't be so funny if you couldn't see them. But even from the pit I can see him patting away. It can throw you off. A Scarpia who paws, now what does that really tell you about Scarpia you don't already know?"

Acting, as Pompelli would expound to the Dettori as they sat in what they were beginning to think of as their café (it was the Giusto), should be used sparingly in opera. "For one thing, there is so little room in a score like 'Tosca.' Puccini carries you note by note. It isn't Mozart where the recitatives allow the time to build character. No such dialogue between arias in 'Tosca.' Not recits at all! And why? The audience listens and the ear helps the eye. You have to look like the Tosca they expect. The great court singer, an actress. But you don't have to act just to keep busy. That is tiresome, *cara*. They will hear Tosca in your voice. You have a color they listen for. Tragic, but may I also say, worthy to kiss."

There began to be many kisses.

About six on the evening of the first Pallas "Tosca," the Dettori helped her husband dress, tying his tie and making sure of his handkerchiefs. Her costumes were already in her dressing room with Othmar's landlady standing by for last minute adjustments. Throwing her fur coat over sweater and slacks, Tosca and her maestro took a stroll down South Main Street and reported for work.

At six, Evey Carruthers Titus had also reported for work. She stood in the ballroom of the Hotel Pallas welcoming opera patrons for a cocktail buffet. The music critics went down the street to a restaurant, the expense accounts of the major dailies feeding the opera mags. Toward seven, the orchestra began arriving to tune and the chorus and extras to be transformed into Romans. By now, the Rev. Weston Macadoo was quite sweet on Sarah Smythe and insisted she help him robe as the cardinal. (She had earlier in the day written up the "society" part of her opening night story and should add details caught at the two intermissions.) In the star's snug dressing room, the Dettori's three costumes were arrayed on dressmaker's dummies and her three hairpieces on wig stands. She made herself up and was fastened into Tosca's act-one dress. Nothing like a seamstress to make you look your best. She could hear the comforting rumble of Bruno Cappetto's voice as he talked to Luigi Luongo in their shared dressing room next door. Then came the vibration of feet as the orchestra climbed down into the pit. Then the gladsome noise of an orchestra tuning.

From stage right, Othmar dressed as the Attavanti and blue contacts making his eyes her blue, slipped into the Attavanti chapel and struck his poise of piety. He could hear the audience beginning to settle in their seats. His audience. The audience he had fought and connived and planned for. The audience he would finally present his "Tosca" to. They smelled pleasantly of perfume and liquor and their voices were high and light and happy. He heard Pompelli rap his baton on his music stands. And rap again. The stage lights came up a hair. The house lights dimmed. The lights for the Attavanti chapel brightened slightly. The Attavanti began slowly to move, to stir from her reverie. With her right hand she gracefully shifted her hood back a fraction so the blond ringlets fell forward. She made the sign of the cross and rose. She glided upstage, her cloak belling out. Gently she swung around, a half turn so she faced down toward the proscenium arch at stage left. Her genuflection to an unseen altar was stately and deep. Away she floated, exiting stage left, as, with a swish, the scrim rose and the ominous chords of the opera loosed themselves forever to change the world.

Tosca was already poised in the darkened wing on stage left as the Attavanti brushed past and disappeared.

"Mario!" Tosca called, the voice liquid fire. *"Mario! Mario!"* Again she called, this time the voice coarsened, vexed. And, to center stage, the Dettori strolled and fixed her staff. There was an intake of breath from the audience and applause, at first scattered, then hearty. The critic from Opera Then and Now was beside himself: Tosca was costumed as she was in 1900. He yelled "Brava!" While seeming to ignore this enthusiasm, the Dettori let it build to a wall of sound. She was pleased of course by the initial reception but she also needed mentally to gauge the distance of the proscenium arch, for all she

could see was a dirty glow. Her strategy was to stay pretty much in one spot and let Cavaradossi play to her. It had worked well at the dress rehearsal, Tosca as diva, she who must be wooed. So she sang straight out to the audience, her voice carrying to the back row of the balcony. That would make the critics sit up and take notice! She found without greatly moving she could vary her pose. She favored Cavaradossi with a languorous gesture to the left and a torrid glance sideways. She could feel the feathers on her hat shake. How they loved in Trieste to see her flirt. *"Rita la civetta,"* Rita the flirt! She felt Cavaradossi's hand on her arm turning her back toward the dirty glow, reorienting her. Better, he thought, for her to face the audience than turn her back on them. She hunted for his voice and homed in.

The audience sat in a trance. For this night they had waited, months it seemed, and not knowing what they would find. It was a civic occasion, of that they were certain, and their noses told them so. You didn't polish your shoes to go to the movies. Opera was new to them. Many factors in their upbringing had represented opera as "difficult" and "exclusive" and "serious." They sought clues that would tell them how to behave, how to listen. Those who had studied the story synopsis for "Tosca" knew what should happen. What they couldn't always tell was whether something important had happened, or was just around the bend, or was still a ways-away from happening, and they'd have to sit tight till this was made manifest. It was not so much the foreign language as being lost in a wilderness of sound. Every once in a while a pretty tune would emerge from the underbrush. Then, time stopped as it did for love songs in the movies. Maybe this was like that, but not a few people wondered that if by enjoying the tune they were missing out on the plot. It was clear that Tosca was madly in love with the young man. He was a puzzle, wasn't he, painting in his good clothes and fooling around with the funny priest. They could see this Mario was a cut above the rest, and that included Tosca—the clothes gave her away. Well, they knew movies like that. The girl who's the chauffeur's daughter catching the boss's son. What you had here was a young man in the clutches of an older woman, and they weren't sure that was a good thing. But being people of good heart, they wanted to give her the benefit of the doubt, and so they sat there patiently, and quietly, and that was the undoing of the Dettori.

She was accustomed in Italy to collaborate with the audience. Her people, as she thought of them, followed where she led. Whenever she was on stage, she could smell them, the wine and later, by the last act, the heavy air of fugitive farts. She could always hear their animal restlessness, the creak of the old seats, the odd hush, the murmurs and muttering; she remembered nights when people talked through the whole performance and the man who hummed. But her people always reacted. What was going wrong here? They were so still. She would have to try harder. She sidled downstage. She began to sell herself to the dirty glow, throwing looks up to the balcony and raking the orchestra seats with dark sightless eyes. She could hear the audience quicken. *Va bene!* Good! In fact, they were startled to be wooed. She flounced back upstage. Cavaradossi caught her with all the grace of an aristocrat and placed her so she could "discover" his painting of the Magdalene. From then on, as though partnering a ballerina, he reeled her in and cast her out, till with one great push he propelled her into the waiting arms of Sarah Smythe, on duty in the wing, and Scarpia could enter.

The audience took at once to Scarpia. They might not know opera but they knew villains and here was the genuine article. Bruno Cappetto too had his *salami* side. He had the bald man's love of stage wigs. For "Tosca" he had two. For Act I he wore his daytime, or working wig of inky black tied at the nape with a big black bow. His makeup was deliberately white to suggest a skull and he was dressed in brown and black which made him strand out against Rome in its light summer garb. On stage he was always an isolated figure. He was the whip hand and one inferred the lashing whip from the way the crowds curled away from him. He played Scarpia very much in profile. He was the master of the flung arm, the disdainful shoulder, the commanding hand, the snapped head. He was particularly proud of the hollowed mouth. The Pallas audience could not get enough of him. Here, they thought, was the man for Tosca.

At the first intermission, Pompelli locked his Rita in her dressing room and sat with her as she changed into her court-singer's gown and jewels. He did not tell her he feared a visit from Othmar over her departure from the staging. A little less playing to the audience, he suggested. That would take care of itself, she thought, with the concentration of scenes with Cavaradossi and Scarpia, and with Scarpia alone. The stage will be brighter too, she said to reassure herself. She was singing well, they agreed. He kissed the daisies on her necklace.

Othmar hid in his darkened office during the intermission. As he now made his way to his seat, another dark figure slipped back to his. For another thing being kept from Othmar was that the Pallas "Tosca" was being recorded.

As with Act One, Othmar had the second act begin with a tableau vivant behind a scrim. A good part of the audience, unaccustomed to opera intermissions, had stayed in their seats. They watched the Palladium curtain rise. For long minutes they peered into the darkened stage trying to see what was going on behind the netting. What would this next scene be, this palace? The rest of the audience shuffled back. The conductor had only to rap once for silence. The lights came up on the Palazzo Farnese as furnished by Evey Titus. From her box, she cast an admiring eye over the gloomy grandeur of the Titus candelabra, the Titus library console, the Titus card table and assorted chairs. She had set Scarpia's supper table herself with big silver serving forks and spoons, dear Bruno advising that an ordinary place setting would look *insignificante, miserabile.* She lent a silver charger to go under his plate and, for the side table, the silver platter that held the Titus family's Thanksgiving turkey and Christmas goose. On this platter was a large prop chicken, one breast carved away, and the carving fork stuck high in the other. For people who read stage sets as they would read a novel, this said Scarpia had dined by himself. Seeing to Scarpia's wine was an extremely thin, tall waiter buttoned into a tight tailcoat. It was the same Ed Nelson, but in his own hair slicked back, whom the audience had laughed at as the Sacristan. You'd never guess, Othmar thought with approval, for it was his idea. Scarpia waved away the waiter. He drew toward him a water pitcher and poured some into a Titus crystal bowl. With a silvery flash of the Titus grape scissors he severed a small cluster and bathed them, deep in thought. Othmar felt anger rise. This was not what they had rehearsed. They had rehearsed peeling a peach.

If there is one thing that Pallas talks of to this day, it's the scene in which Scarpia ate those grapes. He would splay his right hand out and between thumb and forefinger loosen one. This he seemed to inhale in his huge mouth. Then he spat out the skin on his plate. The Opera Mondo critic scribbled "green" in his program. Grapes he could remember; it was significance of the color and variety he needed to ponder. Were they imported? And what does that tell us of Scarpia? Common garden variety Pallas sat transfixed, watching the mound of grape skins build. Here was a territory that lay beyond evil and they sensed it had something to do with elegance. They were almost annoyed when the music broke in and, following a syrupy little tune, Scarpia with terrible satisfaction pronounced Tosca *"un buon falco, "* a good hawk, a good decoy to lure Angelotti into his net.

The Dettori seemed to have her act together and the torture scene was well received. The bloody rag on Cavaradossi's head drew gasps. If few recognized Spoletta's sarcastic quotation of the Dies Irae it wouldn't be the first time. *"Judex ergo sum sedebit Quidquid latet apparebit Nil in ultum remanebit,"* he intones. Tosca tells on, betrays, Angelotti, though just who Angelotti was some people had forgotten. The first act seemed like yesterday. Cries of *"Vittoria! Vittoria!"* burst from Cavaradossi. And cries of *"carnifice!"* as he calls Scarpia a butcher. Scarpia throws him out.

That left Scarpia alone with Tosca.

The audience liked her better in this act. Her jewels were right out of a fairy tale. As a diva (and who knew what else!) she was a better match for Scarpia. Women were always falling for brutes. All that power, and his position. Better in age, too. And he was mad for her. Yearning. He couldn't be the heartless charmer when he offered her the wine with such melting loveliness. She ought to come to her senses and forget the painter. She wasn't helping herself by exposing herself like that. It only brought out the worst in him. He really was something! Never touches her but you just know what he wants. Insinuated right in his voice. Real dirty. Her song is so sad. It won't end well. The audience was not disappointed.

By now Scarpia had moved to his writing table. They'd struck a deal over Cavaradossi. Tosca moves in for the kill. The Dettori felt her way to the serving table where awaited the carving knife with its collapsible blade. It should have been on the platter to the left of the chicken. Ah! No! it was plunged into the chicken. Yes! She pulled it out and advanced with the prongs of the carving fork flashing like fangs.

19.

Othmar's last long ordeal began at the second intermission with a hint of the swamp of congratulations he must cross later that evening. Into his office bounced the Scarpia looking none the worse for just having had a carving fork thrust into his gizzard.

"Gianni, Gianni, we change opera history. Tosca fork me to death!" Bruno Cappetto laughed and presented the lethal weapon. "I, Bruno, see her coming," he said and acted it out. "I pretend as Scarpia I jomp back but not in time. But in time you understand for me, Bruno, to turn. The fork go under my arm. I hold it to me like this," and he clapped his arm across his chest. "Ve-ry-care-ful-ly I fall down dead and it still stick up in the air. *La forchetta fatale.* We laugh and laugh."

Othmar was beyond comment. He opened a desk drawer and drew out four envelopes. Trust the Italians to insist on the old tradition of being paid at the last intermission of each performance. And in cash. Othmar doubted much was declared for Italian taxes. The Scarpia was their *banco.*

"*Grazie,* Gianni," he said, then *"per favore,"* and without waiting for an answer let himself into Othmar's private bathroom. Pompelli had warned of Bruno's "old man" problems.

The final act was without event. Not so the curtain calls. Othmar expected to lead the cast and conductor forward for one final bow, and did, though who would have noticed him? He who had "disappeared" was now caused to disappear. It began with the Pride of Fairstead. They had whipped back down to the dressing room and changed into parade-dress and now marched on to escort the Dettori to greet her adoring public. Toy soldiers! Othmar fumed. "Goddam Rockettes!" Othmar mouthed. He could also have done without the Dettori's "surprise." To the royal curtseys and the "obeisances to art" she now added solo curtain calls to thank the audience. This consisted of her "clapping the house" with weird little cuppings of her hands. "Like castanets," said Gilly later. "Like wind-up false teeth," said Liz, who had small tolerance for diva simperings.

What with a final conference with the box office manager, Othmar was the last to arrive at Old Napoli for the post-curtain buffet.

"Tenn-shunn," bawled Abraham Lincoln King.

His men presented arms. Courtesy required Othmar to take the salute. He seized a Champagne glass.

"To the Pride of Fairstead, Abraham Lincoln King commanding," Othmar entoned. There was a pleased hush as glasses were raised.

"Invincible in peace…" Othmar milked the drama. "…and invisible in war."

People weren't sure about that. In the uneasy silence, the Dettori rushed forward to bestow a kiss on Linc King.

"You don't mean to kill," she said. "I forgive."

"Hip, hip, hooray," bellowed Rollo Shaw. Everybody cheered.

The Dettori, Othmar saw, wore her absurd Sophie Loren eyeglasses.

"Restored miraculously to sight," he said to emptying space.

With her bobbed red hair and black evening suit jingling with black jet, Rita Dettori looked the picture of an opera star. Orchids sprang from each shoulder. "From my Victor and my Bruno," she said.

Evey Titus was resplendent in the first jump suit for evening Pallas had seen. It was panne velvet, black that turned inky blue, and at the simple neckline was a single strand of what all assumed were the Titus pearls. "On me they look real" she was confident. She watched Pallas leave Othmar in isolation. Unforgivable behavior, she thought. Lincoln King was a prize bore but Austin Othmar was a bully, and for this she was sorry. He had talent and potential. She was torn. This morning she had almost decided to give him carte blanche for next year. She would agree to "Traviata"—if he wanted that. And she would raise the money, which would be a considerable amount. Now she thought she had better wait and see.

The party resumed its gaiety. Old Napoli's owner, stunned by the real Italians in his restaurant, circulated with bottles of Asti spumanti. Bruno Cappetto tested the bartender's margaritas. "For Rita." The food was ample but segregated. There were heaping platters of Italian cold cuts and cheeses and caldrons of meatballs for the orchestra and chorus. The Americans had their own table where they chowed down on shrimp scampi. Garlic blessed the air. The Rev. Macadoo watched for Sarah Smythe's arrival with an impatience noticed with interest and approval by his boarders. Mario bobbed up to steer Gilly and Liz toward his own contribution of stuffed veal breast, portions of which were also reserved for the Italian artistes. This had been his first "Tosca" and he was much taken by *la forchetta fatale.*

Having dined before the opera, the flower of Pallas society stuck to highballs and the men prayed for an early departure. Friday was a business day, even if their wives did not seem to remember. Their perfume now ringed Othmar.

"We understand you will give us 'La Traviata' next year," cooed one matron. "Do work us in the ballroom scene," said another tidying his pocket handkerchief.

"'Traviata'?" Othmar was aghast it had reached the public. He smiled without smiling. "You didn't hear 'Traviata' from me," he said.

"Your Othmar is so cute," said the matrons quoting him to Evey Titus. She too smiled, so they knew it must be true, and the next morning there was much excited phoning around Pallas about reviving the old Waltz Evenings so they would be all practiced up.

Unbothered by deadlines, the opera magazine critics staked out a place between bar and buffet. One of the Opera Queens continued his attack on Opera Then and Now for failing to recognize Tosca's first act costume as a replica of that worn by the first Tosca, Ericlea Darclée. Opera Then was not having any of that. "All you know is the studio photo of Darclée dressed like that." One of the Opera Queens sped off to interview the Dettori who surely would know. A third Opera Queen dangled the prospect of lending his Pallas tapes. Opera Mondo brooded about the carving fork. Many months later, he would stun the world with his theory on the deconstruction of opera. The headline read "Murdering 'Tosca'."

The newspaper reviews cannot, of course, be blamed for what happened later. The determining factor really was Evey Titus's tight smile at the idea of a "Traviata" produced by John Austin Othmar. But, in her defense, it must be said she never bore a grudge and if the Italians wanted "Traviata" and Othmar would do it, why, then, she would "have a word with herself" and see that it came to pass. Besides, the Italians owed her a favor for launching Luigi Luongo on his career.

But of the star quality of his voice the big city dailies were not so easily persuaded. The New York Times man, new to the paper and eager to make his mark, had little to say about any of the voices and a great deal to say about the course he felt regional opera should take in America. It was more rhetoric than review. "On the one hand," he wrote, he was for singing opera in the language of origin, and here he dwelt on the coloration that native speakers bring to the lyric art that is opera. Also, "on the one hand," he was for making opera relevant to the American public. Gilly, back in Manhattan by noon, phoned Othmar to read excerpts from the late city edition. "Spare me," said

Gilly, "all this 'one hand clapping' and tell me what the good grey Times wants. 'Tosca' in modern dress? In English? No 'Tosca' as we know and love it but opera about modern problems like mental hygiene and community values?" For the rest, the Times did say the Cavaradossi's "pleasant voice showed promise" and Victor Pompelli "led a workmanlike performance." On the other hand, the Tosca and the Scarpia were examples of acting that gave opera a bad name and the New York Times expressed surprise that this should have been tolerated by an experienced director like John Othmar Austin.

"At least they could have gotten my name right," said Othmar stiffly.

The Boston Globe was more frisky and knowing, managing in the case of the Tosca to slaver over her remaining vocal gifts (and coyly predicting brisk circulation of the illegal tapes) while raising a jaundiced eye at her "Bo Peep" costume for Act I and condemning the provincial look of the entire production, for which the director alone was responsible. The Cavaradossi showed promise, said the Globe, and proceeded to tell him exactly what he should do about furthering his gift. But there were generous and apt things said about the orchestra and chorus and especially about the grand old man who was their maestro. The young American singers were each accorded a colorful adjective or two for future publicity flyers, for which Gilly was grateful. Jonce Jones was called a "talent deserving of bigger things." Alex Avery, who kept count, informed the breakfast table at "Padre" Macadoo's, that printed praise for his "resonance" had drawn even with printed praise for his "full-bodied voice." The Baptist minister's resemblance to a certain Boston cardinal never made it into print, circulating instead on the priestly grapevine. Trying to cheer them up, Sarah Smythe said What do critics know anyway?

The Italians knew nothing of their critical reception (only Pompelli read English with any facility) and Gilly thought, why upset them? Othmar could not wait to shake the dirt of Pallas from his feet.

"Traviata." So once more he had been ignored. No! Worse! He had been betrayed by the one person he trusted. Pompelli! There was nothing he would not do for Pompelli. The extra orchestra rehearsals, the ringers which cost a pretty penny. All he asked was a little time with Pompelli to go over other music. What did he get from the maestro but one "tomorrow" after another, and all because of the clandestine coaching of Luigi Luongo. And when he had finally confided the German experience, Pompelli had laughed at him, and thinking about it now, Othmar swelled with hurt and self-importance. If such a confidence had been made to him, he, Othmar, would have been the figure of consolation. "Shitheads," he would have said to this young singer. "That's what the audience is." *Stronzi!* But, of course, the word bought him back to Pompelli's perfidy.

Pompelli must be in on this "Traviata" deal. How could he talk that way about rehearsing "Elixir" all the time knowing it was in the bag for "Traviata."

"They've got to be stopped!" he muttered.

If they did let me do "Elixir," he argued, you can bet it would be with their cast. Another one of the Dettori's pupils for the Adina. Cappetto's pupil for the Belcore. How many more of these pupils! "It will be *autentico,* Gianni, you will like." He could just hear Pompelli making the pitch. He hated Pompelli. Hated him, when he, Othmar, ventured a suggestion that Tosca move around the artist's platform in such a way, to be told by Pompelli thumping the score "it is already in the music." He could imagine Evey Titus on choosing "Traviata" for next season: "It's a musical decision for Victor to make and I never interfere."

"They've all gotta go," Othmar said to Othmar. "Get'em where it hurts. Vengeance is mine."

All these thoughts ground at Othmar as, on Friday, he made for Albany.

He had slept without refreshment and awoke heavily, the sun slanting in his window. As he backed down the driveway, Mrs. Keohane came hurrying out.

"Not now," he yelled.

"…radio…" she called and waved.

At the theater, people appeared from nowhere to jump him with their problems. The box office manager was short a pair of tickets. When could Othmar release his house seats? Hunt Smith wanted one more choral rehearsal, and wanted it on stage. To save Othmar the trouble, he had gone ahead and scheduled it for Saturday just before the matinee.

Potts was the worst, out of his goddam mind to say the business with the fork should stay in.

"I never believed she would do it with that little knife."

Where had it all gone so wrong?

Amateur Hour, that's where it started. It began with them thinking they could be part of a professional production. It began with Sarah Smythe's assinine articles, her paeons to "community participation." Peons is what they were. "Pee-ons," he roared. "Pee-ons." But it didn't make him feel any better and he began to notice that every twenty feet the Rambler's old shocks bumped where the cement sections of road. The tinsel in his ears was almost deafening.

Just as once he could not find downtown Albany, Othmar now could not escape it, and for almost an hour he was trapped among the grand and curious monuments to civic order and commercial health. In a final, desperate spiral he came to the intersection where he had seen the two unisex beauty parlors and there they were bedizened like rival gas stations in a price war. Later, he promised, and pressed on. He was hungry. He found Burke's gun shop first and it was not until he had been buzzed in that he learned why the tavern across the street was closed.

"By order of the district attorney," said Burke without preamble. Through the dusty rows of fishing rods in Burke's show window, Othmar saw the tavern was dark and a police sawhorse stood across the sidewalk.

"Your friend the cop is in disgrace."

Not my friend, Othmar wanted to say.

"In disgrace for being found on the premises where betting slips were in plain view and him doing nothing about it." Burke laughed. "In dis-grace."

Othmar, his hands going clammy, wondered if Burke had something to do with this turn of events, and if so, if he—Othmar—ought to get out of there right now. But Burke had seized his right hand and pressed a handgun into it, and Othmar was calmed by the cool smooth metal. He followed Burke down to the shooting gallery. Burke came and went, bringing him other guns to try. If there were other customers, Othmar heard or saw none, and he was beginning to worry again if he should be here at all. But the more he shot, the more he shot, as Burke knew he would. And the more he shot, the more he came to prefer one gun in particular, as Burke also knew. "Like an extension of me," Othmar grinned, and he was about to bid it a fond farewell when Burke made his move. First, he named such a ridiculous price that Othmar gagged and then, as if that was settled, gave him the most agreeable of terms.

"Half now, and the other half when you have it. I can't do better than that. These things are not cheap."

When still Othmar hesitated, Burke plucked the gun away and took it upstairs. Another decision made for me, Othmar thought bitterly. Burke now unlocked a drawer and casting an expert eye over the contents withdrew a dark cylinder.

"For the same price," Burke said screwing it on. It was a silencer, and he feigned surprise Othmar had never seen one. Well, why not a silencer? asked

214

Burke. It would save "Jack" the long journey from Pallas, was it? "Jack" could take the silencer into any woods and set up cans and bottles and shoot away, and who'd be the wiser.

Othmar locked the gun in the Rambler and went to have his hair restored to the shining blond it was when he arrived to take Pallas by storm. Several fogs lifted as he joked with Randy the stylist. "Just visiting?" Lucky man, said Randy: Albany was the pits, which Othmar was glad to hear and added a few bucks to the tip. At every stop light, he admired himself in the mirror. The old Othmar was back, Othmar the Magnificent, Othmar the outsider, Othmar packing lead. It had been a mistake to think he could play any part of their game, to do as Pallas does. He drove to the theater.

At his desk sat a blonde. "I came in through the box office," said Sarah Smythe. Then taking him in, she squealed, "Twins, we're twinsies, like the ad!" Blonde she was and monstrously blue-eyed from eye shadow, an apparition of the Attavanti she was going to play at tomorrow's matinee. "I was just leaving you a note to say your landlady had made me my own cloak for the Attavanti. Isn't that sweet, and Aunt Evey and I are going to share it as an evening wrap." Sarah batted her big blues at Othmar. Not because she was flirting but because the makeup weighed on her lids.

"You know, Johnny," she said, and Othmar cringed that this form of his name was so universal, "you could do something so wonderful for Aunt Evey after all she has done for 'Tosca' and let her be the Attavanti for the final performance. And she could take a solo bow. It would mean so much to Pallas. My idea, not hers, and don't ever say I suggested it, promise? Must dash."

"They've both got to go!" said Othmar quietly. "They've got to be removed. Expunged. Erased." The Titus must go first, so Stupid will be wiped out. No! Better still, just the Titus, so Stupid will have to live with it. But make Stupid do it. Make her poison her. Put poison in her whiskey. "A dark one for me, darling!" Or serve her poisoned cheese, cheese she thinks Gilly sent from New York.

There was a problem with this, Othmar quickly realized, and it came down to the fact he knew nothing about poisons or where to get them. He certainly couldn't ask Burke. Not Burke's business. Burke was either a cop or a fence, and certainly a rat-fink, but he was not into poison. Rat poison? Hardware stores probably carried it, though he certainly didn't want to ask old Keohane where he got his. Did it work on people? Rat poison killed dogs; stories about that were always in the newspapers. He supposed he could read up on poisons in the library. He laughed at the niceness of this: To use the Titus Memorial to take care of the Titus.

But poisoning? Was it good enough? It was small, what women did, Othmar thought, and the deed that needed avenging was larger and demanded a larger, grander solution. What the Tituses and Pallas did destroyed not just him but an institution.

Yes! He was beginning to see the solution. He could almost see it in his mind's eye. The process was not unlike the way he gathered ideas for staging anything, say, his late lamented "Elixir." He was a great believer in form. If you got the form right, the production followed. It did not matter he did not really know the story of "Elixir." That would come. It was a romantic comedy and he knew what should go into it. There would be the obligatory "crowd scene." And hadn't haunting museums paid off for that! Some day, when he had made his name, he could aspire to the richly detailed scenes he knew only as flat paintings. The crowd at some English race track with the picnics and the stagecoaches. And those Dutch pictures! He remembered a skating scene on a canal that was complete down to the dog turds on the ice. He could imagine painters blocking their scenes with models and props just as he blocked his with singers and supers.

That was the solution! He would stage the vengeance that was due them. The great Evey Titus would watch it unfold from her box, and Sarah, too, and they would be powerless to stop it, and they would have to live with it for the rest of their lives. It was only right and fitting that he should do something nice, something artistic, for his benefactor. "Surprise me!" she had said.

Saturday was Sarah Smythe's big day. For several weeks now she had been hanging around the theater watching rehearsals and "kibbitzing"—or "kibbutzing," as Jonce Jones first taught her to say—and reflecting in her good-hearted way on how "artists" are different from the people she had known in Pallas and elsewhere. Not that she had any great understanding, she knew, of the world of commerce and industry, say, and the kind of talents summoned to make the better mousetrap. But if everything went well, mousetraps poured off the assembly line and that was that. Everyone had mice; everyone needed a mousetrap.

Opera wasn't something everyone needed, though she felt guilty even thinking the thought. The other thing was, it had to be performed or it didn't exist. It wasn't like a painting or a sculpture in a museum which existed for centuries. So she had the utmost regard for the singers. What a hard life it must be never knowing if someone loved opera enough to want the help of your vocal gift spiritually and emotionally to put it on the stage. (To say nothing of the money it took to put opera on, and God bless Aunt Evey!) She was impressed that the singers were always working on their "instrument" and the care they took of it. At first she thought this was somewhat sissy. No, not sissy, but "taking too good care of yourself" or always playing to win, when the point was to have a good time. She was also struck by how fragmented visually and aurally this world of opera was. She had come to appreciate what Othmar said about theatrical illusion and the ideas you can put in people's mind—the High Altar because that's where the procession is headed. Equally curious is how people saw what they expected to see. So she was as astonished as anyone in the opera that so few of the critics realized Tosca stabbed Scarpia with a fork. Scarpia is always stabbed with a knife, so a fork is a knife. You saw what you knew to expect.

The other puzzlement was the singing voice. Each of the American singers had a distinctive speaking voice. You could hear them talking from a mile away. Up close there was a sort of static in the singing voice, and to Rita Dettori's, a shimmering metallic edge. Sarah never failed to wonder how the voice all came together. Also that it could be so different depending where you heard it. She had been so disappointed listening from the wing, where the vocal sound was close up but sideways, and raw, nothing like the full glory she heard when she sat well back in the theater. She wondered what singers heard, and if they were surprised by hearing themselves on records. Also, from the wing, you saw the voice being produced, the throbbing muscles and rubbery face and the saliva, and that only reinforced how loud and grainy it was. Even Luigi Luongo with his high smooth voice couldn't make it effortless. She thought of the first time she watched Alex Avery sing really deep and how the first idea that popped into her mind was that he was gnawing a bone.

The other thing she realized, and it made her a bit sad, was how tired of it all she was. Tired of "Tosca" and writing her stupid little stories. Tired of dashing, "schlepping"—she wished she had never heard the word.

She looked long into her mirror. "The show must go on."

Second performances of anything are in a category of their own. Opening night is another country with its own time zone and emotional climate, its own history and poets to tell that story. Which is not to say that subsequent performances are not as good. A second performance will often surpass the first. Energy replaces torpor. The cast is more confident, perhaps basking in rave reviews or baring their collective teeth to fight bad notices. In a long run of performances, there comes a time when the director does, or should, return to the production to pump the cast up, to chastise or correct, to inspire, get them excited again. Not so the Pallas "Tosca" with its puny four performances. This time next week, Othmar knew he would see the end of this sorry tale, this travesty of opera, and for this he was grateful.

So it was with disdain bordering on disgust that he made his face up as the Attavanti for the matinee. A mere precaution, for Sarah Smythe was going to do this Attavanti. She had arrived an hour ahead of the costume call, bursting in on the choral rehearsal, insisting on modeling her cloak for whoever she came across. But, as Othmar knew, there was no telling about stage fright. He was prepared; he was the professional.

At five minutes to two, Othmar led Sarah on stage and posed her as the Attavanti at prayer.

"Break a leg," giggled Sarah as he went off.

Down went the stage lights and up went the black curtain behind the scrim. It was a long five minutes she had to wait till a flashlight from the wing opposite would signal her to start. She could hear the audience arrive. She even thought she knew certain voices. That had to be Gretchen's silly laugh. Would they recognize her? Another thought brushed up against this. Why was Othmar in makeup? Had he forgotten he said she could be the Attavanti? Was it his way of saying she shouldn't be up there on stage at all? She had rehearsed the little scene. How difficult could it possibly be! She shook off the thought and straightened her shoulders. She would show him.

Now came the flashlight signal to move. Despite makeup which made her face feel huge and eyeliner which caused tearing, she had quickly adjusted to stage lighting. She could perfectly see where she was meant to go, and she did, precisely moving along those space-defining angles that made the audience think they were seeing aisles and altars where none existed. But it was also like a bad dream and her little minute in the limelight—they had put a very low follow-spot on her—was an eternity.

From the manager's box, Othmar watched with satisfaction. He was right. Amateur Hour! She can't walk. She had jiggled while kneeling at prayer, had gone out of character. He would have a lot to tell her when he gave the cast their performance notes! She couldn't even hold the pose he had devised for himself because he knew, from experience, how long it is to wait.

With anticipation he saw the scrim rise. With joy he awaited the magic of opera to begin. He heard Puccini introduce the character who must set the stage. He saw Angelotti materialize from the shadow of the chapel crypt. Othmar hugged himself. This was almost his favorite scene in the opera. He was prepared to be entertained by another man's fright.

But even in the dim light, Othmar could tell there was something wrong. He heard it first in the voice, which was dark but muffled by the orchestra when it should have cut through. Then he saw it confirmed in the figure of Angelotti. Was he drunk? Was Jonce Jones drunk? But, no! it wasn't Jonce. The voice told him that and the movement which was a cartoon of the character that Jonce had made Angelotti. Musicians say they can tell about a soloist or conductor by the first three measures. If you get the Angelotti right, Othmar believed, you get "Tosca" right, and Jonce Jones's voice and very being—his bright "hoarseness" and the excited stillness of a hunted man— proclaimed that Rome lived under a despot. There was none of that now! The gestures were over-broad and the jerky posture a parody of fear. Not that the audience would know—in fact, they watched Angelotti with fascination— but Othmar knew, and he was buoyant with rage. Without telling him, Alex Avery had gone on for Jonce Jones.

"Where is Jonce?" Othmar demanded when he caught up with Alex after a migraine-causing number of the Dettori's curtain calls.

"New York," said Alex, greasing off his makeup. "The big auditions."

"Why wasn't I told?" Othmar asked before he realized the words were out of his mouth.

"We thought you knew. Anyway, I'm famous. My hat trick. I'm going to be on the radio Monday." He chortled. "Matter of fact, I'm going to send it in as question for the Met broadcast." And mimicking the fruity tones of the opera quiz host: "Panel members, in which performance of 'Tosca' did one singer play three roles, one in each act?"

Huddled further along the makeup bench, Sarah heard all. She was blinded by cold cream and she was having trouble seeing where she had smudged her mascera. She was humming *"Vissi d'arte."* At the company's first curtain call, one of the boys paging the curtain had come forward to thrust a floral tribute at Sarah. The donor's intent had been a spring bouquet but there was confusion at the florist's and she was handed a single tall Easter lily in a pot. She stood it next to the cold cream jar, and wondered who would have sent it? for the purple florist's foil still hid the message: "With love from West."

Othmar was now shouting. It was nasty, violent, Sarah thought. She gave a final swipe to her eyes. She must intervene. She rose and stepped forward just in time to get Othmar's hand full across her face as, with a last cry of rage, he ran out. Blood raced from her nose.

It was hardly to be expected that the second post-performance party would be as glamorous as the first. The orchestra had split, as had most of the chorus, but it was "great fun," Sarah insisted, with much being made of the boychoir by their parents, though a son in lipstick was not to every father's liking. Sarah spotted the little kid with the big voice who sang the offstage shepherd's song. "You'll never forget this," she promised and began to weep.

"Next time," said Othmar deliberately seeking her out to give her a performance note, "please remember not to walk on your cloak. We thought you would never make it across the stage."

That stung, as it was meant to, and she wandered over to the table where the Americans were hanging out with Ed Nelson's girl and Rollo Shaw's fiancee. Plans were afoot to drive over Lebanon mountain to a roadhouse called the Showboat. "Come along with us and 'Forget yo'troubles,'" Rollo sang to Sarah. He had overheard Othmar and was appalled by the cruelty. That is why Sarah Smythe found herself slow-dancing with Alex Avery and it was so wonderful and natural snuggling with him in the car driving back. "Come home with me," she decided she would whisper, and he would whisper back, yes, yes, he would; and so she said it into his ear.

"Why, Miss Sarah," replied Alex Avery in his comic Rastus voice, "Ah thought yo'knew Ah was saving ma self fo' marriage."

20.

On Sunday Othmar went shooting. It was a low grey day, warm, and moist underfoot. He drove through the state forest and decided against stopping because of the public aspect of its footpaths and trash bins. Further along he saw the well-kept forest unravel. Othmar pulled the Rambler into the beginnings of a lane and followed a stone wall deep into woods. Burke had been right about the quiet of the gun. The crunch of leaves was louder than its hiss. At first Othmar popped away, content to splinter tree limbs. A curious squirrel present himself as target. Othmar took aim, then dropped his hands. He was not here for squirrels. Walking on, he came to a long stretch of ice, perhaps a pond. He expended three precious bullets trying to make them skitter on the hard grey surface the way he used to skip stones on water. The ice wasn't as much a target as a puzzle, a working out of angles. He became aware of the sun dipping, of the chill in his fingers. And that he was as alone as he had ever been. He could well believe no one had been in these woods except himself, and, with regret, he retraced the small disturbances in the fallen leaves that his own feet had made an hour ago. Regaining the Rambler and the dusty warmth of its radiator, he drove on letting the road take him where it would, and all the while he made lists.

He was well along in his plan to make "Tosca" his instrument of justice. He cast himself as the Roberti in this, a role he once thought of taking, Scarpia's tame judge, the one who hears the evidence and renders the judgment that Scarpia wants to hear. "Fit the punishment to the role," Othmar now sang.

Save for the odd refinement or two, he knew how it would be accomplished.

There was a certain poetic justice in staging it in his beloved theater. There wasn't a one of them who hadn't profaned the lyric art the Palladium stood for and they had to answer for sabotaging his goal of ensemble opera. Ensemble! Ha! He would make sure in his next production he auditioned each and every singer. With the exception of Alex Avery, he had been able to do that for the small roles and it had paid off. Furthermore, those four had reason to be grateful: Not every production spends so much time on diction and coaching. And they had thanked him—he gave them that. All except Jonce Jones.

That figured, didn't it! Jones was too grand for poor little Pallas. What use could Othmar possibly be to him when he was auditioning for the big time. What did Angelotti matter to him? An inconvenience. As Angelotti was to Scarpia, Othmar thought. Then, mimicking The Titus as inspiration struck, he said: "Everyone forgets about Angelotti."

Angelotti was a sign. Angelotti was a warning signal lest he fail to complete the grand pattern of "Tosca." Not as showy a death because it happens off stage, but the first. Let Alex Avery boast about his pathetic hat trick, a different role in each act. From the wreckage of "Tosca," he, Othmar the Magnificent, had plucked a four-leaf clover. His rage had cooled to more useful anger, and anger was calming, anger made life effortless.

"To review," he said. The road stretched on. His headlights danced across country intersections. "Must not leave anybody out."

The rot began with Pompelli, the maestro whom he worshipped, whom he had indulged with extra orchestra rehearsals and uncounted numbers of (paid) ringers to make the best of the meager orchestral talent available in Pallas. How could Pompelli do that to him? And it got worse. How could Pompelli foist his wife on a production he must know she was not up to. Who's blind here? Who's the blind man? So she could still sing. But you don't hear the singing when she's so grotesque it blots it out. "Bo Peep!" That critic nailed it on the head. And a tenor who came to the first rehearsal without even one performance under his belt. It wasn't professional. He blamed not just Pompelli but Cappetto who was putting his own selfish interests ahead of the ensemble.

And Evey Titus. "You know I never interfere in musical decisions." Ha! Interfering bitch from the start. She lets Cappetto horn in on my rehearsal time to teach his precious nephew what he should have arrived already knowing. Of course, "darling Victor" and "dear Bruno" would be only too glad to eat her repulsive food and laugh at her awful stories. One hand washes the other. She plays the grand patron and takes the credit for Luigi Luongo. The critics may be right: he's just another pretty face from Italy who will get cut down to size the first time he sets foot in a major house.

No! They are all in on it. Even the Americans who contrived to get her around on stage. And Potts, too, for thinking up the system of flashlights to guide her.

I will wreak vengeance. I will bring my temple down upon them.

"Me, Sampson!" Othmar shrieked as he drove.

His plan, the more he thought about it, had elegance and integrity. It as worthy of him, for he believed in being true to the creator's intentions. He would follow the text. They would die in the order and manner as they do on stage. His "Tosca" would be a memorial to art betrayed.

Early on Monday Othmar phoned Evey Titus.

"Sorry for the hour," he said, "but I've got to take Old Paint in for a lube. And I want to make some plans for closing night. What I'd love to do is to have you take a curtain call with the whole company. Without you—as the saying goes."

Evey thought that was less than gracious.

"I'd be delighted."

"Just as soon as the curtain comes down, you should find your way to the stage manager's corner. That's to the left of the stage as you look at it. The cast bows first. Then we begin the solo bows for the small roles. Well, you know the drill! I wouldn't be surprised if there were bouquets. The boys paging the curtains will bring them on."

Would he take much longer, she wondered. She had a full day ahead.

"The other thing I want to discuss is 'Traviata.' It's all over town you want to do it next year. I've talked to the maestro about it. It would seem we've got the Alfredo and the Germont right here in the 'Tosca' cast. The gals I talked to at the opening night party are dying to appear in the ball scene."

Evey was annoyed. Next year was not as settled as Othmar seemed to think.

"What if I got the costume sketches to you next month and you got Mrs. Keohane busy on making the gowns. The cloak she made for Sarah gave me the idea. She does terrific work, she could even head the costume shop, and it'll save us money."

Evey snorted at the "us." Efforts to enlist Othmar in fund-raising had come to naught, in part, because she found him so surly.

"I'm pretty sure I can find decent sets to rent. 'Traviata' is a repertory piece. But the whole schmeer will cost more than 'Tosca' because there has to be more music prep. Luigi Luong hasn't done Alfredo yet. I'd really like to have them here for a month again so Bruno can work with him. That turned out really well, though I have to confess I still think we were a bit short on rehearsal time for the kind of ensemble opera I want us to stand for."

The "us" again.

On and on he went. Once again he struck Evey as someone who had no one to talk to.

"I'm glad to hear of your interest," she said when she could get a word in. "Victor has mentioned 'Traviata' to me. But, especially because of the expense, I do think I will have to have to present it to the opera board." That did not commit her, she thought.

Othmar gave a sultry laugh. "I imagine what Evey Titus wants she gets." The nerve!

Then he was back to talking about the closing night of "Tosca," making sure she knew where to go.

"I want the last curtain to be a curtain call to remember."

By late morning, Othmar was out shopping. It was raining and he pulled a Navy watch cap over his blondness. He drove north of Pallas. In a big town in the next county of he found another gun and tackle shop that seemed more geared to the sportsman than Burke's. He made two purchases, the second because he deliberately let the clerk talk him into it. "You'll be glad you picked this up now," said the clerk in the way clerks have of reassuring customers they got a bargain. "Deer season will be here before we know it." Striking east, Othmar hit two hardware stores. In a matter of minutes he bought two dark tarps and canisters of spray paint.

At the next store, he spent almost an hour in his guise as the new owner of a fishing camp. It was a real dump, he told the clerk, and he didn't know what he was going to do for a dock. A good buddy told him to go with a float and said he would help him make it out of oil drums. Not a bad idea, Othmar confided, but his pal failed to solve the problem of what to do with the float when the pond froze. "All granite ledge so it's dammed hard to pull a float up on shore," said Othmar, and the clerk said, yes, ledge sure was a problem around here. He, Othmar, said he was thinking of a little plank wharf you could winch up with a come-along at the end of the summer, and what did the clerk think about that? And was chain better for the come-along than cable, and why? Cable, said, the clerk, no question, and got out a pencil and drew a little wharf on brown wrapping paper, and showed him a good way of hinging it by using metal pipe which ran the width of the planks, and two ways of weighting it, one with a bucket filled with cement. Cable, Othmar reflected as he lugged the wire coil back to the Rambler, was quieter than chain.

His final stop was at a five and ten. He was back in the boyhood smells of frying donuts and talcum powder, and for sentimental reasons, he paid a visit to the turtles. Still boring, despite the Disney decals on their shells. They were out of black crepe paper, the motherly clerk apologized. All bought up for Hallowe'en, and the store really should reorder. Othmar settled for six yards of navy and six of spruce.

With the opening night of "Tosca" behind them, the good people of Pallas moved on to other concerns. Merchants changing their windows for Easter discarded the opera posters along with the St. Patrick's Day shamrocks. Along Main Street, "Tosca" might never have been. Sarah Smythe wrote next to nothing, too dispirited by the reviews to do the round-up of critical reaction she had intended. Nursing her own hurts she no longer stopped at the Rev. Macadoo's kitchen for a second breakfast.

Every Titus ordered a headstone for Maida. Her poor frozen little body had been recovered by Dr. Brielman who wrapped it snugly in butcher's paper and took it to the community meat locker. "What we got here? Deer meat?" said the locker man, and Brielman said that was so.

The cast was beginning to break camp. Jonce Jones was still in New York and the other Americans scattered for a day or two. While Othmar was out shopping on Monday, Evey Titus drove Bruno Cappetto and Luigi Luongo down to New York for an audition that Gilly had arranged in the Fifth Avenue apartment of mutual friends. Gilly also managed to trade of copy of Victor Pompelli's own pirate tape of Luigi's big numbers from the Saturday performance for a copy of Opera Queen's complete tape, which was unaccountably marred in places. Gilly was the picture of politesse listening to Victor try to sell him Rita's best pupil for the Pallas "Traviata."

"I return to coach," promised Rita.

"Here we go again," groaned Gilly to Liz. Later, over dinner at a new fish place, they spent long minutes hashing over Evey Titus's request to Gilly. "Tell Othmar it's fine with me if he wants to do 'Traviata' next year. Tell him it really would go. I would tell him myself but he thinks I'm a meddlesome old bag who doesn't know anything. Just tell him to go slow on it. I don't want to find I've created a monster."

"Poor Evey," said Liz. "The fun has gone out of her."

Othmar had five full days to convert the Palladium into his instrument of revenge. "Always begin with the hardest part," he could hear his mother say. Accordingly, Monday evening found him on stage and in the two levels underneath.

"I'll lock up," he told Potts. "I've got to get in that bottom cellar and make sure we have a full set of sections for a raked stage. The inventory says we do but I need to be sure for next season. There is talk of a theater company coming for a month. The more they can rent the Palladium the better for the bottom line."

Potts knew speechifying when he heard it. If Othmar got his jollys messing in cellars, so be it! Potts thought he would take the pretty interne out for dinner. He was right: She had the makings of a stage manager. He would encourage her, bring her along, make sure she got hired for his next job.

Othmar worked expeditiously. He loved a project. Although of short gestation, this one was unfolding with the sureness of long careful planning. The first task this evening was to verify a crucial spacing on the stage itself. With his carpenter's tape, he measured just how far over he would have to shift the stage piece in the last act that the audience knew as the angel figure crowning the Castel Sant'Angelo. Not quite eighteen inches would do it, and it might not even have to be re-lit. He would blame the move forward on the need to bring the shepherd boy downstage. "The audience can't hear the kid," he would say. No one would notice that the move now fully exposed the trap door.

Next, he went into the basement beneath the stage and, working the pulley, eased the trap door down till it hung vertically. The trap was exactly how he remembered it from his very first tour of the theater nearly two years ago. One of the mushroom cellar vents lay directly under the trap. How fixed was that vent? he wondered. He let himself into the cellar and played his flash upwards. To his great relief, he found the vent was nothing more than a wooden grille, and, better still, it was hinged so it too was a trap door. Goddam clever of the architect, Othmar thought, to put a trap under a trap. A stage crew could lower pieces of scenery and furniture from stage level to the mushroom cellar without carting the stuff outside and around to the cellar gangway. At a guess, it was a two-story drop from stage level to bottom-most cellar floor. "About three from the Castel," he said to be on the conservative side.

He spent the rest of the evening oiling hinges. He located the extension ladder and stowed it for future use. Odd how one task lets you think about another, he mused, as his mind wandered back to something he thought he had seen in Keohane's barn.

On Tuesday he went to yet another hardware store and bought more cable as well as a sack of pre-mix cement, two pails and a bunch of eye-hooks.

Tuesday evening, Potts took the pretty interne to the movies. She was ambitious and he was hungry; and if Othmar wanted to lock up again, well, let him. Potts was not one to say he never listened to gossip but from what he heard and saw (and passed on to other ears) he was pretty sure Othmar was dead meat. None of the singers exactly warmed to him, and as a man and an American, Potts was ashamed of Othmar's treatment of the Italian lady. Her eyes weren't her fault and everyone else had helped out. Difficult to say who spotted the trouble first, but the word spread like wildfire. He heard it from Ed Nelson who usually played cribbage with him during the second act. As the Sacristan, Ed had to kill the next two acts while waiting to take his bows in costume at the end. Ed probably heard it from Bruno Cappetto. The Sacristan and the recently-deceased Scarpia played gin during the second act. "And from heaven above, Puccini smiles down," said the pretty interne.

The interne, as it happened, was the source of the rumor that Othmar had killed a singer on stage. She got this from someone who had gone to the college where it was supposed to have happened. "Do you think it's true?" she asked Potts, fount of all knowledge. Potts ran it past Ed Nelson who said he heard from someone at Eastman that it happened when Othmar flew the Witch in "Hansel and Gretel."

But it was an accident, Ed was sure. "Accidents can happen."

"Ay-yuh," said Potts and scooted ahead of Ed on the board.

With Potts again out of the way, Othmar spent Tuesday night hard at work. That afternoon when he saw Keohane drive off, he had slipped into the barn. What he sought was on a high shelf almost out of sight. He made a mental note to buy talcum powder. The theater was as Potts had left it, the ghost light in its accustomed place down stage. The glow played off the proscenium arch with its ropes of laurel in gilt plaster. Othmar saluted with a bow. "The gods are good," he said. "The gods smile. Athene smiles. This is her temple." Then he went below to where the evening's task lay.

His plan required a mechanism to close both traps upon command but without his direct intervention. "I will of course be in full public view the whole evening."

That night he built it, a system as simple as it was effective. It was a slightly extended version of the way a sash weight will raise and lower a window. Not that reclosing the traps was strictly needed but it was a refinement he enjoyed devising. He came very close to whistling as he worked, then remember it was one of the theatrical superstitions, such as wearing purple on stage brought bad luck, or his mother's conviction that a hat on the bed meant a death. Strange, his mother's generation. Best not to think about that.

Mixing the cement in the pails, he set each to harden with an eye-hook plunged in the center. Then he addressed the traps. "Measure twice, cut once," he murmured. It all came back to him, though he'd never worked on a project as richly complicated as this. With a time table, and contingency plans. He loved the sound of "contingency plans." Had to be British, some war film, where war was like a chess game. Not a cowboy flick which was all action, and throwing rifles around, and how, just how, did Burke know he could catch a long gun tossed to him? He had been incredibly flattered, but, the more he thought about Burke, it scared him, What did Burke know?

Once again he opened the traps so the doors hung down.

To the underside of each, on its blind or downstage side, he now intended to attach lengths of cable. That the cable was downstage meant it was less likely to be seen from above. Not by her, but by the stage crew. He ran the wire from the stage trap through eye-hooks screwed under the stage floor. "Right-y tight-y, left-y loose-y," he caroled as he turned the screws till they sank home.

On to the mushroom cellar. The wire from that trap he ran through eye-hooks along the cellar ceiling. These two tributaries flowed to join the main stream. He thought of it as the map of a great river system, the Ohio and the Missouri fetching up with the Mississipi. He had loved geography class and making maps. The Missouri was the vertical cable, each end of which was attached to a cement-filled pail. He had so rigged it that when the weights were in equilibrium, the cable was slack and the trap doors flapped down, or open. But if you freed the main cable of its top pail, the bottom pail would plummet, yanking at the horizontal wires which, in turn, would draw the trap doors up till they closed. It was so simple, and so exhilarating. He sniffed his palms. He liked the smell of the metal cable. It smelled like guns.

The cement took longer. It would harden by tomorrow evening. For a tiny moment, Othmar wished he had someone to show his handiwork to.

On Wednesday morning, Potts stopped by Othmar's office to beg leave to go back to Boston for a couple of days. There was a job he wanted to see about for the summer. The pretty interne could handle tomorrow night's performance. He would return Friday noon for the grand finale on Saturday.

Take the interne, too, Othmar said jovially, and offered to work in her place. Potts colored. "We'll see."

As soon as Potts left the room, Othmar did Liz's "dirty old man" routine.

The whole of Wednesday evening Othmar spent in the cellar constructing a new mattress. He thought of it as the ghost of the old. The old one had come off someone's double bed a million years ago. He and Potts had found it at

Goodwill and lashed it to the Rambler's roof. That was when he and Potts were still speaking. But Potts had taken the Italians' side and joined the conspiracy about her eyesight. It was Potts who came up with the idea of flashlights in the wigs, a glare toward which the Dettori could home in on. And it was Potts who recruited stage hands or singers, whoever was free, to catch her as she exited and get her in position for her next entrance.

"Without so much as asking me!" said Othmar as he unrolled the crepe paper. "What did they think I was going to do? Fire her? Cancel the run?" Othmar could not very well pursue those thoughts without implicating himself. For it was his dirty little secret he had let himself be persuaded this Tosca did not need a cover. "My Rita never miss a performance," Pompelli told him. For form's sake, there were covers for the principals about whose availability Gilly had inquired. But it was understood the covers would not actually come to Pallas.

Bill Potter's defection was, in some ways, more hurtful than Pompelli's deceit. Potts was the only true outsider. "My guy," Othmar said. The others all had links. Links to Gilly especially. Who else but Gilly had landed him with this cast? He would have cast it himself, but Gilly had dangled Pompelli, and Pompelli came with his own Tosca. How could Pompelli have fallen for that joke of a Tosca? Bill Potter took her side.

Bill Potter was the only one of the backstage staff whom Othmar knew from other productions. He went back to Othmar's Boston days and—it seemed months ago now—as Potts worked with him rigging a mattress to catch Tosca, they traded Sarah Caldwell stories, and "Tosca" stories, and opera and theater stories. Potts was tops, a quiet man, a perfectionist who sat "out front" once a week to spot any deviations from the director's wishes. Lazy actors thought he was a fink. Of theatrical content, Potts had no opinions. He was a problem-solver not a critic: the ghost of Hamlet's father was the same to him as Madame Arcati's blithe spirits. Almost his first words to Othmar had concerned Tosca's jump.

"A murphy should do it," Potts had said.

"A what?"

"Murphy bed."

Potts was always two jumps ahead of you. He'd had his tape out and he knew the castle ramparts came within eight feet of the cyclorama. There was plenty of room for a mattress to catch Tosca. The beauty of the Murphy wall bed, or Potts' version of it, was that it folded up against the set for storage. That meant you did not have to built it its own tower and roll the tower up to the scenery.

The morning that Othmar help build the Murphy bed he learned just how encyclopedic Potts' mind was. Potts could name every Tosca who did not "jump." The Toscas who walked into the wing, Toscas who ducked behind the angel statue and hid, the Tosca who slid down a chute. He knew about stage hands catching Tosca in their arms, about stage hands catching her in a blanket, about the Tosca who jumped into a firemen's canvas circle.

"And the famous time," grinned Othmar, "where she jumped onto a trampoline and bounced right back up in full sight."

"So I have been told and do in part believe."

A mattress would work but Potts worried about accidents. There had been the Tosca who overshot and broke her back. He would equip the Murphy with cloth sides to guide this Tosca.

"It will be like jumping into a bag or box." Potts thought some more. "She won't really have to jump far. Like jumping off a curb and sliding onto to her, on her fanny, and curling up."

It was Othmar's turn to ponder this. "Won't her body be seen from the second balcony?" Othmar had pledged to give the cheap seats the full value of his production. He promised empty Roman air when his Tosca jumped. But, goddam, if Potts hadn't already been up to the highest row in the balcony to make sure.

"No," said Potts, "especially if her cloak falls over with her. Or some of it. It'll cover her. And the part left on the rampart will nail the impression she jumped. It's still pretty dark on stage at that point. You've got the cyke brightening up at the top as the sun rises. And there's the distraction of whoever they are moiling around."

"The soldiers and Spoletta."

"Them," Potts conceded, "and a fast curtain does it."

Othmar hid his version of a Murphy under tarps. He would install it Friday night.

21.

On Thursday morning Othmar made a close, final inspection of the artist's platform that the Cavaradossi uses to paint in the Attavanti chapel. It would serve admirably, and he himself would supervise and refine its position on stage. "Gotta be moved," he could hear himself say. "They can't hear the kid."

That afternoon, with the idea of causing trouble for Evey Titus, he stopped in to see his landlady, Mrs. Keohane. The radio on, she had been sewing in the kitchen, which smelled stuffily of baked beans, and Othmar was not sorry to be bustled into the little living room.

"This is nice," she said, more like his mother than ever, for she was able to listen to at least two things at once. "She's as good as her word," and Mrs. Keohane nodded toward the radio blasting in the kitchen. "She promised to have each of the American singers on her show." Othmar cringed to hear Jonce Jones parry a question about his future plans. He gestured for her to turn the sound down.

"It isn't too soon to plan for next season," he bellowed. "I hope you will rent me the same place."

"Imagine that!" she exclaimed, when Jonce said, fatuously Othmar thought, that his debut would be in "a major German opera house." Othmar held his cup out for more tea. "Jonce is only going to Wupperthal," he said making the name sound absurd. "Where I used to sing—but we all have to start somewhere. Now about next season…" And here Othmar began reciting the script in his head about Mrs. Keohane making the costumes for the ball scene in "Traviata."

"You know about singers having to audition?"

She guessed she did.

"Well, when I saw the workmanship, the art, in that cloak you made for Sarah Symthe, a little light bulb went on, and I said to myself, we've got the costume maker we need right here in Pallas, and that's you. You know

'Traviata' and how it has these two party scenes and they're all in formal dress? The idea would be for you to make the ball gowns. Mrs. Titus is going to invite her friends to appear as the party guests. But don't let her know I told you this."

Mrs. Keohane pursed her lips and went to turn down the radio.

"To put on an opera like 'Traviata' is very, very expensive but Mrs. Titus thinks she can raise the money. You can understand why she doesn't want to announce 'Traviata' till she's got most of the money in the bank."

Mrs. Keohane could see the wisdom of that.

"But between you, me and the lamp post"—Othmar sold this with a sly wink—"it's on for next season. Then, I had my most brilliant idea, and that is, why not make you head of the costume shop. In charge of the cutters, and fitters, and sewers. Men's tailoring you might not want to do, and we might rent those. Even so, getting the ball gowns done here would save us a bundle. There is just one thing…" Othmar looked sternly at Mrs. Keohane so she would know who was in ultimate charge of the production. "You probably know that the stars bring their own costumes."

"The signora," Mrs. Keohane managed to slip in.

"But with the ball scene and the gambling scene, for Mrs. Titus's friends and the rest, the chorus ladies, I figure a total of twenty gowns, thirty max." Othmar was making this up and so he hurried on. "I would get the costume designs to you this summer."

Mrs. Keohane made as if to ask a question.

"No, not now," he said, "Not till I get the okay from Mrs. Titus. Our little secret," he said, luxurious in deceit. Then, quickly, for he had noticed Mrs. Keohane was a talker, he let out the sigh he had been practicing and leaned forward.

"Now, I've got something to tell you that embarrasses me. "It's about the theater and maybe I should ask you husband. We have a rodent problem."

"Rats," said Mrs. Keohane.

"People bring food to the rehearsals. I'm ashamed to say Signora Dettori has seen one in her dressing room."

Mrs. Keohane rose and went into the dining room. From the china cupboard she fetched a white tin.

"Cyanide," she said.

Othmar blanched. What, then, was in the white tin in Keohane's barn? Keohane was always talking about rats. "You?" he sputtered.

Mrs. Keohane enjoyed his reaction. "What you do is buy hamburg meat, the cheapest, and dish washing gloves, and you take a flower pot, I've probably got one of those, and you make the hole bigger. And you mix it in the meat. Then you put the pot upside down over it, and secure it to the ground, so dogs won't get at it. Find a dark, quiet place—that's important. Did you know they're shy? The rat will climb in but will be dead before it can get out. That way they don't die in the walls and make a terrible smell. My husband," Mrs. Keohane gave a sweet smile, "thought it was the best idea I ever had."

She handed the tin to Othmar. "Go on!" she said, sensing a reluctance. "There's plenty more. Jewelers keep it for cleaning. I do the bead stringing for Kay's, pearls mostly and garnet necklaces for babies, and they give it to me for my husband."

In a light sweat, Othmar drove to the theater. He had been prepared to steal old Keohane's tin with its skull and cross bones promising poison. Take some out and replace it with talcum powder. No one the wiser, except later when it didn't matter. "Do the rats a favor." It was unnerving to be offered it by his smiling wife. "Complete with recipe." She was sure to keep after him. "She will ask what I paid for the hamburger." Othmar disliked being pushed. He might just forget Angelotti.

But Jonce Jones had not forgotten him.

About six o'clock came a knock at Othmar's office door.

"As I live and breathe!" said Othmar forcing a laugh. "I suppose I should have your hide. But come in and tell me all about it."

"Just for a minute. I'll give you the gory details later." Jonce Jones stood alert but easy, round-featured and deep-chested, and Othmar, who needed to know everything bad about everybody, suspected Jonce worked out. And probably had lessons in "Alexander Technique" for stress. Confidence and duplicity oozed—Othmar's word—from Jonce's every pore.

"I want to clear something up," said Jonce. "Alex thinks you didn't know he was going to cover me. It was in my contract I could be away if I got a cover."

"Only for a rehearsal."

"Actually, not specified. So I got Alex to do the matinee."

"Without asking me? How do you suppose I felt? Suppose Alex couldn't hack it? What was I going to do? You made me feel like a goddam fool."

"We thought you knew," Jonce said with maddening clam. "So I taught it to Alex, and Potts let us rehearse it on stage. Angelotti is only on in the first act. It looked safe. The reviews were already in. And it was just the matinee."

"Even so, Jonce, it wasn't professional." But so little contrite did Jonce appear that Othmar refused to ask about the "major German opera house" that Gilly had already told him he was negotiating with on Jonce's behalf. It wasn't Wupperthal. There was a hanging silence. Far off, a door banged. The cast was beginning to arrive.

"You should know," said Jonce, "about Gilly and how he sings your praises all over New York. People can't wait to work with you. And there's one more thing I've got to tell you. Before it's too late and we all go away. I've liked working with you. You listen. I've learned a lot and the others have too. You cannot imagine the luxury of having Rita as coach. Do you have any idea that that would cost in the city?"

At seven, to allow for his eyes to tear, Othmar inserted his blue contact lenses. The evening's performance went without incident.

On Friday morning, Othmar went to the bakery next to Kulda's. "Only the best will do," he said as he bought a pan of brownies. At a superette he bought a can of chocolate frosting. "This is a budget production," he joked with himself, and totted up the hardware. He would bring his "Tosca" in well under five hundred bucks.

On Friday afternoon, Gilly arrived by train and found Othmar in his office. Liz would drive up tomorrow.

"You've got a hit, mon vieux, a palpable hit!"

Othmar boxed the air.

"Rival managements are, as we speak, checking into the hotel to check out Luigi baby."

Othmar shrugged.

"Let's clear the decks on this one," said Gilly. "Just so you know: I got there first. I talked with him in New York on Monday and an hour ago I signed him."

On Monday? Talked with him Monday? Othmar tried to register, to think what that meant. "On Monday," he said.

"On Monday. Evey Titus drove him down, drove them down, for an audition, which I'll tell you about later. It went very well."

No response from Othmar.

"So I would appreciate it, old friend, if you didn't say anything. They'll try to pump you. That creep from Gotham Artists is here, and both partners in

'Toil & Trouble.' Which means the 'SUMI wrestlers' will get here by curtain time. You can be very proud of yourself, Johnny."

Still no response. This wasn't playing out the way Gilly thought it would.

"You can have him next season for 'Traviata.' Please take him for a month, if you want. You deserve it. And, between us, he'll need the coaching. Just let me know which month or months it might be."

Othmar continued to look fixedly at the floor. At last he said: "My preference for next season is for 'Elixir' which he could also do. And which we could tour."

Gilly danced away from that one. It would be better if Evey Titus told Othmar what she had been persuaded to tell him herself at dinner after the final curtain.

"Which ever. He's yours. Can I take you to dinner? I owe you."

Othmar begged off. He was tired, he said. "And looked it!" Gilly told Liz when he phoned to crow over signing Luigi Luongo to his exclusive management. Free of Othmar, Gilly paraded the Italians though the hotel, making sure they were seen in the hotel bar as his guests. Bruno Cappetto tried the Olympus martini. On their way out to dinner, Gilly waved merrily at "Toil & Trouble," otherwise Boyle who did all the work and Hubble who, as someone said, had a Ph.D in intrigue.

Friday evening found the Rev. Macadoo looking over his text for Sunday's sermon and wondering what shape he would be in to deliver it. There had been so many distractions of late. But his mind was resolved on one point. He intended to escort Sarah Smythe to the gala party afterward, and, moreover, he intended to take her arm in his and keep it there for as long as she would let him.

As he sat poking at his sermon, he rehearsed her face, feature by feature. He was sure the mascara would vanish like a bad dream, and, likewise, the startling blonde she had become. Her slang too would revert to language he could understand. He would miss his four lodgers and the side income from renting them rooms: the big old house that the parish provided assumed big families as well as room for lodgers to supplement the meager stipend paid a minister of God. The Rev. Macadoo's earliest predecessor in Pallas could also count on the stud fees from his horse.

Visions of Sarah kept getting in the way of the sermon, which was entitled "In His Feet." In truth, he had given it before, in his first year in Pallas, when he preached on the crooked path that leads surely to abiding faith and salvation. Shining words when writ in the fire of confidence. On this Sunday, could he rise to the occasion? It was so long since he had a-wooing gone, and the rules were so different now: that first one had run just fast enough to let him catch and marry her. Did Sarah even know he existed? Apart, that is, from his flapjacks and the cardinal "gig." He still put suchlike words in quotation marks, such as "recycle," which is what he was doing by foisting an old sermon on his unsuspecting congregation. Wasn't that "crooked" in another sense? He sighed.

Supposing she was the smallest bit interested, courting her in Pallas meant doing it under the watchful eyes of his parishioners. "I might as well hire a hall." There was an element, he was sure, who would say he ran with the wrong crowd. They would point to his appearance on stage as a Roman cardinal. "Thank God it isn't Lent yet." Which was worse, he wondered, to play a Catholic during Lent, or play a Catholic at all? For that matter, for a man of the cloth to be up there on stage at all. Where had his mind been? Well, he knew the answer to that: He had just gotten so swept up in Sarah.

He would be strict with himself this Lent: Silence…Study…Service. He vowed he would think of Sarah only on Sundays in Lent. Surely Lenten refreshment allowed him that as well as a big Sunday dinner. He might ask her home for one of those and invite, from the vestry, let's see…But tomorrow night, he would take her arm—and her hand, if she let him; and if there was the slightest response, why, he would treasure it as a gardener does a seedling, as believers do the mustard seed of faith. He would buy himself a new necktie.

"I never thanked you for your Valentine," Othmar said to Sarah on the phone after Gilly left.

"How did you know it was me?"

"Had you written all over it."

The valentine was so long ago that Sarah could scarcely remember.

"Was it Raggedly Andy? There were two gingerbread people left over but there was something wrong with the girl's skirt, and I never know with valentines if you're supposed to send a boy to a man or you send him a girl. I mean, is the picture on the valentine meant to be you? Or me? I can understand why they go in for lovebirds and cupids."

That off her mind, Sarah asked, as Othmar was sure she would: "Any news?"

"As a matter of fact! Can we talk? Coffee? Kulda's in half an hour?"

Coffee at Kulda's had a certain rightness, they both thought.

"Where we first met," said Sarah always mindful of history.

"Different booth," said Othmar, and to himself: but no cleaner.

"Yer usual?" asked Catherine.

"Mr. Othmar will be leaving us soon."

"So I heard."

"Catherine listens on the Keohane network," giggled Sarah. "She's a Keohane, you know. The sister of your landlord."

Othmar pretended to see a family resemblance. When it came to good looks, Fairy Godmother had favored her sister, and Catherine's glare acknowledged that. Serves her right, Othmar thought. Goddam spy!

"Now about next season, Sarah."

She tapped him playfully on the hand. "As they say, 'Off with the old before on with the new.' I've got a surprise to tell you. I've got the paper to send a photogragher for the final curtain call. After the audience leaves, we all go back on stage. He shoots from the first balcony. He's going to try color. He's got this neat wide-angle lens. So we'll get everybody in the picture, and in costume, and the orchestra standing up in the put. And—don't tell anybody but Aunt Evey is going to have copies made up for everybody."

She was positively giddy, Othmar thought. Was she in a condition to get what he wanted in the paper? He patted her hand. "Where would this whole thing be without you! You've given us the kind of publicity money can't buy."

Sarah flushed. That was nice to hear.

"But look at all you've done for Pallas," she said. Best to deflect praise lest you come to believe it. Believe your own reviews, as Othmar would say.

"Keep this under your chapeau for now," he began, "but the name of the enterprise will change to Opera Prima and we will tour one production."

"One production?" Sarah, like everyone else, knew about the "Traviata."

"In fact Sarah, there will be two. In repertory, if you like. I'm adding 'L'Elisir d'amore.' Do you know it? A honey. A romantic comedy by Donizetti." And since Sarah seemed hazy on the meaning of repertory, he explained casting both operas with two of the "Tosca" principals and most of the Americans, and they would sing them in rotation.

"But not a word of this in print till it's official. Your aunt said she had to get the board's approval. But a done deal, don't you think? She gets what she wants, doesn't she! She has been a revelation. I couldn't have done 'Tosca' without her. She has made me what I am. You'll see at the curtain calls."

Sarah knew there was a question she ought to ask but it wouldn't come. "You're changing the name of the company," she said instead. "Why?"

"Opera Prima means Opera First—ensemble, first and foremost. And it doesn't tie us geographically." There was much more along these lines and Sarah scribbled away, gladdened at the way he looked. Charged. Happy. The old Othmar. The Othmar she remembered from the first time at Kulda's when he explained how he was going to stage "Tosca." Aunt Evey was right. People do best when they have a project. So there was hope for next year.

"I don't want to think our 'Tosca' wasn't ensemble opera. Despite what the critics said about the staging, which was not my fault, and I'm sure you understand."

Shrugging, Sarah was going to say, what do critics know?

"The more important thing, you heard, we heard, in every single role, a devoted and dedicated singer who put the music first. One day you may hear more thrilling voices but our Tosca and our Scarpia are as authentic as it gets."

Sarah was having problems with "authentic." It sounded like a weasel word and would take some explaining.

"But Luigi Luongo is special."

Sarah breathed in. Knowing what she knew and the gossip she had heard, she waited to hear Othmar say how special. In the back of her mind was something about a toothpick, a story she couldn't quite credit. From her one time on stage, she knew she couldn't see into the auditorium.

"He is very, very special. He's the wave of the future. Again, something you are not supposed to know, but Gilly has just signed him to his exclusive management. You can ask Gilly later what that means. The point is, Gilly saw Luigi Luongo's promise, and snapped him up before someone else did, a big outfit like SUMI. Luigi Luongo was born to be up there on stage. Sure he can sing. But he's not just a voice, he's a presence. And you witnessed it happening right here in Pallas."

"Gosh!" said Sarah. But she wrote down "jelly," which was the family word for "jealous."

22.

"His bags are packed," Othmar's landlady had observed to her husband earlier in the week.

"Make sure you get the last rent." City fellas who wore lady's capes were not to Mr. Keohane's taste. And what was he up to, messing around in the barn?

"His bags are packed." Liking the expression, Mrs. Keohane repeated it when her sister Catherine got home Friday from waitressing. "Here but not here, you know?"

"Good riddance," said Catherine. "Mrs. Smythe had to leave the tip."

Othmar's bags were packed. It was time to move on. He awoke on Saturday, bone weary and mortally tired of "Tosca." The final performance would take a supreme effort.

Taking down a show, he knew from long experience, required as much effort as putting it up. More, he thought, because the drive of creation wasn't there to carry you. But it had the same endless details. If he could just press a button and "Tosca" would jump back in the "Tosca" box. It made him think of the Hindemith opera he had considered doing in the days when he really was "John Austin Othmar Presents," a twelve-minute sketch called "Hin und zurück,"or "There and Back." The husband discovers his wife's love letter to another man and shoots her. Then decides to jump to his death. High melodrama. Enter a Wise Man. This is all too sad for words, the Wise Man thinks, and makes time run backwards. And like a home movie in reverse, it rewinds in frantic hilarity to the beginning. They even sing backward, not note by note but phrase by phrase. He had always meant to look Hindemith up in Grove to see if he liked movies, or if this was just his having fun with what you could do with film. God, he missed the city and being able to take in a new flick anytime you wanted. The Hindemith was still a possibility. The trick was what to put it with, and a few years back when he and Gilly had kicked it around, they had not succeeded either in finding another work to fill the bill, or, more crucial, a cast who could sing both. Liz, who thought she knew everything, said the perfect first half would be the Hindemith plus some of Brahms's "Liebeslieder Waltzes. Love then and Love now, she had said, and you could use the same two pianists and add a mezzo to make up the vocal quartet in the Brahms. Othmar wished she wouldn't add her two cents worth, keep horning in.

Anyway, German expressionism was definitely not for Pallas. Pallas lusts for "Traviata" with ball gowns and Champagne. So they can show themselves off, Othmar thought with disgust. "Oh, pretty please, let us be in the ball scene," they pleaded. "We'll practice all winter," they promised. Don't they have the least idea that opera isn't the Pallas Players or whatever they call their pathetic theater group. "Over my dead body!" If he came back, he vowed, it would be under his own terms. With a cast of his own chosing. And a conductor without a wife. How could Pompelli have done that to him? Othmar threw himself out of bed. So much to do before curtain time.

That morning, Othmar went to the bank, the Titus Trust, of course, and emerged with four envelopes filled with cash. Monopoly money would do just as well, he thought, then reproached himself. For his plan to succeed, he must act as though this was a performance like any other. In his office, he checked his master list of the tasks ahead. The crew would strike the show tomorrow afternoon and have the sets ready for shipment on Monday. Ditto the costume people packing up the costumes in their wicker trunks. Evey Titus's furniture would find its own way back to Spring Side. He wrote down "fork." He wrote down "fan" and put a question mark.

And he had a fence to mend. He phoned Bill Potter. He knew he'd been a royal pain, said Othmar to Potter, but he had not expected a Tosca who couldn't see. It had thrown him: he had acted badly. He wanted Bill to know it couldn't have been handled better, and he was phoning to say so. He hoped they would work together again. Et cet ter ra, et cet ter ra. Would Bill do him the enormous honor, asked Othmar, of sitting out front tonight?

"There is no one like you for remembering a show," said Othmar trying not to pile it on. "If I ever do another 'Tosca' I'll be able to pick your brains on how I did this one."

There was a long silence. Othmar dared not breathe.

"I like to sit back of the cross aisle."

"Done," said Othmar. And, to himself: "Out of my hair."

In the late morning, he iced the brownies and wrapped them for delivery. In the early afternoon, he went into the empty theater to check on things. The stage was already set up for Act I. Othmar smiled to see how the painted drop for the Attavanti chapel exactly covered the stage-right trap. His next stop was the mushroom cellar. It looked undisturbed. Sections of the old raked stage, coated with grime, lay stacked on the hard dirt floor, as they had been for eons. Behind this pile of bygone stage equipment he had found ample space to run his cables and pails. How nicely the spray paint blackened the silvery metals of his river system. He heaved on a pail and felt the thrill of invention as the cable played out to let the trap door fall open. Othmar now loosened the light bulb nearest. More here he could not do.

All was in order also in the basement immediately under the stage. The downstage trap was closed. Already in position for Act III was the set of steps that would be shoved into place at the second intermission. Up these would climb the tenor hero, *il pittore* the aristo Mario Cavaradossi, to his execution—mock, Tosca believes—on the ramparts of the Castel Sant' Angelo. Upstage from this trap, tarps hung, curtaining the rest of the basement off. This had been Bill Potter's idea. He ran a tight ship: he didn't want musicians going back there to smoke. "Who was I to argue?" Othmar mouthed as he slipped behind the tarps.

Twinned by cable to the mushroom cellar trap, the upstage trap hung open. He flashed his light upward. It was, what? at least four stories to the top of the fly loft, and his beam barely reached there. He played the flash up to his Murphy. It had not been quite the snap to install that he supposed, but it was up there, and goddam! it looked just like Potts's Murphy. By his calculation, it was a three-story drop from the top to the castle scenery to the very bottom of the theater. He returned to the mushroom cellar and bade the cable and pails draw both traps shut. "Master of all I survey," he mouthed. There was pleasure in telling secrets.

The day was not without other light diversions. With relish he left a note in Bruno Cappetto's dressing room about returning the Titus fan to him at the second intermission. As for the great Evey Titus, she would just have to watch this last "Tosca" from her box. "Somehow," he said to himself, "somehow, I just didn't get around to asking her to be tonight's Attavanti." He smiled into the mirror where he was making up. "Tonight is my show, all mine. John Austin Othmar Presents…"

He had expected time to drag. He really had nothing more to do. The Rambler was loaded. As "Tosca" hurtled to its close, he would leave by the stage door and, as a final touch, pull the fire alarm. He had even written the headline for the first edition of the Clarion Voice:

FALSE ALARM MARS OPERA FINALE

There remained putting his signature to this "Tosca." Artists signed their work—why not he? He pulled the long desk drawer all the way out and turned it over. As he expected, it was unvarnished, virgin wood. He inscribed the date. In India ink, he wrote out the verse of the Dies Irae that Spoletta mutters:

> *Then shall the judge his throne attain*
> *And every secret sin arraign,*
> *Till nothing unavenged remain.*

"Nothing unavenged…" At one point in his musing he had considered signing it "The Attavanti." Although unseen in Puccini's opera, she has her own musical motif. And why not? As a character she has as much reason as Tosca to kill Scarpia. He has caused the suicide of her brother. "By an unnamed poison," Othmar murmured. How easy that had been to procure! There was something after all to be said for small towns. Yes, the Attavanti had reason to fear Scarpia. "She was an Angelotti, you know," Othmar fluted. As an encore: "She was a Carruthers, you know."

He was in a good mood. "In the manner and in the order. In the order and manner." With a grand flourish he signed himself John Austin Othmar.

He could hear sounds grow in the theater. An hour remained till "Magic Time," as Sarah Caldwell called it. A knock came at the office door. It was Rollo Shaw already costumed and made up as Scarpia's black spider, Spoletta.

"Speak of the devil!" Othmar was manic. As if the writing of Spoletta's prophecy, for that was how he thought of it, would summon the man himself.

"We thought you would like to see Joey," and from behind him Rollo Shaw pulled the small choir boy with the big voice who sang the offstage shepherd.

This was Joey (for Joseph) McLaughlin, and at the auditions Othmar thought he had never seen an uglier kid. Big ears. Big teeth and crooked. But blessed, for Othmar's purposes, with a big edgy voice that carried out into the theater. Beautiful it wasn't. Other productions used a female alto with a butch sound. Joey was a born belter. And a big nuisance. The trouble started when he realized he would not be dressed as a shepherd. When Othmar nixed the costume idea, Rollo brought the boy to plead his case.

"You don't need a costume, Joey, because no one sees you," Othmar had told him flatly. "That's how it is in opera. But, of course, you will take a bow with the company at the end."

"All the other boys are in costume. I'll look stupid."

"Not at all, Joey. Everyone will know you're the offstage voice for the simple reason you are not in costume. If you were in costume, you would look just like the choir."

Joey saw through that. "Shepherds don't wear choir robes."

If Joey had broken into tears, Othmar might have relented, but this kid stared at him, dared him. "The answer is No, and if you don't like it, I'll replace you."

So Joey sang dressed in his parochial school uniform and had his picture in the Clarion Voice. Sarah Smythe made sure the story explained the situation.

But Joey—and Othmar—reckoned without Rollo Shaw. Big, tall, kind Rollo, who was not at heart a Spoletta. Rollo, who loved singing Schubert more than anything. Rollo, who had volunteered to be the offstage conductor for the shepherd, leading him across the back of the stage by flashlight. "Like the usher in a movie theater," Rollo told Joey. "Follow me, young sir, the best seats are this way." Rollo also gave Joey a few musical pointers. It was too late to do much about the poor voice teaching but he could help with phrasing and diction. Joey worshipped Rollo and as soon as the school bus arrived at the theater he would race down to the dressing room Rollo shared with the American singers and watch Rollo make up. Then he'd go out front, and hide till the performance, and watch the first two acts trying to find his friend in Spoletto's shadowed face.

"He is not a nice man," Joey had said to Rollo, anxious for him.

Now Othmar looked down and tried to find Joey in the apparition before him. His hair was matted and his cheeks weathered. On the lids either side of his nose was the red dot of makeup that Rollo told Joey accentuated the eyes. Joey wore sandals, Rollo's fiancée having vetoed bare feet. It was she who designed the costume after a Nativity scene. At Goodwill she found a pair of boy's corduroy knickers and an old brown shirt. Better than nothing. Then Rollo had his inspiration. Shepherds wore sheepskins, didn't they, and he found what he wanted at an auto supply store. To this sheepskin, intended as a seat cover, Rollo applied shoe polish to antique its tawny curls. It now fell picturesquely from one of Joey's small shoulders.

"Can he really sing in that get-up?" Othmar's sneer left Rollo speechless.

"And another thing," said Othmar. "I want him singing as far upstage as you can get, as near the cyke as possible. The scenery is muffling him."

A bit before eight, the stage lights went down and, for the last time, Othmar took up his position as The Attavanti. One thing he would be glad of and that was, he would never again have to kneel for so long. Goddam the audience for taking their time. Finally the house lights went down. He ran through all his Attavanti stuff, the dropped fan, the hurried sign of the cross, the light swaying walk that belled her cloak out. The picture of aristocratic piety. Where he usually kept in profile, so the follow spot would catch his blonde ringlets as he turned into the imaginary aisle that led to the invisible High Altar, he now veered "just a teensy bit" downstage. He flung his final sign of the cross over the footlights and dropped to one knee. "A sneak preview." It was Rita Dettori's obeisance to art without the innocence.

From her box, Evey Titus watched Othmar's performance with narrowed eyes. "Showy," she thought. She wondered if he fooled anyone. Tonight, however, she had her own role to play. She was going to eat crow and appear to like it. She was going to fawn all over Othmar, and she herself would make the announcement he had been re-engaged for next season. She would let him describe the production. He was good at that. People liked hearing from the top man. It would give Sarah a real piece of news for her last story. Poor girl had worked so hard to pump this final "Tosca" up. She would put Othmar on her right at her table. Pompelli and dear Bruno would understand.

In the sanctity of his office, Othmar ridded himself of the Attavanti. Off came her pink cheeks. Out came her blue eyes. He tied on black sneakers. He rolled his dark turtleneck up under his chin. One more time he unlocked a small drawer and felt his watch cap for its contents. Then he stepped into the wings and watched the cast play the Dettori like a game of skittles. Sarah Smythe was there, dressed for the apres-opera party. She, too, had "diva duty." When the final curtain came down, she would "bomb on up" the Castel Sant'Angelo ramparts and fetch the Dettori and make her nice for her bows. The wig tended to tilt.

"Tosca divina," sang Bruno Cappetto's Scarpia. (Nasally, Othmar thought.) And Tosca showed her surprise, the Dettori doing her "taken aback" thing. ("That 'shudder' you could see in Albany," Othmar muttered.)

A mano mia," sang Scarpia, suavely offering his hand, *"la vostra aspetta piccola manina,"* waiting for your little hand, *"non per galanteria,"* not for flirting, *"ma per offrirvi l'acqua benedetta,"* but to offer you holy water. And Tosca, doubtful but afraid to offend, bends to his will, as, warily stepping forward, she stretches a finger toward his to complete her seduction. Another Scarpia might have indulged the Dettori's poor eyes and brought his hand up under hers. Cappetto waited and made her come to him, and as her hand hestitates his way, the audience sucked its breath in joyful anticipation.

"Grazie, signor!" she sang, and crossed herself.

At the first intermission, Othmar made himself "useful" backstage. He took charge of parking Cavaradossi's painting platform in the wings. He helped guide the painted drops down. As the stage assumed the guise of Scarpia's rooms in the Palazzo Farnese Othmar fussed with the tableware. He took the assistant stage manager aside. He had taken the liberty, he told her, of putting a chair upside down on the upstage right trap to warn the off-stage chorus people off. The trap dropped a bit when he'd walked across it, he said. Can't be too careful. Right-o, she said. Another "funny" about Othmar to tell Potts at tonight's cast party.

Othmar made a final inspection. "Two down, one to go." He went back to his office. Tosca could kill Scarpia without his help. He pulled the brownies out from hiding.

The stage lights came up behind the scrim and Pallas watched in fascination as Scarpia executed each green grape as though it were an enemy of state. Othmar slipped down to the dressing room the Americans shared.

"Mind if I sit for a while," he said to Jonce Jones. Alone of the Americans, Jonce did not have diva duty getting the Dettori around stage.

"I still think you were wrong not to tell me," Othmar began. "But I don't want hard feelings. And, just between you and me, Alex wasn't up to you. You can act with your voice and the world is going to know that. And you, you stick with Gilly. He will really put out for you. He's hungry, too."

Jonce smiled and stretched. "All will be revealed."

"I hear it's Germany. And don't let me forget, these are for you. I think they're from the old bag on the radio." He slid down the makeup bench a box fenced in with a WPAL bumper sticker. "They were left with the box office."

"Mary Ellen has been at every performance," said Jonce. "Gave me hell for missing the matinee."

"Discerning of her," said Othmar, beginning to enjoy the performance. "Not for me." He waved away the brownies. "Chocolate gives me migraines. Do me a favor and eat mine."

And just when Othmar was scared almost breathless that it wasn't working, Johnson Jones began to clutch at his throat. "Help," he meant to say. And "breath." And "water." And, in the few minutes he could still focus, he saw Othmar making his same gestures as though also seized. "Help," he pleaded. "Help," said Othmar in echo. His eyes rolled wildly. "The eye bit coming right up," said Othmar. "I'm a quick study, like Alex. But I will never be as good as you in the part."

When Jonce Jones was still at last, Othmar dragged him over behind the wicker costume trunks and threw a stage cloth over him. He plunged the remaining brownies deep in the trash can. He looked at his watch. In the theater, the good people of Pallas had just heard Spoletta break in on Scarpia's cresting lust for Tosca to inform his boss:

"Angelotti al nostro giungere s'uicise!"

Rather than be taken prisoner, Angelotti had poisoned himself.

Othmar slipped back to his office.

The intercom brought him a "Tosca" dramatized by the faithful promiscuity of a single sentinel mike. It was an opera of creaking footfalls and chipmunk voices. For long stretches nothing seemed to be happening. The orchestra was tinny. Of *"Vissi d'arte"* he heard little, Tosca facing in the wrong direction. The audience applause was like the flapping of birds. Finally came the thud he'd been waiting for as the curtain fell on the second act.

Quickly he stepped on stage, eager to be seen so "helpful" with shifting scenery. The painter's platform was still where he wanted it. The Titus silverware went into its leather case and Othmar carried it away. He felt wonderful. He was giving it his all and it was working. He had broken through to the other side.

"Just behind you," he said to Bruno Cappetto who was at the office door waiting to pick up the pay envelopes—as Othmar knew he would.

"Gianni, there is some mistake." Cappetto was wheezing. "You ask Rita to return the fan. You do not know that the signora Titus has given it to her, a souvenir of friendship." Cappetto sat down heavily. He was still in costume but had peeled off his wig. Makeup ceased at the pale dome of his bald head. The dark coat, so elegant and so evil on stage, was not in its first youth and gave off a sour smell. He was in no hurry. Scarpia is dead and must while away the last act. He might play gin with Angelotti who is also dead. Cappetto pocketed the money. Still he did not rise.

"Gianni, about 'Traviata.'"

"What about 'Traviata'?"

"The signora say we do it here next year."

"Does she?"

"You do not know? Ah! I ruin her surprise at the party. She say she raise the money. Expensive for 'Traviata.' She make Luigi promise to come back. His first Alfredo. I teach it to him. You will like. So handsome! Yes!"

Othmar said nothing.

"Gianni, now I ask a favor. I do Germont, how many times? so many times. With your permission I will end my career here. I will sing Germont the father and Luigi sing Alfredo the son. In our life, the uncle and the neph. Everybody think it is so nice. Victor will conduct. It is OK with him but he say to ask you. So I ask."

Othmar still said nothing.

"I go now and you think. Tonight the signora make it a surprise."

With a heave he was up out of the chair. He nodded toward the bathroom.

"Sure," said Othmar. "Be my guest."

Hammering from the stage came over the intercom. They were securing the Castel Sant'Angelo. Othmar threw on the Attavanti's cloak. From a drawer he took the deerskin gloves and the deer knife. He put the Titus fork in his back pocket. He walked into the bathroom. He heard Cappetto flush. The stall door squeaked open. Othmar lunged forward, left hand on Cappetto's chin as the right drove into his gut. He twisted the blade. Once, twice, and again. Like winding a clock. He hadn't known what to expect, deliberately hadn't thought about it. It was easy. Too easy. No outcry—not even a gasp. Othmar shoved Cappetto back on to the toilet and banged home the Titus fork. He yanked the stall shut. He slid off the cloak and wadded it under the stall door. He washed his hands. He listened. Still nothing. He filled the gloves with water, drained them and put them on the hissing radiator. He turned out the lights and, locking the office door, stepped into the wings. As Othmar walked across the stage, the crew lowered the monumental figure of the archangel Michael onto the ramparts of the Castel Sant'Angelo.

"The plague is almost over," Othmar said to the assistant stage manager. She grinned. Another "funny" to tell Pottsy.

In the days when he used to think about such things, Othmar wondered if he would like Puccini if they met. He could think of composers he would rather know. Just to be able to look at Mozart! Othmar would not presume to talk to him—even if, as in a day dream, everyone spoke everyone else's language. He would be prepared for Mozart's bathroom humor. But that was probably Mozart talking to friends. He would settle for a glimpse of the public Mozart. He would sit in the chair next to him at the barbershop. He had read Mozart went every day to the barber. Figaro would shave the count. At home, of course. Would he ever do "Figaro"? He had definite ideas. The one "Figaro" he had seen was too la-di-da. The Almavivas lived as though they lived in the same style right in the palace with the king. Too public. And should be a bit seedy, in the private rooms. The thing that never failed with "Figaro," if you just listened, was the strange sadness. They were all somehow a family, even though half the people on stage were servants or peasants, and that is what made it so excruciating, and so funny. They were all in it together, with no way out. Except death. Was there another composer who would open an opera with a man measuring for his marriage bed? All the time knowing his beloved Susannah was his only by gift of their betters, and the count could renege at any time. He saw the count as no better a man than Figaro, as he supposed Mozart did, Mozart with his vast experience of the hundreds of people he had to please who had none of his talent; and this could be the difference, he would make the count not much better off than Figaro. His count would be Masetto in "Don Giovanni," but a few generations later. Masetto, the rich peasant, who has his own peasants; and here is why Masetto is so angry: the gall of Don Giovanni to suppose he can have his way with Zerlina! Count Almaviva knows he is stuck with servants and peasants as his lot on earth. He has to live with people who depend on him for their food. They let him know it everyday. This was real. They talk about Puccini being the realist. With his operas about everyday people. Cowboys, police, Mimì who sews for a living. Pinkerton in a Yale sweater tossing a football—no way he's going to take Butterfly to America. Not a dry eye in the house but none of Puccini has Mozart's grit. There was only one thing that made him want to meet Puccini. It was not the soprano stuff in "Tosca." Not the sheer theatrics of laying out the body or her jumping. Both were in the play. It was how Puccini began the final act. Before the shepherd sings.

Othmar could see Victor Pompelli's face in the pit. He had brought the players to their feet for the orchestra's traditional bow to the audience. He was applauding them and smiling. He rapped his baton lightly.

This is music of dawn, music of a new day. Never mind that a man has just been stabbed to death. And, as many in the audience already know, there's a suicide to come. This is music that says the sun will come up, as it must. It is music of a city getting up and going about its business. Gershwin's New York but with cowbells instead of taxi horns. In a different world, one sort of god would have called everyone together and made a judgment and struck the murderer dead right then and there. But this world was too big for that tidy justice. You knew what you knew, and who you knew, and for the rest of it, there were things you would never know or care about. Othmar knew that was also real, and was afraid. But fear was in the real world, not the world he now inhabited. He was an artist with art's own rules.

To his left he saw a tall man propel a lump of something furry upstage. It was Rollo Shaw escorting Joey for his offstage shepherd song. Costuming Joey, as Othmar would not be told, had had one unforeseen result: the boy was limp with stage fright. He had come out of Othmar's office in tears. "He never looked at me," he wailed. Rollo took him in his big arms and rocked him. Now was not the time to explain the Othmars of this world.

"He says I can't sing."

"No, he said he wondered if you could sing dressed that way. A good question. I'm not sure I could sing with sheepskin on me. Too heavy."

"Then I won't be a shepherd."

"It's morning. The sun is about to come up. Your sheepskin was your blanket. Now you're awake and you have to get your flock ready to change pasture. You know about sheep? They walk a while and then they put their heads down and graze. You know the music with the cowbells? What we hear when we walk to the back of the stage? That's the cows and the other animals, goats and your sheep, as they move to their day pasture. You can wear your sheepskin then. The sheep will think you're a sheep and follow. Sheep are very dumb." Rollo poked Joey in the ribs. "Then, you will put the sheepskin on the ground, and the sheep will stop, and you will sing."

A part of Joey knew this was a story for his little sister. His eyes filled.

"What's wrong now?"

"What I sing, is it girl stuff?"

"Yes, it is," said Rollo. "This is opera, kiddo. You don't think I am really Spoletta, do you? You're not Joey but a shepherd. Shepherds don't sing to their sheep."

Othmar watched them go, Rollo with flashlight and carrying a piano-vocal. This would be a "Tosca" for the books, thought Rollo. Spoletta doubling as moony shepherd and he, Rollo Shaw, who had only sung falsetto in fun. "But only if Joey can't," he had assured the maestro.

As the shepherd sang, the Cavaradossi and a sergeant of the guard made ready to climb up through the downstage trap as though they were coming from the dungeon cells in the Castel Sant'Angelo. This was Othmar's cue to move to where he had stationed the painter's platform. The tarp was as he had draped it, fussily telling the crew it was needed to protect Cavaradossi's paint pots stored underneath. He ducked in. Up into the platform he climbed, bracing himself on the struts. He reached up to a ledge and patted his watch cap. He pulled on black rubber gloves. He peeked out. The prisoner approached, Cavaradossi in his bloodied finery; and the jailer jerked awake. Othmar smiled. You'd never know The Jailer was Alex Avery. He enjoyed watching Alex's little touches. Fighting a yawn. It is what? four in the morning, sunrise in an hour. Peering at the official papers the guard hands him. Writing in his prison register with the labored intensity of the unlettered.

"Mario Cavaradossi?" he sings. Sign here.

The wonderment of Alex's Jailer when Cavaradossi refuses a consoling hour with a priest. The worried glance he will have to spend that hour alone with the prisoner. The palpable relief that all the prisoner wants to do is write a farewell. His reward of Cavaradossi's last possession, a gold ring, if he brings him paper. The stray thought that this gold ring might be worthless brass.

Far more difficult, Othmar thought, to play the soppy lover. As Luigi Luongo now pretended to struggle with the inspiration for his letter, Othmar tensed. "Show time," he mouthed.

"*È lucevan le stelle,*" the prisoner sang. The stars were shining.

Not for very much longer, Othmar mouthed. Already the cyclorama was softening for dawn. Othmar could hear the hum of the stage lighting. High up behind the silhouetted angel the night sky was fading. Then would come the first bulge of color, a dirty pink under the mists. Then, inexorable gold. He drew the watch cap out of hiding and put it on. In the wing opposite he saw the Dettori's launching party assemble.

First came the prison guard with lantern. Then, Spoletta aiming Tosca at Cavaradossi with a push forward, this guidance system disguised as officious contempt.

She really is a very annoying woman, Othmar thought, as Tosca teaches her lover how to die.

"*Tieni a mente: al primo colpo giù,*" she sang. Remember at the first shot to fall down, she instructed.

*"Giù, "*down. Cavaradossi was playing along.

"Ne rialzarti innanzi ch'io ti chiami. " And don't get up before I call you. *"E cadi bene. "* Fall down properly.

"Come la Tosca in teatro, " like Tosca on stage, he teased her.

As the execution squad marched on, Othmar slipped the safety off the gun.

The squad marched off.

"O Mario, non ti muovere, " Tosca sang. Don't move yet.

Othmar swung down lightly from the platform. "Walk, do not run! To the nearest exit," he mouthed. He stopped cold. Someone was there.

It was Sarah.

And, next to Sarah, was someone it took him a long time, precious moments, to identify. He nodded to both, and, for good measure, gave thumbs up. It wouldn't look right to be in a hurry. The man was minus his kepi or shako or whatever the hell he thought made him a soldier, but there was no mistaking Linc King, goddam Abraham Lincoln King, goddam Pride of Fairstead. Dammit, what was he doing there? He was supposed to have marched his squad off and down the stairs to the dressing rooms to wait for the curtain calls.

Othmar headed upstage. Toward the end of the wing he paused, casually he hoped, and looked up at what passed for the Castel Sant'Angelo. It was no more than a scaffolding of boards crudely (but effectively) braced. Very high up was what appeared to be a padded shelf. This was the Murphy, the mattress and "pouch" that would guide and catch Tosca. From where Othmar stood he swore he could not distinguish where mattress became cloth and paper. He smiled. He was about to walk along the cyclorama to the stage door and freedom when an object caught his eye.

"Damn!" The chair he had upended over the trap was still there. "Naughty, naughty!" he sang. He would spirit it away.

"Stop!" he heard a voice squeal. As he reached for the chair, he felt his arm twisted. He heard Sarah call his name. "Stop! Stop!" Wrenching himself free, he stepped forward.

Obedient to its creator's design, the stage trap snapped to attention, dropping its door down.

Othmar fell hard and the second trap sprang. He fell further. The cables sang, restoring the traps smartly to position. In the dark below, Othmar lay stunned. He could feel nothing. He could not lift his head. Scintillas of light showered down. He had no idea where he was but he knew he should not be here.

There was a rumble of thunder above, and a blaze. Hurtling down, her cloak like the wings of an avenging angel, Tosca fell and the cables sang their last song.

Sipario rappido, fast curtain, *fine dell'Opera*, end of the opera. In the pit, Pompelli closed the score and clasped his hands over it, bowing to Puccini. Then he bowed to the orchestra. His eyes glistened.

In her box, Evey Titus gathered herself and waited for the telltale parting of the curtain that announced the first bows. She'd gotten the hotel to send Artie Mason and Herbie Pennell in their bellmen's finery to page the curtain. She must now make her way backstage for the company bow. What was holding things up?

There would be no curtain calls that night. Linc King, hugging Sarah to him, ran back to the stage manager's corner. "I didn't mean to. I smelled gun powder. We weren't armed." He could hardly get the words out. "A terrible accident back there."

In his arms, Sarah shrieked and shrieked. Wherever she looked she saw a cloud of something dark falling. Like a parachute. There would be a thud when the feet landed—there always was a thud. Then it vanished. It shouldn't have done that. She must be wrong. "Linc," she moaned, and burrowed into his heaving chest. "Shots," he kept saying. "I smelled."

The cast had piled on stage for the curtain calls and they were all there when the Spoletta found the Cavaradossi's body. Weston Macadoo, in his cardinal's costume, closed the sightless eyes. He went to Linc and Sarah first, and huddling them together, murmured a prayer. Sarah's tears ran down his neck.

When the police broke into the manager's office, they found Scarpia stuffed in the toilet. And, later, when they searched the theater, they found Tosca lying theatrically, as though her death had been staged, hand flung over her eyes, grotesque in art. Only when they lifted her up did they find Othmar. He too was dead, his face smashed from her fall. One blue eye winked and shut.

The End
Fine dell'opera

Acknowledgments

This tale has been long in the making, and grateful thanks go to my family and to these friends:

The late Annabelle Bernard-Mercker, James and Joceyln Bolle, the late Mario Bonelli, Richard Buell, Marshall Burlingame, the late Sarah Caldwell, Mark and Anne Willan Cherniavsky, Frances Crane Colt, the "Core," William N. Cosel, James Logan Cramer, Francis and Katharine Cunningham, Phyllis Curtin and the late Eugene Cook, Colin and Shamsi Davis, the late Peter Davison, the late José de Varon, Paul Driver, Richard Dyer, Mark Jay Ellenbogen, David R. Elliott, Salvatore Liugi Fierro, the "Finnegans Wake," Anthony Fogg, Robert Gartside, the late Boris Goldovsky, Bill Greene, D.Kern Holoman, Paul Hsu, Lucilla Wellington Fuller Marvel, the late Louis Menand III, Thomas J. McMullin, Helen Pond and the late Herbert Senn, Andrew Raeburn, Cynthia Robbins and Stephen Rubin, Peter and Lucy Rosenfeld, John Saumarez Smith, the late Roland Shaw, the late Geraldine Sheehan, the late Beverly Sills and Peter Greenough, the late Craig Smith, Mary Hunting Smith, Michael Steinberg, Donald S. Stern, the late Edith R. Stern, Pamela Stevens, the late Brier and Alexander Stoller, and the late Frank E. Upton, Jr.

8/08

COOLIDGE CORNER BRANCH
BROOKLINE PUBLIC LIBRARY
31 Pleasant Street
Brookline, MA 02446

Printed in the United States
122082LV00006B/33/P

9 781604 749939